SEXCASTLE

a graphic novel by Kyle Starks

SEXCASTLE. FIRST PRINTING. MARCH 2015. Published by Image Comics, Inc. Office of publication: 2001 Center Street, 6th Floor, Berkeley, CA 94704. PRINTED IN THE U.S.A. For information regarding the CPSIA on this printed material call: 203-595-3636 and provide reference # RICH – 608432

FOR MY DAD

who taught me how to be a man through both his own actions,
and by allowing me to see far more action movies
than I should have as a little dude.

Special thanks to Adam P. Knave whose constant encouragement
made this book both as real and as good as it is.

Eternal thanks to my Wife and her support and
my beautiful children for their inspiration.

Additional thanks to Matt Fraction, Michel Fiffe, Chris Sims, Dylan Todd,
Andy Hirsch, Karla Pacheco, Rich Barrett, anyone who has been so kind
enough to help this book, and everyone at Image Comics.

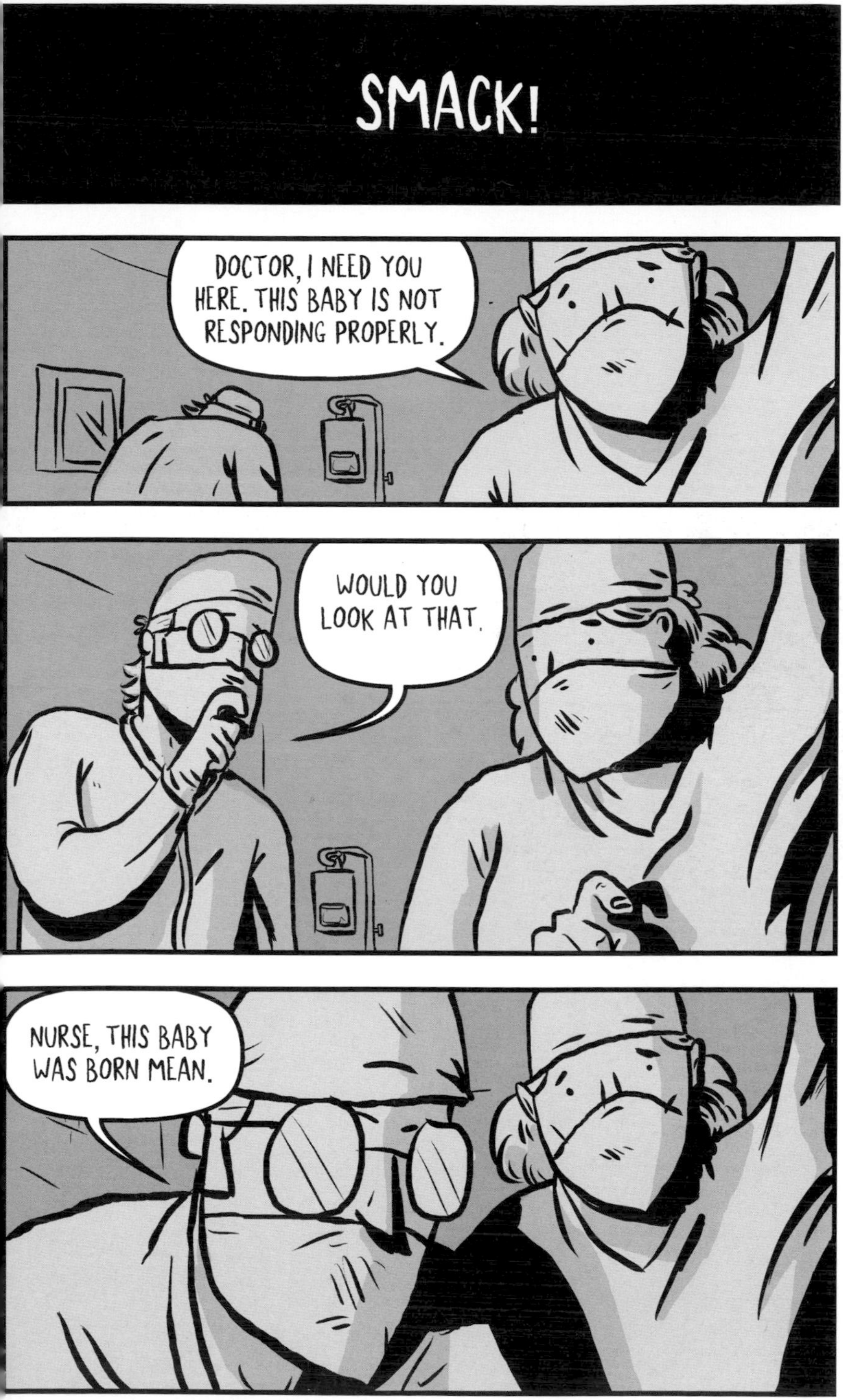
SMACK!
DOCTOR, I NEED YOU HERE. THIS BABY IS NOT RESPONDING PROPERLY.
WOULD YOU LOOK AT THAT.
NURSE, THIS BABY WAS BORN MEAN.

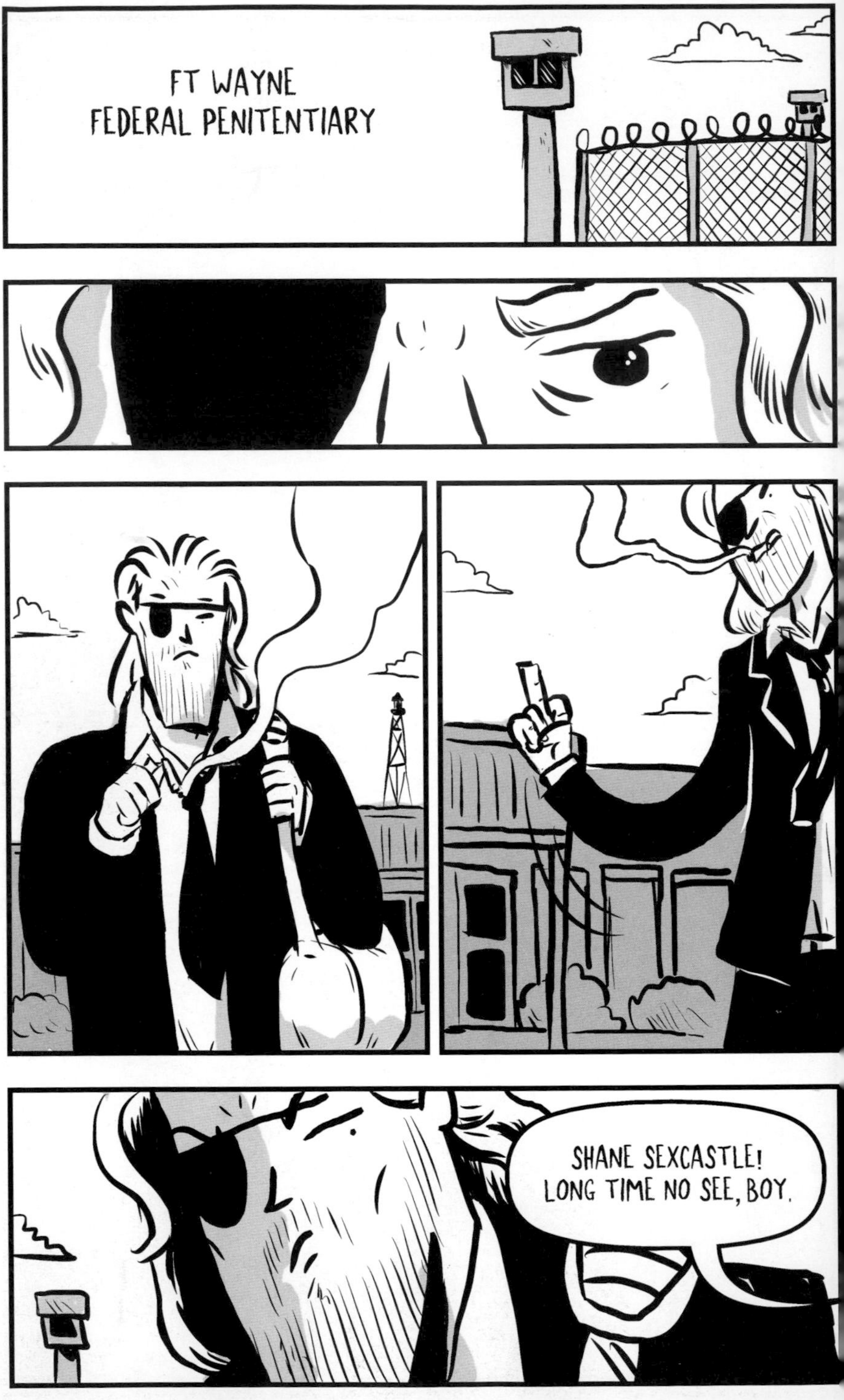
FT WAYNE
FEDERAL PENITENTIARY
SHANE SEXCASTLE!
LONG TIME NO SEE, BOY.

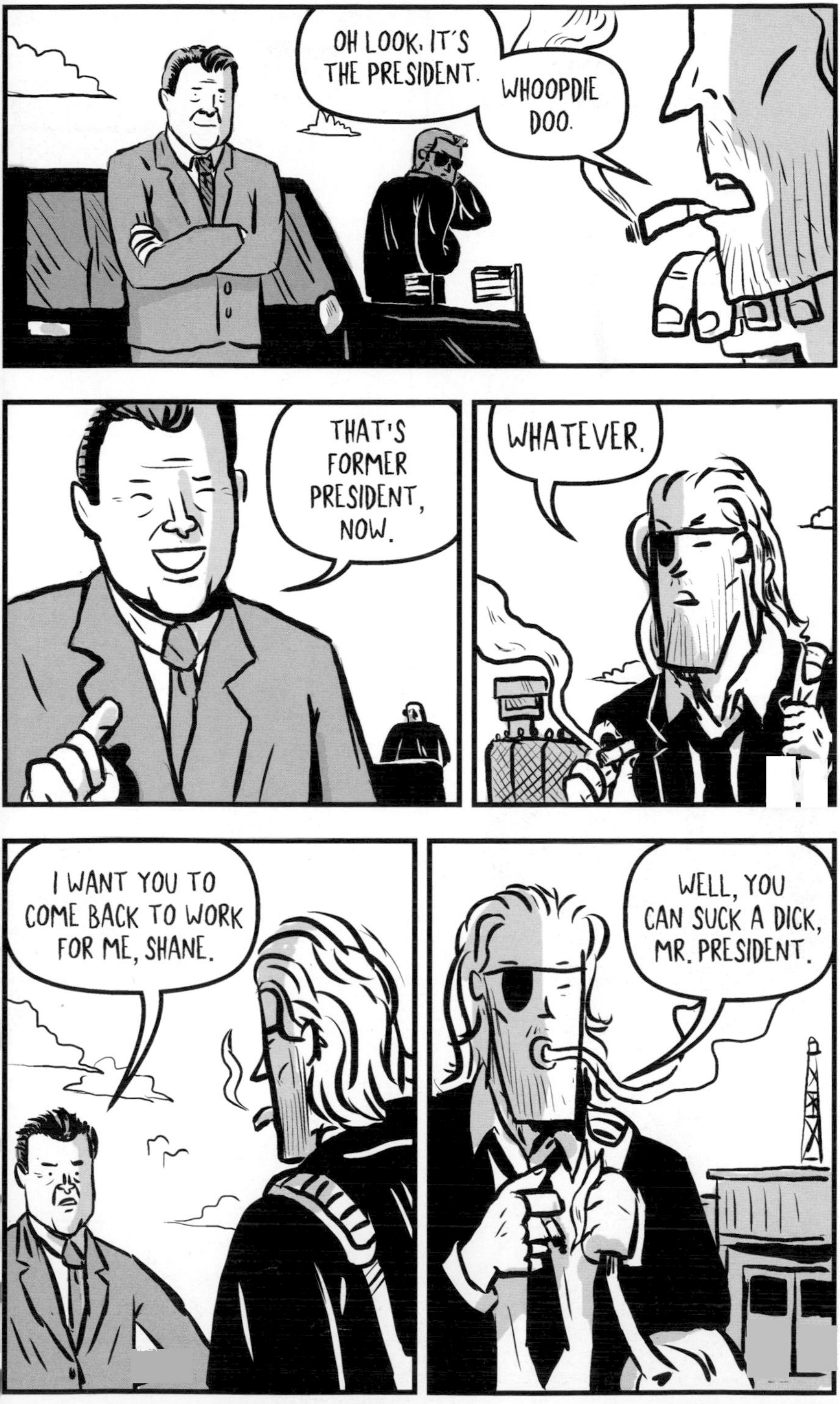
OH LOOK, IT'S THE PRESIDENT.
WHOOPDIE DOO.
THAT'S FORMER PRESIDENT, NOW.
WHATEVER.
I WANT YOU TO COME BACK TO WORK FOR ME, SHANE.
WELL, YOU CAN SUCK A DICK, MR. PRESIDENT.

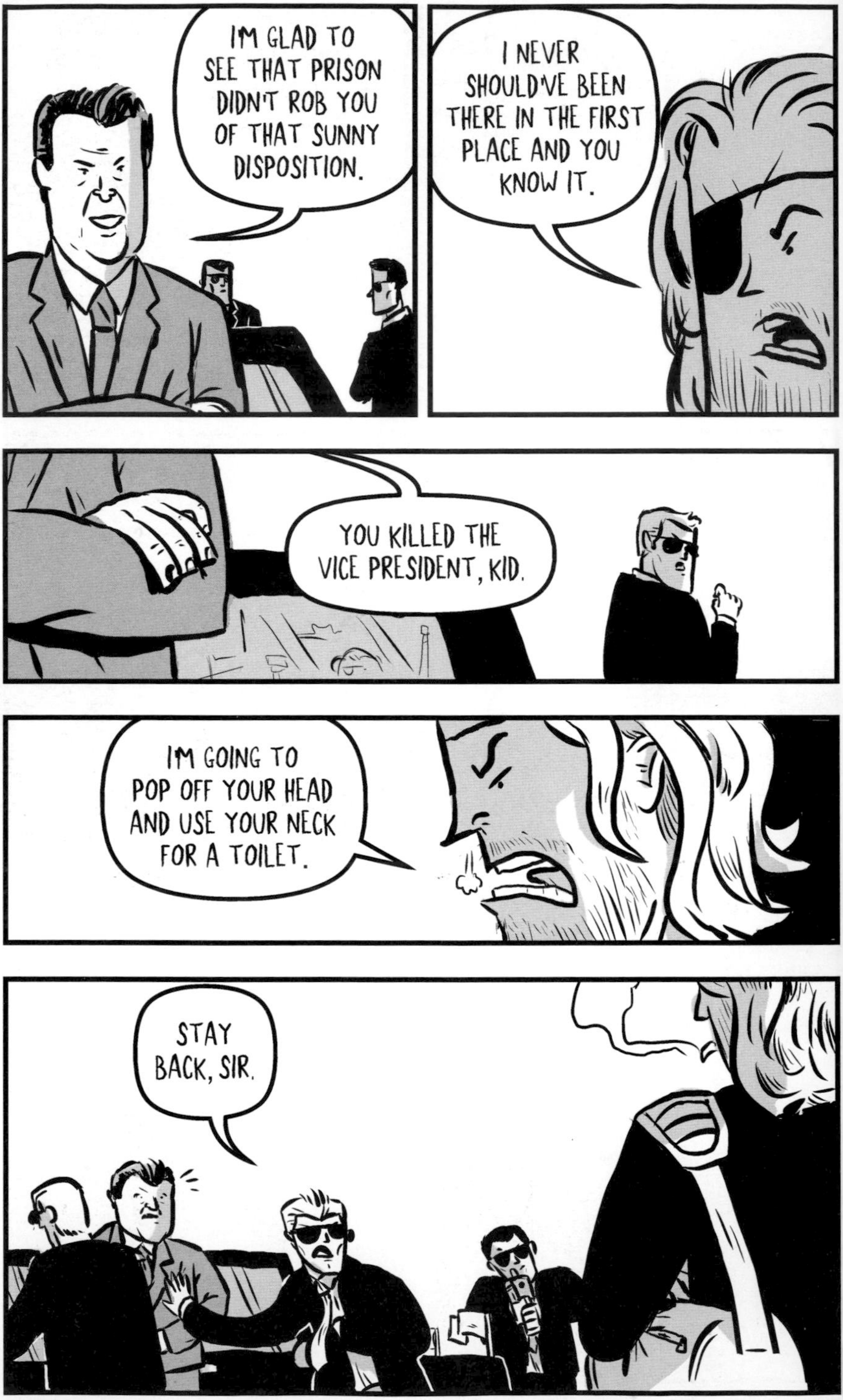
I'M GLAD TO SEE THAT PRISON DIDN'T ROB YOU OF THAT SUNNY DISPOSITION.
I NEVER SHOULD'VE BEEN THERE IN THE FIRST PLACE AND YOU KNOW IT.
YOU KILLED THE VICE PRESIDENT, KID.
I'M GOING TO POP OFF YOUR HEAD AND USE YOUR NECK FOR A TOILET.
STAY BACK, SIR.

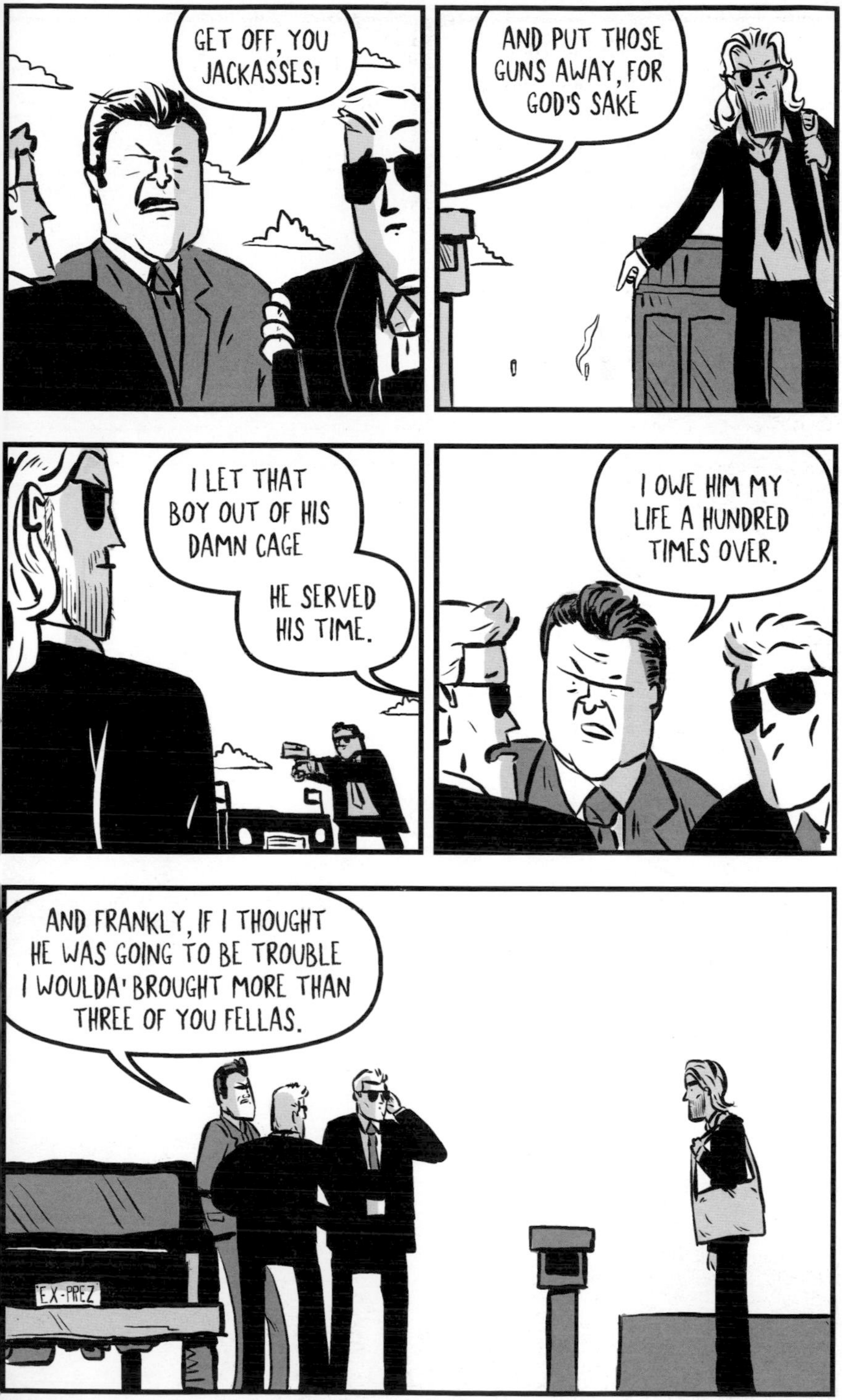
GET OFF, YOU JACKASSES!
AND PUT THOSE GUNS AWAY, FOR GOD'S SAKE
I LET THAT BOY OUT OF HIS DAMN CAGE
HE SERVED HIS TIME.
I OWE HIM MY LIFE A HUNDRED TIMES OVER.
AND FRANKLY, IF I THOUGHT HE WAS GOING TO BE TROUBLE I WOULDA' BROUGHT MORE THAN THREE OF YOU FELLAS.
EX-PREZ

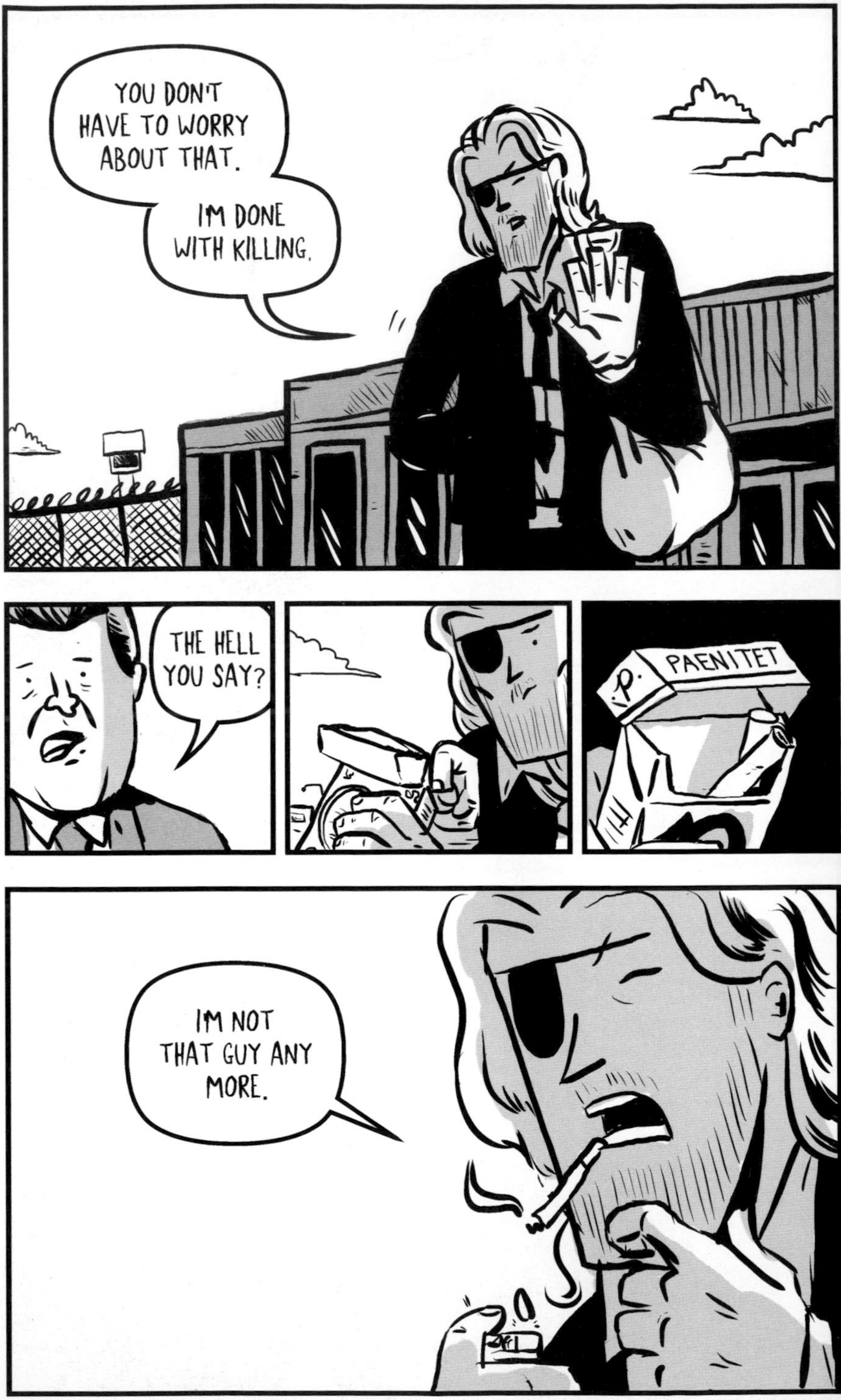
YOU DON'T HAVE TO WORRY ABOUT THAT.
I'M DONE WITH KILLING.
THE HELL YOU SAY?
PAENITET
I'M NOT THAT GUY ANY MORE.

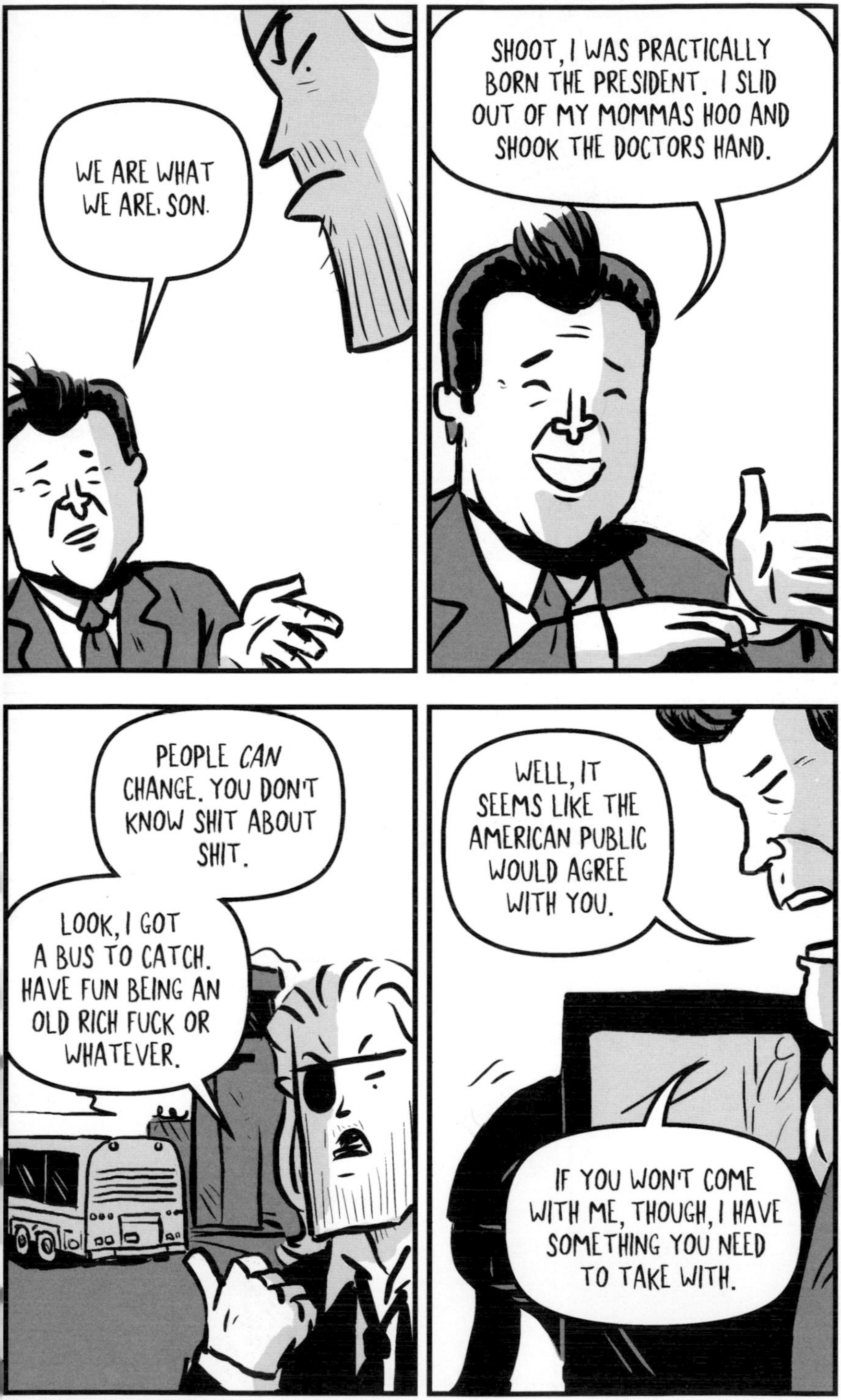
WE ARE WHAT WE ARE, SON.
SHOOT, I WAS PRACTICALLY BORN THE PRESIDENT. I SLID OUT OF MY MOMMAS HOO AND SHOOK THE DOCTORS HAND.
PEOPLE *CAN* CHANGE. YOU DON'T KNOW SHIT ABOUT SHIT.
LOOK, I GOT A BUS TO CATCH. HAVE FUN BEING AN OLD RICH FUCK OR WHATEVER.
WELL, IT SEEMS LIKE THE AMERICAN PUBLIC WOULD AGREE WITH YOU.
IF YOU WON'T COME WITH ME, THOUGH, I HAVE SOMETHING YOU NEED TO TAKE WITH.

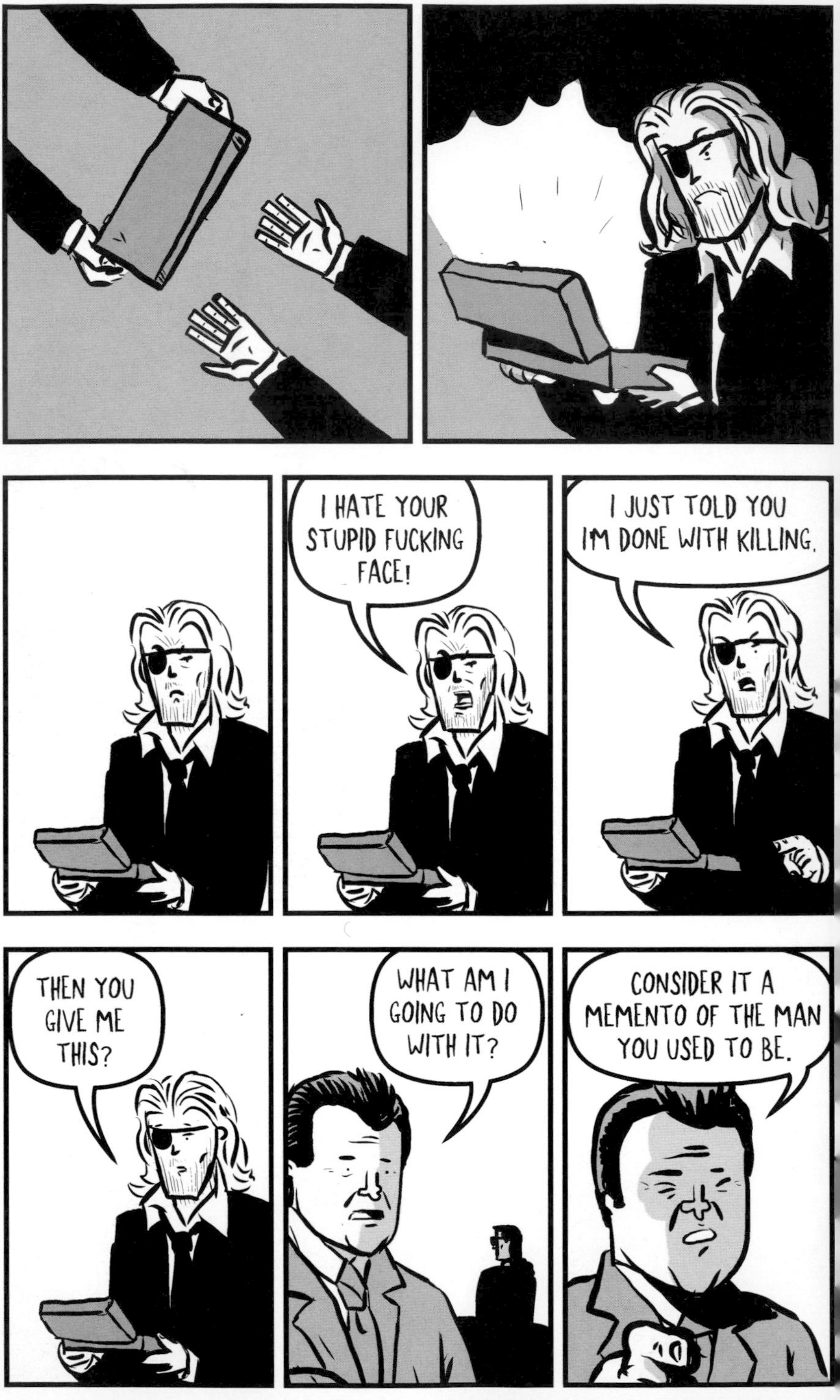
I HATE YOUR STUPID FUCKING FACE!
I JUST TOLD YOU I'M DONE WITH KILLING.
THEN YOU GIVE ME THIS?
WHAT AM I GOING TO DO WITH IT?
CONSIDER IT A MEMENTO OF THE MAN YOU USED TO BE.

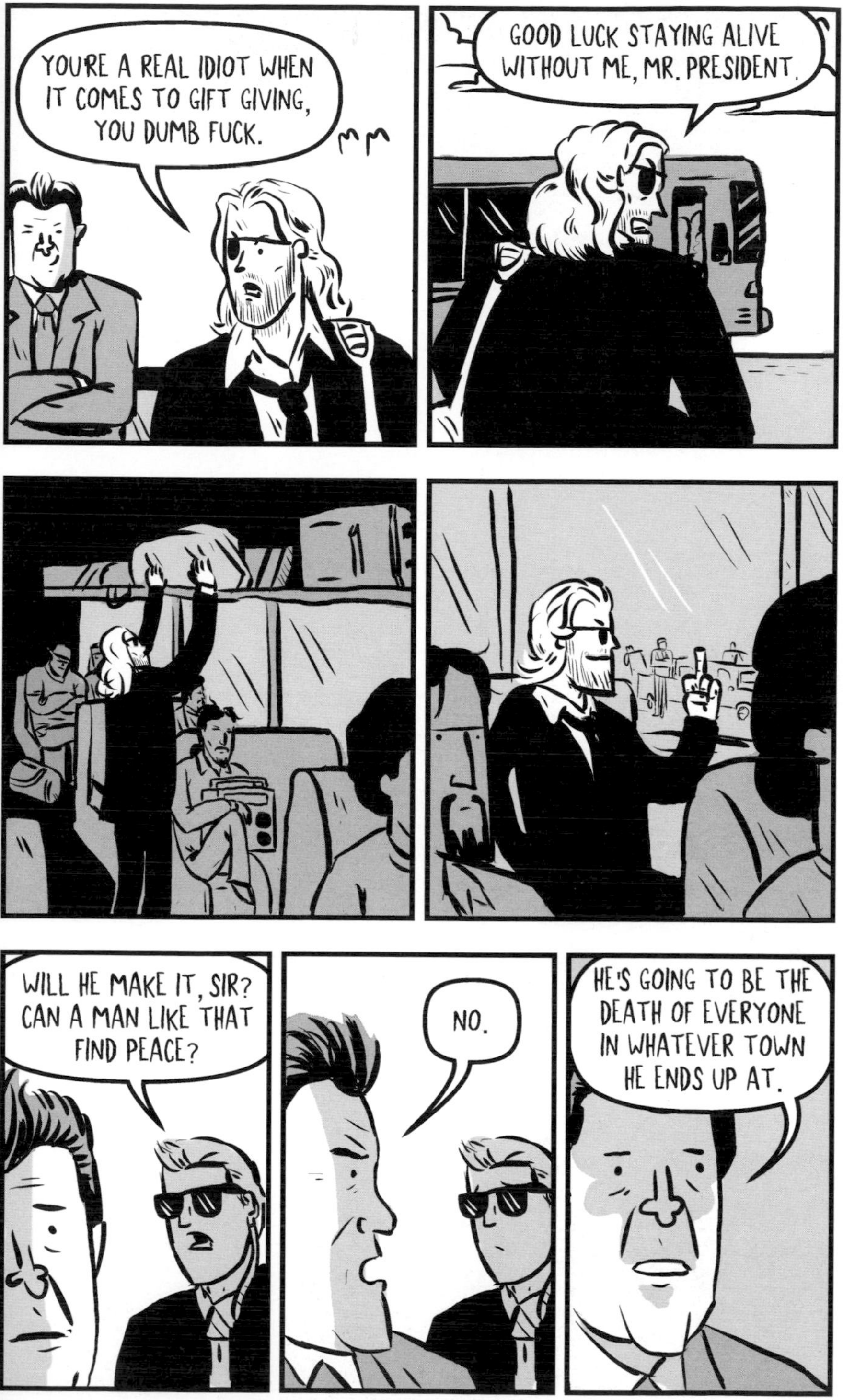
YOU'RE A REAL IDIOT WHEN IT COMES TO GIFT GIVING, YOU DUMB FUCK.
GOOD LUCK STAYING ALIVE WITHOUT ME, MR. PRESIDENT.
WILL HE MAKE IT, SIR? CAN A MAN LIKE THAT FIND PEACE?
NO.
HE'S GOING TO BE THE DEATH OF EVERYONE IN WHATEVER TOWN HE ENDS UP AT.

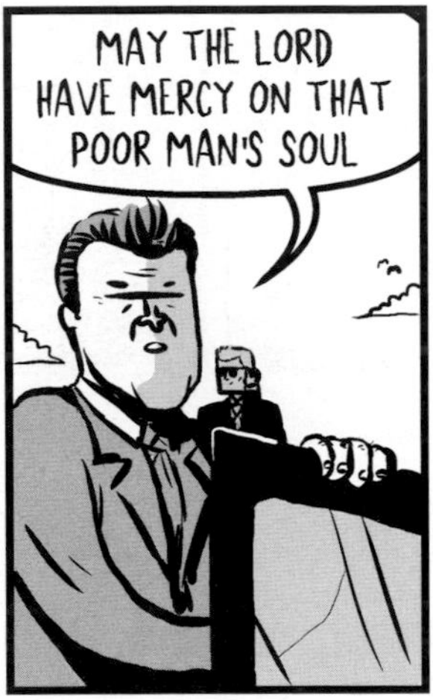
MAY THE LORD HAVE MERCY ON THAT POOR MAN'S SOUL

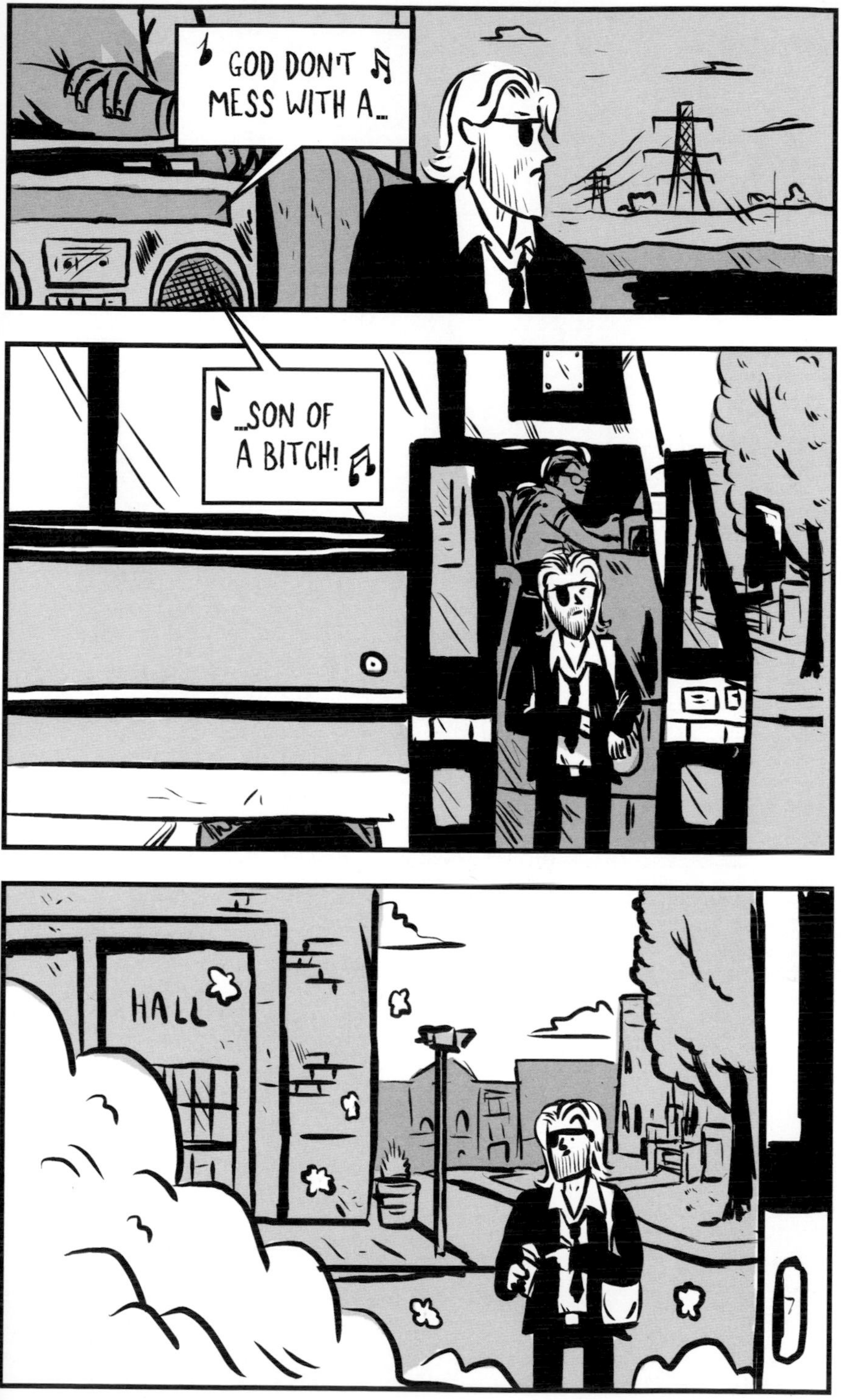
GOD DON'T MESS WITH A...
...SON OF A BITCH!
HALL

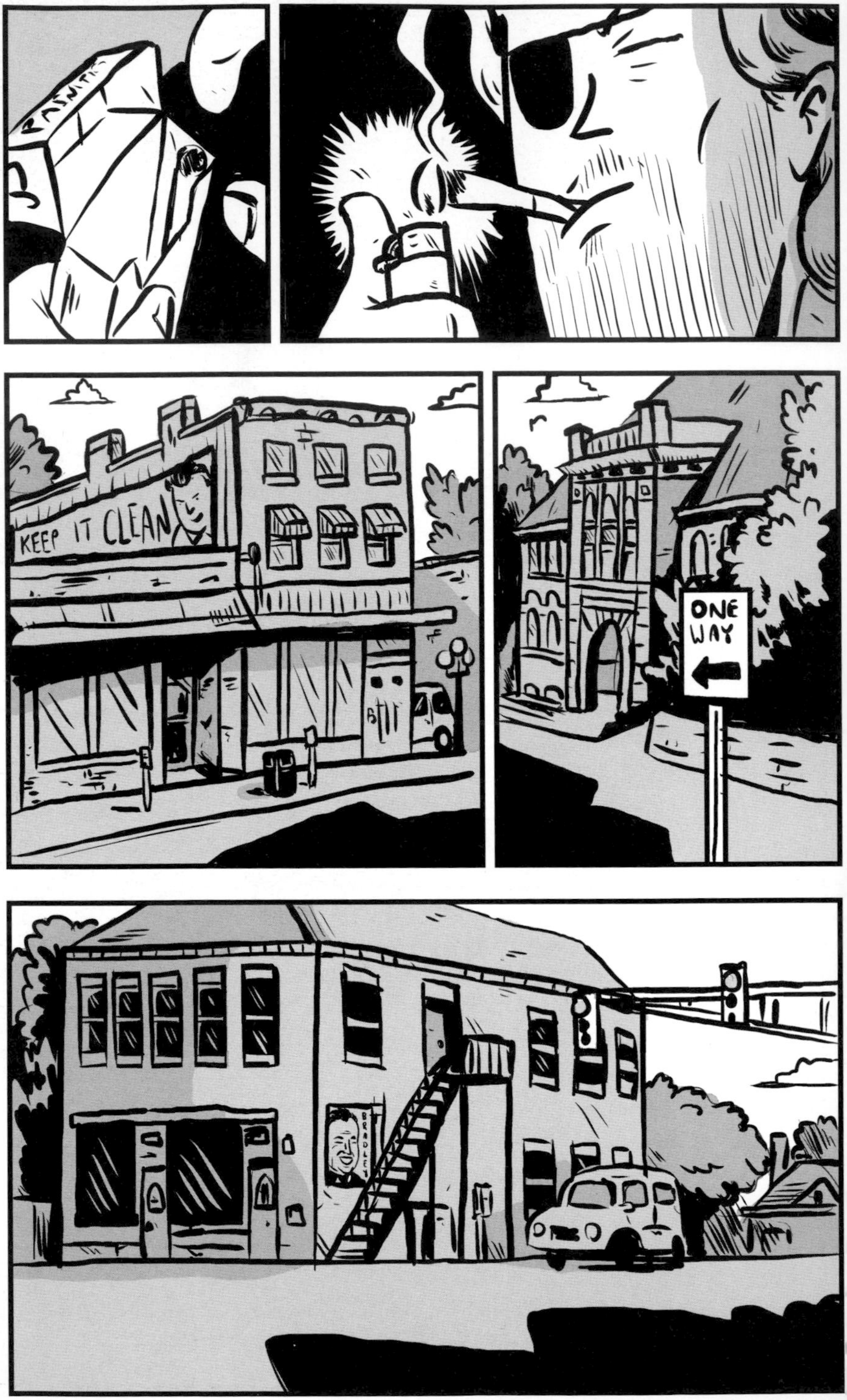
KEEP IT CLEAN
ONE WAY
BRADLEY

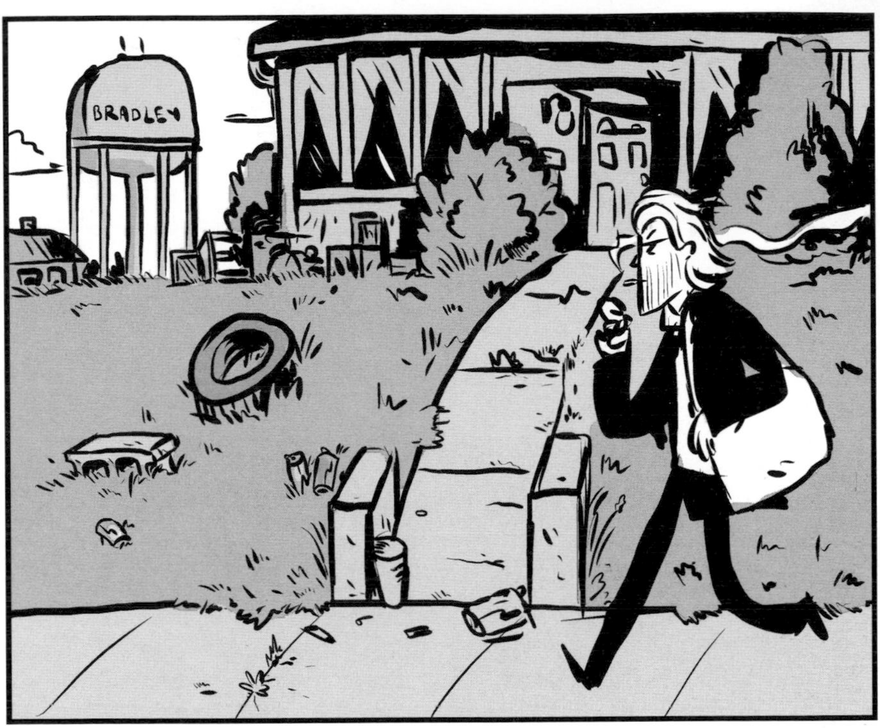
BRADLEY

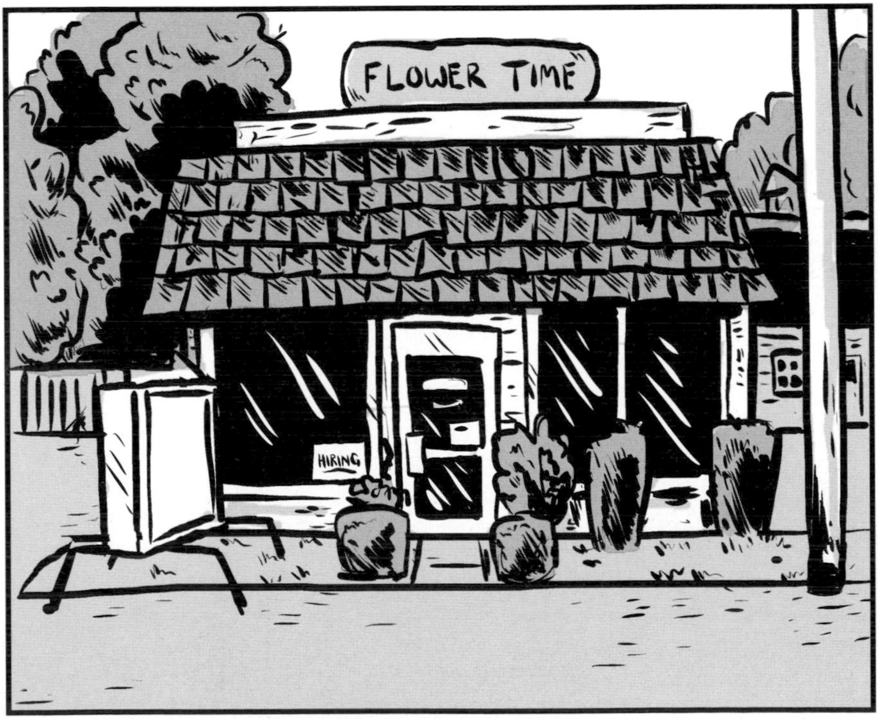
FLOWER TIME
HIRING

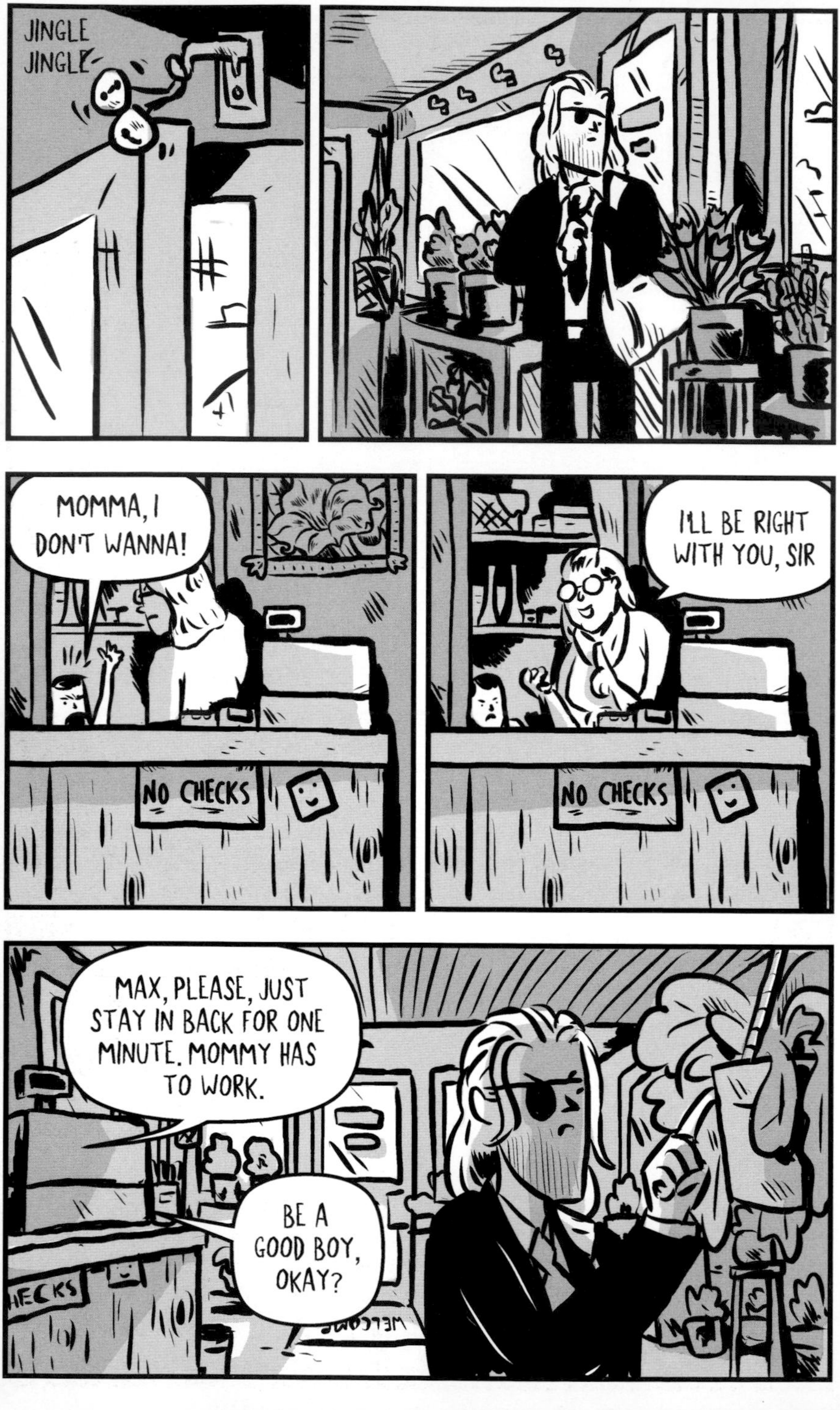

JINGLE JINGLE
MOMMA, I DON'T WANNA!
I'LL BE RIGHT WITH YOU, SIR
NO CHECKS
NO CHECKS
MAX, PLEASE, JUST STAY IN BACK FOR ONE MINUTE. MOMMY HAS TO WORK.
BE A GOOD BOY, OKAY?

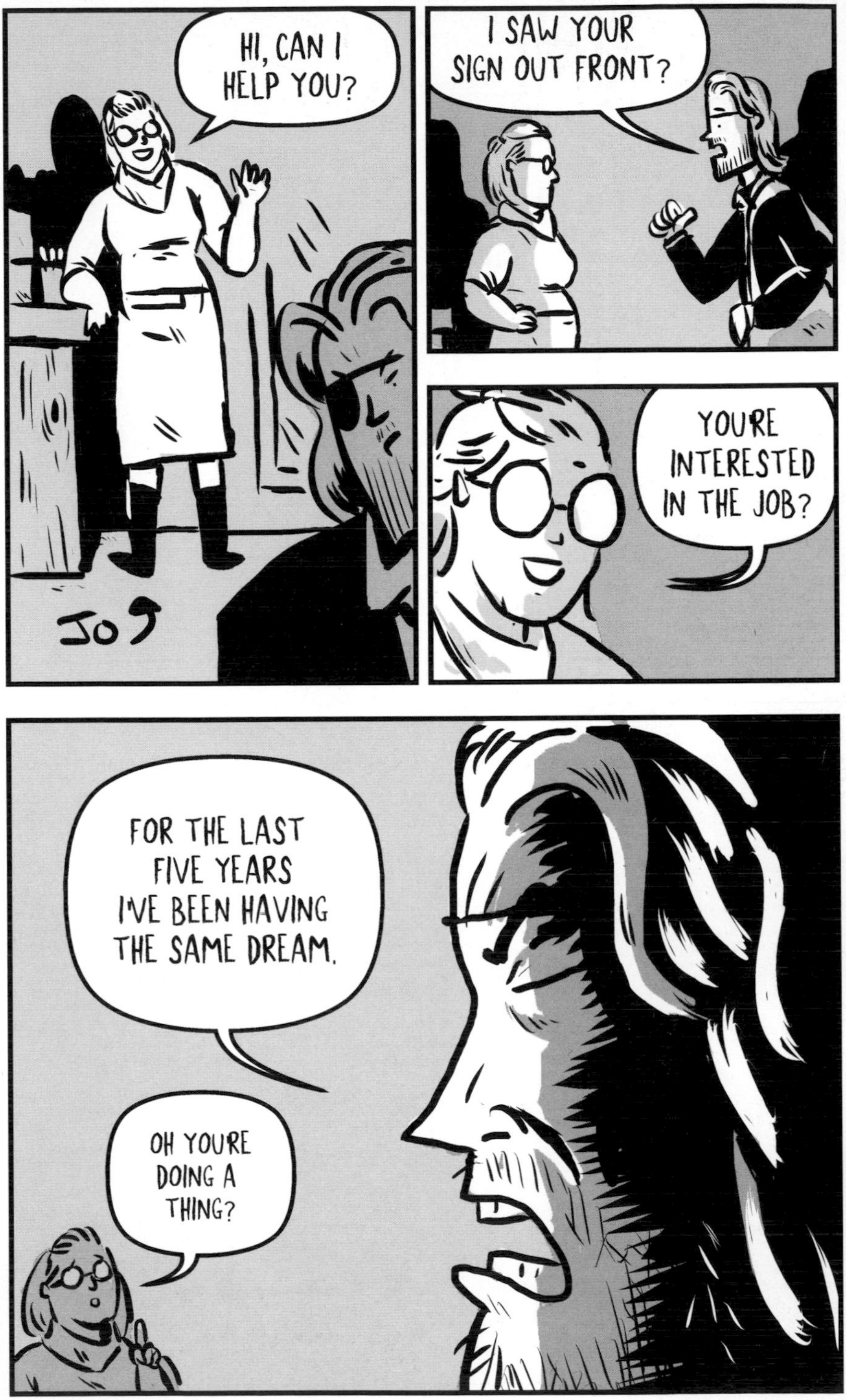
HI, CAN I HELP YOU?
JO
I SAW YOUR SIGN OUT FRONT?
YOU'RE INTERESTED IN THE JOB?
FOR THE LAST FIVE YEARS I'VE BEEN HAVING THE SAME DREAM.
OH YOU'RE DOING A THING?

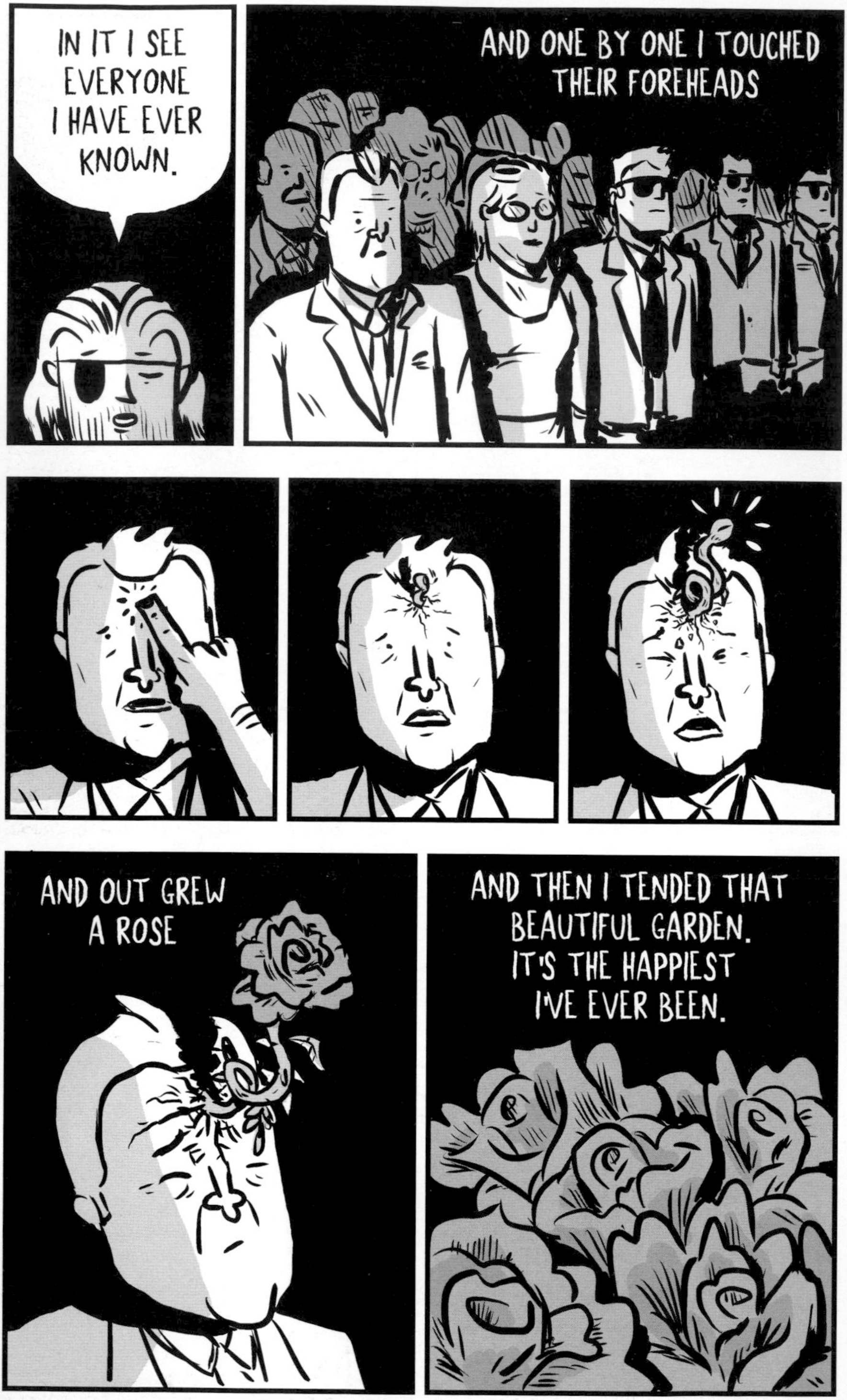
IN IT I SEE EVERYONE I HAVE EVER KNOWN.
AND ONE BY ONE I TOUCHED THEIR FOREHEADS
AND OUT GREW A ROSE
AND THEN I TENDED THAT BEAUTIFUL GARDEN. IT'S THE HAPPIEST I'VE EVER BEEN.

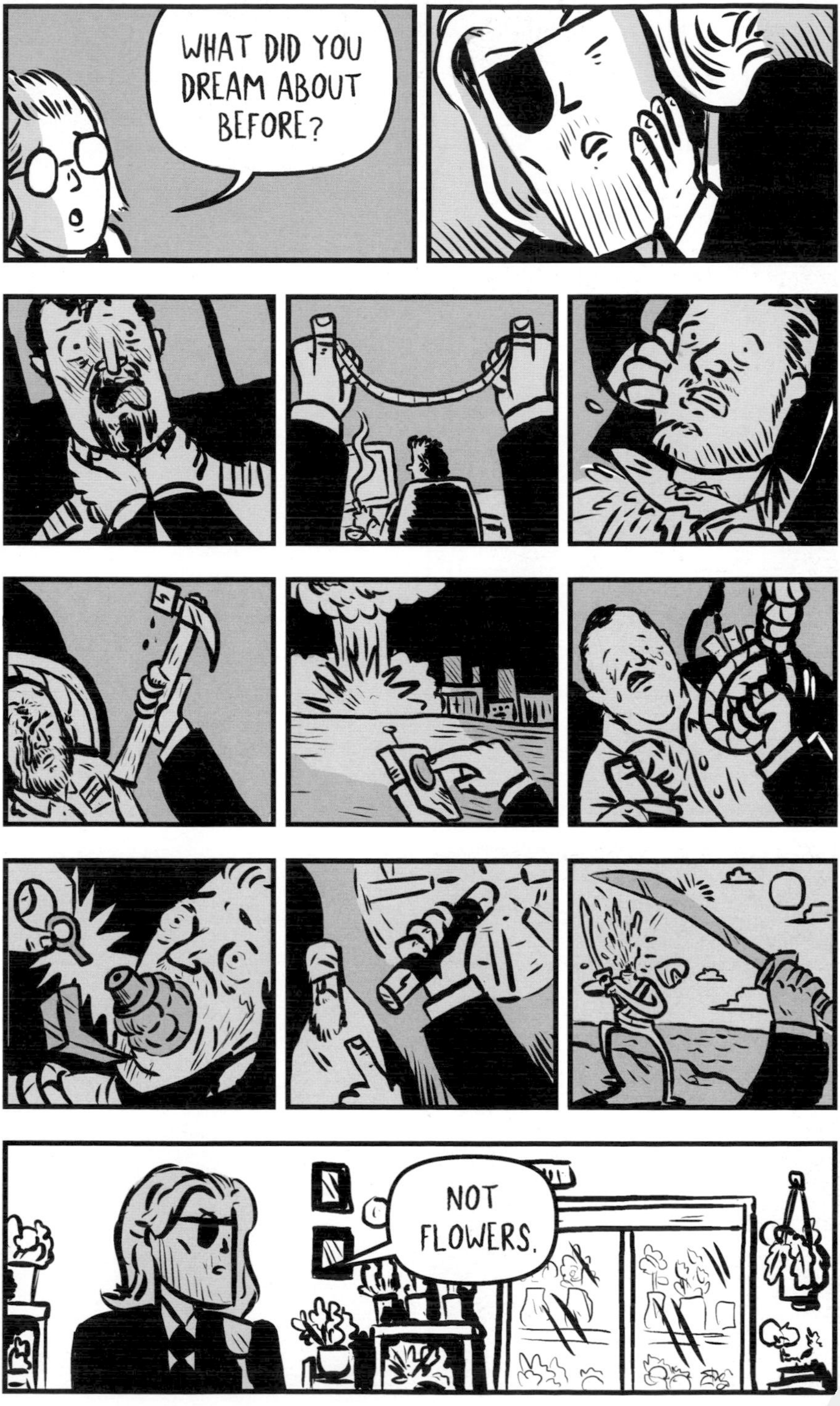
WHAT DID YOU DREAM ABOUT BEFORE?
NOT FLOWERS.

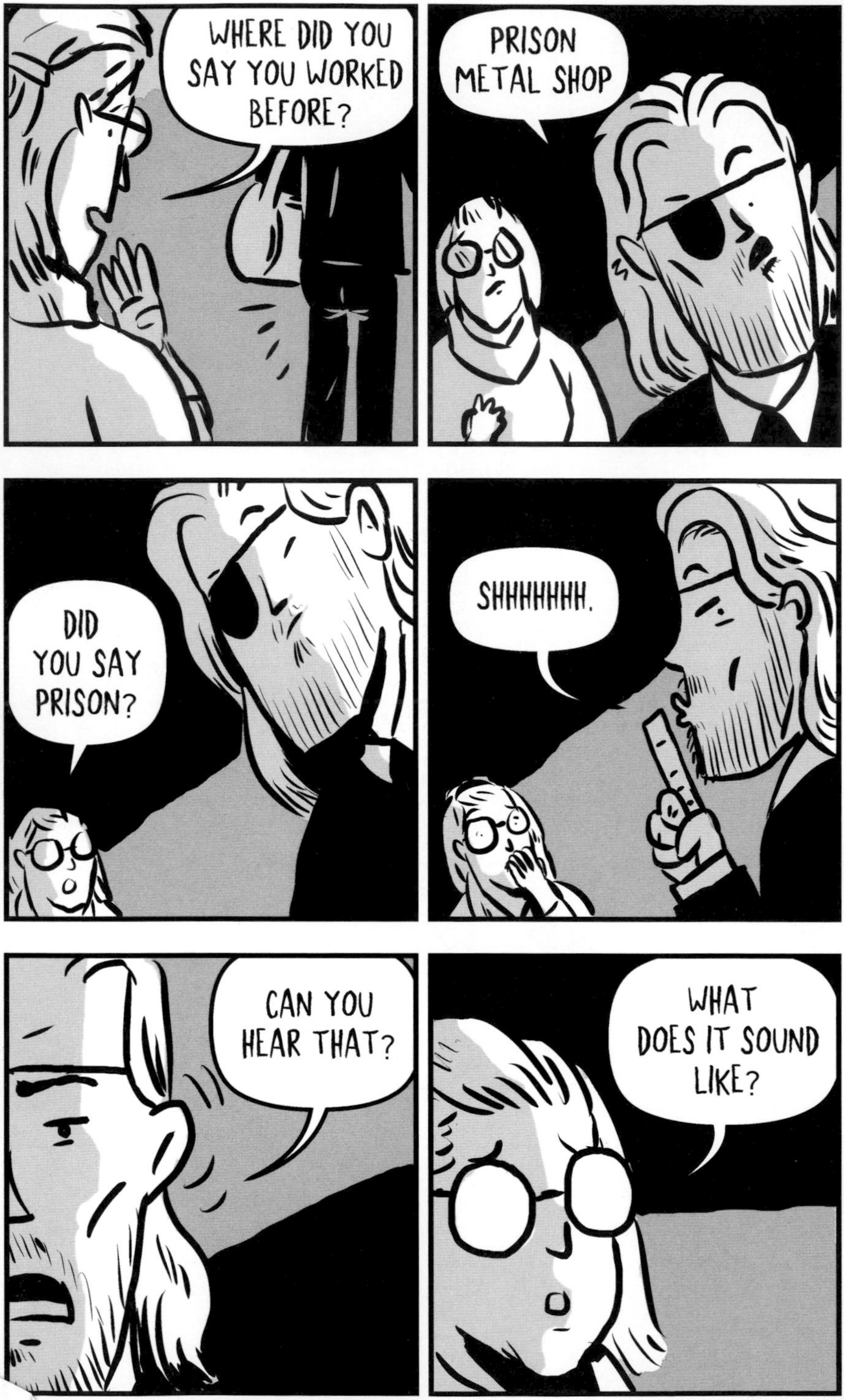
WHERE DID YOU SAY YOU WORKED BEFORE?
PRISON METAL SHOP
DID YOU SAY PRISON?
SHHHHHHH.
CAN YOU HEAR THAT?
WHAT DOES IT SOUND LIKE?

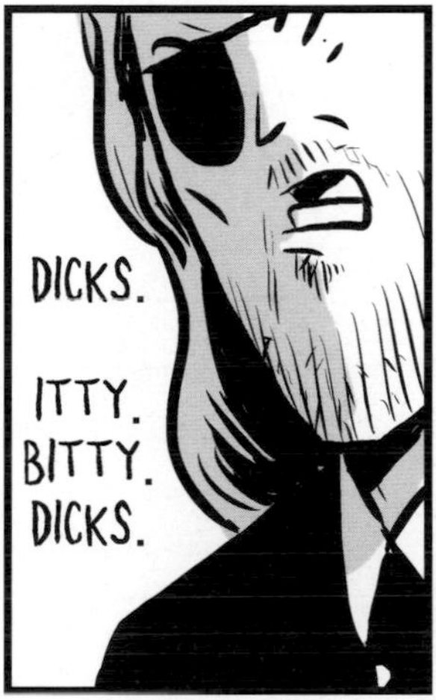
DICKS.
ITTY. BITTY. DICKS.

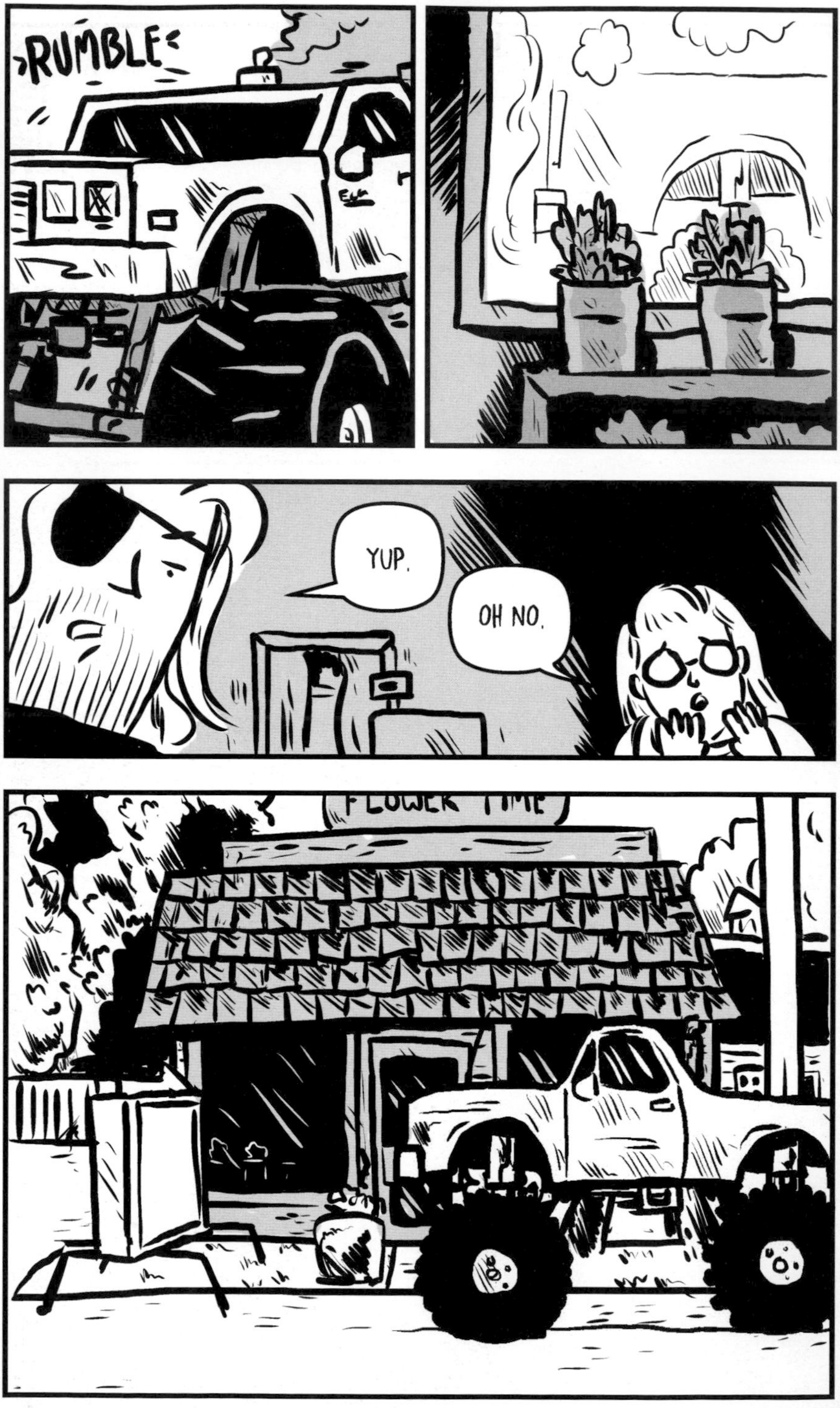
RUMBLE
YUP.
OH NO.

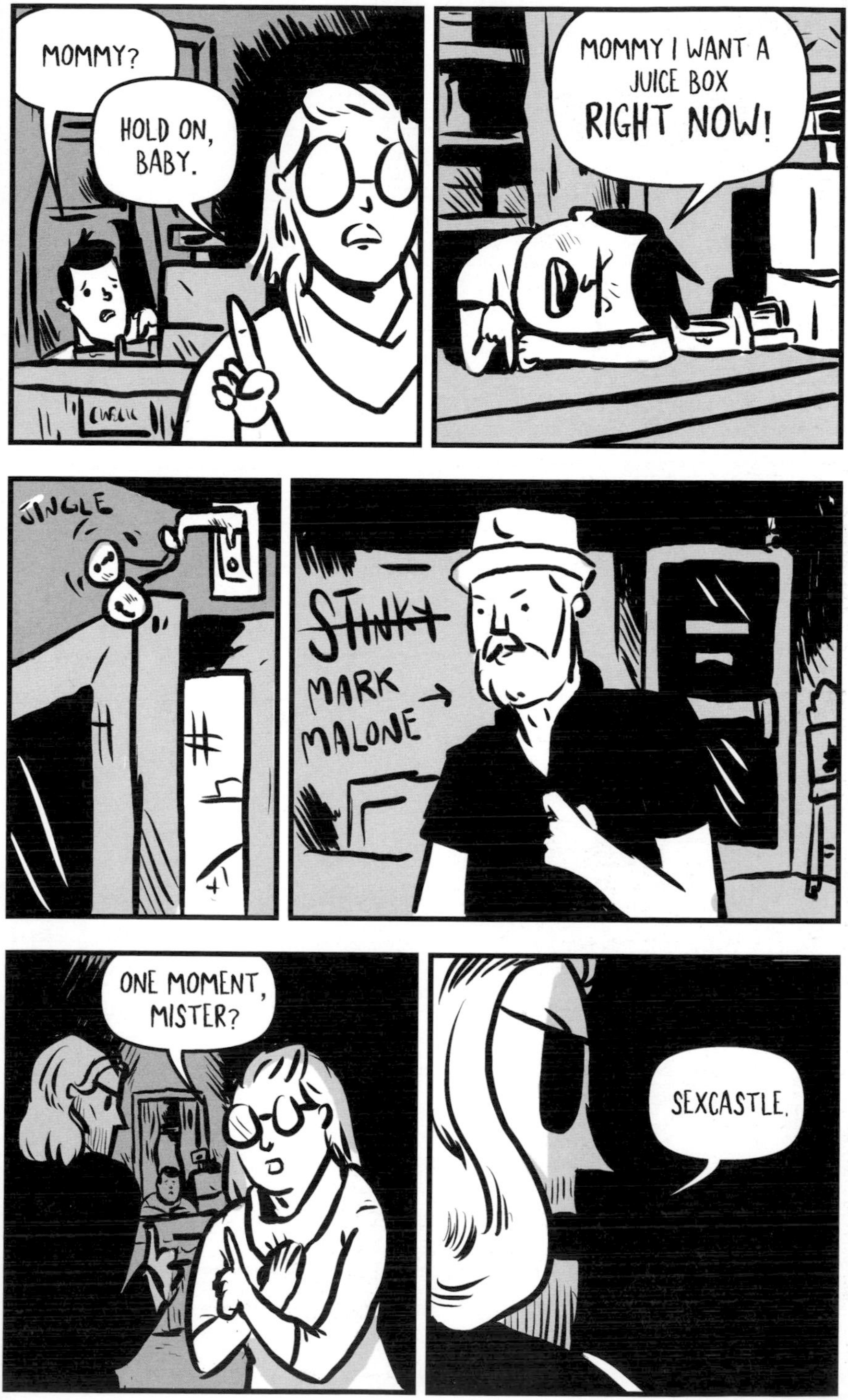
MOMMY?
HOLD ON, BABY.
MOMMY I WANT A JUICE BOX RIGHT NOW!
JINGLE
STINKY
MARK MALONE
ONE MOMENT, MISTER?
SEXCASTLE.

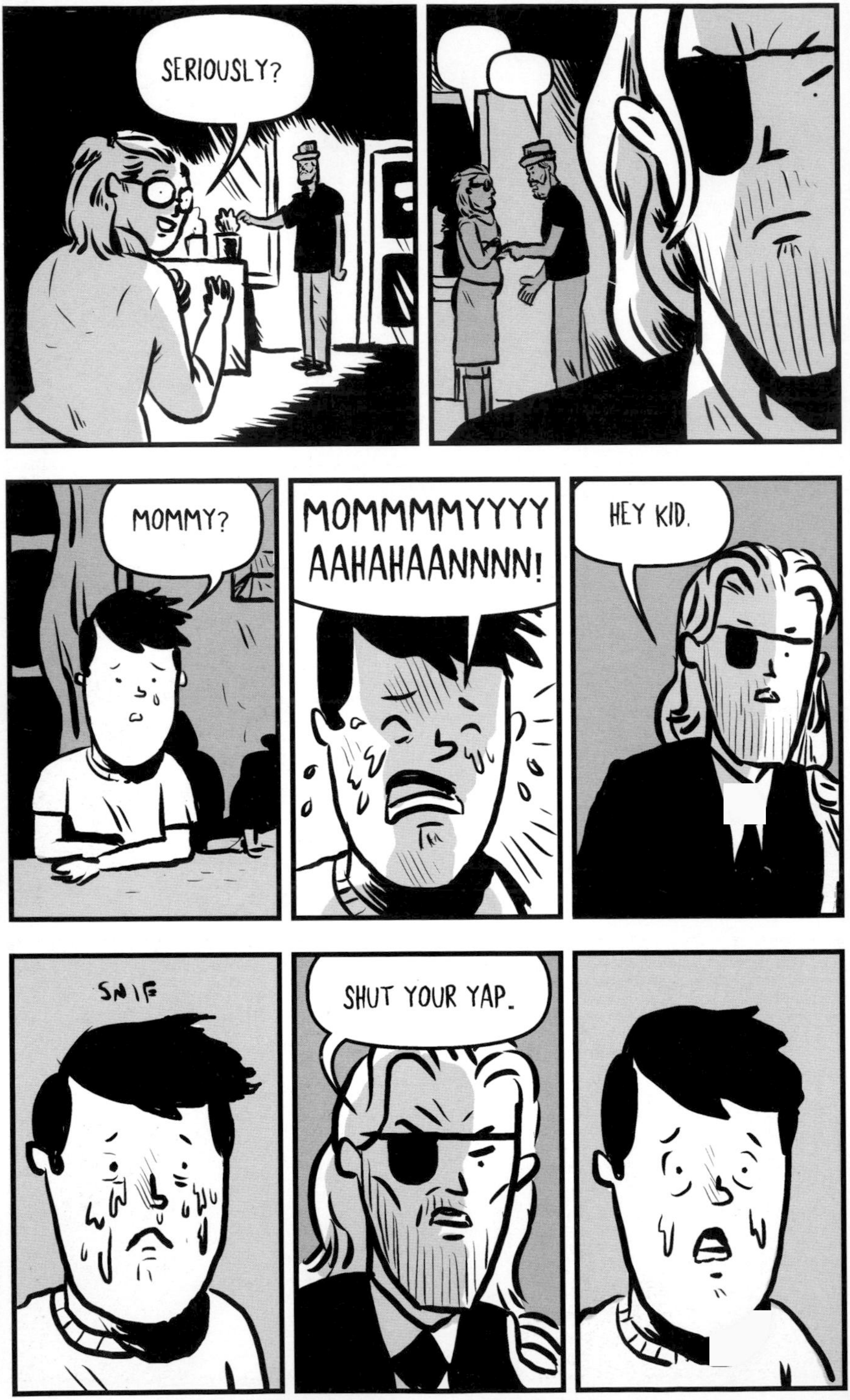
SERIOUSLY?
MOMMY?
MOMMMMYYYY AAHAHAANNNN!
HEY KID.
SNIF
SHUT YOUR YAP.

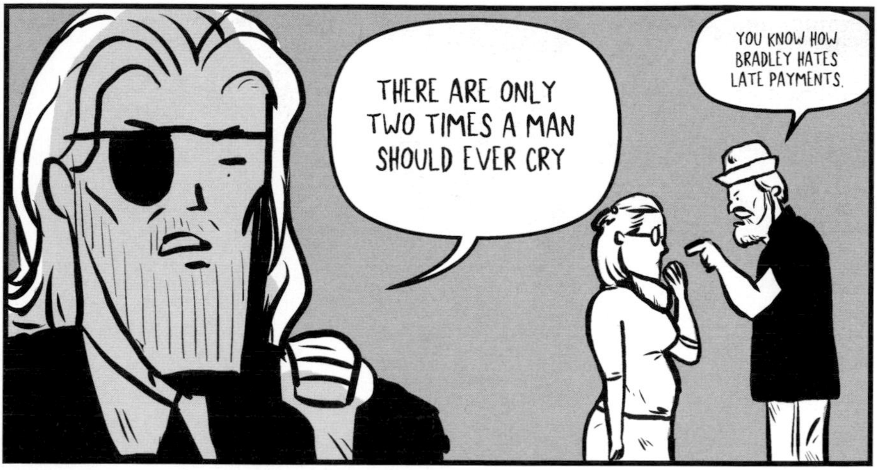
THERE ARE ONLY TWO TIMES A MAN SHOULD EVER CRY
YOU KNOW HOW BRADLEY HATES LATE PAYMENTS.

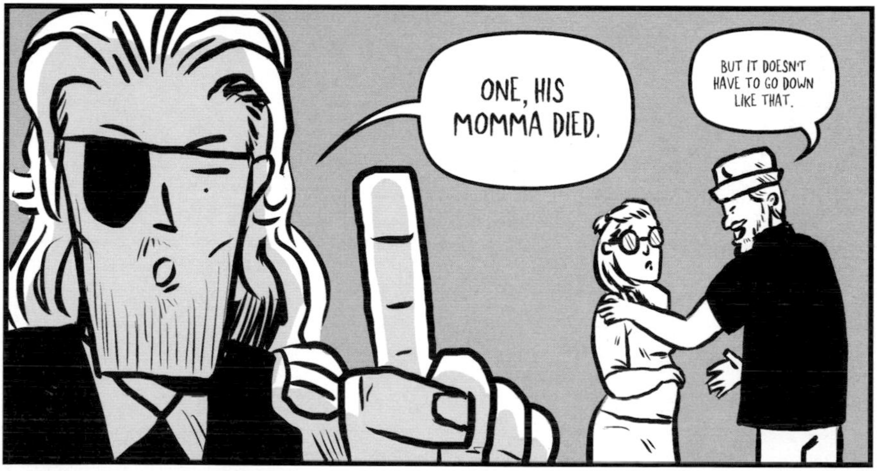
ONE, HIS MOMMA DIED.
BUT IT DOESN'T HAVE TO GO DOWN LIKE THAT.

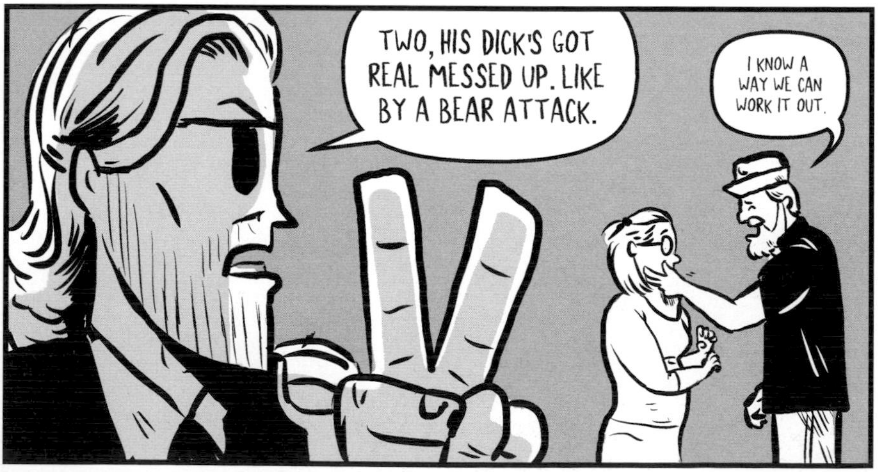
TWO, HIS DICK'S GOT REAL MESSED UP. LIKE BY A BEAR ATTACK.
I KNOW A WAY WE CAN WORK IT OUT.

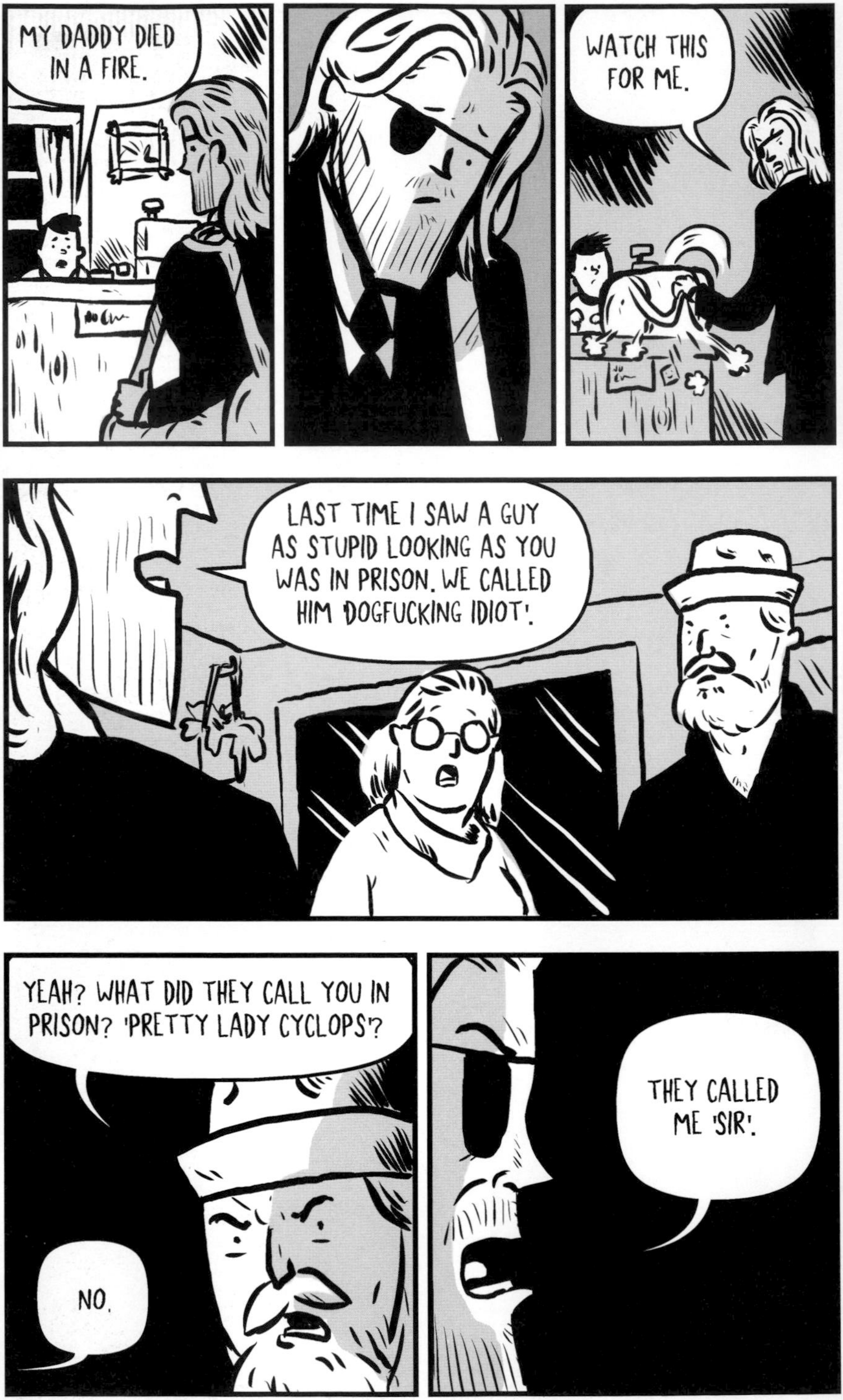
MY DADDY DIED IN A FIRE.
WATCH THIS FOR ME.
LAST TIME I SAW A GUY AS STUPID LOOKING AS YOU WAS IN PRISON. WE CALLED HIM 'DOGFUCKING IDIOT'.
YEAH? WHAT DID THEY CALL YOU IN PRISON? 'PRETTY LADY CYCLOPS'?
NO.
THEY CALLED ME 'SIR'.

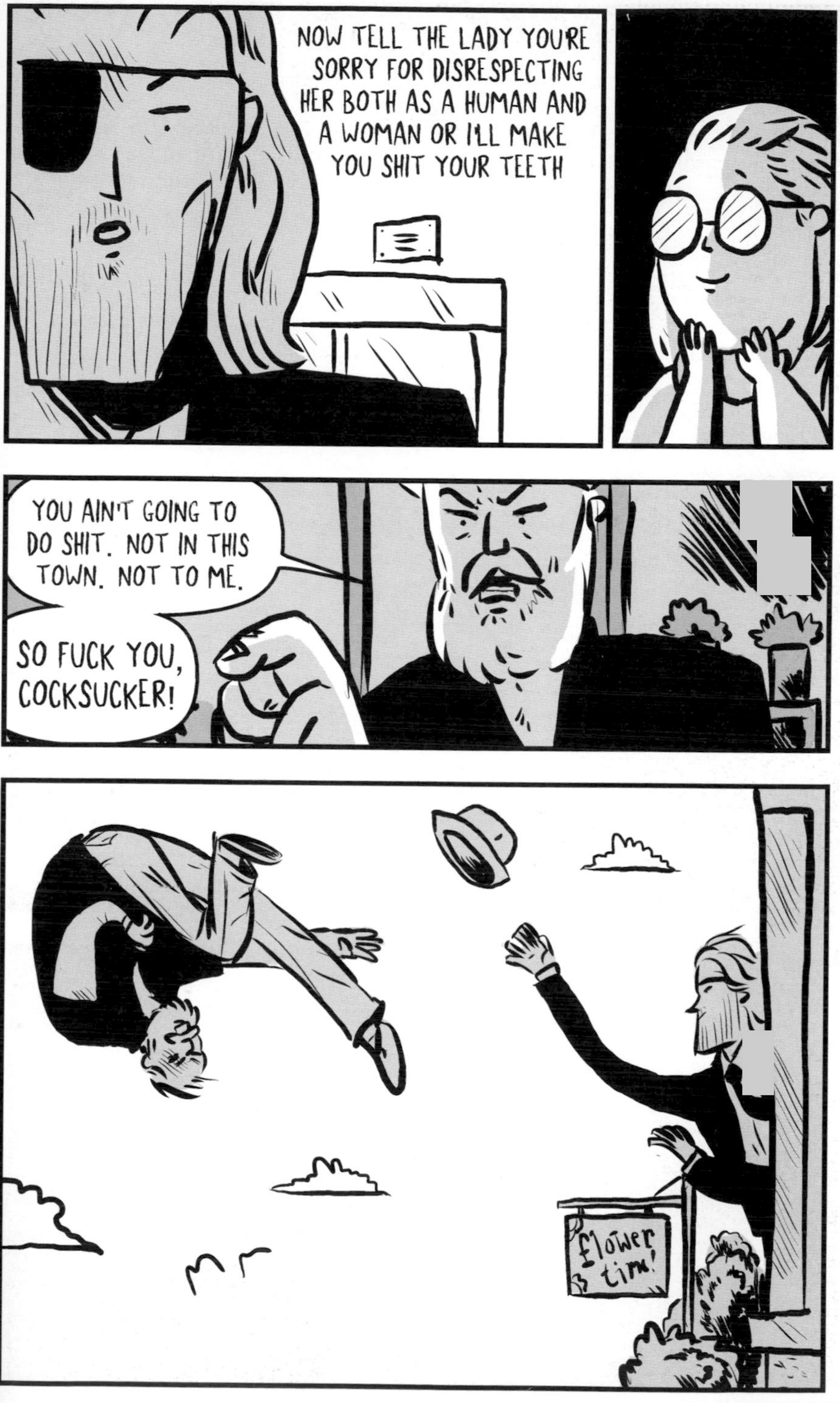
NOW TELL THE LADY YOU'RE SORRY FOR DISRESPECTING HER BOTH AS A HUMAN AND A WOMAN OR I'LL MAKE YOU SHIT YOUR TEETH
YOU AIN'T GOING TO DO SHIT. NOT IN THIS TOWN. NOT TO ME.
SO FUCK YOU, COCKSUCKER!
flower time!

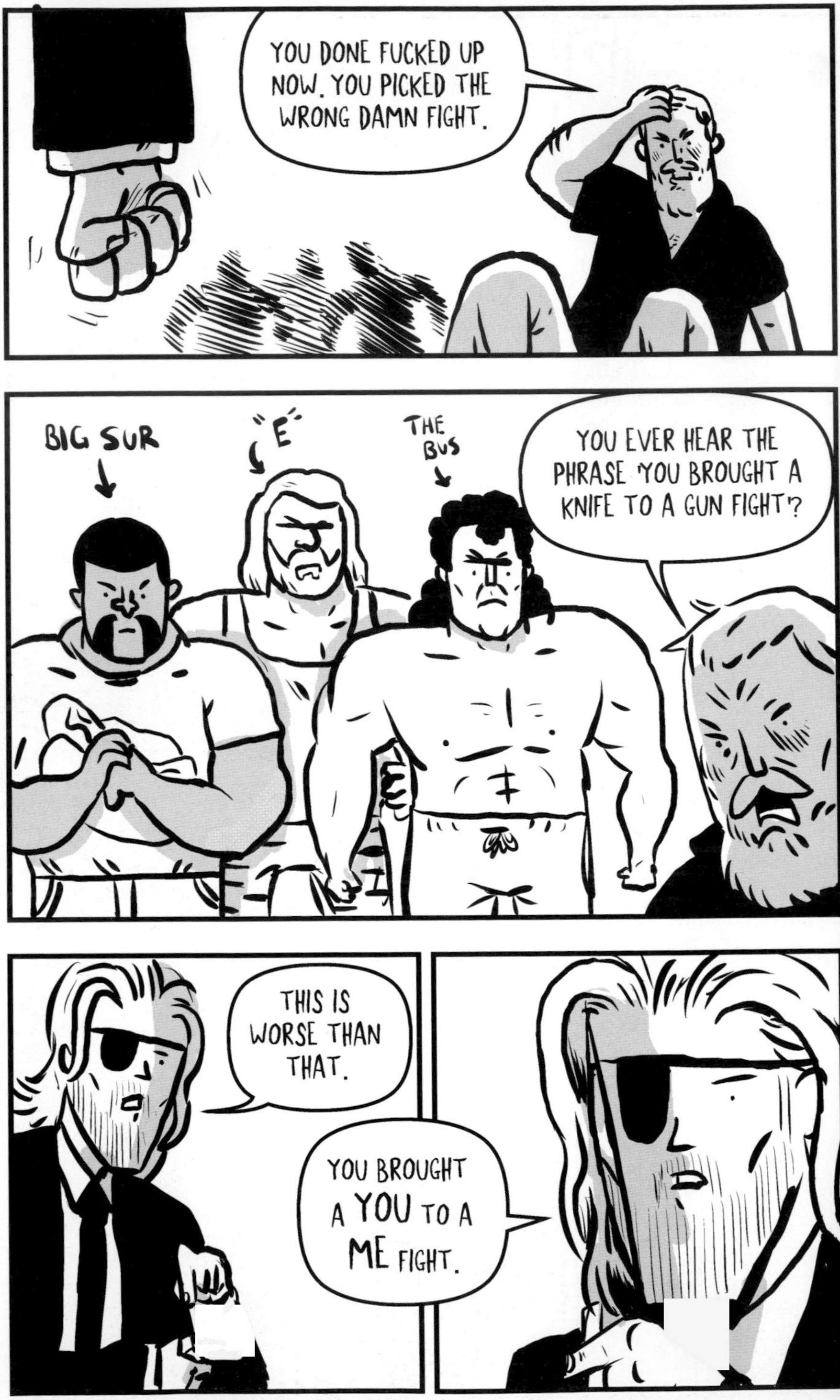
YOU DONE FUCKED UP NOW. YOU PICKED THE WRONG DAMN FIGHT.
BIG SUR
"E"
THE BUS
YOU EVER HEAR THE PHRASE 'YOU BROUGHT A KNIFE TO A GUN FIGHT'?
THIS IS WORSE THAN THAT.
YOU BROUGHT A YOU TO A ME FIGHT.

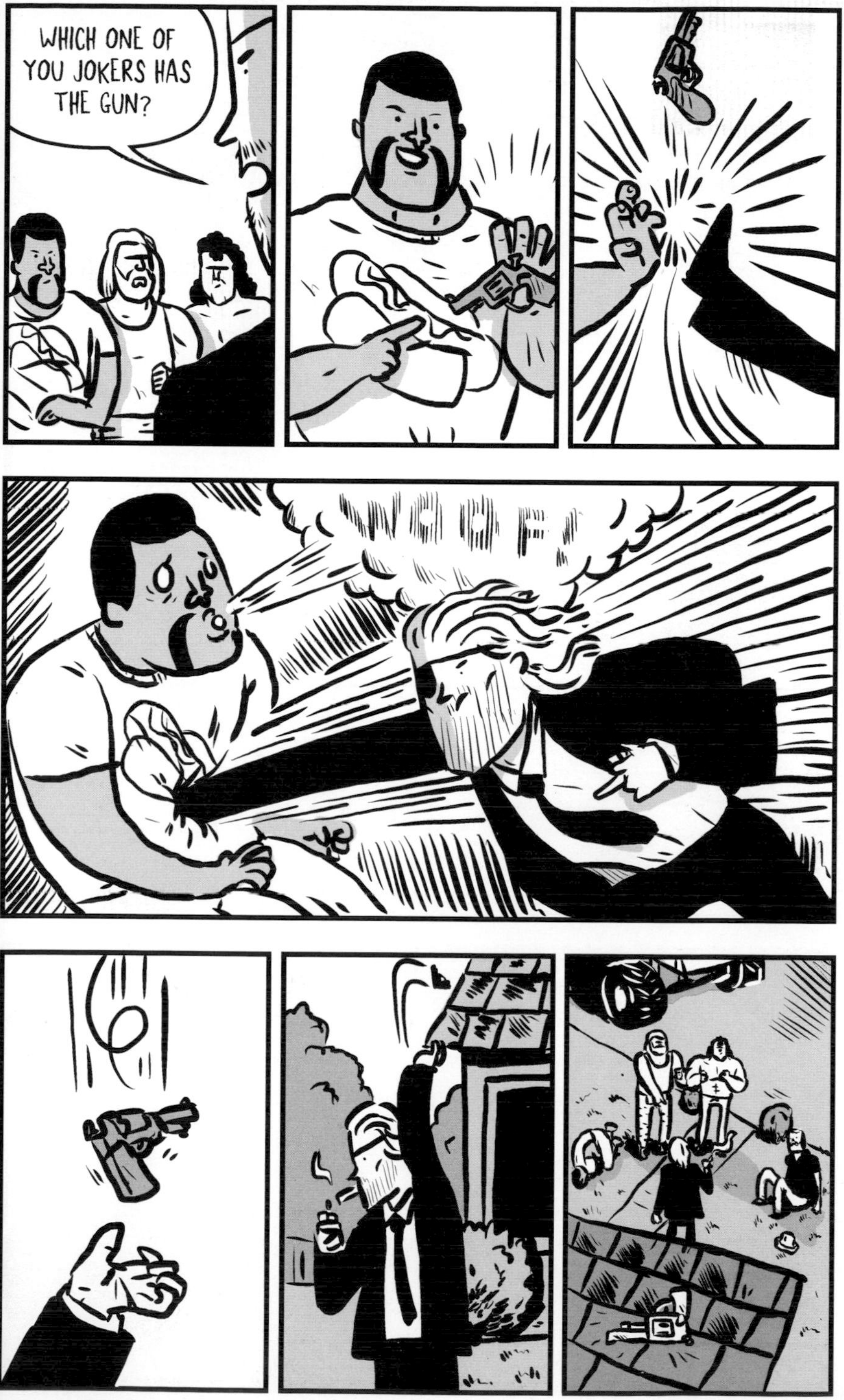
WHICH ONE OF YOU JOKERS HAS THE GUN?
WOOF!

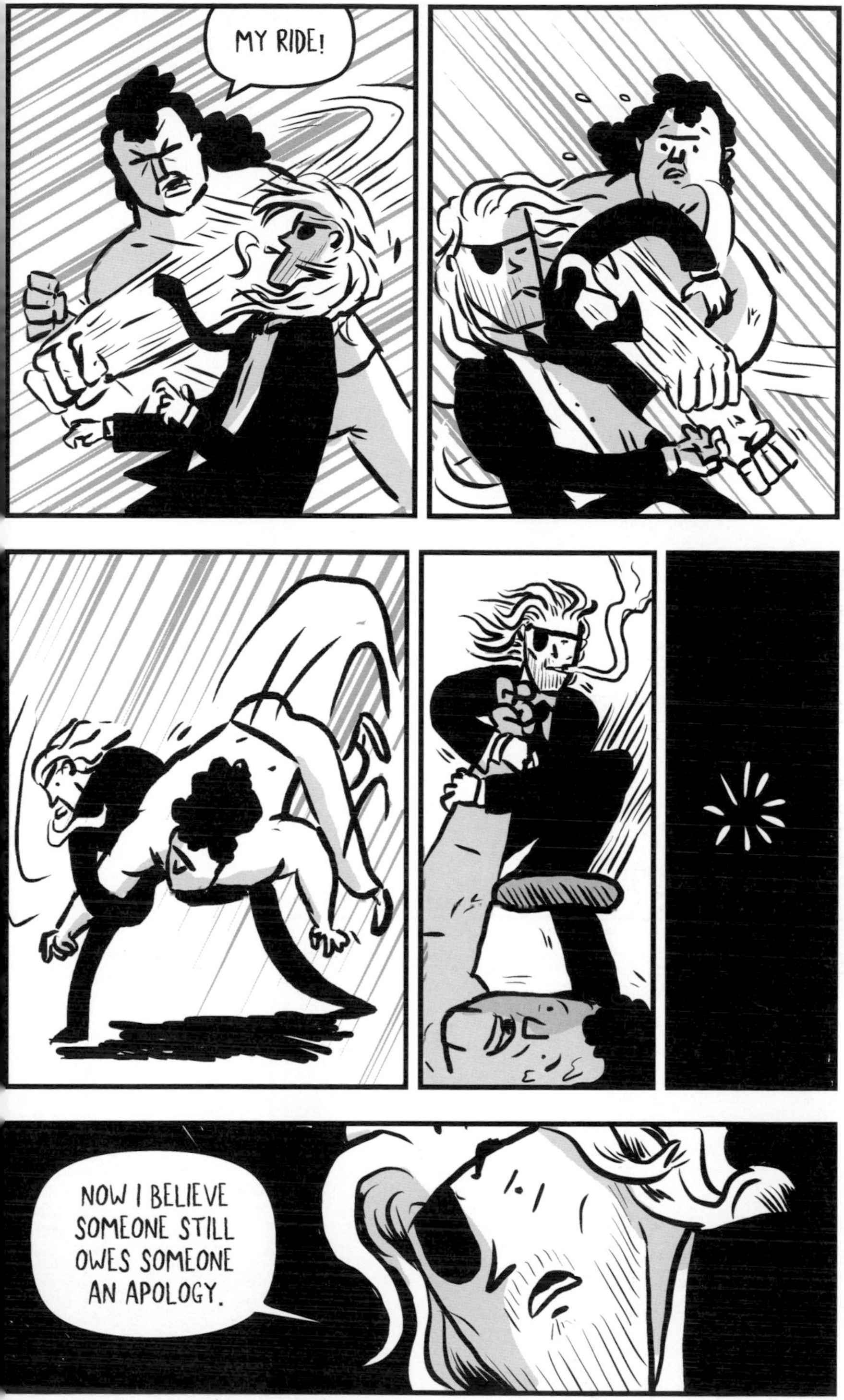
MY RIDE!
NOW I BELIEVE SOMEONE STILL OWES SOMEONE AN APOLOGY.

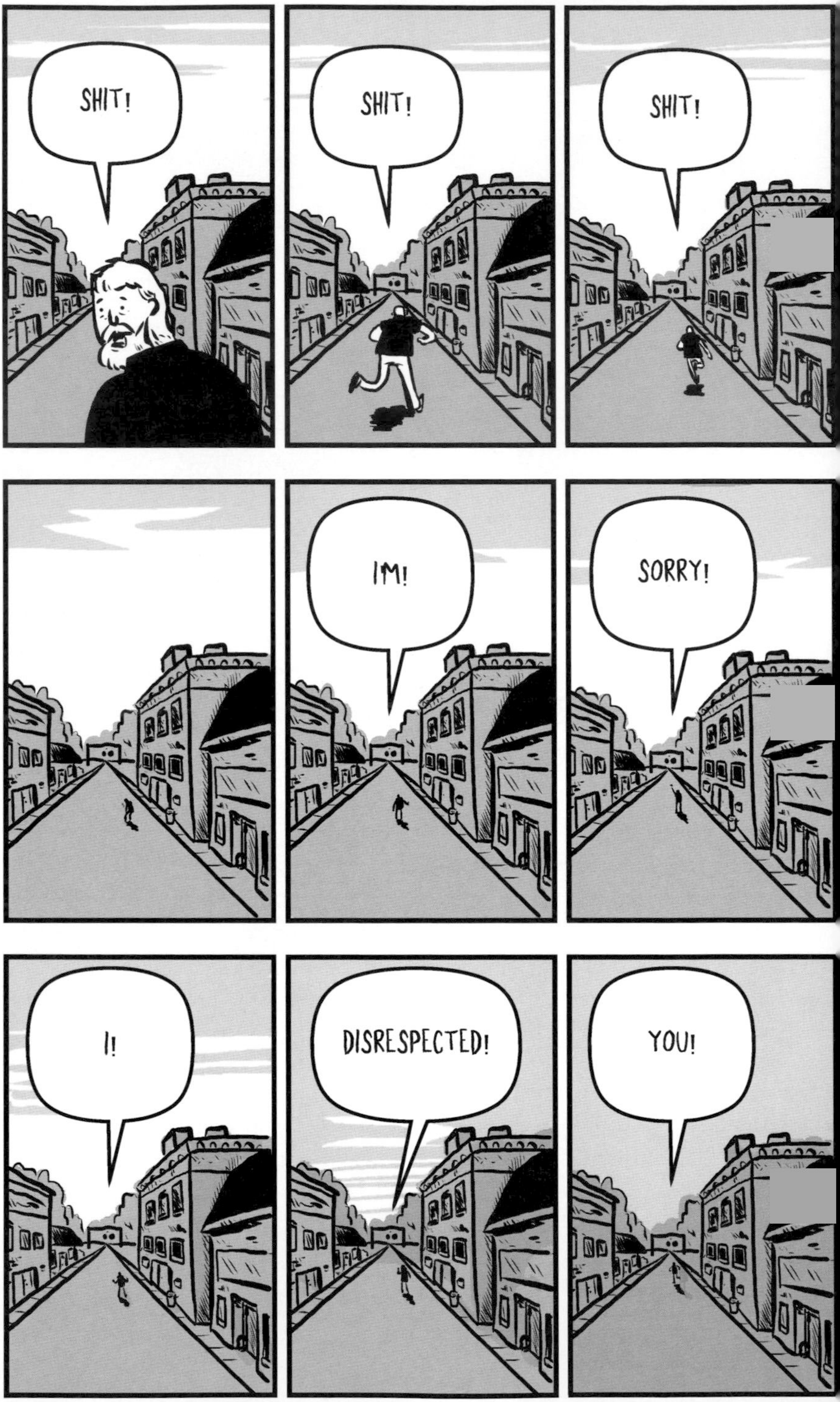
SHIT!
SHIT!
SHIT!
I'M!
SORRY!
I!
DISRESPECTED!
YOU!

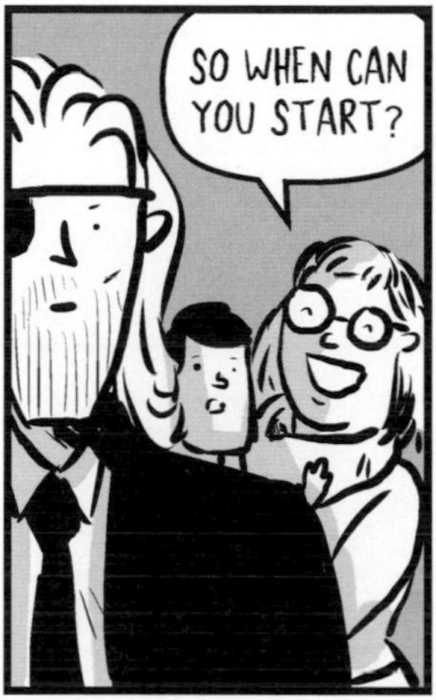
SO WHEN CAN YOU START?

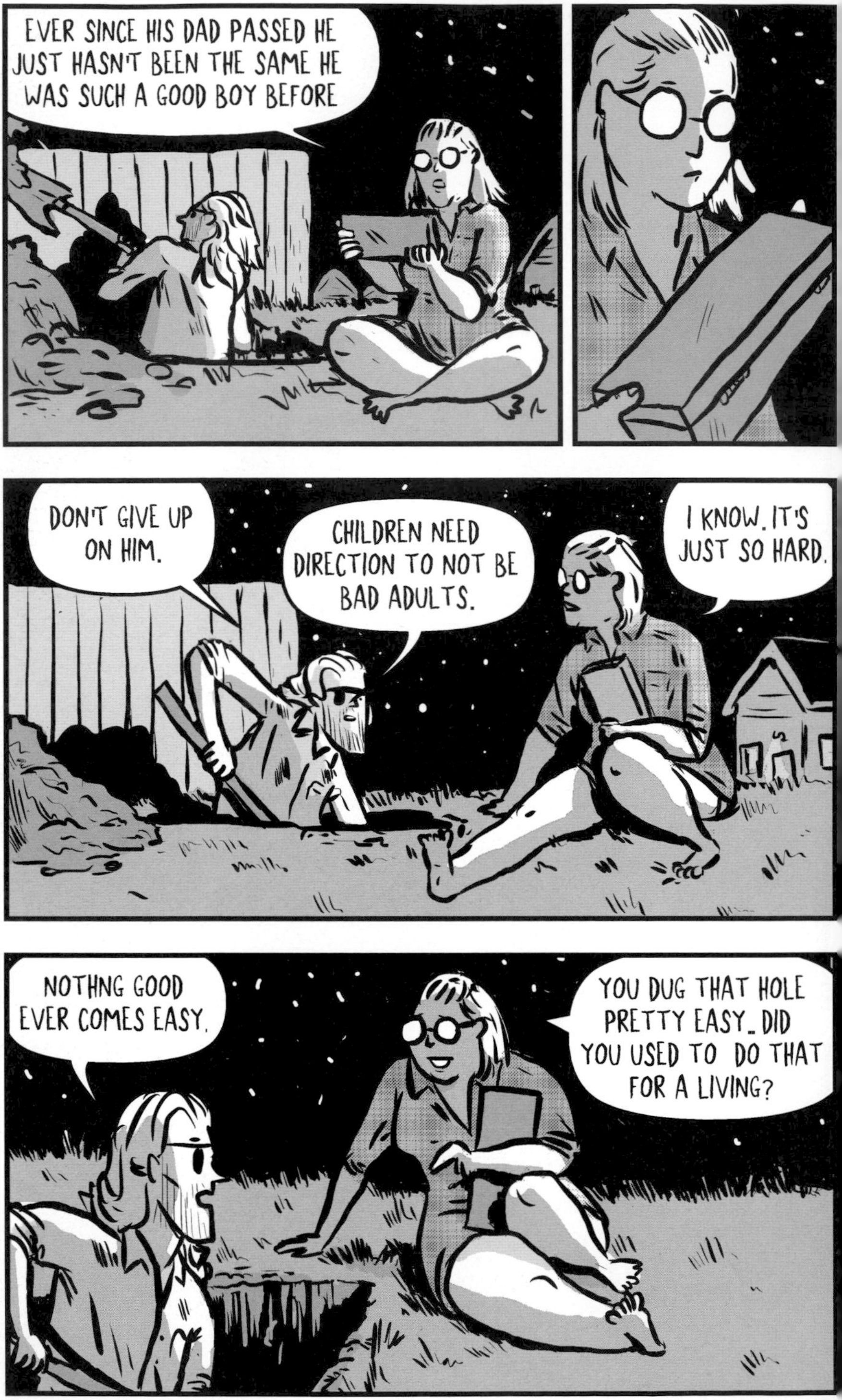
EVER SINCE HIS DAD PASSED HE JUST HASN'T BEEN THE SAME HE WAS SUCH A GOOD BOY BEFORE
DON'T GIVE UP ON HIM.
CHILDREN NEED DIRECTION TO NOT BE BAD ADULTS.
I KNOW. IT'S JUST SO HARD.
NOTHNG GOOD EVER COMES EASY.
YOU DUG THAT HOLE PRETTY EASY.. DID YOU USED TO DO THAT FOR A LIVING?

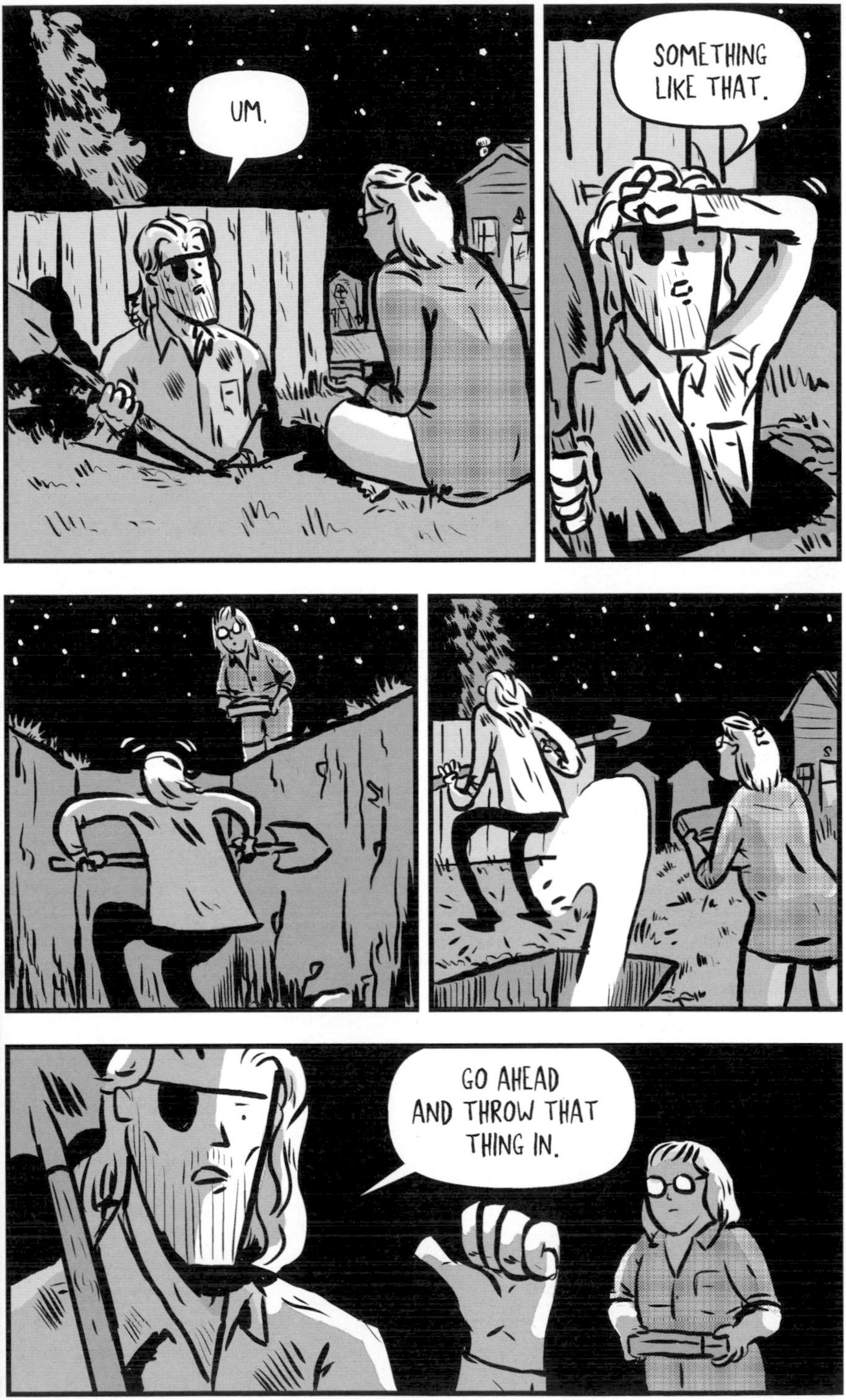
UM.
SOMETHING LIKE THAT.
GO AHEAD AND THROW THAT THING IN.

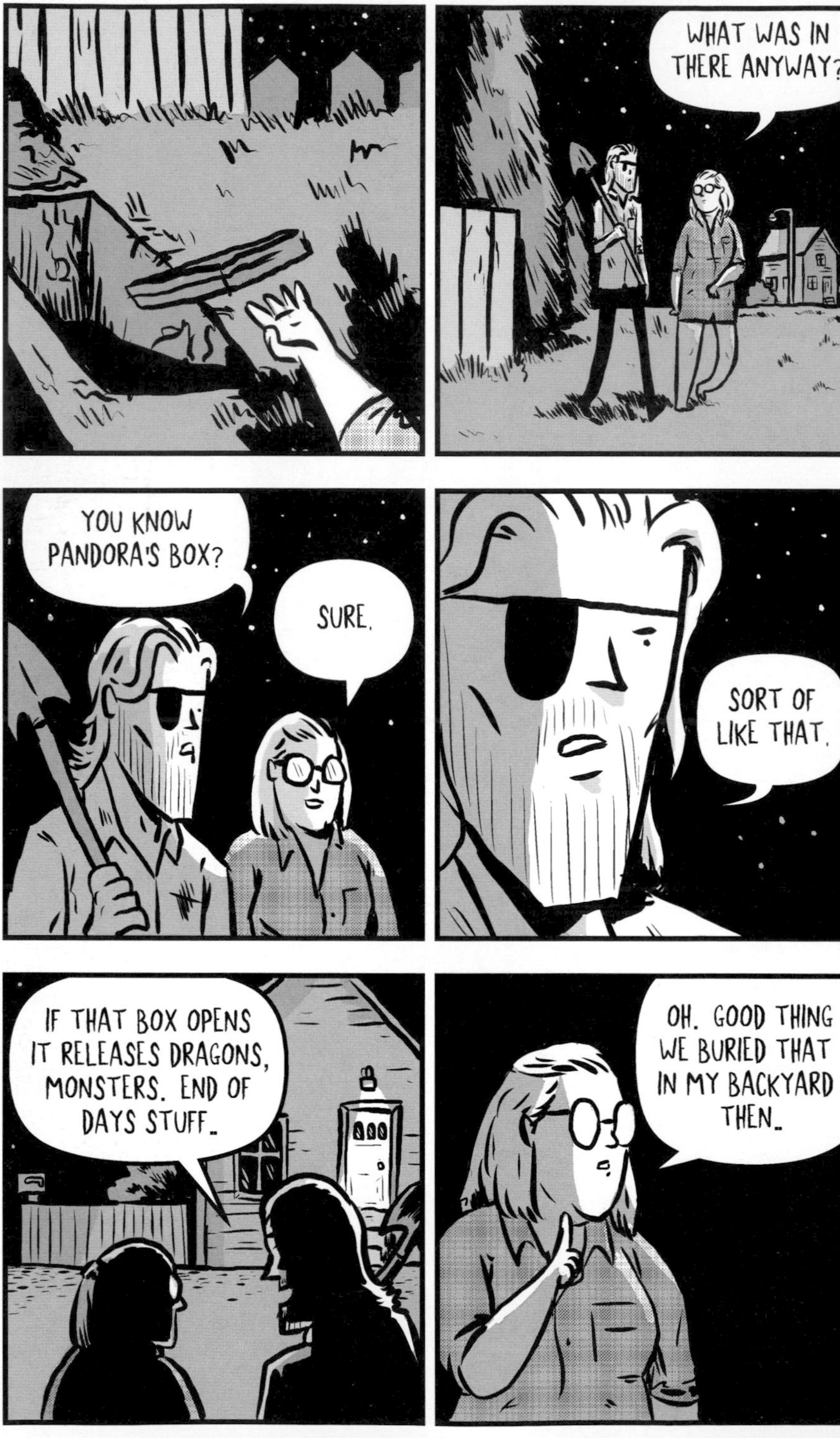
WHAT WAS IN THERE ANYWAY?
YOU KNOW PANDORA'S BOX?
SURE.
SORT OF LIKE THAT.
IF THAT BOX OPENS IT RELEASES DRAGONS, MONSTERS. END OF DAYS STUFF..
OH. GOOD THING WE BURIED THAT IN MY BACKYARD THEN..

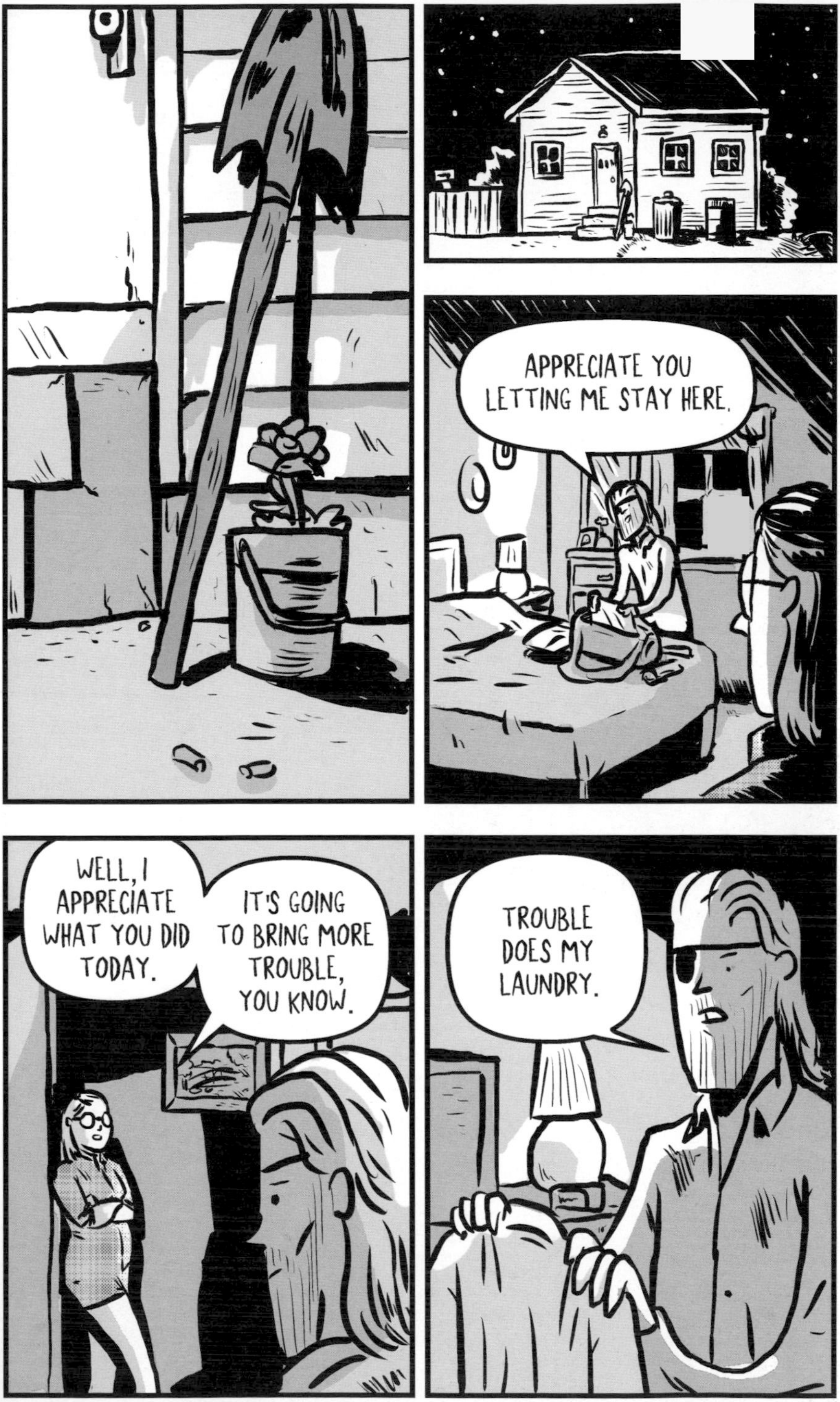
APPRECIATE YOU LETTING ME STAY HERE.
WELL, I APPRECIATE WHAT YOU DID TODAY.
IT'S GOING TO BRING MORE TROUBLE, YOU KNOW.
TROUBLE DOES MY LAUNDRY.

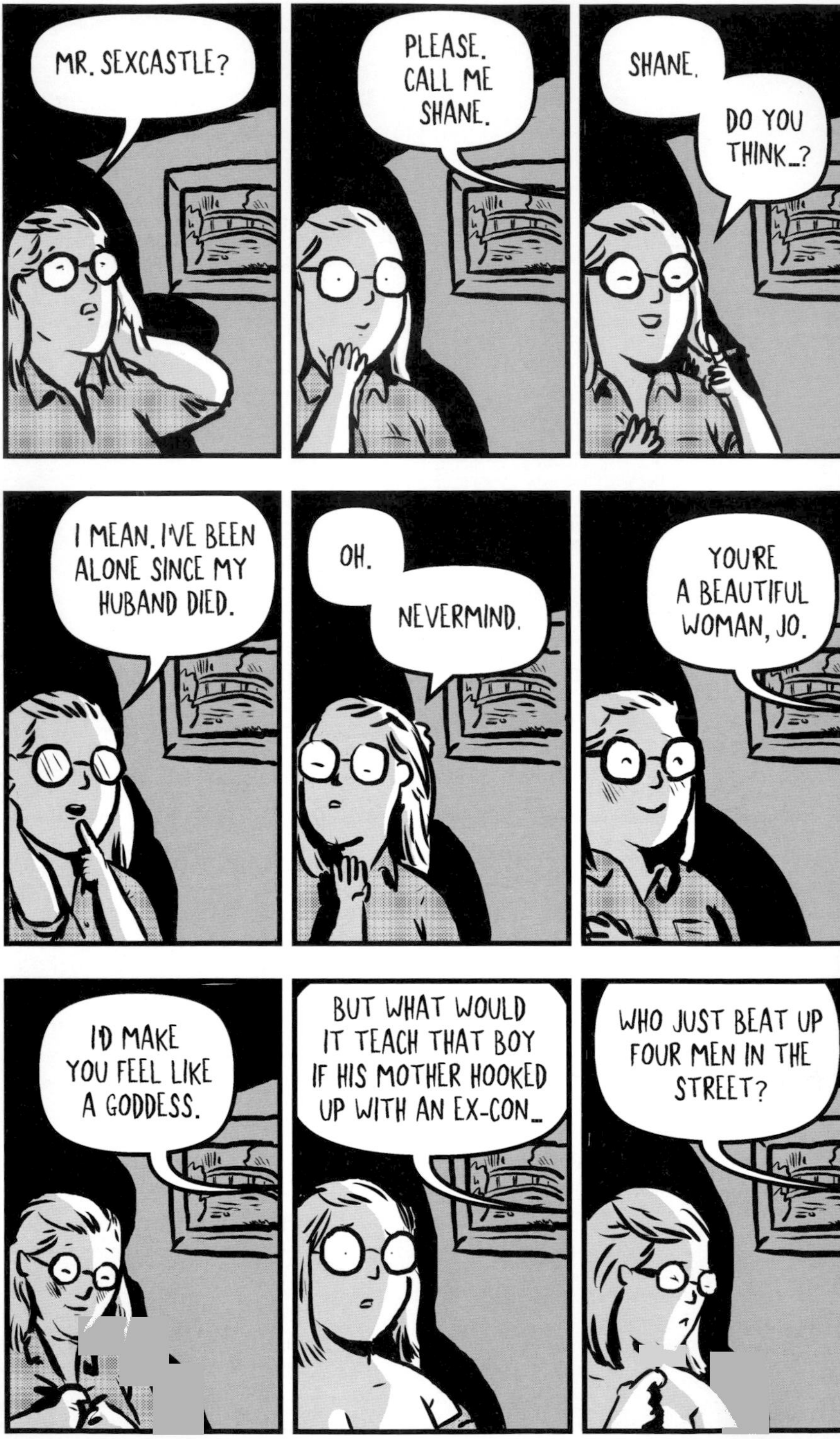
MR. SEXCASTLE?
PLEASE. CALL ME SHANE.
SHANE.
DO YOU THINK...?
I MEAN. I'VE BEEN ALONE SINCE MY HUBAND DIED.
OH.
NEVERMIND.
YOU'RE A BEAUTIFUL WOMAN, JO.
I'D MAKE YOU FEEL LIKE A GODDESS.
BUT WHAT WOULD IT TEACH THAT BOY IF HIS MOTHER HOOKED UP WITH AN EX-CON...
WHO JUST BEAT UP FOUR MEN IN THE STREET?

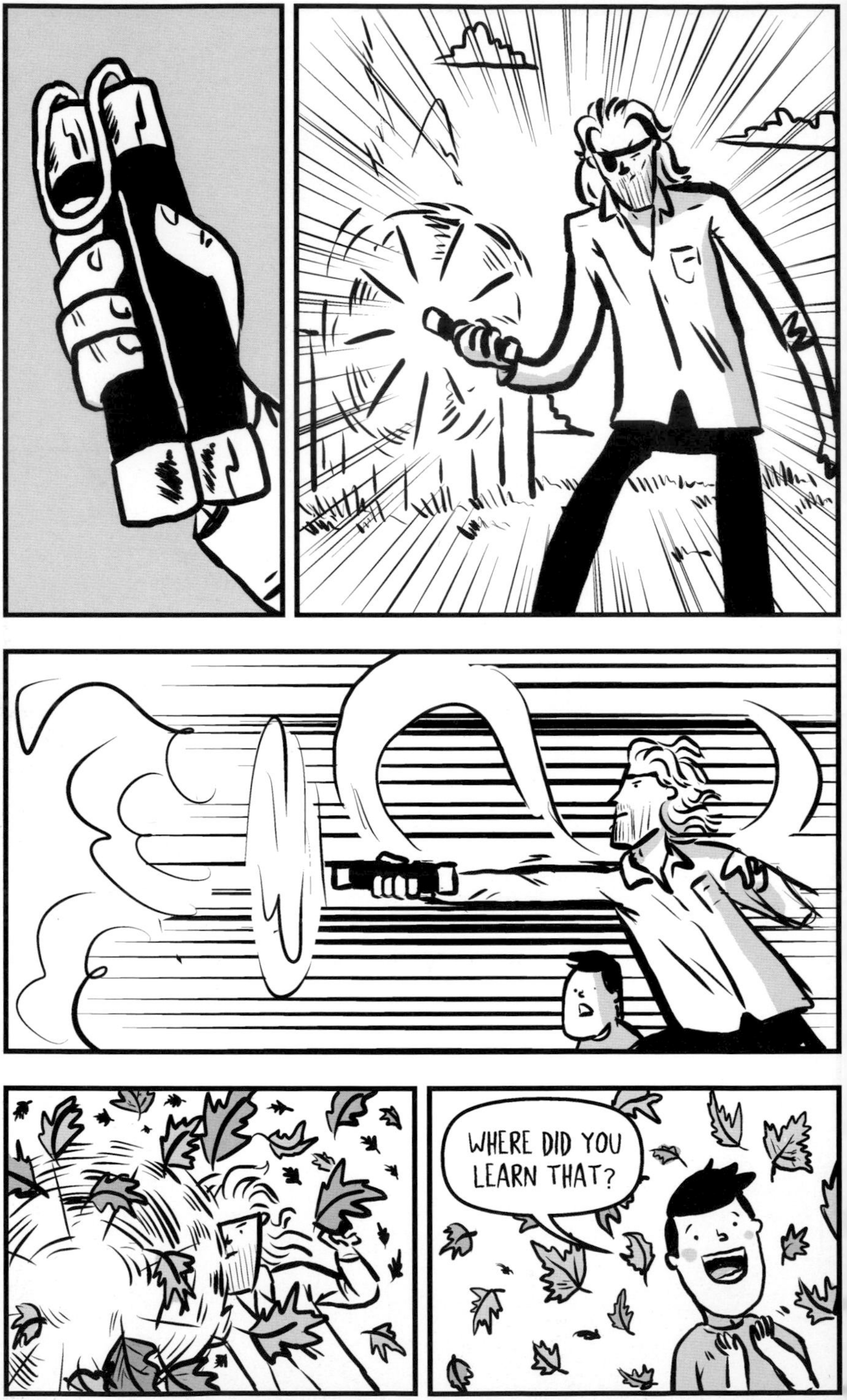
WHERE DID YOU LEARN THAT?

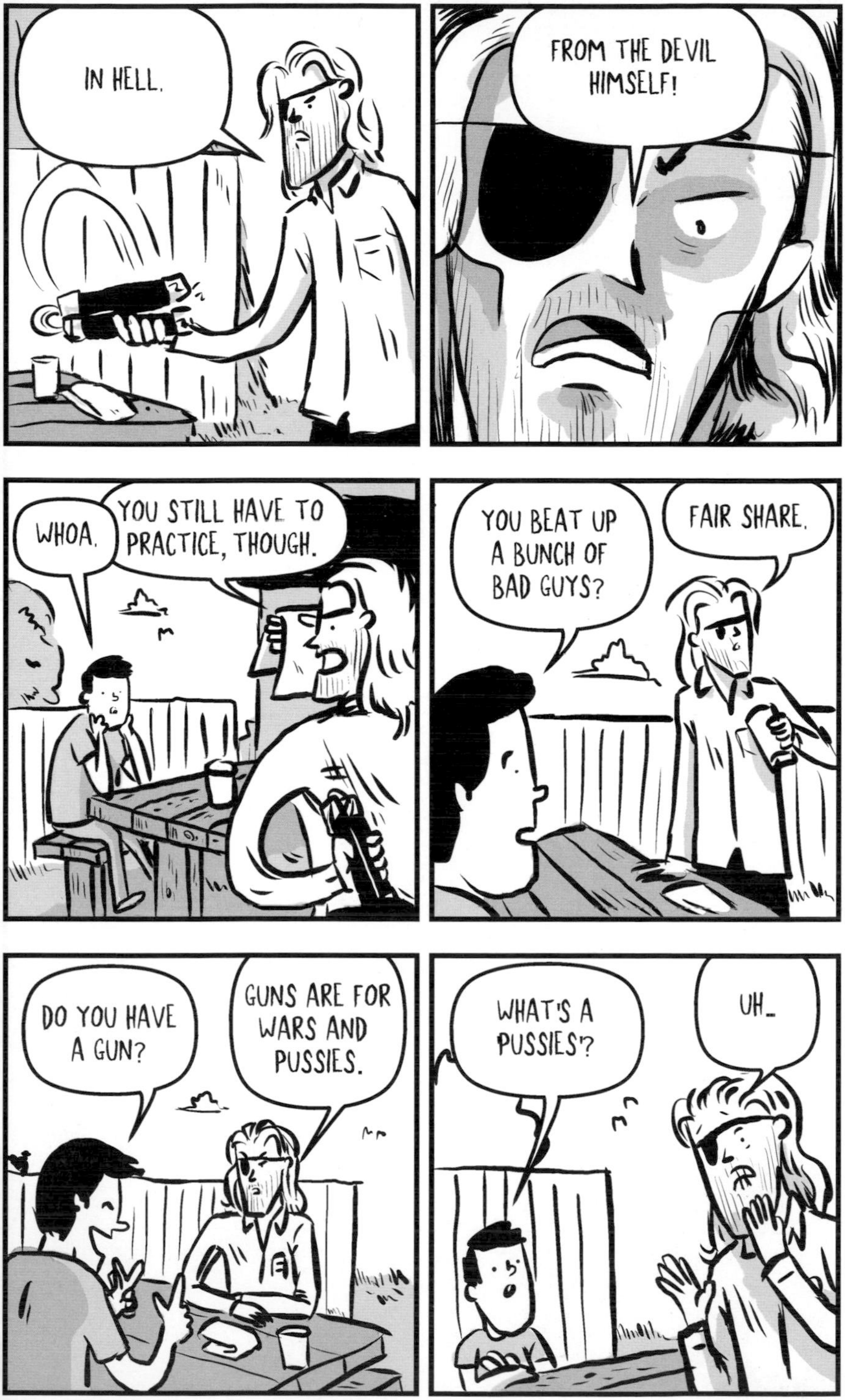
IN HELL.
FROM THE DEVIL HIMSELF!
WHOA.
YOU STILL HAVE TO PRACTICE, THOUGH.
YOU BEAT UP A BUNCH OF BAD GUYS?
FAIR SHARE.
DO YOU HAVE A GUN?
GUNS ARE FOR WARS AND PUSSIES.
WHAT'S A 'PUSSIES'?
UH...

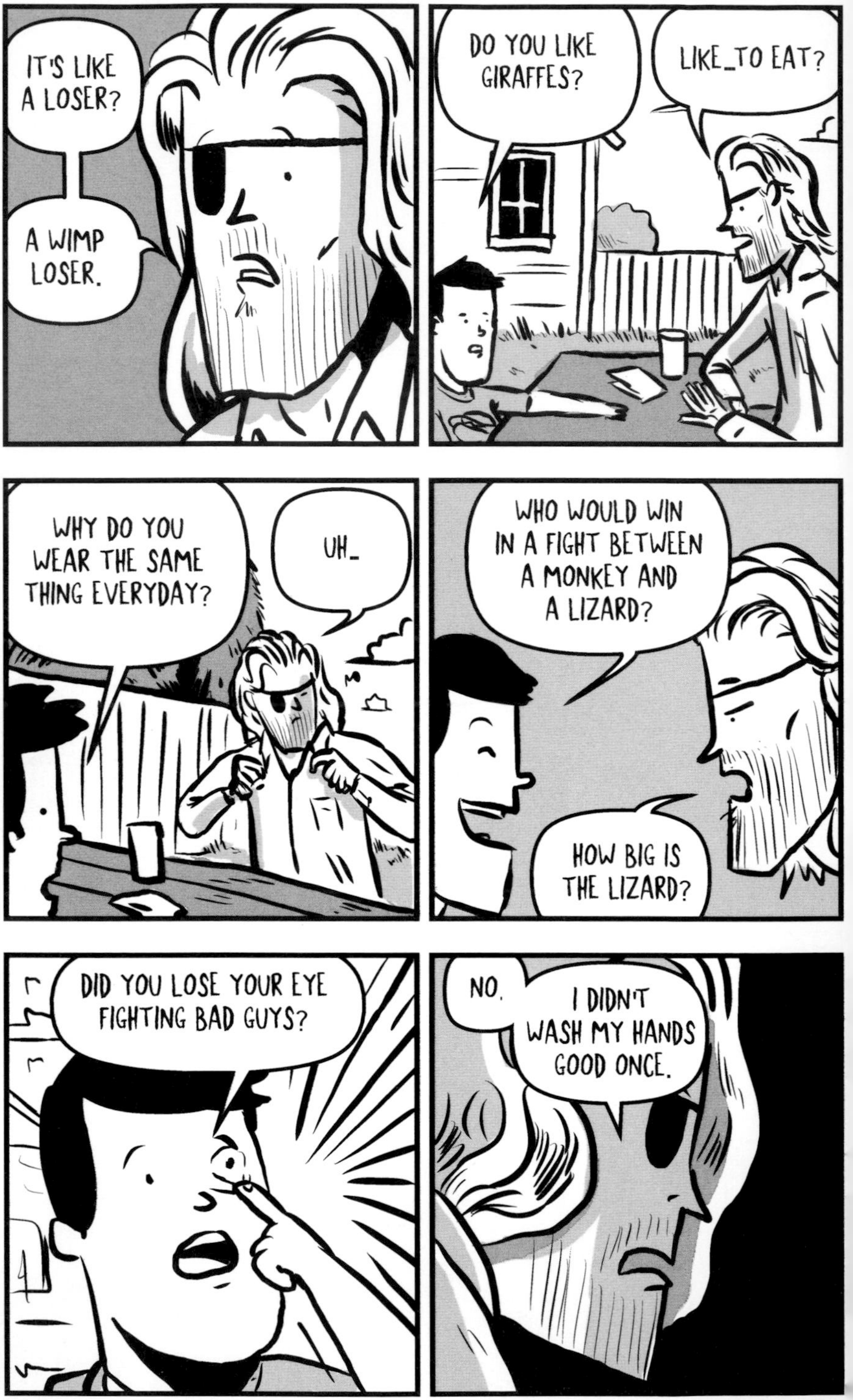
IT'S LIKE A LOSER?
A WIMP LOSER.
DO YOU LIKE GIRAFFES?
LIKE_TO EAT?
WHY DO YOU WEAR THE SAME THING EVERYDAY?
UH_
WHO WOULD WIN IN A FIGHT BETWEEN A MONKEY AND A LIZARD?
HOW BIG IS THE LIZARD?
DID YOU LOSE YOUR EYE FIGHTING BAD GUYS?
NO.
I DIDN'T WASH MY HANDS GOOD ONCE.

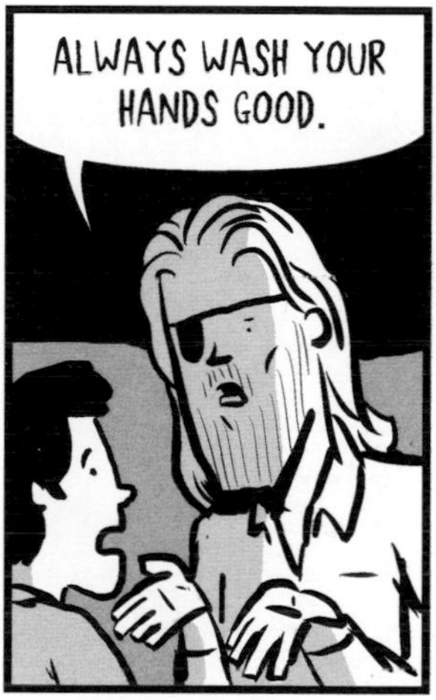
ALWAYS WASH YOUR HANDS GOOD.

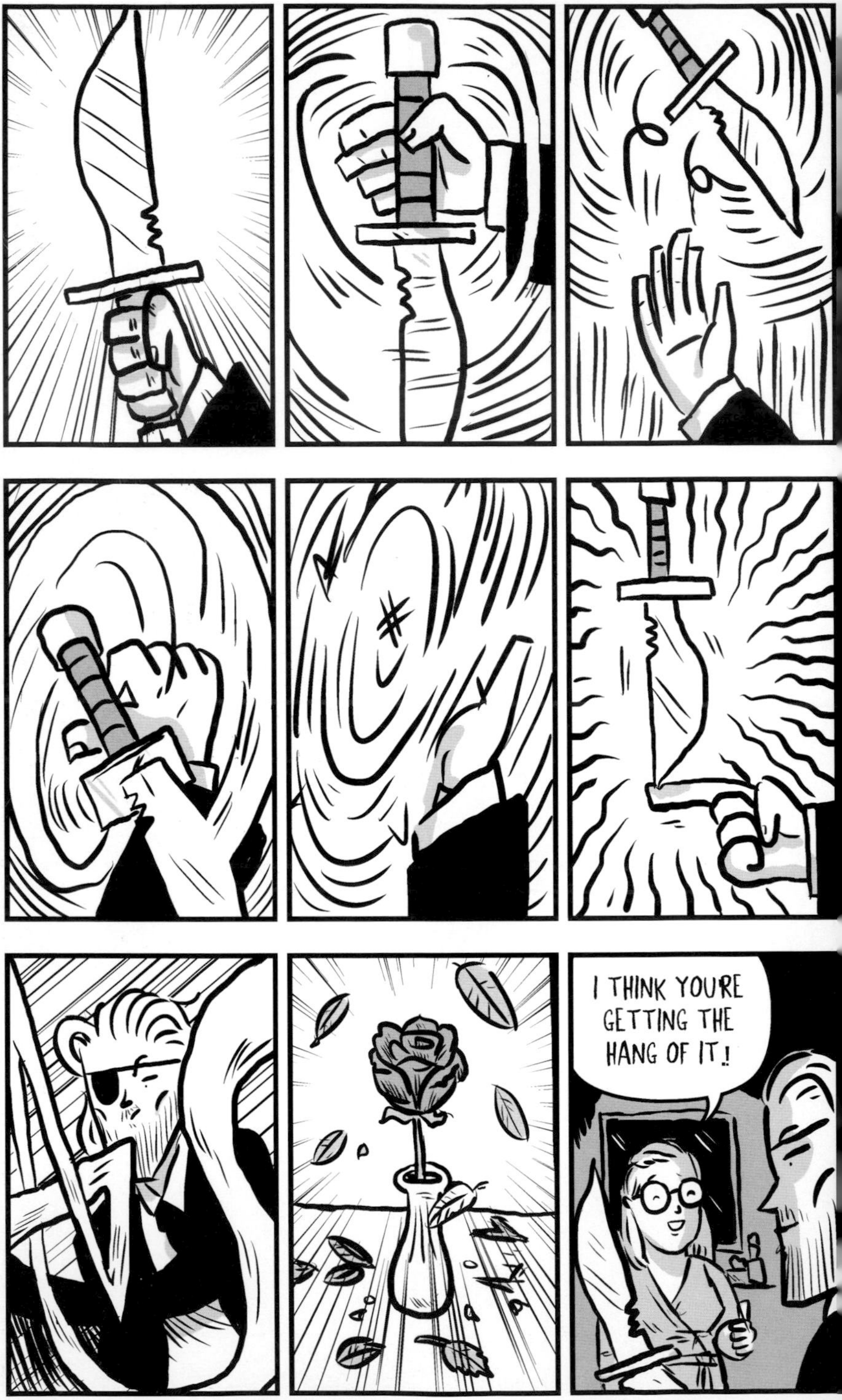
I THINK YOU'RE GETTING THE HANG OF IT!

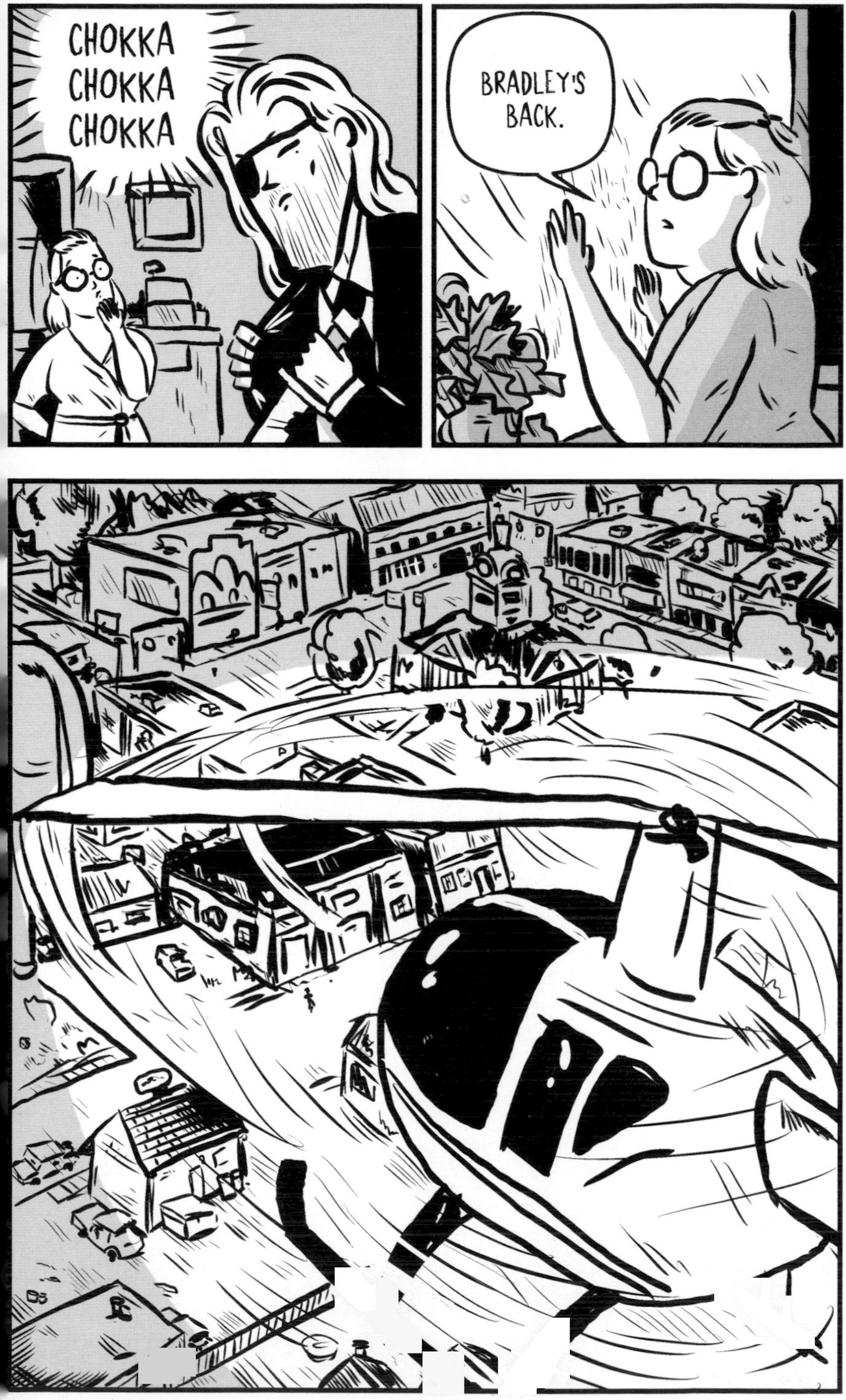
CHOKKA CHOKKA CHOKKA
BRADLEY'S BACK.

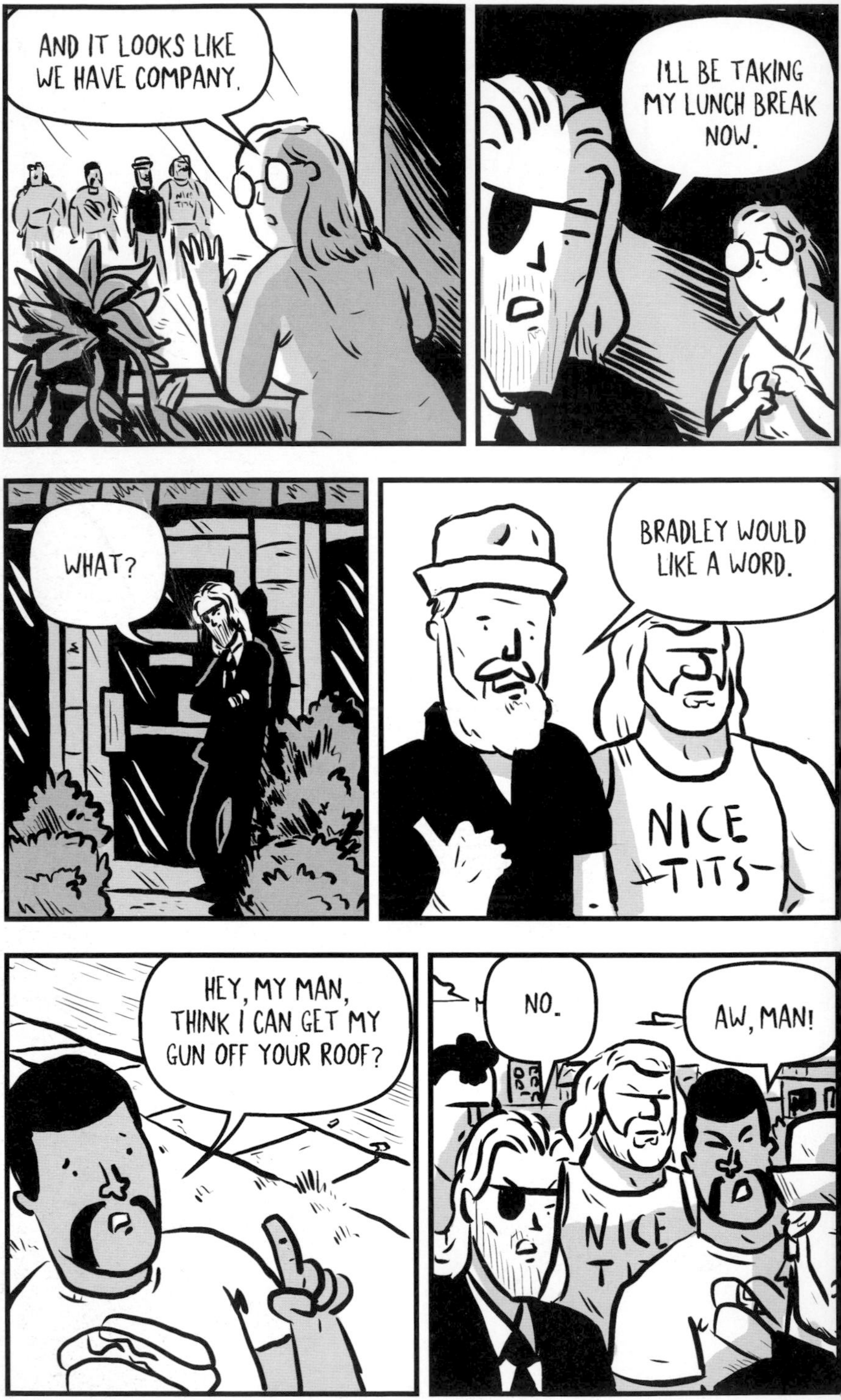
AND IT LOOKS LIKE WE HAVE COMPANY.
I'LL BE TAKING MY LUNCH BREAK NOW.
WHAT?
BRADLEY WOULD LIKE A WORD.
NICE TITS
HEY, MY MAN, THINK I CAN GET MY GUN OFF YOUR ROOF?
NO.
AW, MAN!

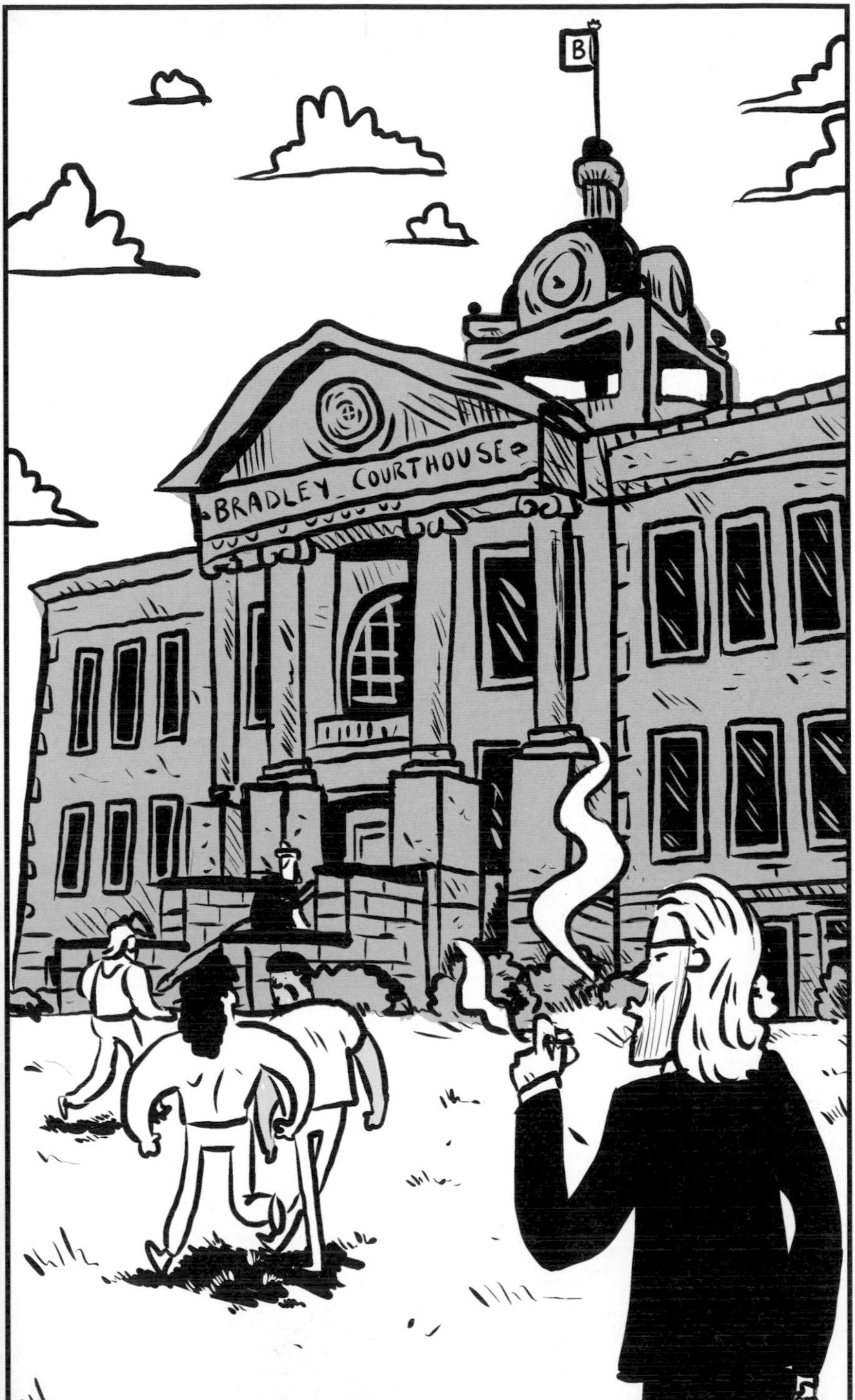
B
BRADLEY COURTHOUSE

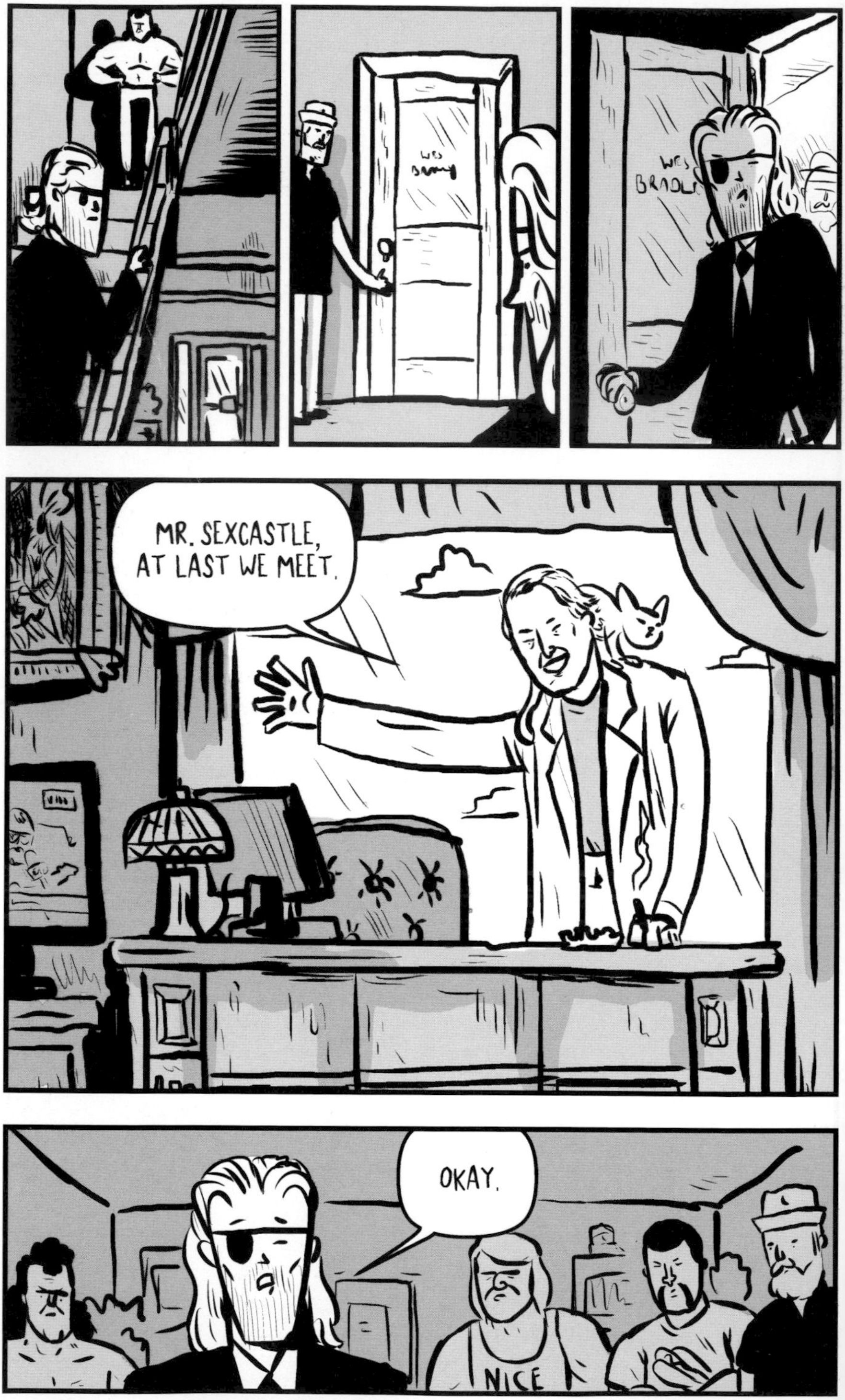
MR. SEXCASTLE, AT LAST WE MEET.
OKAY.
NICE

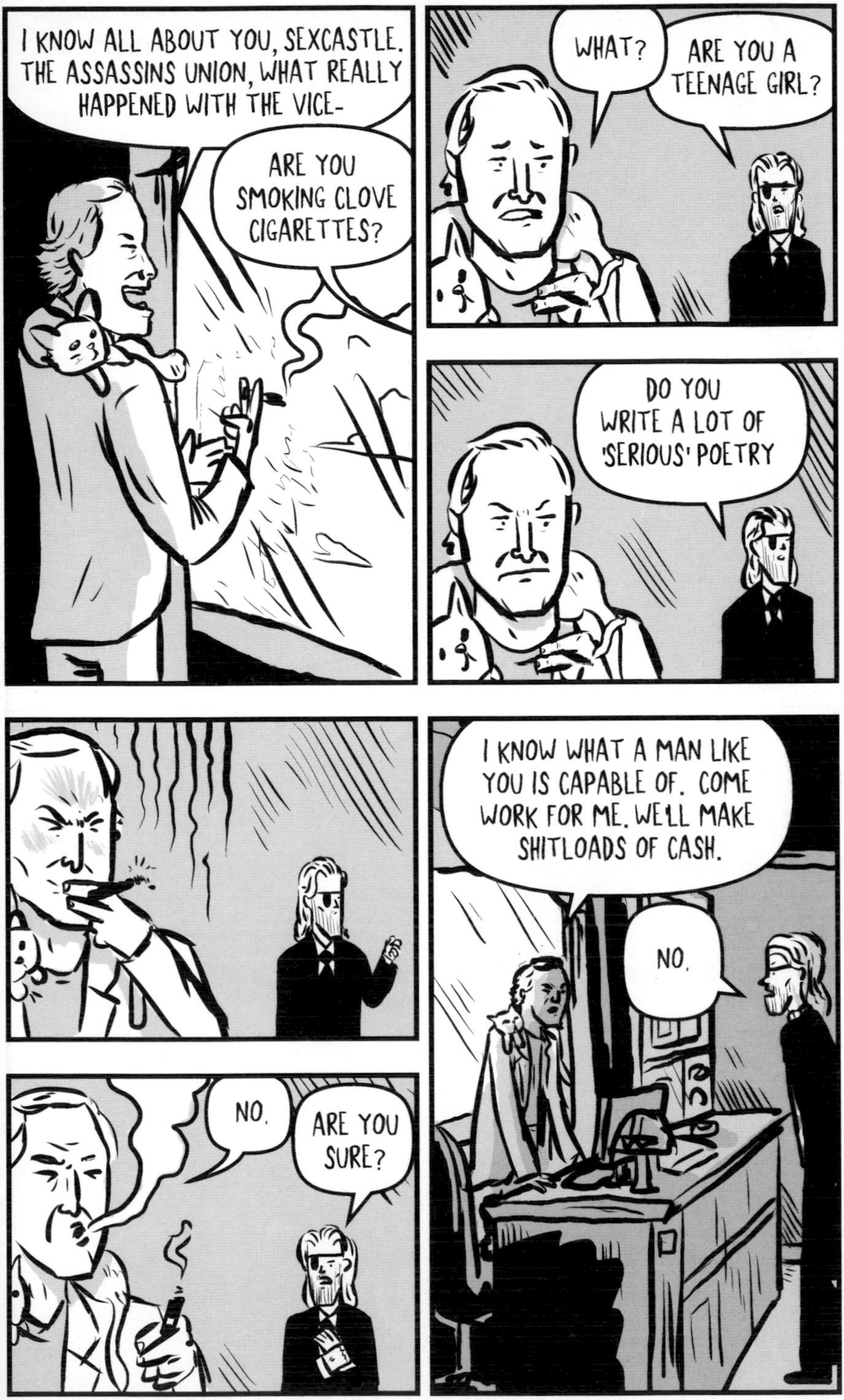
I KNOW ALL ABOUT YOU, SEXCASTLE. THE ASSASSINS UNION, WHAT REALLY HAPPENED WITH THE VICE-
ARE YOU SMOKING CLOVE CIGARETTES?
WHAT?
ARE YOU A TEENAGE GIRL?
DO YOU WRITE A LOT OF 'SERIOUS' POETRY
NO.
ARE YOU SURE?
I KNOW WHAT A MAN LIKE YOU IS CAPABLE OF. COME WORK FOR ME. WE'LL MAKE SHITLOADS OF CASH.
NO.

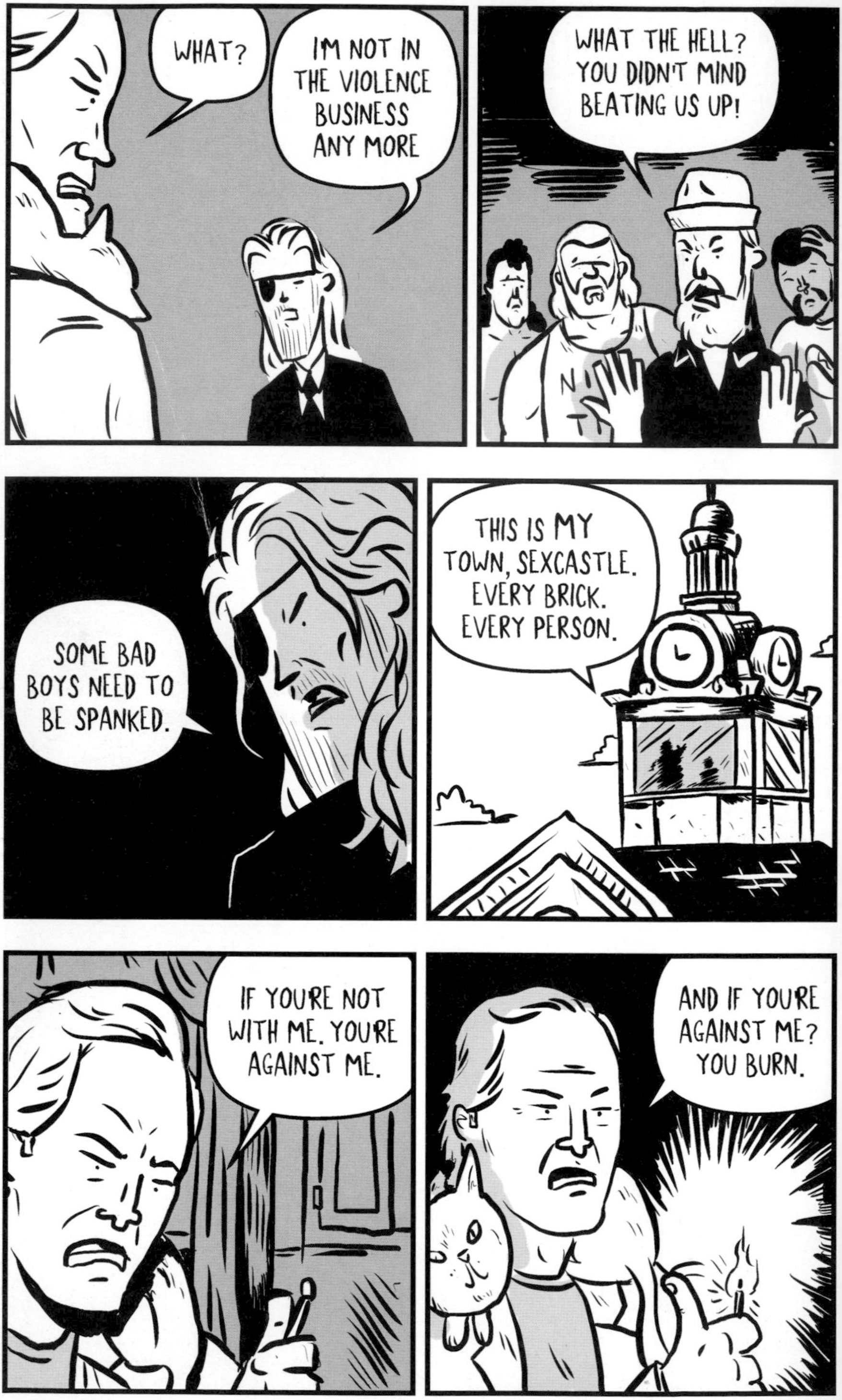
WHAT?
I'M NOT IN THE VIOLENCE BUSINESS ANY MORE
WHAT THE HELL? YOU DIDN'T MIND BEATING US UP!
SOME BAD BOYS NEED TO BE SPANKED.
THIS IS MY TOWN, SEXCASTLE. EVERY BRICK. EVERY PERSON.
IF YOU'RE NOT WITH ME. YOU'RE AGAINST ME.
AND IF YOU'RE AGAINST ME? YOU BURN.

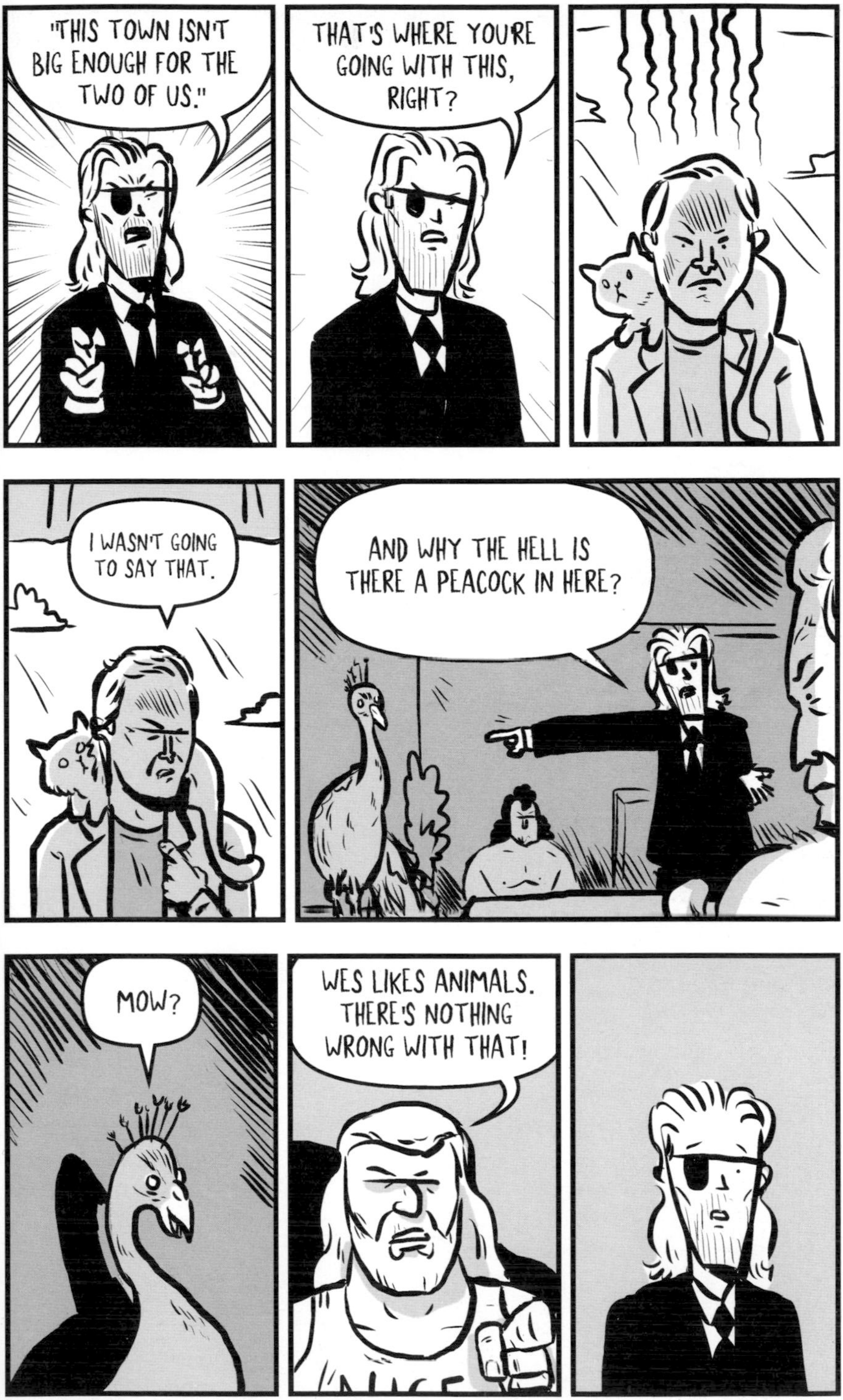
"THIS TOWN ISN'T BIG ENOUGH FOR THE TWO OF US."
THAT'S WHERE YOU'RE GOING WITH THIS, RIGHT?
I WASN'T GOING TO SAY THAT.
AND WHY THE HELL IS THERE A PEACOCK IN HERE?
MOW?
WES LIKES ANIMALS. THERE'S NOTHING WRONG WITH THAT!

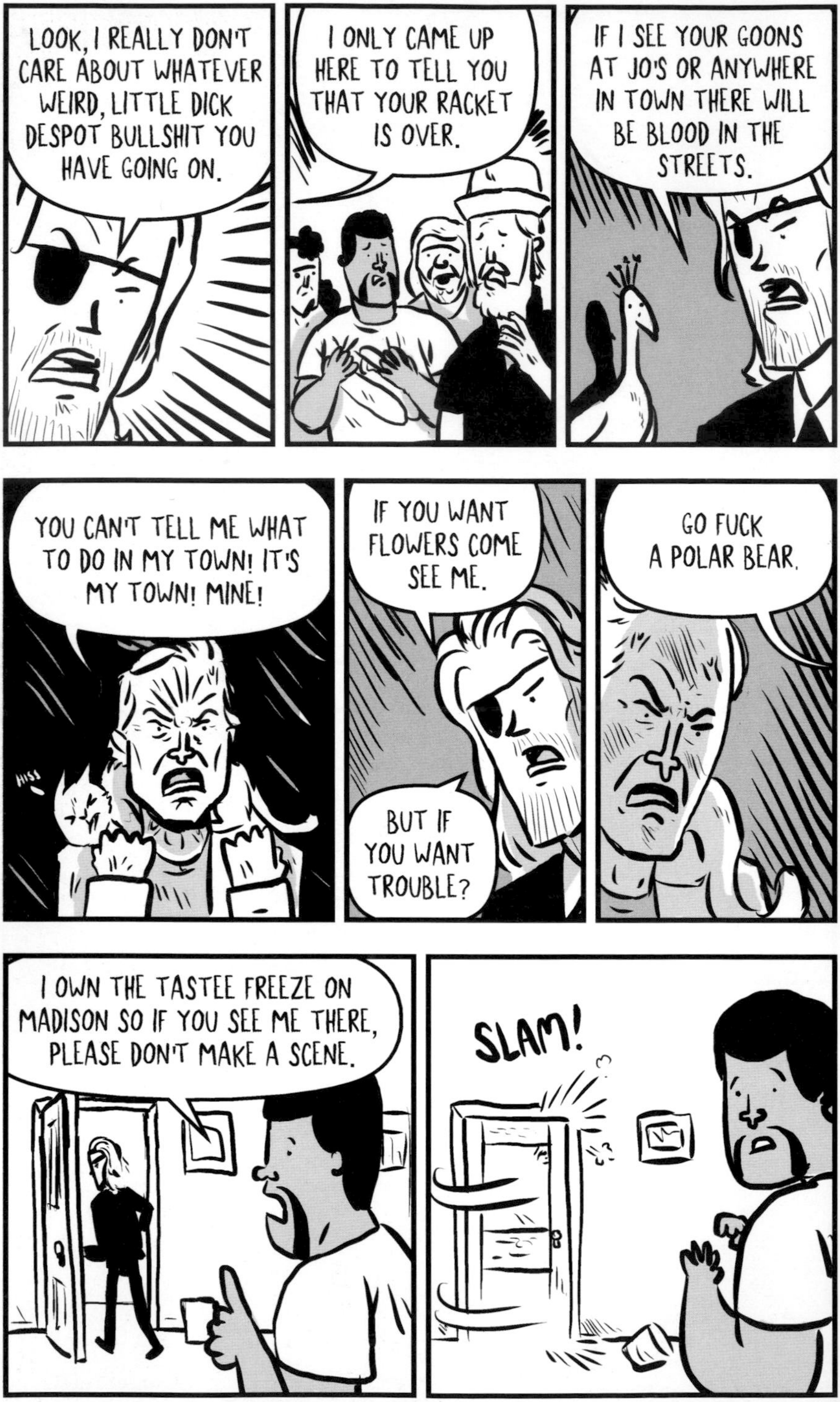
LOOK, I REALLY DON'T CARE ABOUT WHATEVER WEIRD, LITTLE DICK DESPOT BULLSHIT YOU HAVE GOING ON.
I ONLY CAME UP HERE TO TELL YOU THAT YOUR RACKET IS OVER.
IF I SEE YOUR GOONS AT JO'S OR ANYWHERE IN TOWN THERE WILL BE BLOOD IN THE STREETS.
YOU CAN'T TELL ME WHAT TO DO IN MY TOWN! IT'S MY TOWN! MINE!
HISS
IF YOU WANT FLOWERS COME SEE ME.
BUT IF YOU WANT TROUBLE?
GO FUCK A POLAR BEAR.
I OWN THE TASTEE FREEZE ON MADISON SO IF YOU SEE ME THERE, PLEASE DON'T MAKE A SCENE.
SLAM!

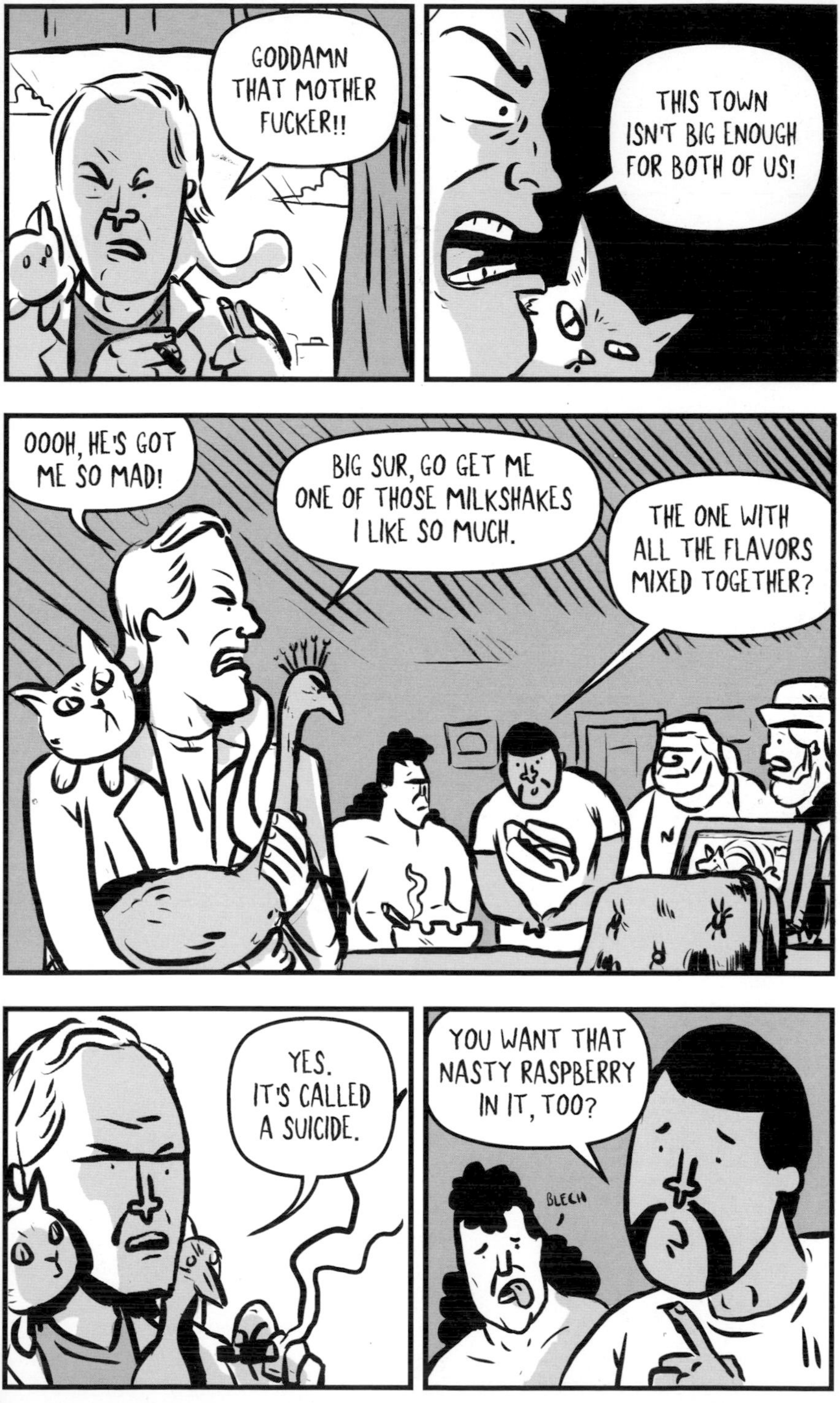
GODDAMN THAT MOTHER FUCKER!!
THIS TOWN ISN'T BIG ENOUGH FOR BOTH OF US!
OOOH, HE'S GOT ME SO MAD!
BIG SUR, GO GET ME ONE OF THOSE MILKSHAKES I LIKE SO MUCH.
THE ONE WITH ALL THE FLAVORS MIXED TOGETHER?
YES. IT'S CALLED A SUICIDE.
YOU WANT THAT NASTY RASPBERRY IN IT, TOO?
BLECH

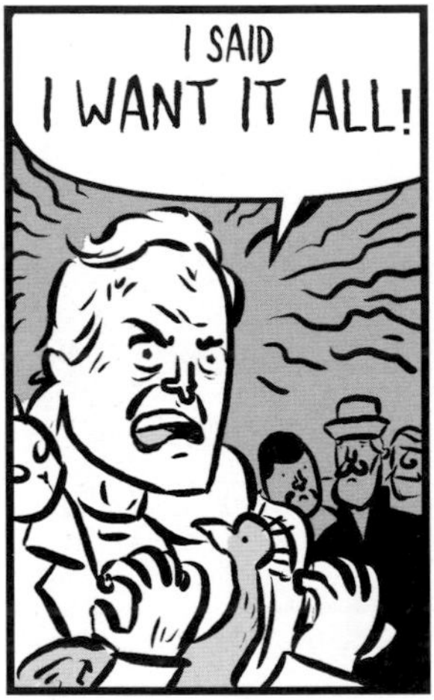
I SAID
I WANT IT ALL!

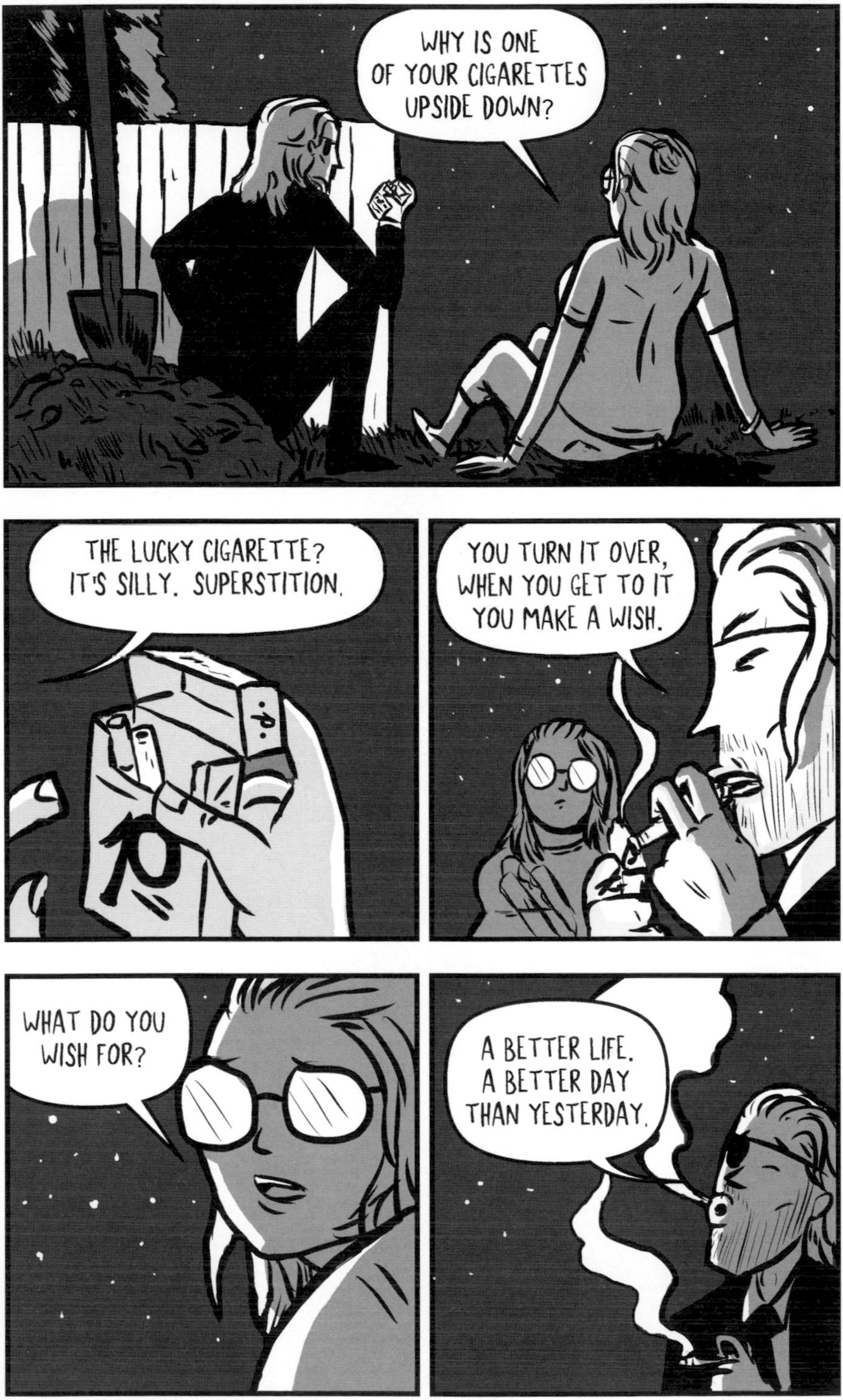
WHY IS ONE OF YOUR CIGARETTES UPSIDE DOWN?
THE LUCKY CIGARETTE? IT'S SILLY. SUPERSTITION.
YOU TURN IT OVER, WHEN YOU GET TO IT YOU MAKE A WISH.
WHAT DO YOU WISH FOR?
A BETTER LIFE. A BETTER DAY THAN YESTERDAY.

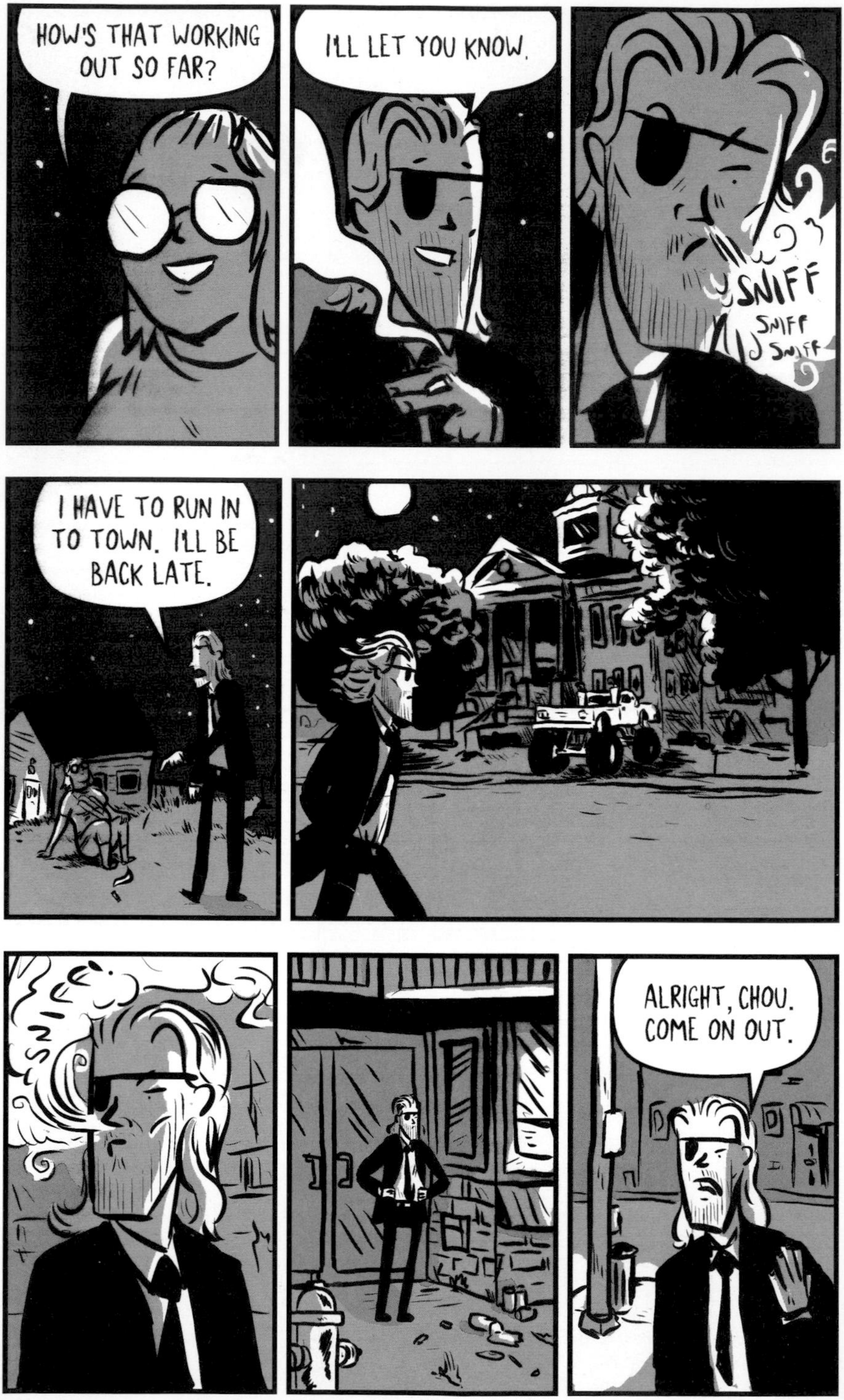
HOW'S THAT WORKING OUT SO FAR?
I'LL LET YOU KNOW.
SNIFF
SNIFF
SNIFF
I HAVE TO RUN IN TO TOWN. I'LL BE BACK LATE.
ALRIGHT, CHOU. COME ON OUT.

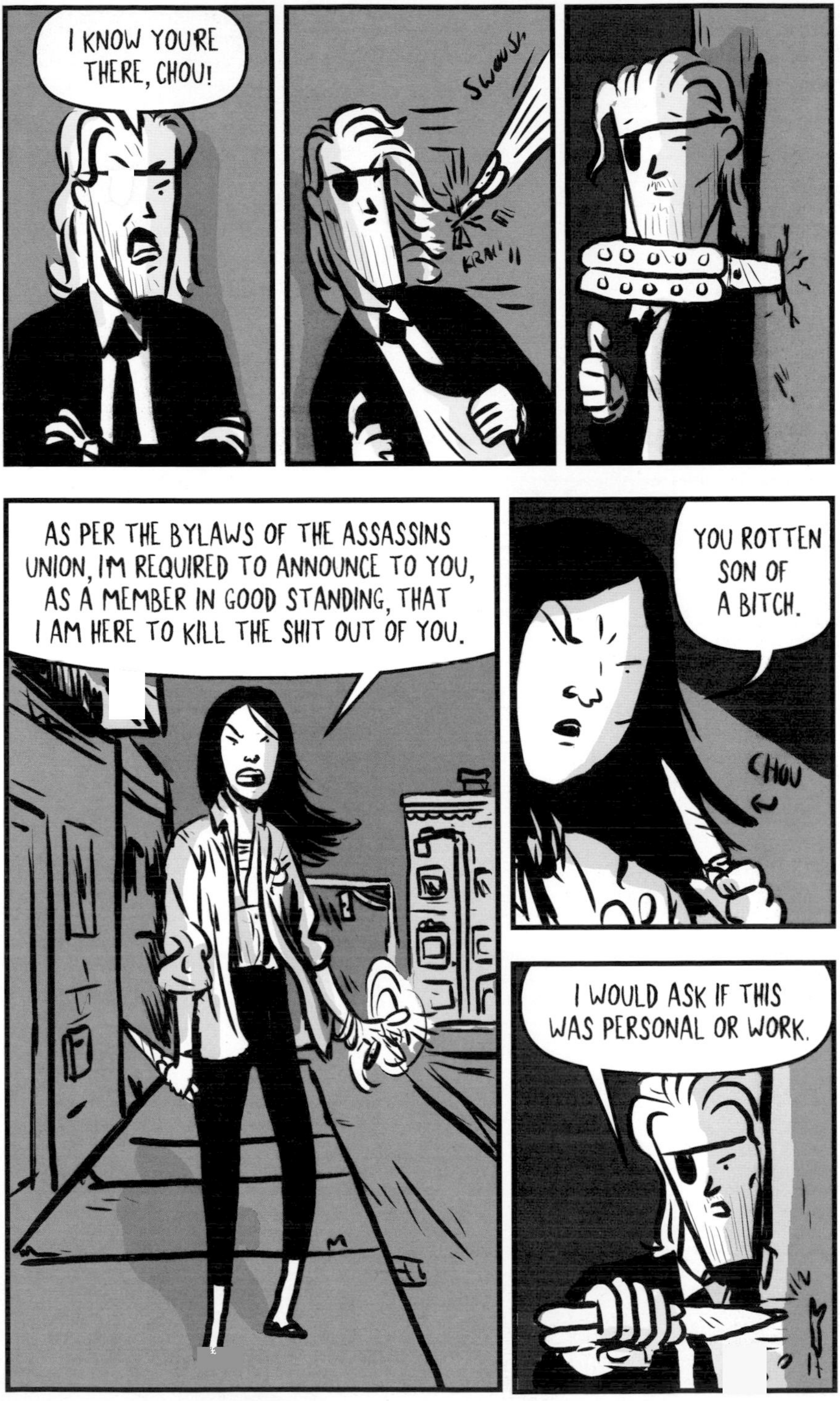
I KNOW YOU'RE THERE, CHOU!
SWOOSH
AS PER THE BYLAWS OF THE ASSASSINS UNION, I'M REQUIRED TO ANNOUNCE TO YOU, AS A MEMBER IN GOOD STANDING, THAT I AM HERE TO KILL THE SHIT OUT OF YOU.
YOU ROTTEN SON OF A BITCH.
CHOU
I WOULD ASK IF THIS WAS PERSONAL OR WORK.

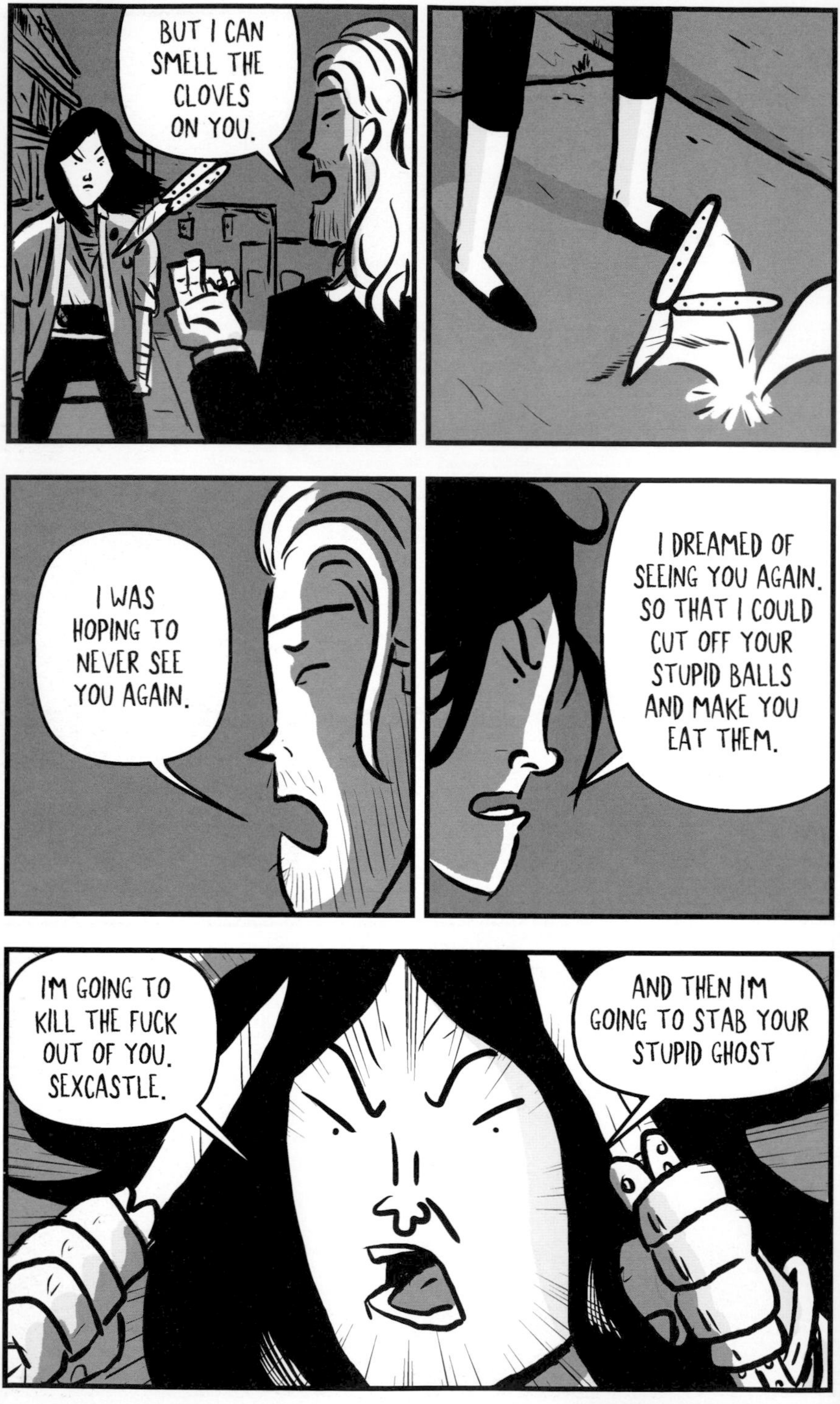
BUT I CAN SMELL THE CLOVES ON YOU.
I WAS HOPING TO NEVER SEE YOU AGAIN.
I DREAMED OF SEEING YOU AGAIN. SO THAT I COULD CUT OFF YOUR STUPID BALLS AND MAKE YOU EAT THEM.
I'M GOING TO KILL THE FUCK OUT OF YOU. SEXCASTLE.
AND THEN I'M GOING TO STAB YOUR STUPID GHOST

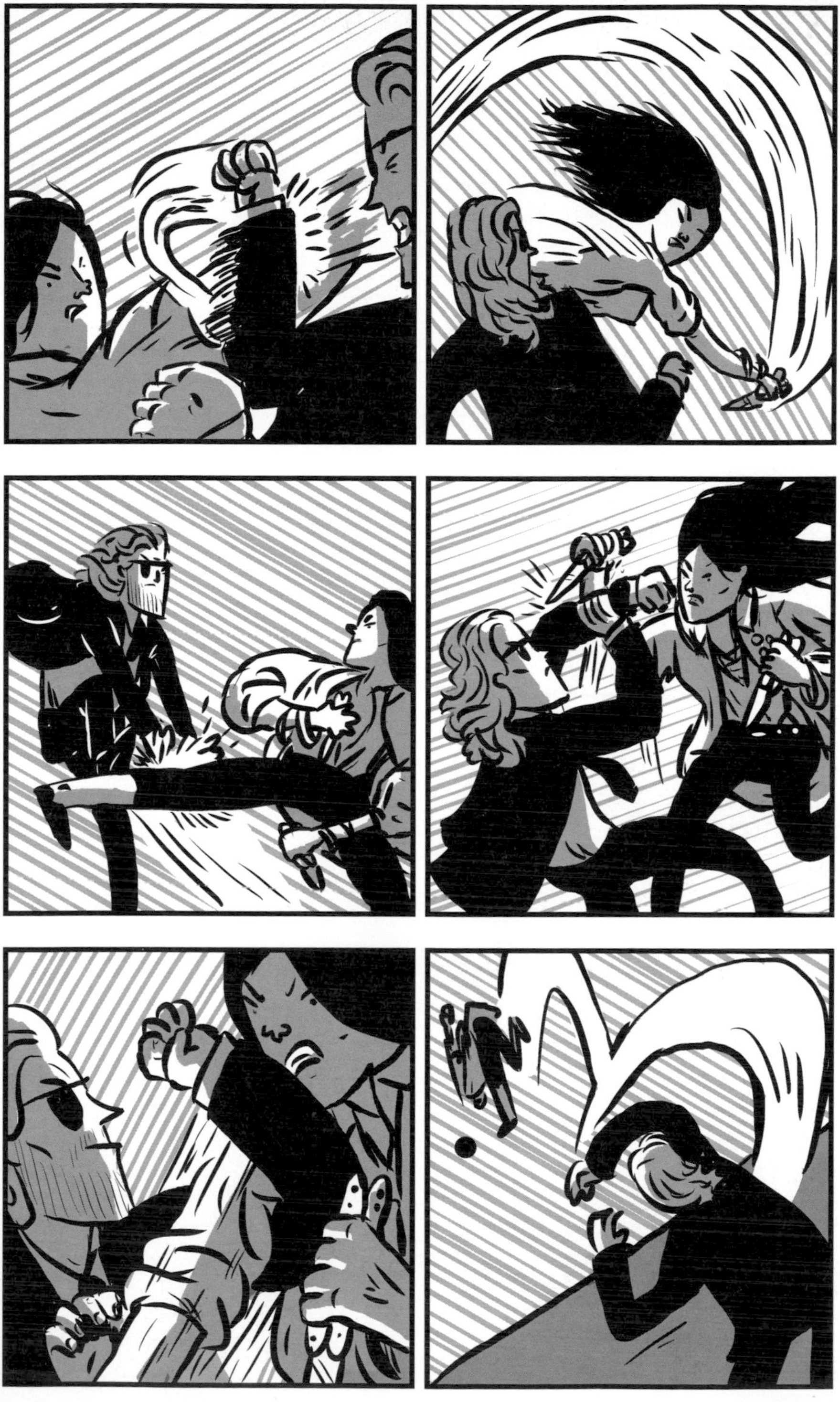

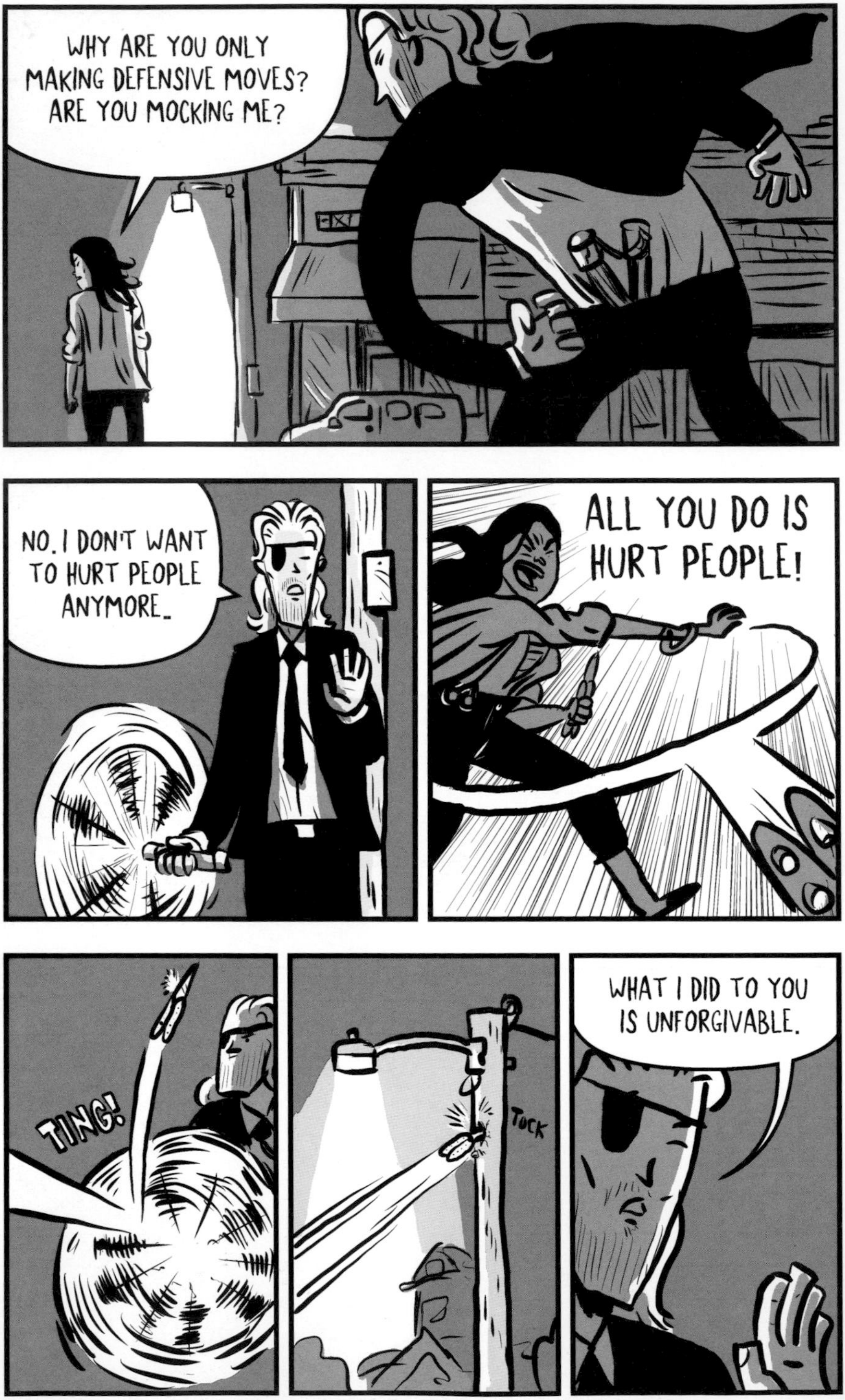
WHY ARE YOU ONLY MAKING DEFENSIVE MOVES? ARE YOU MOCKING ME?
NO. I DON'T WANT TO HURT PEOPLE ANYMORE...
ALL YOU DO IS HURT PEOPLE!
TING!
TOCK
WHAT I DID TO YOU IS UNFORGIVABLE.

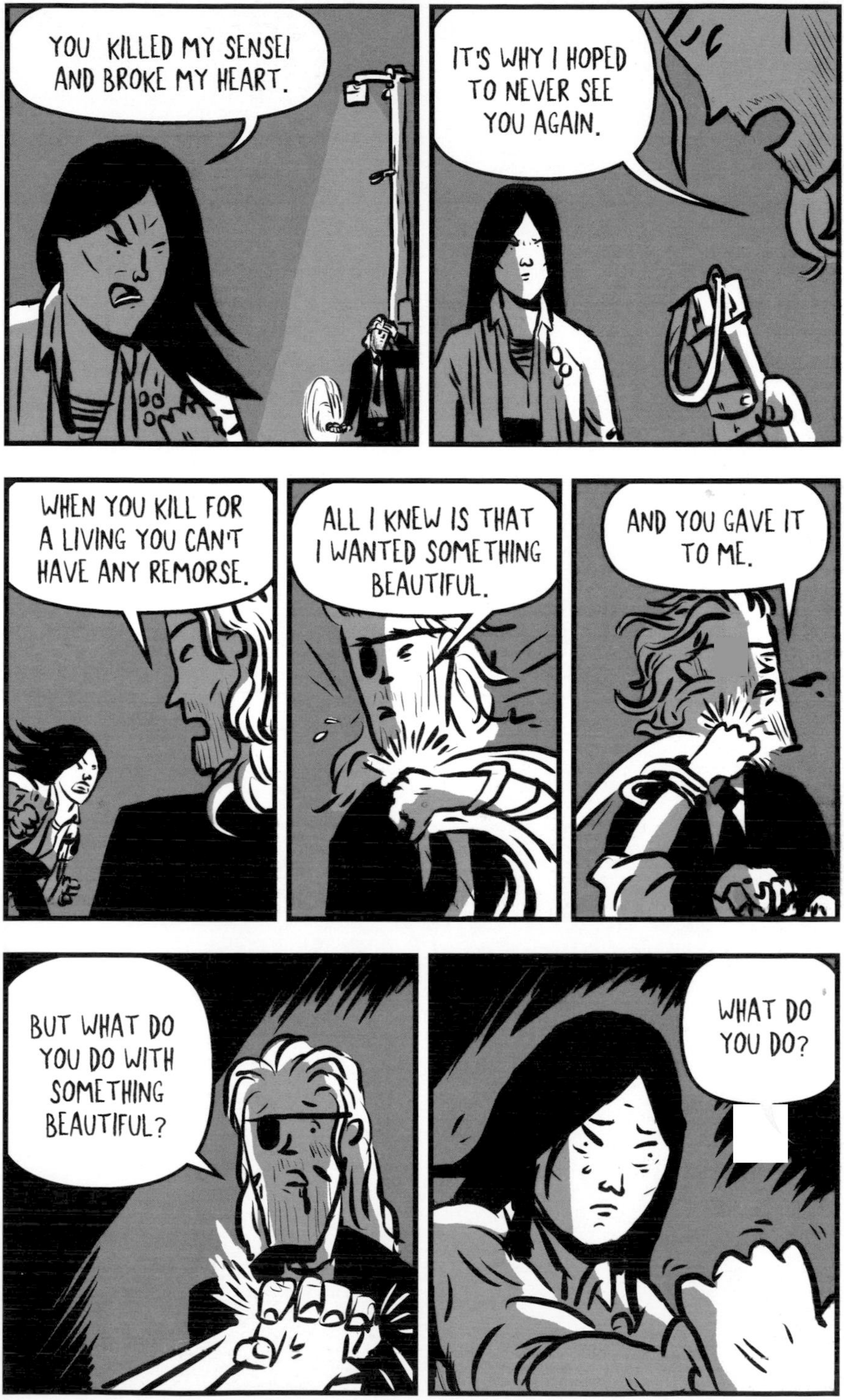
YOU KILLED MY SENSEI AND BROKE MY HEART.
IT'S WHY I HOPED TO NEVER SEE YOU AGAIN.
WHEN YOU KILL FOR A LIVING YOU CAN'T HAVE ANY REMORSE.
ALL I KNEW IS THAT I WANTED SOMETHING BEAUTIFUL.
AND YOU GAVE IT TO ME.
BUT WHAT DO YOU DO WITH SOMETHING BEAUTIFUL?
WHAT DO YOU DO?

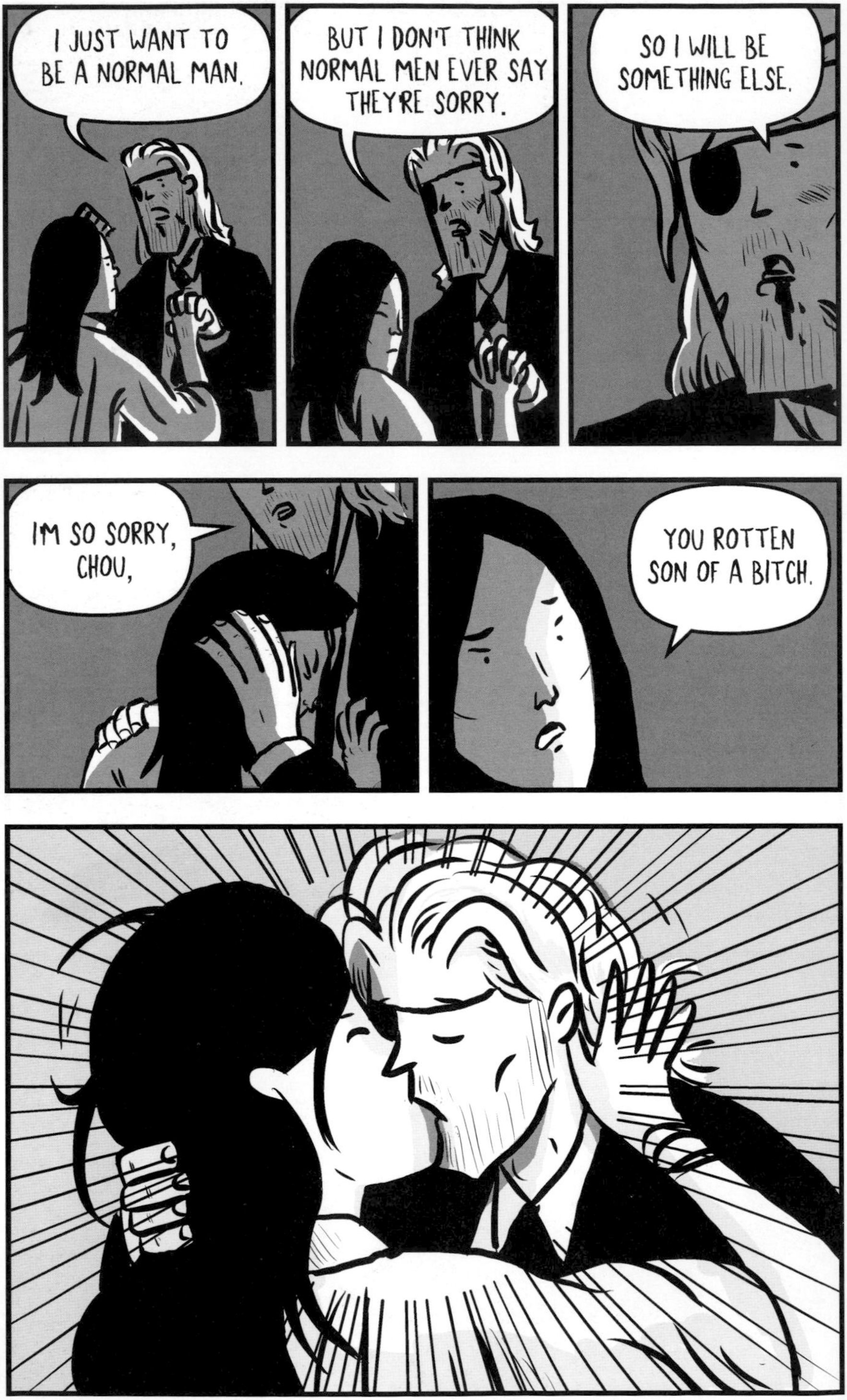
I JUST WANT TO BE A NORMAL MAN.
BUT I DON'T THINK NORMAL MEN EVER SAY THEY'RE SORRY.
SO I WILL BE SOMETHING ELSE.
I'M SO SORRY, CHOU,
YOU ROTTEN SON OF A BITCH.

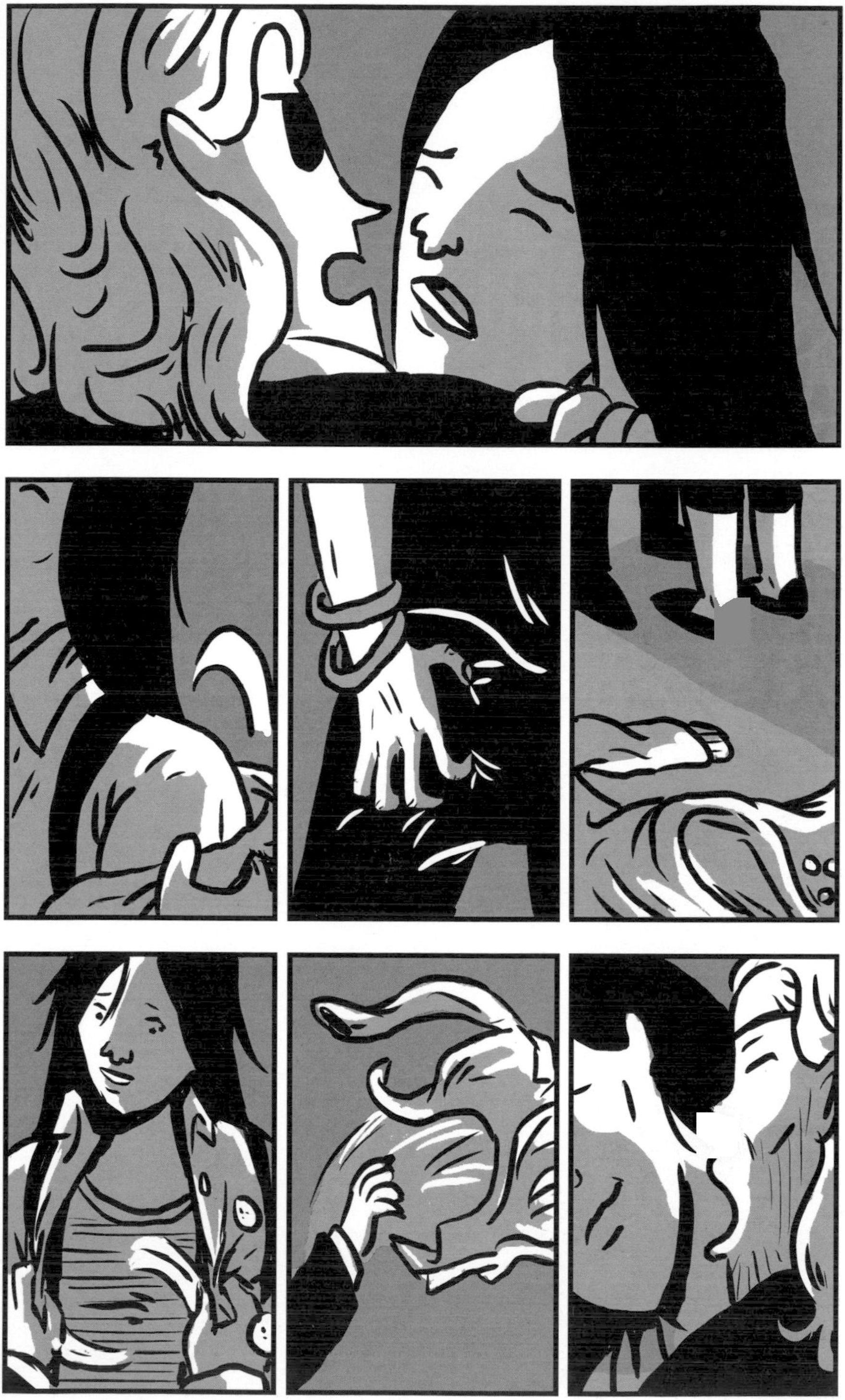

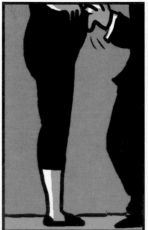

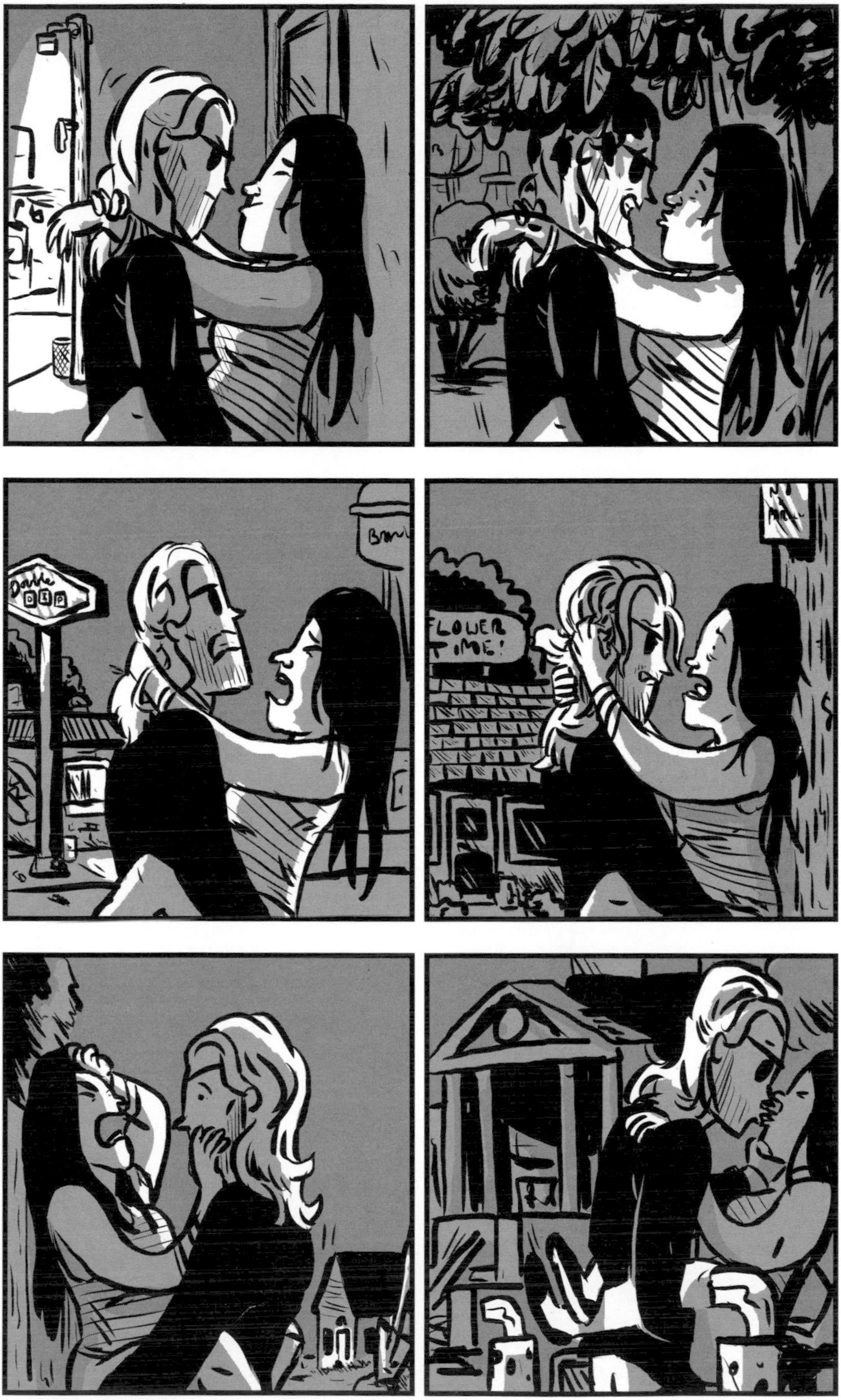
FLOWER TIME!

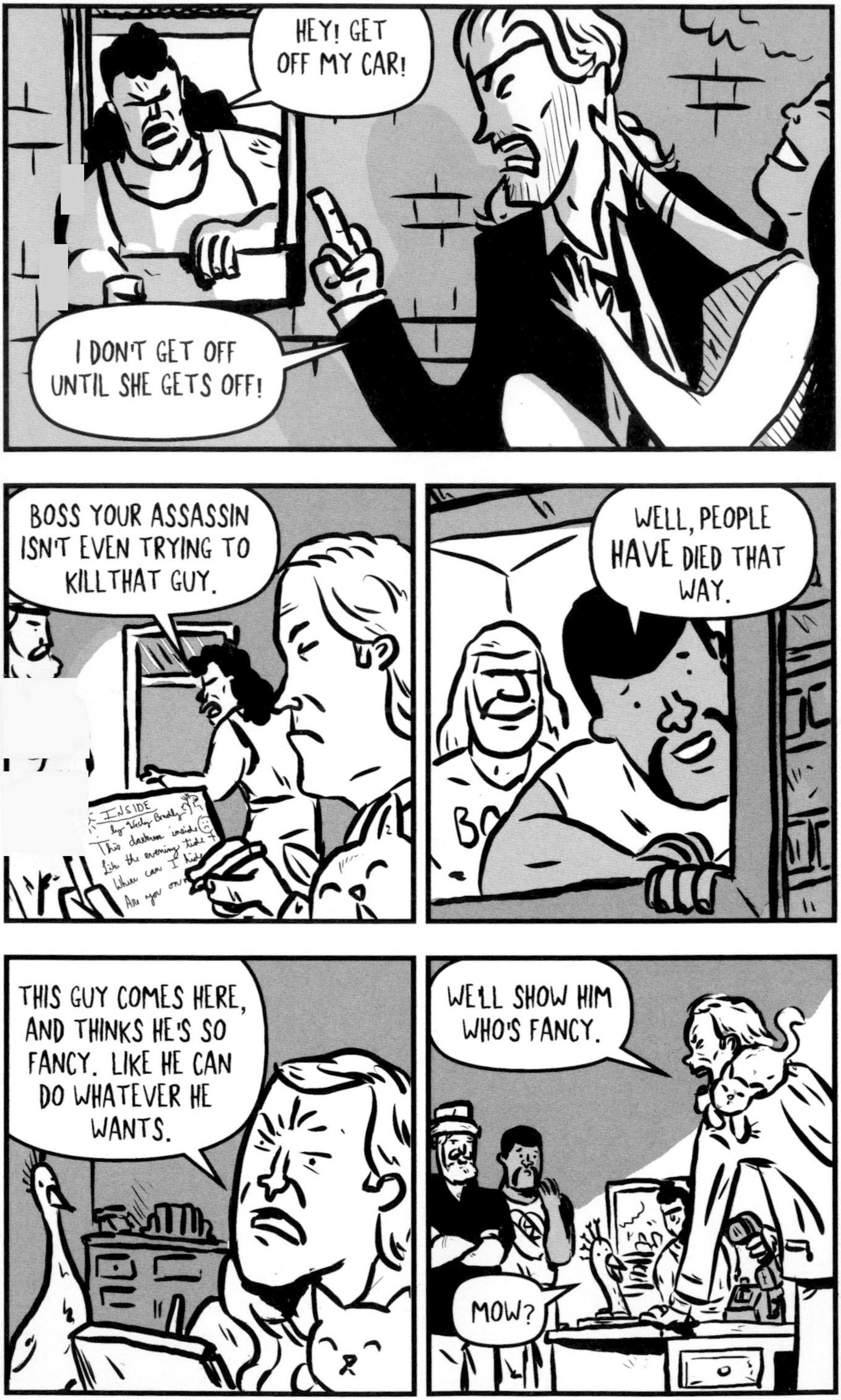
HEY! GET OFF MY CAR!
I DON'T GET OFF UNTIL SHE GETS OFF!
BOSS YOUR ASSASSIN ISN'T EVEN TRYING TO KILLTHAT GUY.
INSIDE
WELL, PEOPLE HAVE DIED THAT WAY.
THIS GUY COMES HERE, AND THINKS HE'S SO FANCY. LIKE HE CAN DO WHATEVER HE WANTS.
WE'LL SHOW HIM WHO'S FANCY.
MOW?

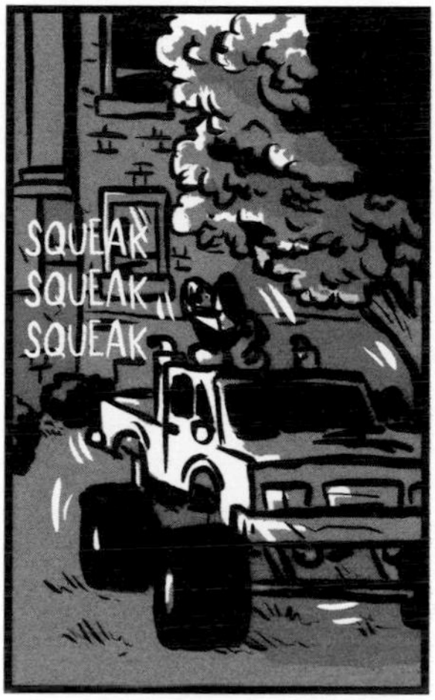
SQUEAK
SQUEAK
SQUEAK

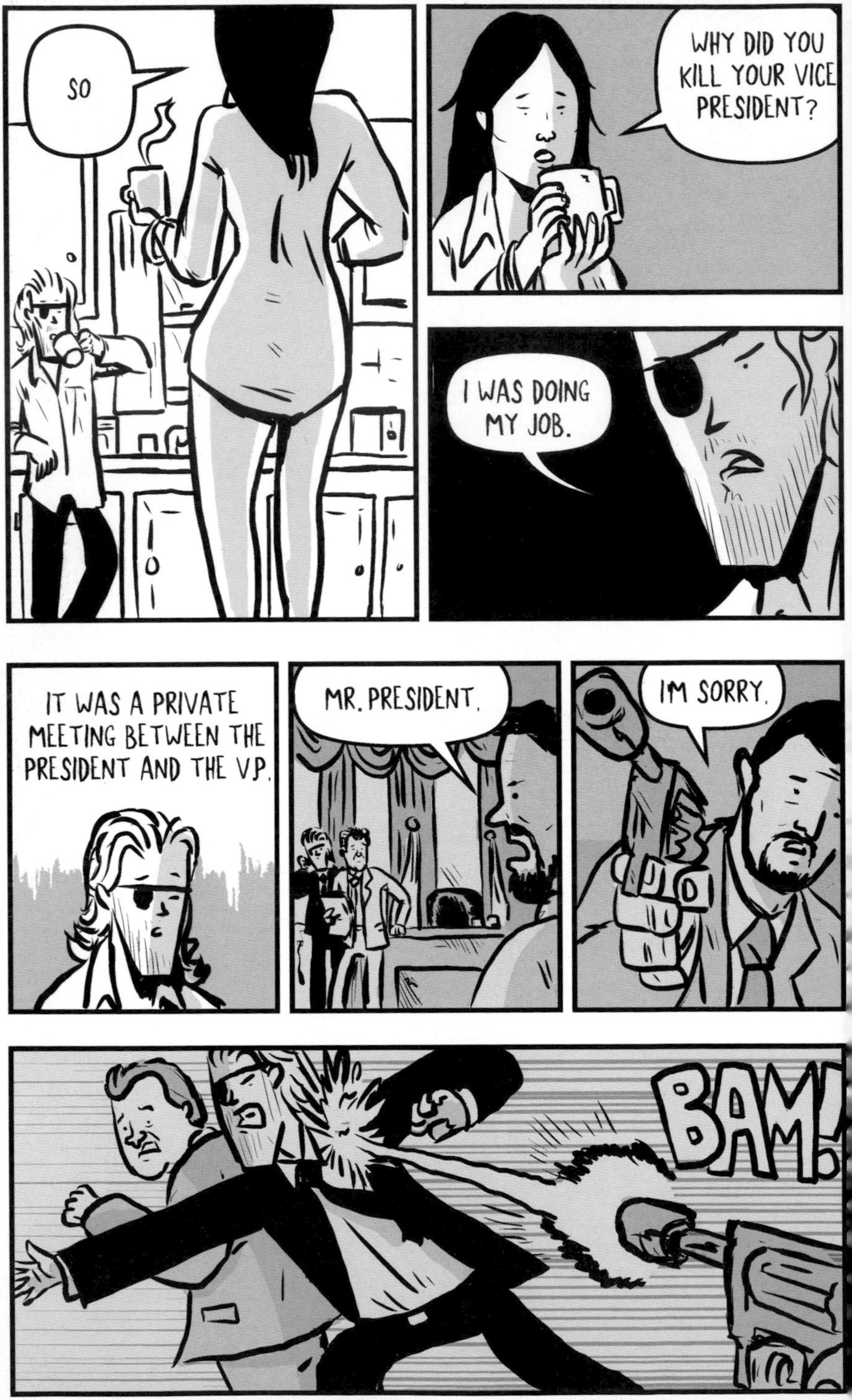
SO
WHY DID YOU KILL YOUR VICE PRESIDENT?
I WAS DOING MY JOB.
IT WAS A PRIVATE MEETING BETWEEN THE PRESIDENT AND THE V.P.
MR. PRESIDENT.
I'M SORRY.
BAM!

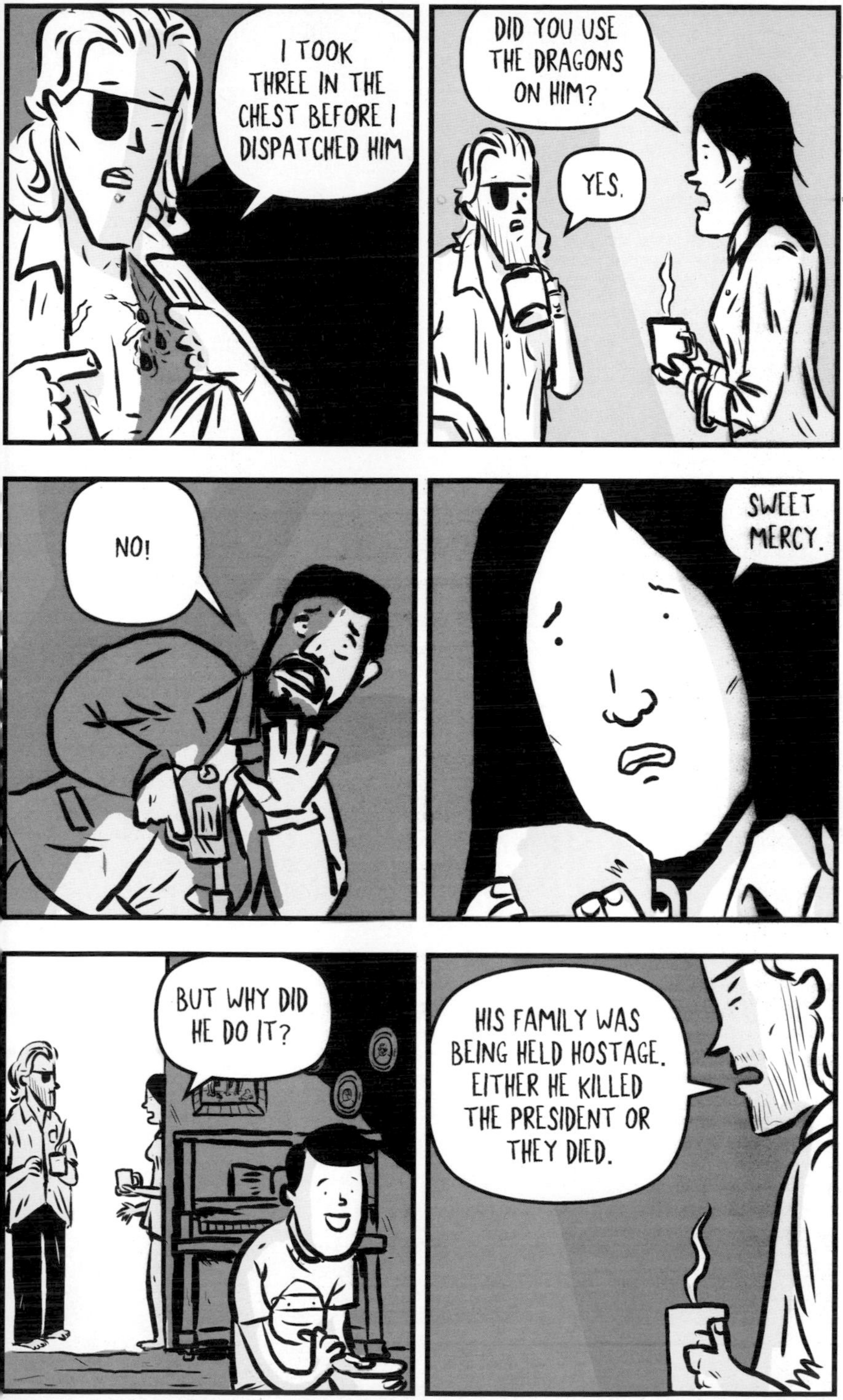
I TOOK THREE IN THE CHEST BEFORE I DISPATCHED HIM
DID YOU USE THE DRAGONS ON HIM?
YES.
NO!
SWEET MERCY.
BUT WHY DID HE DO IT?
HIS FAMILY WAS BEING HELD HOSTAGE. EITHER HE KILLED THE PRESIDENT OR THEY DIED.

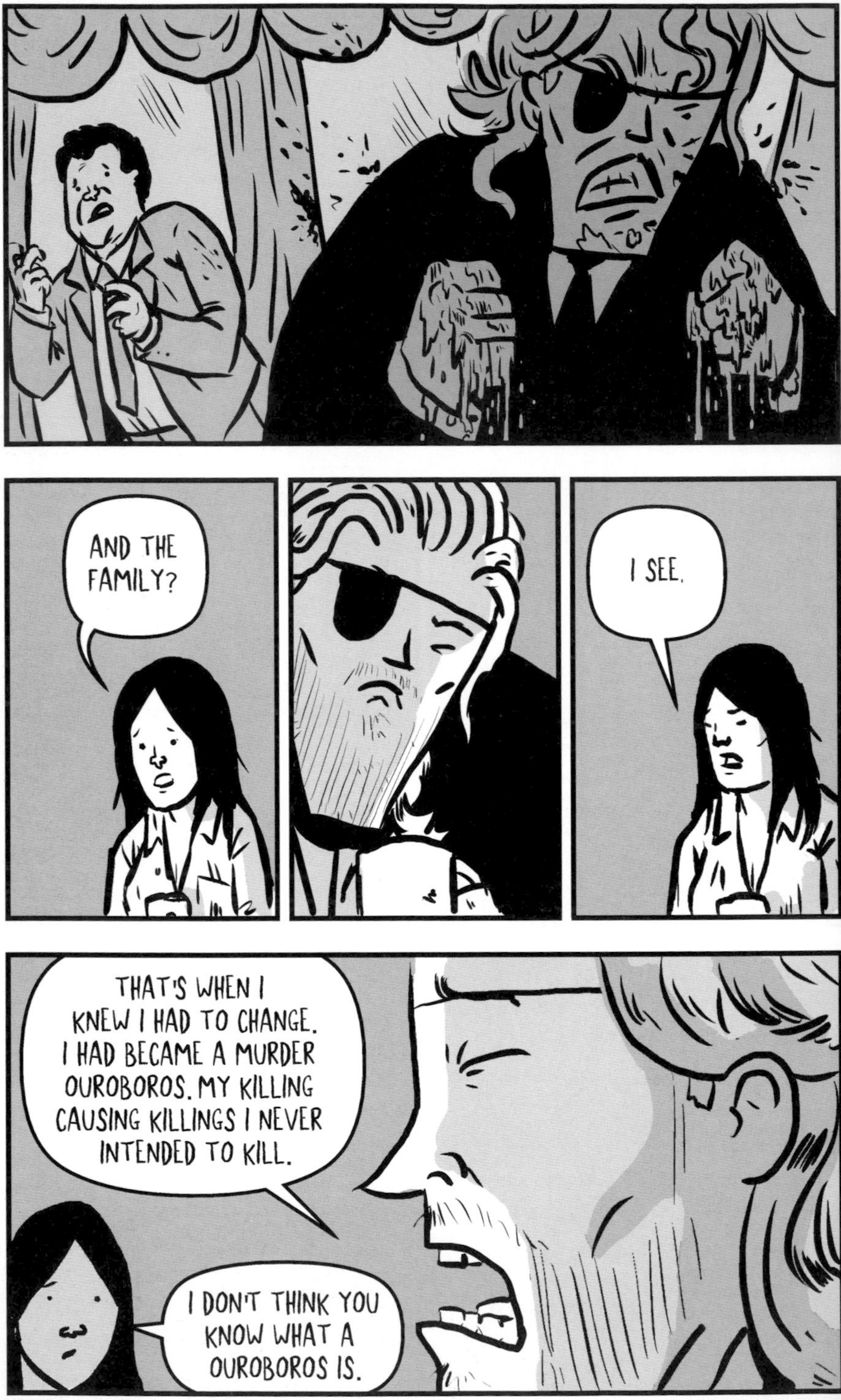

AND THE FAMILY?
I SEE.
THAT'S WHEN I KNEW I HAD TO CHANGE. I HAD BECAME A MURDER OUROBOROS. MY KILLING CAUSING KILLINGS I NEVER INTENDED TO KILL.
I DON'T THINK YOU KNOW WHAT A OUROBOROS IS.

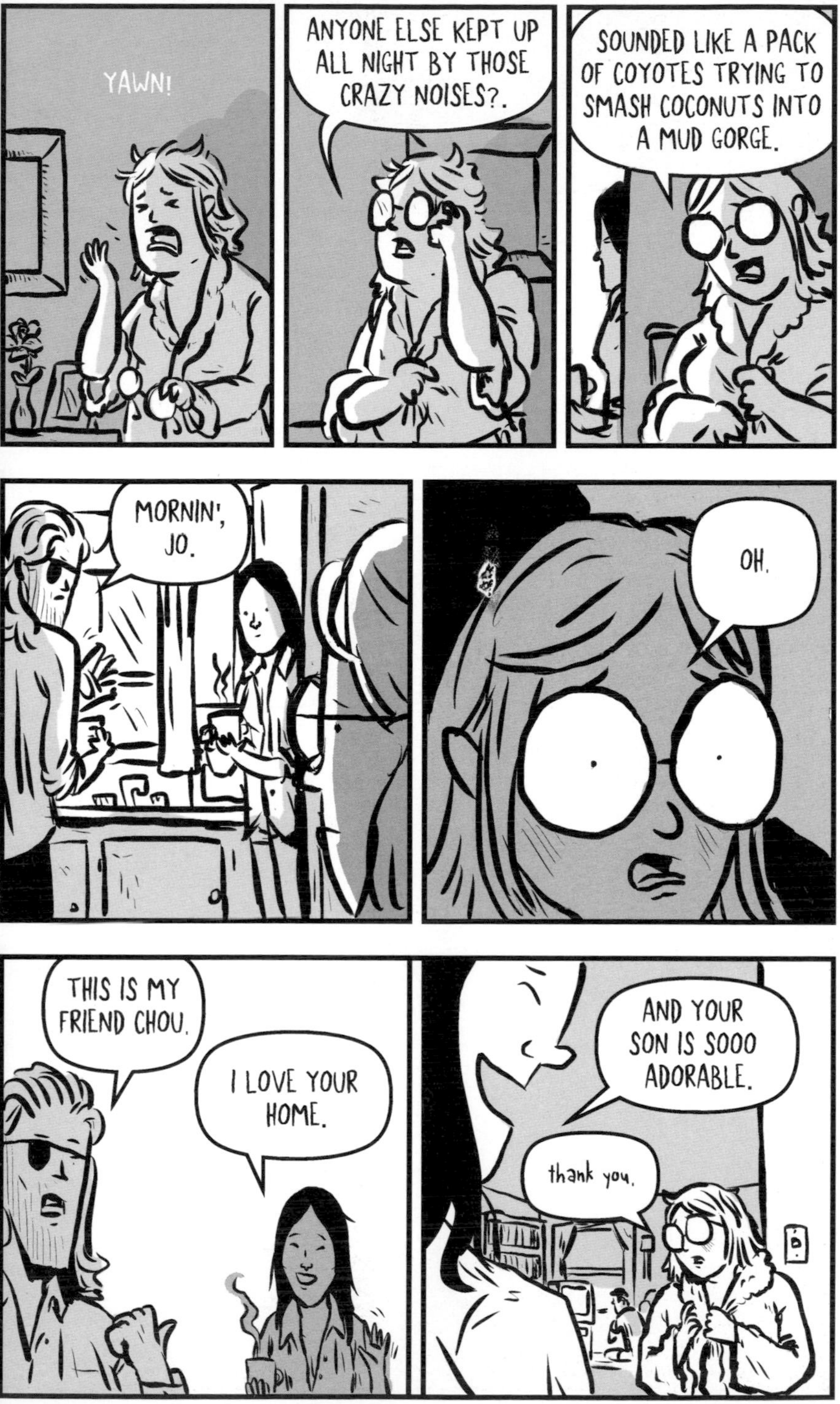
YAWN!
ANYONE ELSE KEPT UP ALL NIGHT BY THOSE CRAZY NOISES?.
SOUNDED LIKE A PACK OF COYOTES TRYING TO SMASH COCONUTS INTO A MUD GORGE.
MORNIN', JO.
OH.
THIS IS MY FRIEND CHOU.
I LOVE YOUR HOME.
AND YOUR SON IS SOOO ADORABLE.
thank you.

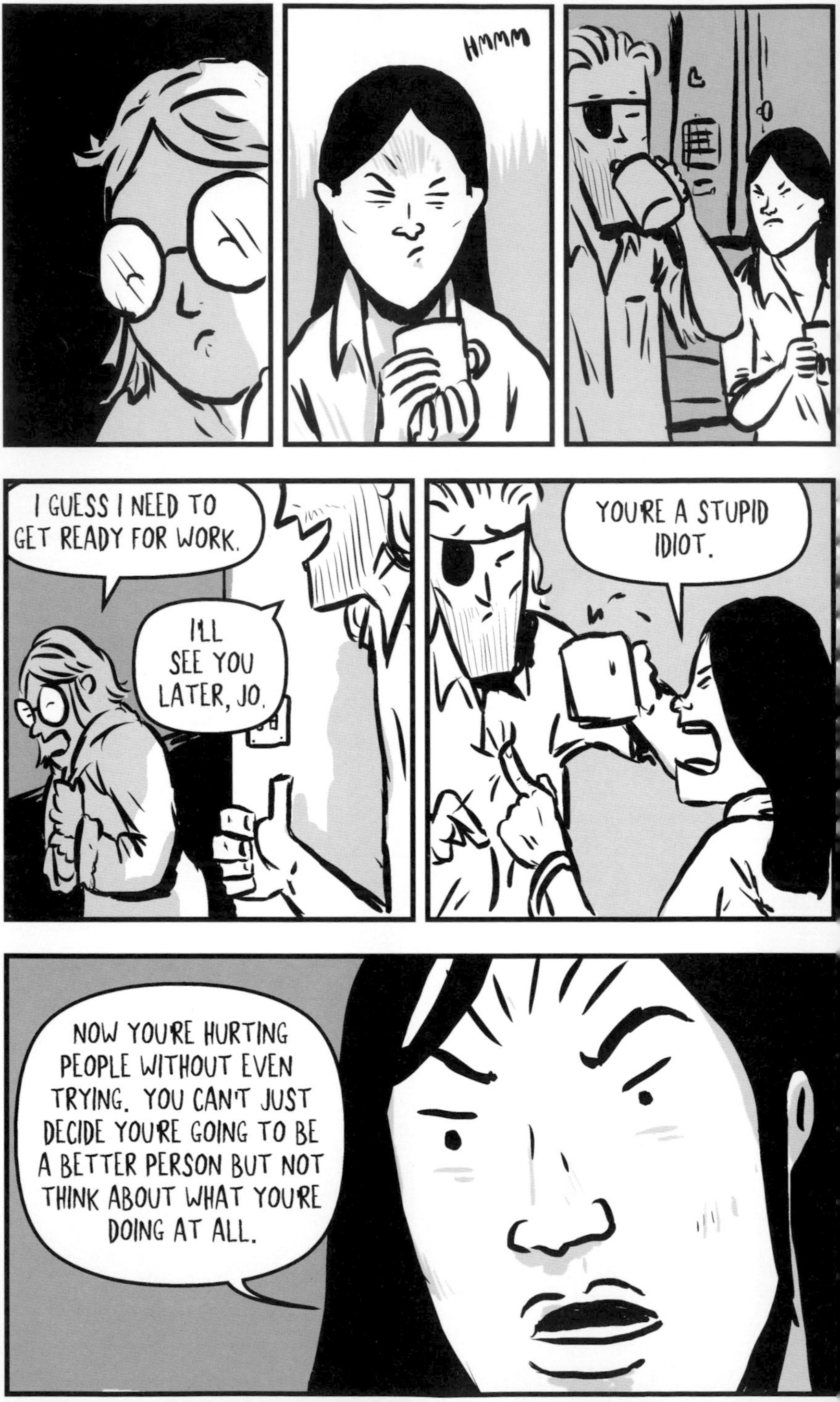
HMMM
I GUESS I NEED TO GET READY FOR WORK.
I'LL SEE YOU LATER, JO.
YOU'RE A STUPID IDIOT.
NOW YOU'RE HURTING PEOPLE WITHOUT EVEN TRYING. YOU CAN'T JUST DECIDE YOU'RE GOING TO BE A BETTER PERSON BUT NOT THINK ABOUT WHAT YOU'RE DOING AT ALL.

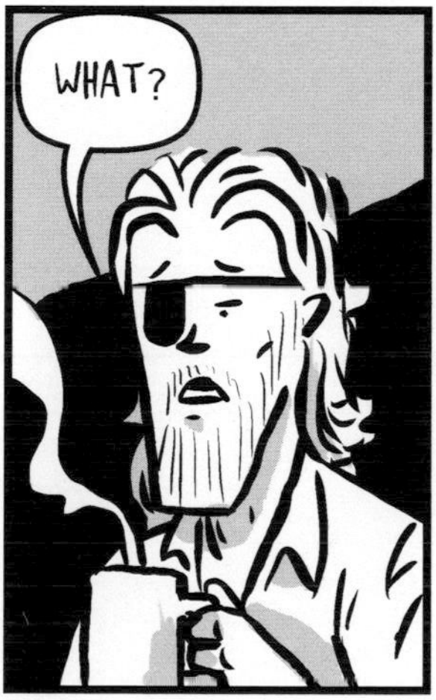
WHAT?

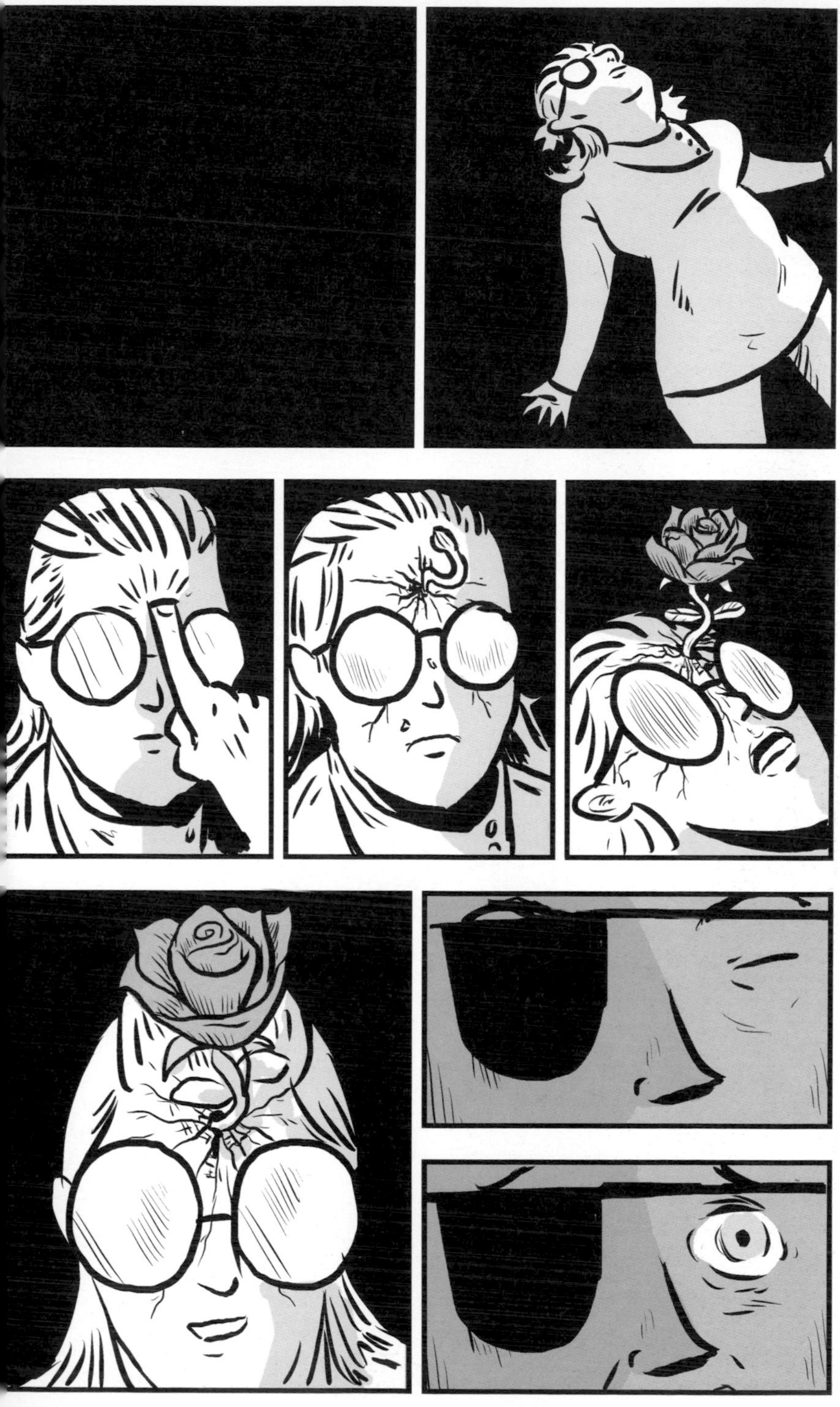

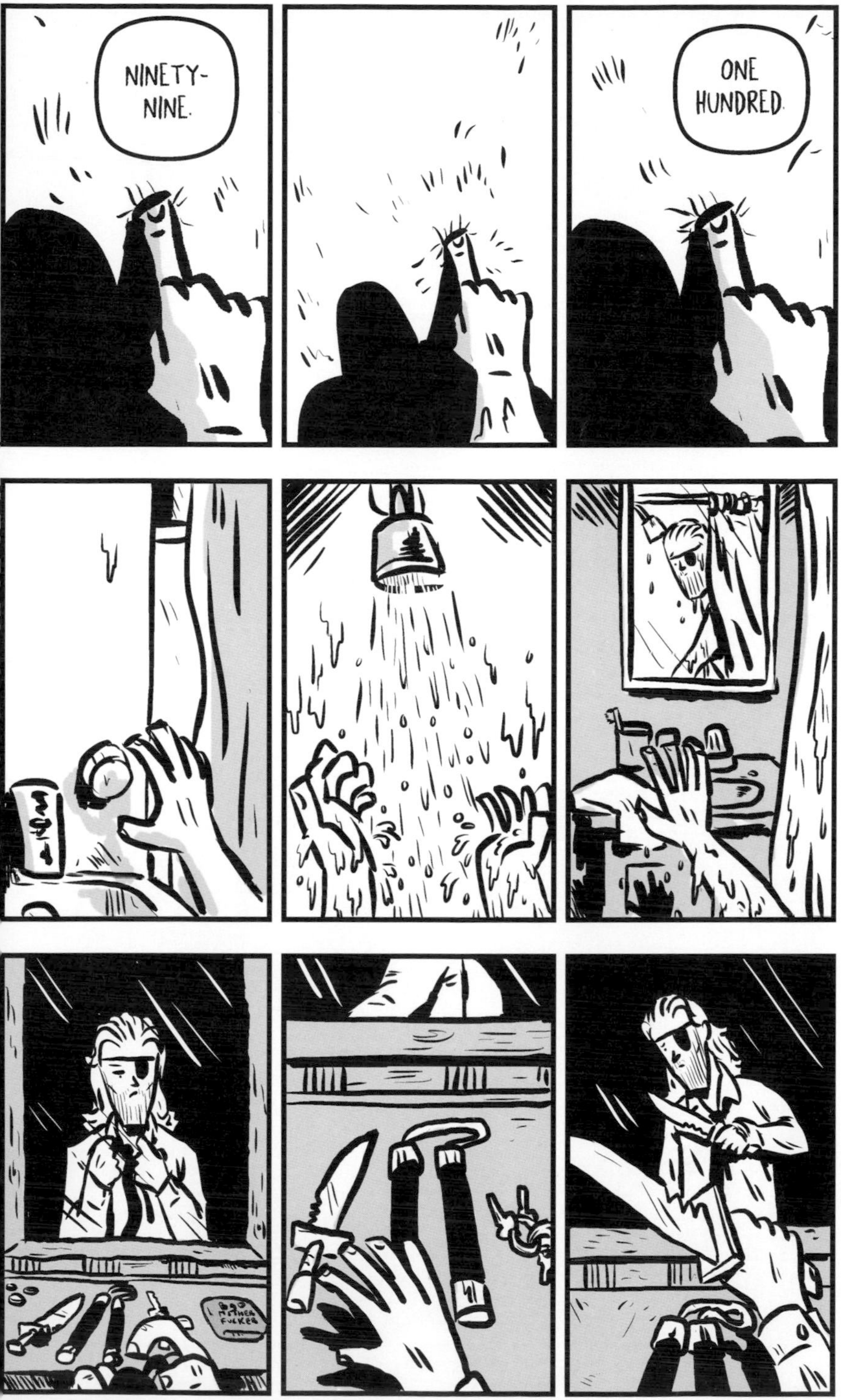
NINETY-NINE.
ONE HUNDRED.
BAD MOTHER FUCKER

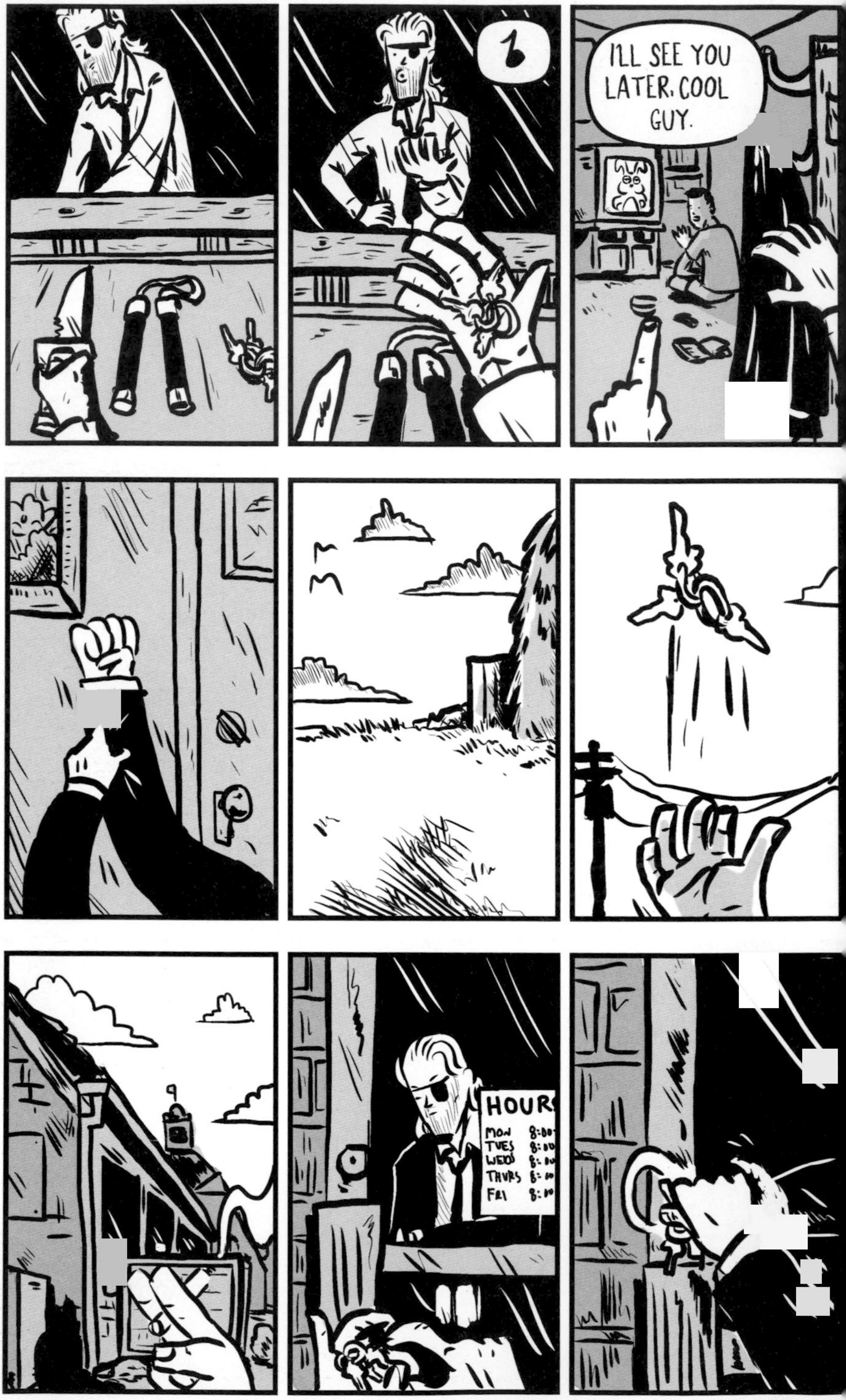
I'LL SEE YOU LATER, COOL GUY.
HOURS
MON 8:00
TUES 8:00
WED'S 8:00
THURS 8:00
FRI 8:00

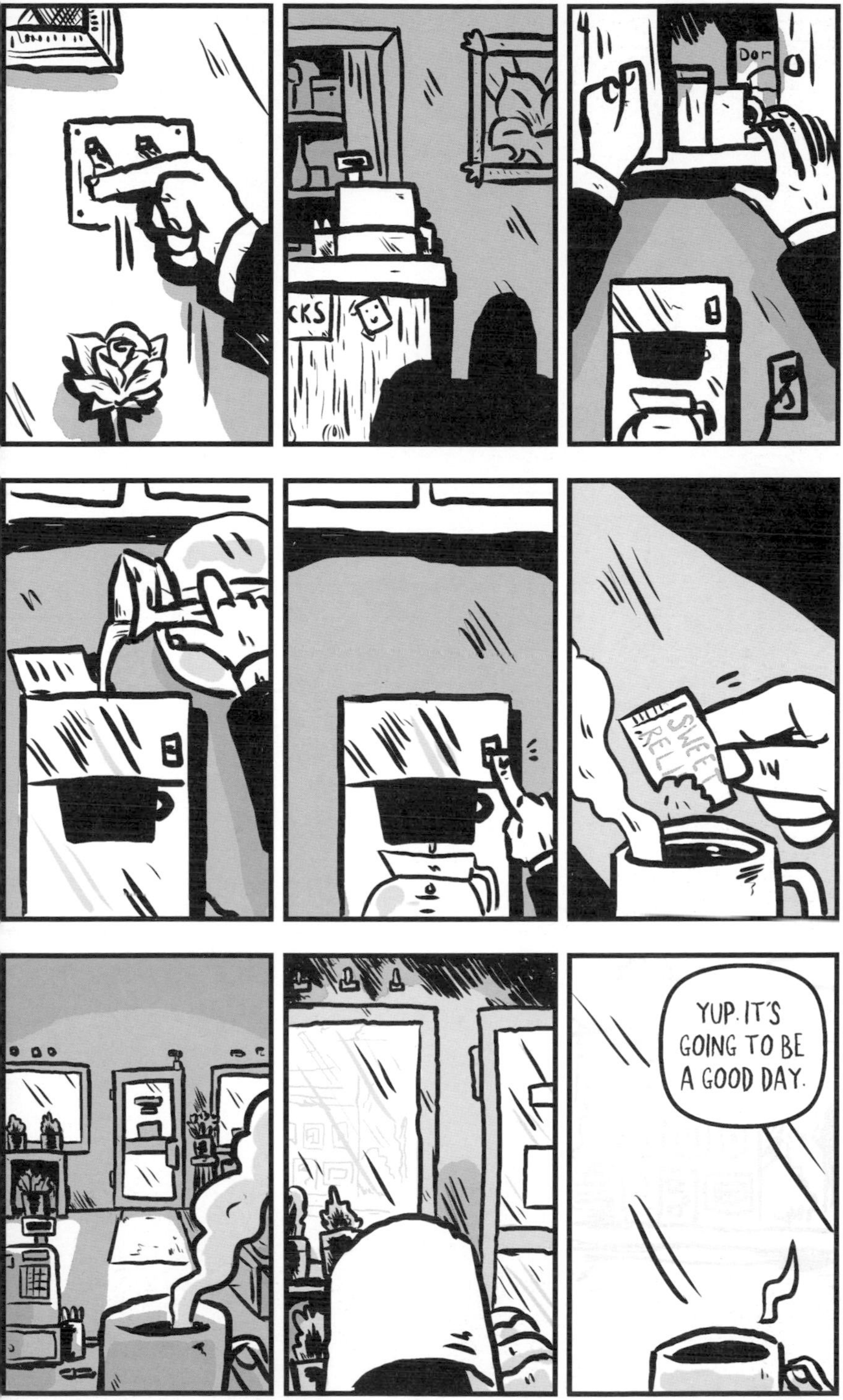
YUP. IT'S GOING TO BE A GOOD DAY.

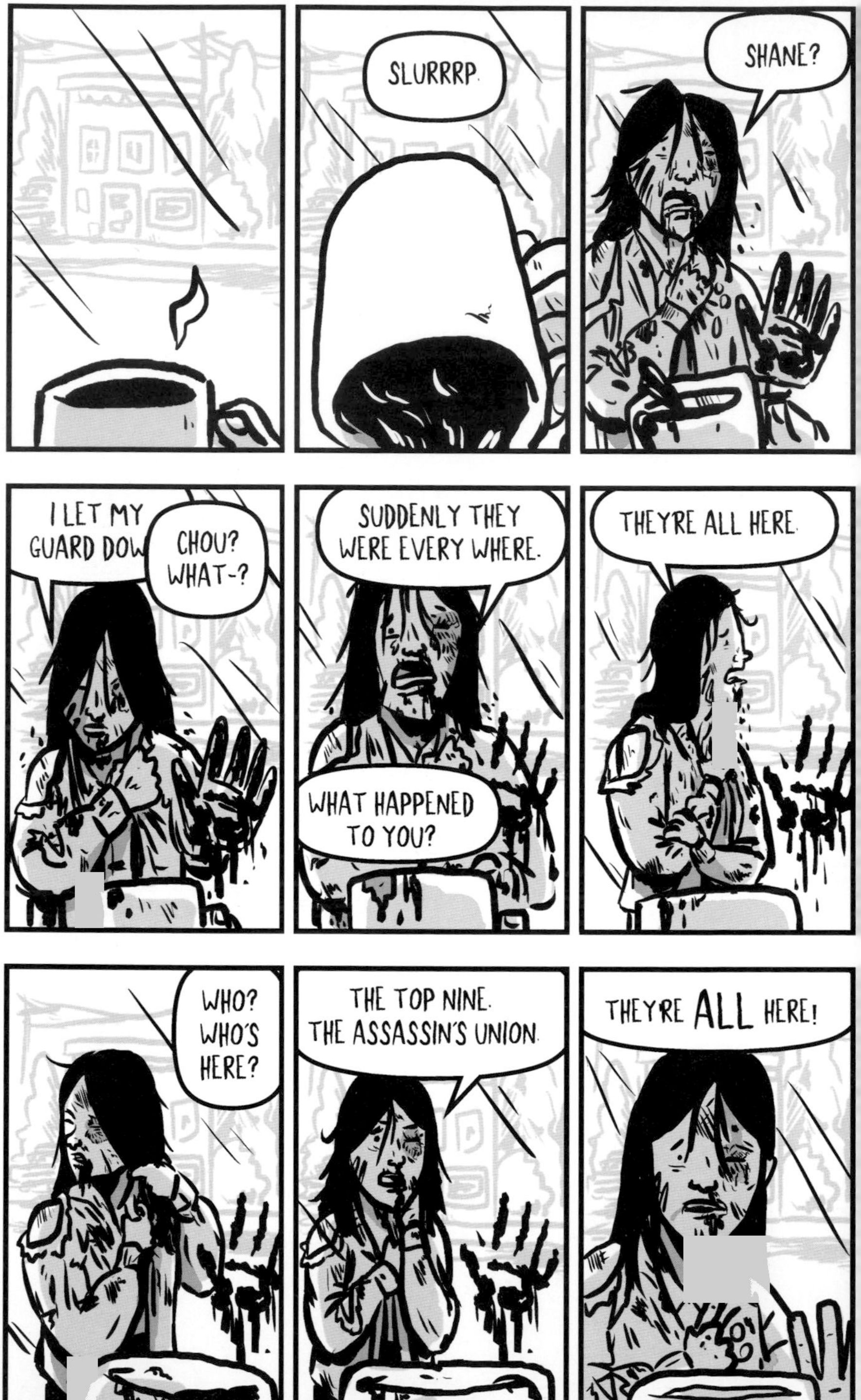
SLURRRP.
SHANE?
I LET MY GUARD DOW
CHOU? WHAT-?
SUDDENLY THEY WERE EVERY WHERE.
WHAT HAPPENED TO YOU?
THEY'RE ALL HERE.
WHO? WHO'S HERE?
THE TOP NINE. THE ASSASSIN'S UNION.
THEY'RE ALL HERE!

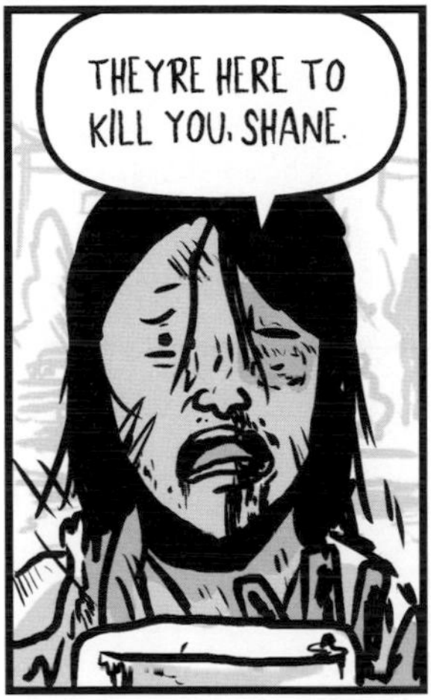
THEYRE HERE TO KILL YOU, SHANE.

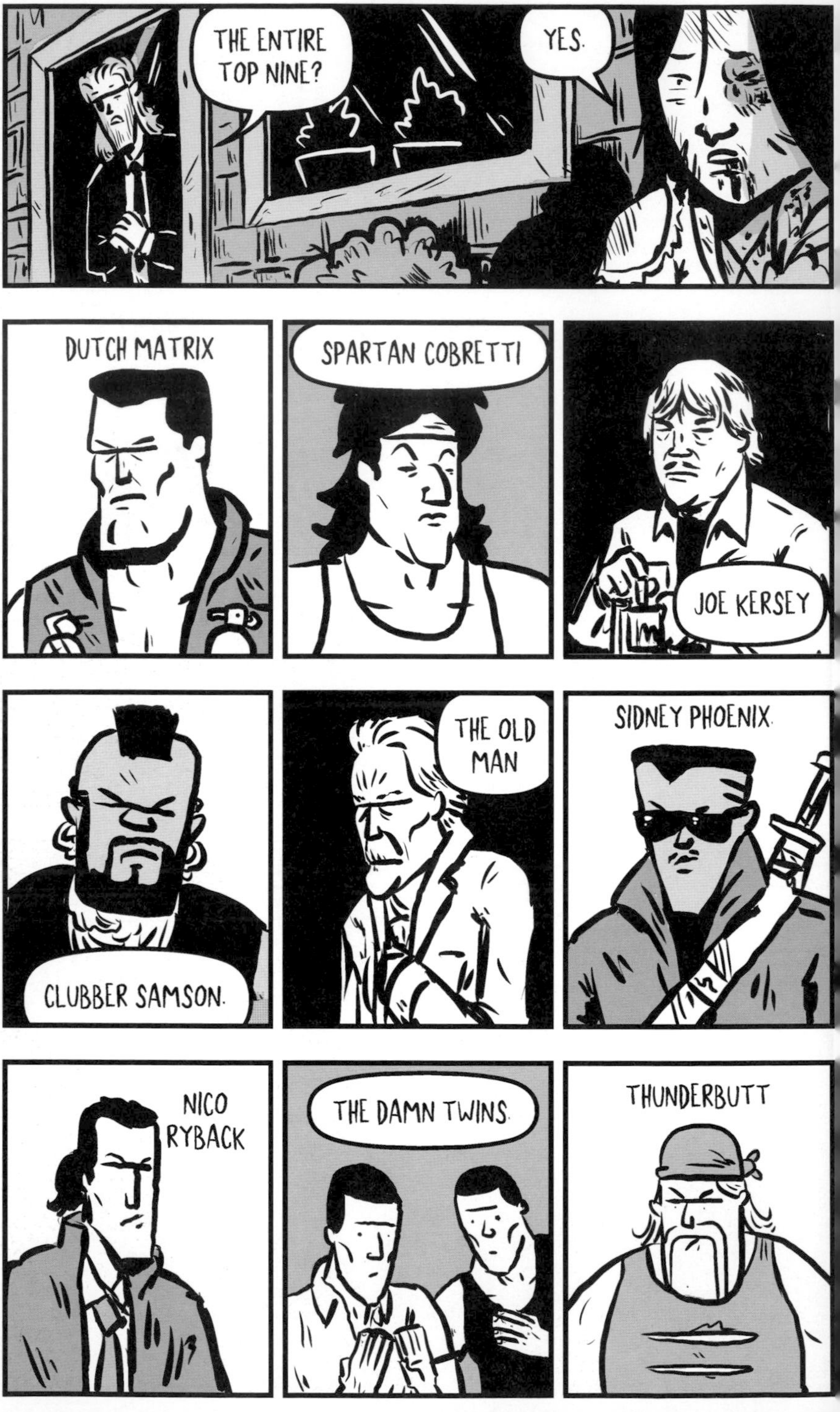
THE ENTIRE TOP NINE?
YES.
DUTCH MATRIX
SPARTAN COBRETTI
JOE KERSEY
CLUBBER SAMSON.
THE OLD MAN
SIDNEY PHOENIX.
NICO RYBACK
THE DAMN TWINS.
THUNDERBUTT

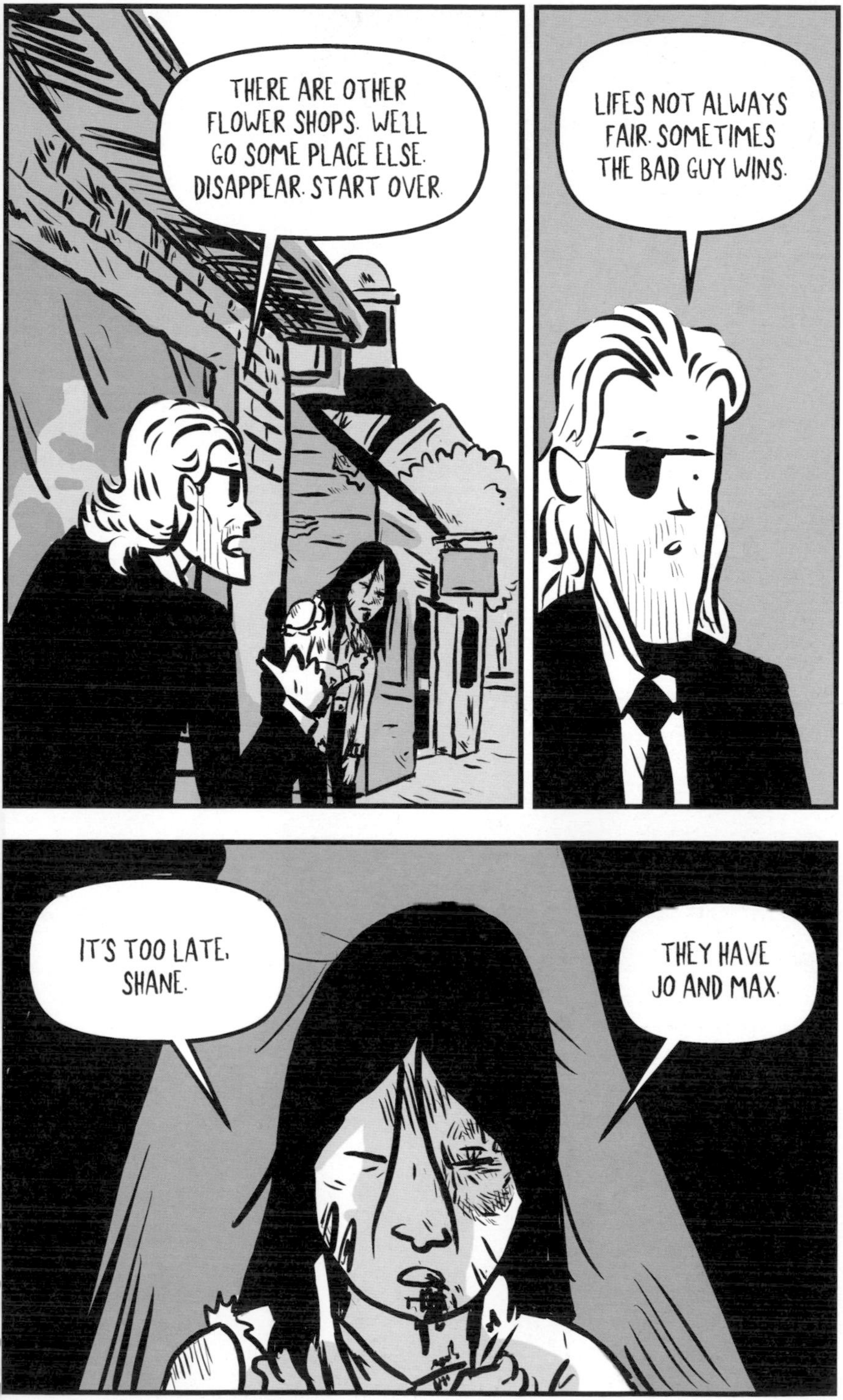
THERE ARE OTHER FLOWER SHOPS. WE'LL GO SOME PLACE ELSE. DISAPPEAR. START OVER.
LIFES NOT ALWAYS FAIR. SOMETIMES THE BAD GUY WINS.
IT'S TOO LATE, SHANE.
THEY HAVE JO AND MAX.

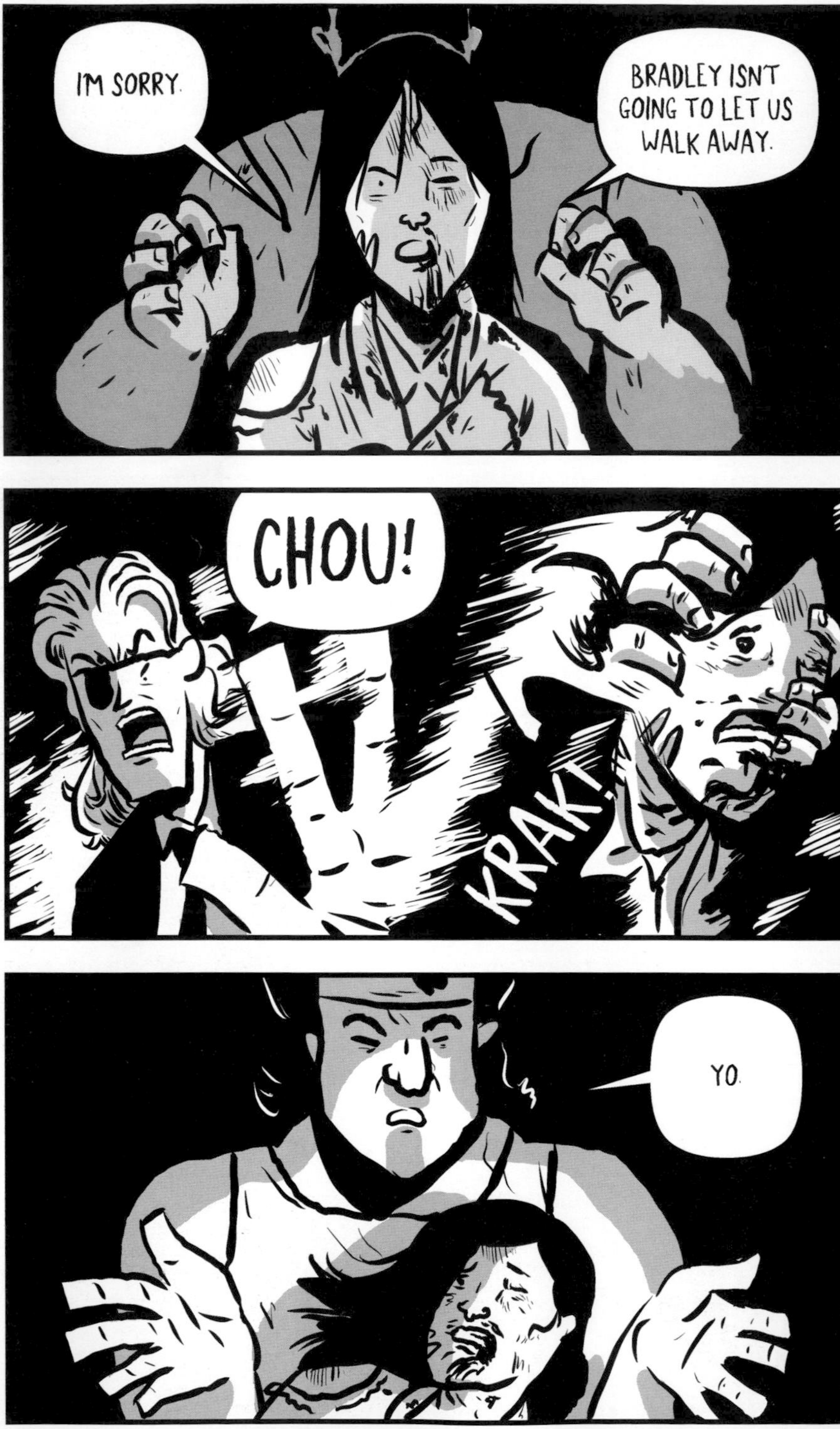

I'M SORRY.
BRADLEY ISN'T GOING TO LET US WALK AWAY.
CHOU!
KRAKT!
YO.

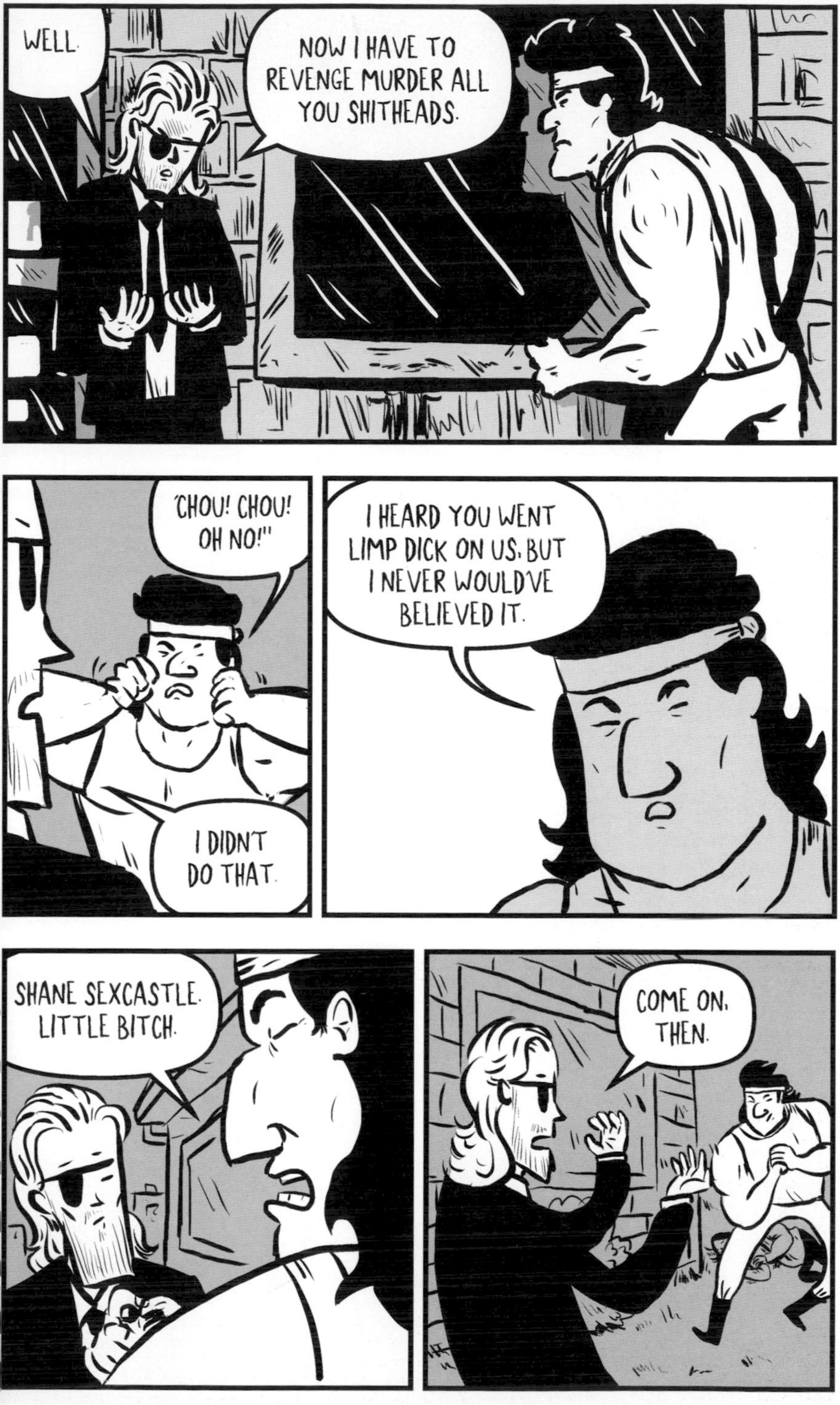
WELL.
NOW I HAVE TO REVENGE MURDER ALL YOU SHITHEADS.
"CHOU! CHOU! OH NO!"
I DIDN'T DO THAT.
I HEARD YOU WENT LIMP DICK ON US, BUT I NEVER WOULD'VE BELIEVED IT.
SHANE SEXCASTLE. LITTLE BITCH.
COME ON, THEN.

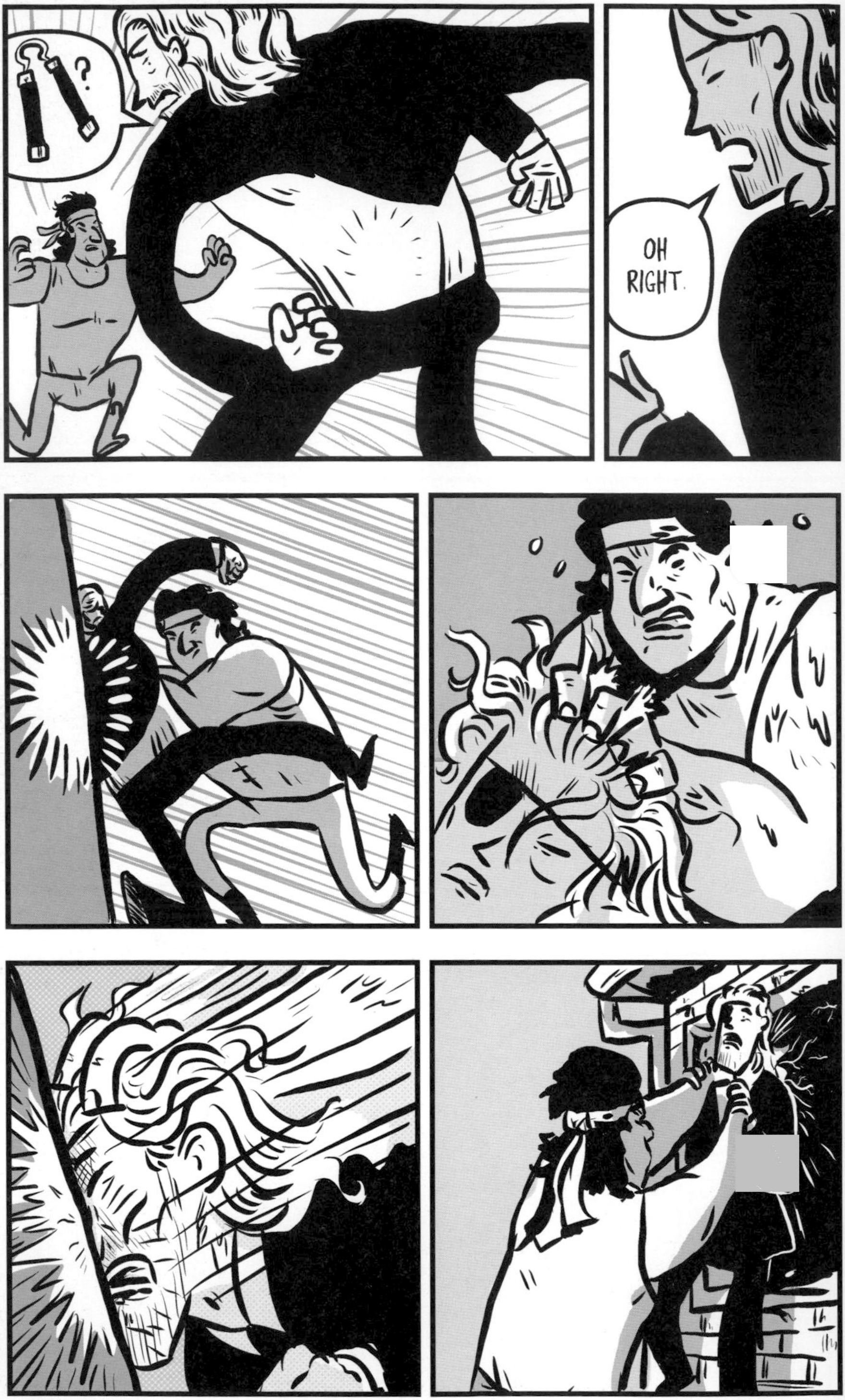
?
OH RIGHT.

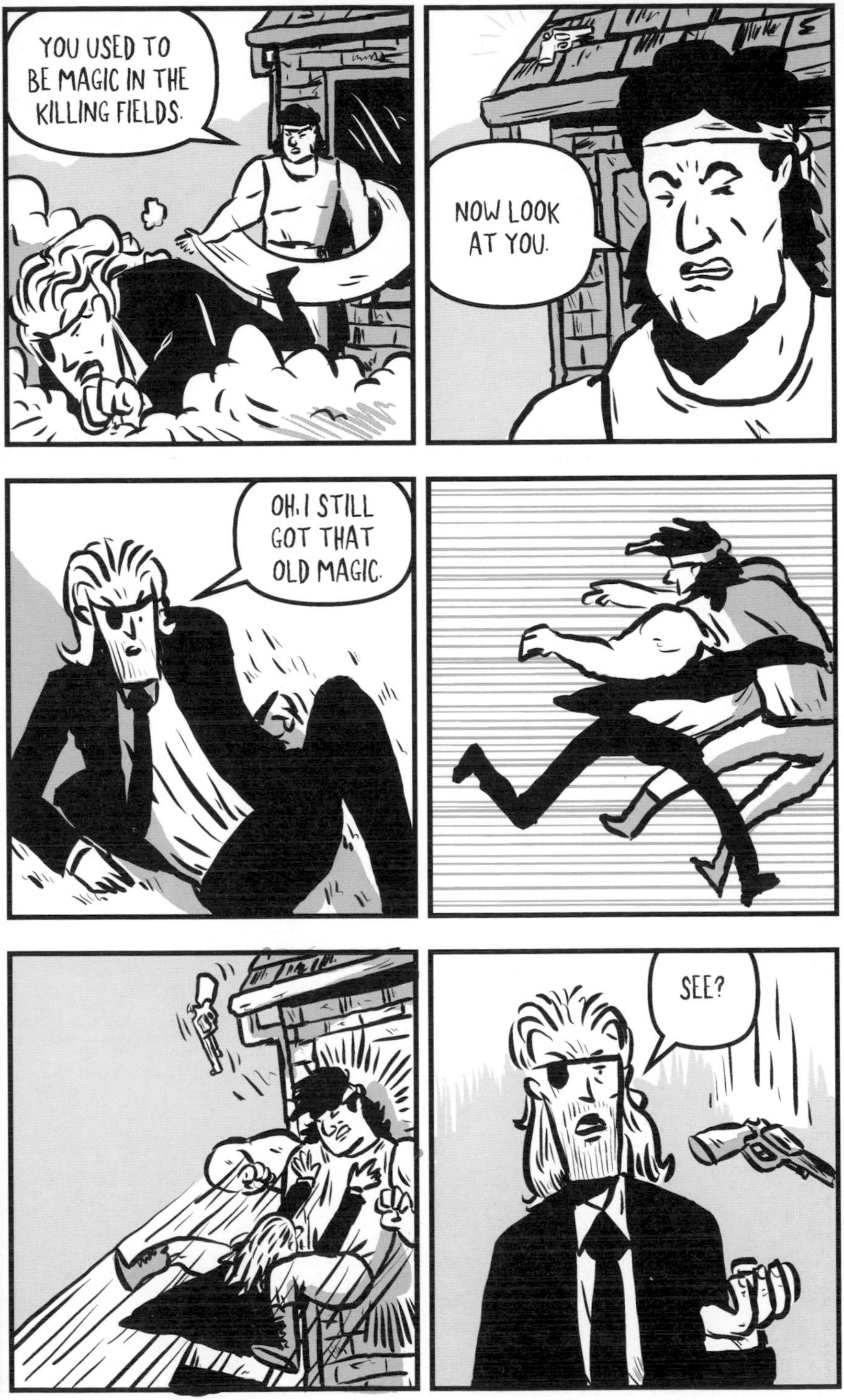
YOU USED TO BE MAGIC IN THE KILLING FIELDS.
NOW LOOK AT YOU.
OH, I STILL GOT THAT OLD MAGIC.
SEE?

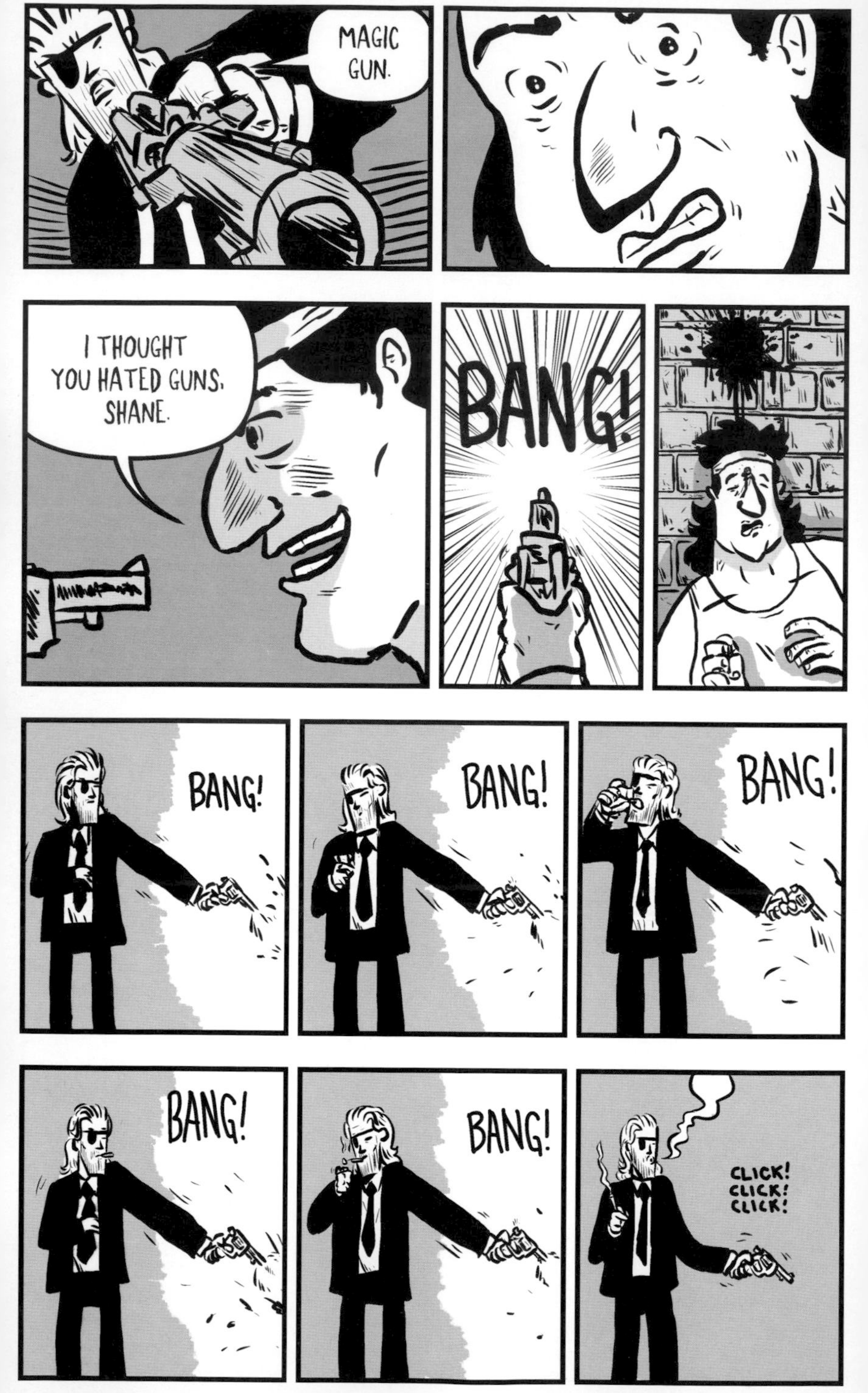
MAGIC GUN.
I THOUGHT YOU HATED GUNS, SHANE.
BANG!
BANG!
BANG!
BANG!
BANG!
BANG!
CLICK! CLICK! CLICK!

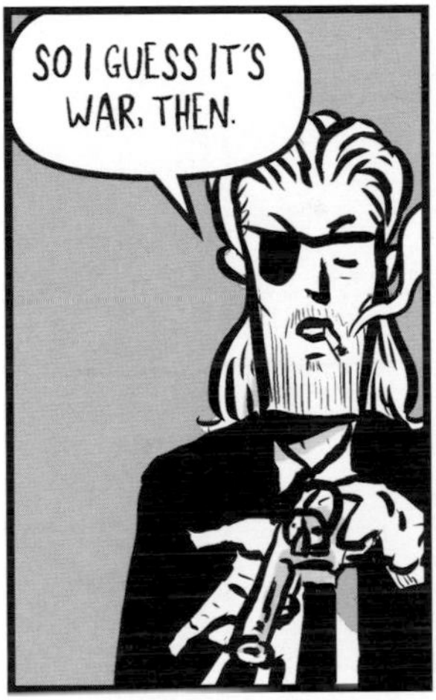
SO I GUESS IT'S WAR, THEN.

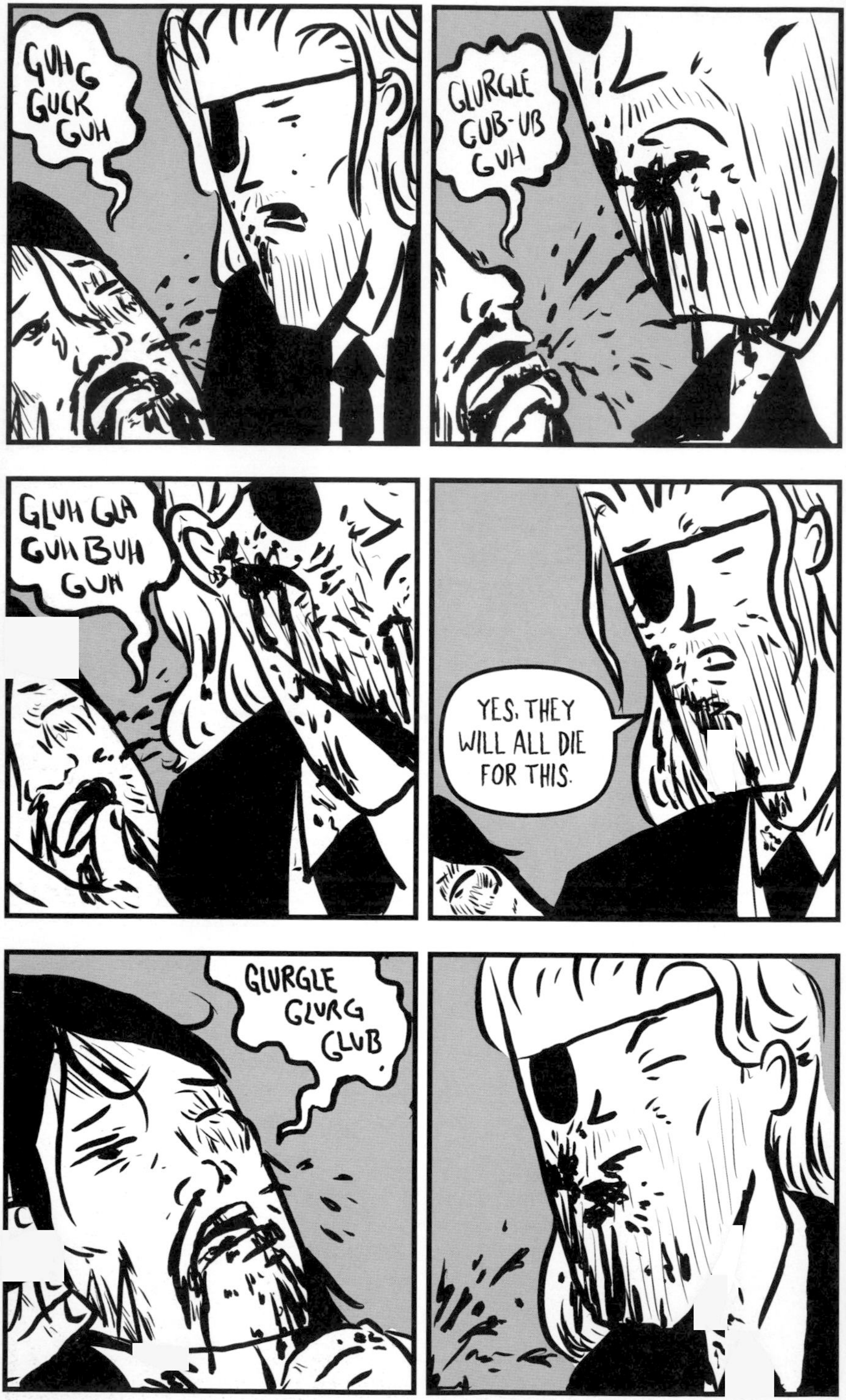
GUHG
GUCK
GUH
GLURGLE
GUB-UB
GUH
GLUH GLA
GUH BUH
GUH
YES, THEY WILL ALL DIE FOR THIS.
GLURGLE
GLURG
GLUB

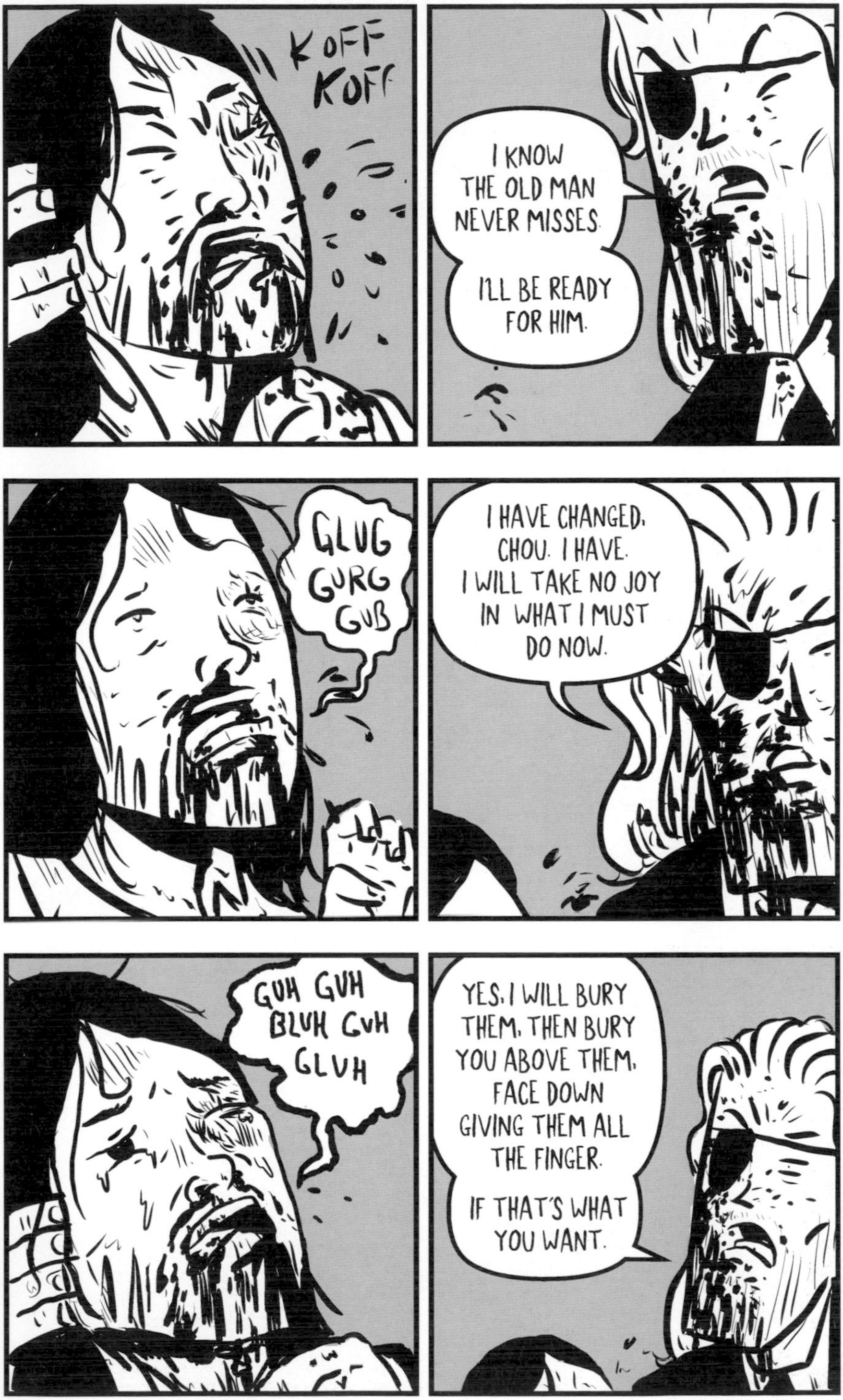
KOFF KOFF
I KNOW THE OLD MAN NEVER MISSES.
I'LL BE READY FOR HIM.
GLUG GURG GUB
I HAVE CHANGED, CHOU. I HAVE. I WILL TAKE NO JOY IN WHAT I MUST DO NOW.
GUH GUH BLUH GUH GLUH
YES, I WILL BURY THEM, THEN BURY YOU ABOVE THEM, FACE DOWN GIVING THEM ALL THE FINGER.
IF THAT'S WHAT YOU WANT.

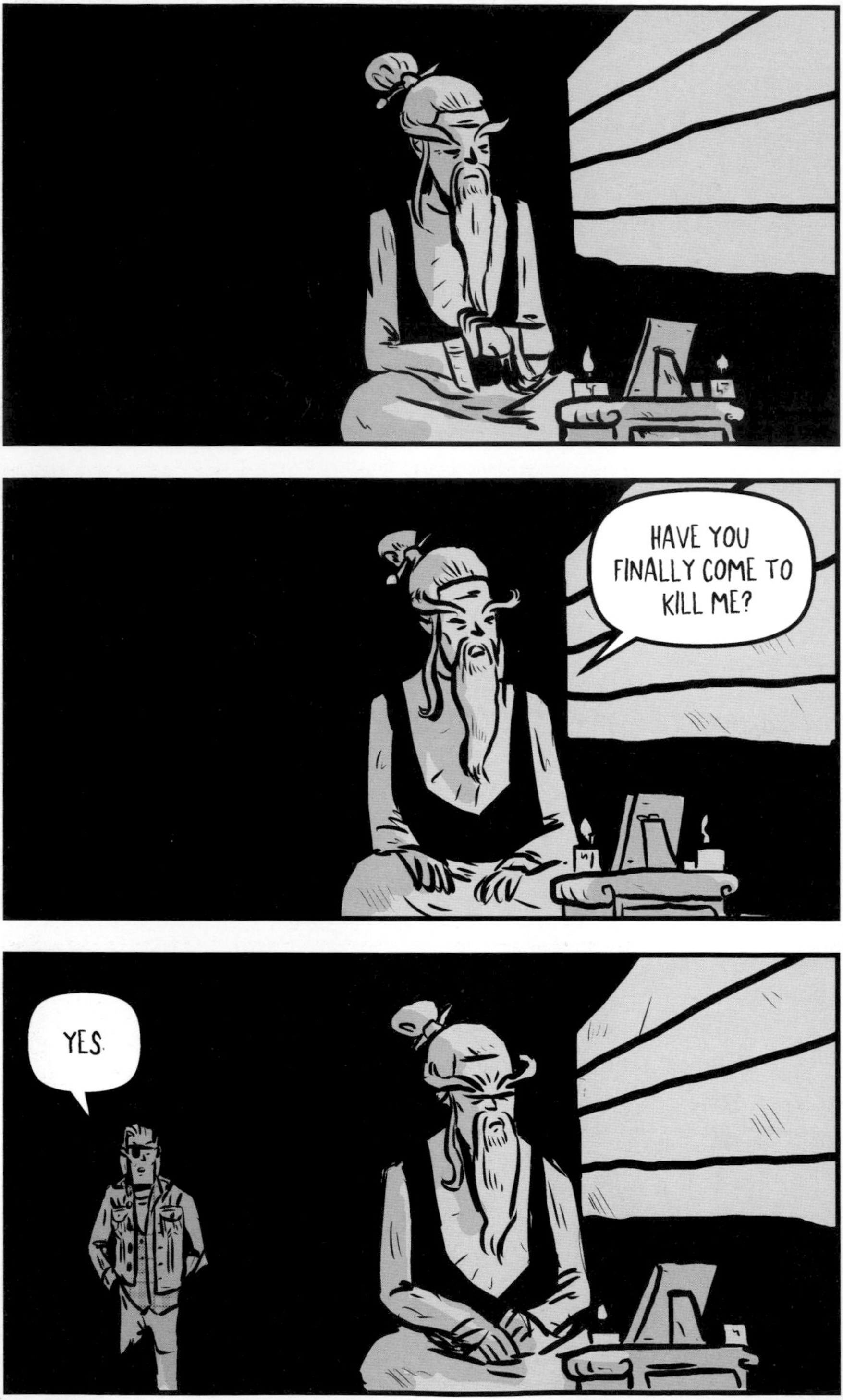
HAVE YOU FINALLY COME TO KILL ME?
YES.

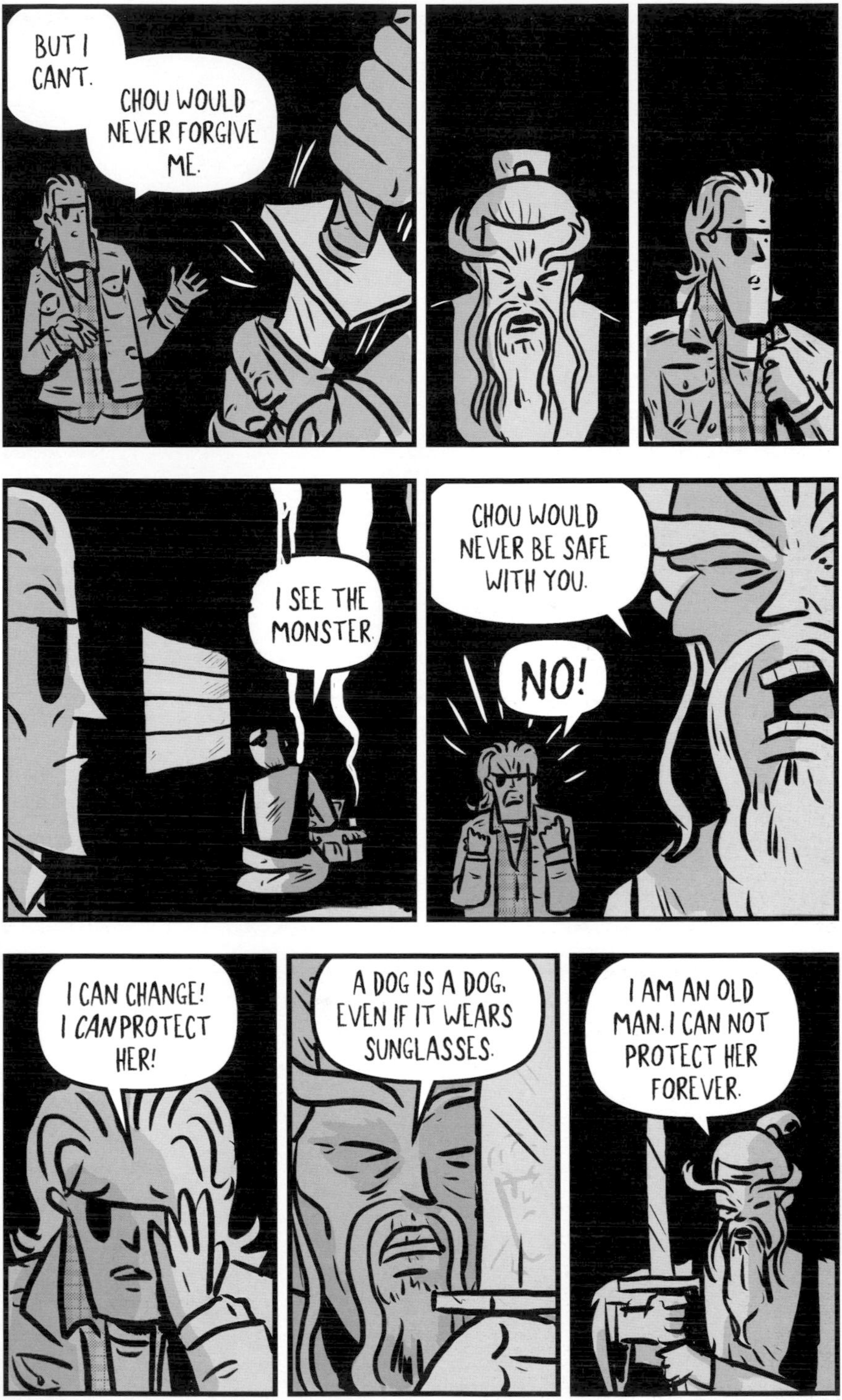
BUT I CAN'T.
CHOU WOULD NEVER FORGIVE ME.
I SEE THE MONSTER.
CHOU WOULD NEVER BE SAFE WITH YOU.
NO!
I CAN CHANGE! I *CAN* PROTECT HER!
A DOG IS A DOG, EVEN IF IT WEARS SUNGLASSES.
I AM AN OLD MAN. I CAN NOT PROTECT HER FOREVER.

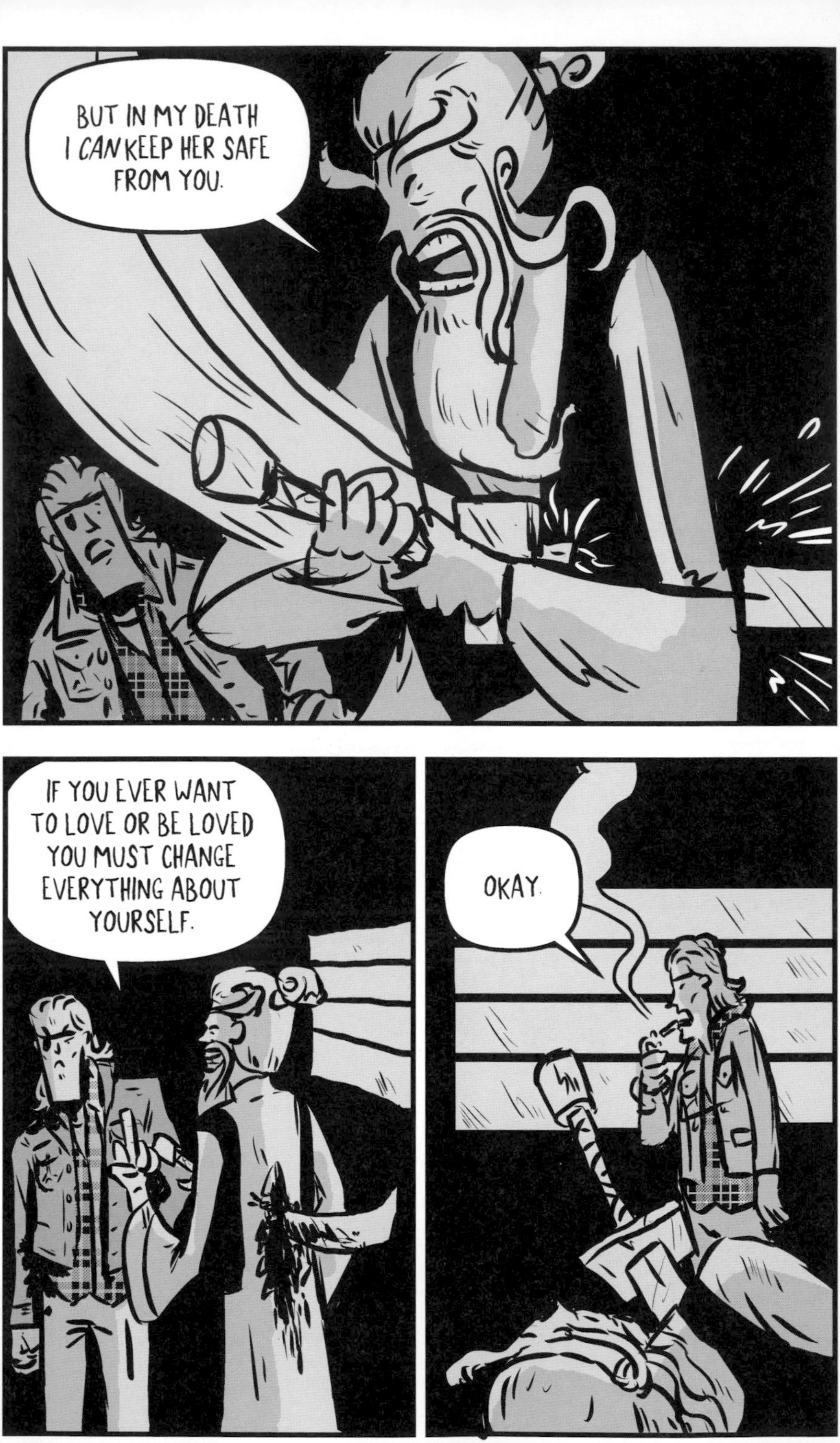
BUT IN MY DEATH I *CAN* KEEP HER SAFE FROM YOU.
IF YOU EVER WANT TO LOVE OR BE LOVED YOU MUST CHANGE EVERYTHING ABOUT YOURSELF.
OKAY.

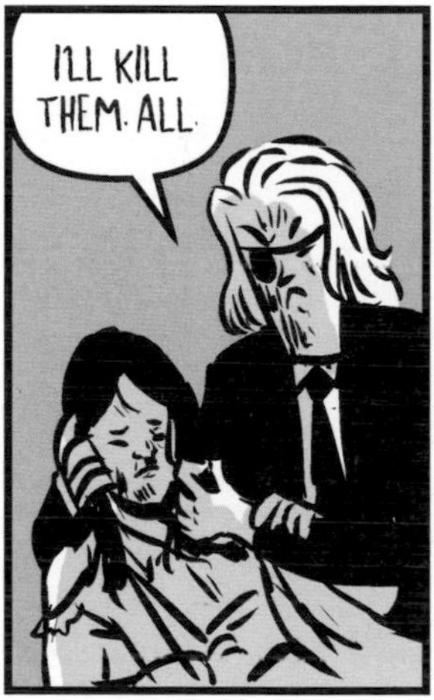
I'LL KILL THEM. ALL.

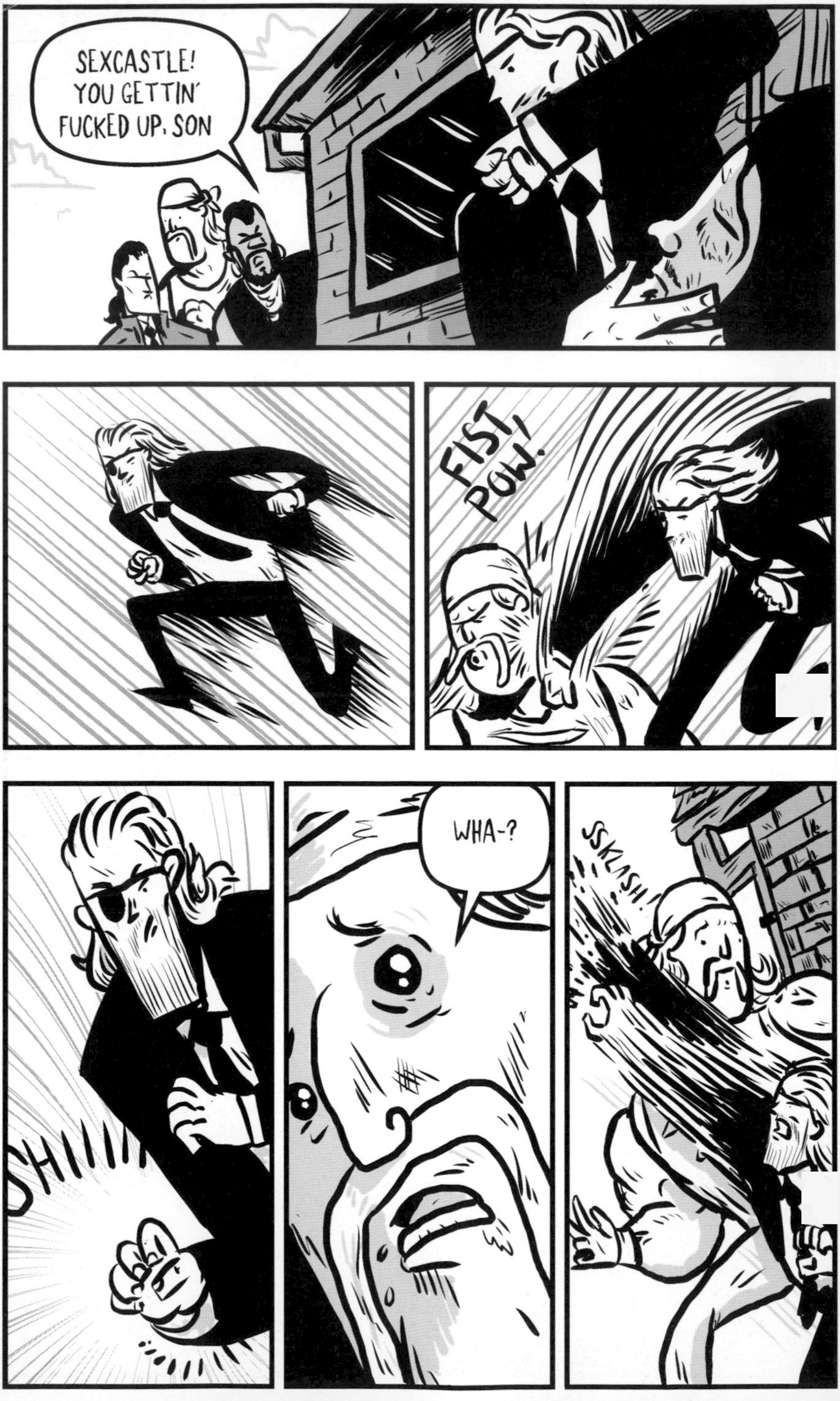

SEXCASTLE! YOU GETTIN' FUCKED UP, SON
FIST POW!
SHIIII
WHA-?
SSKLASH!

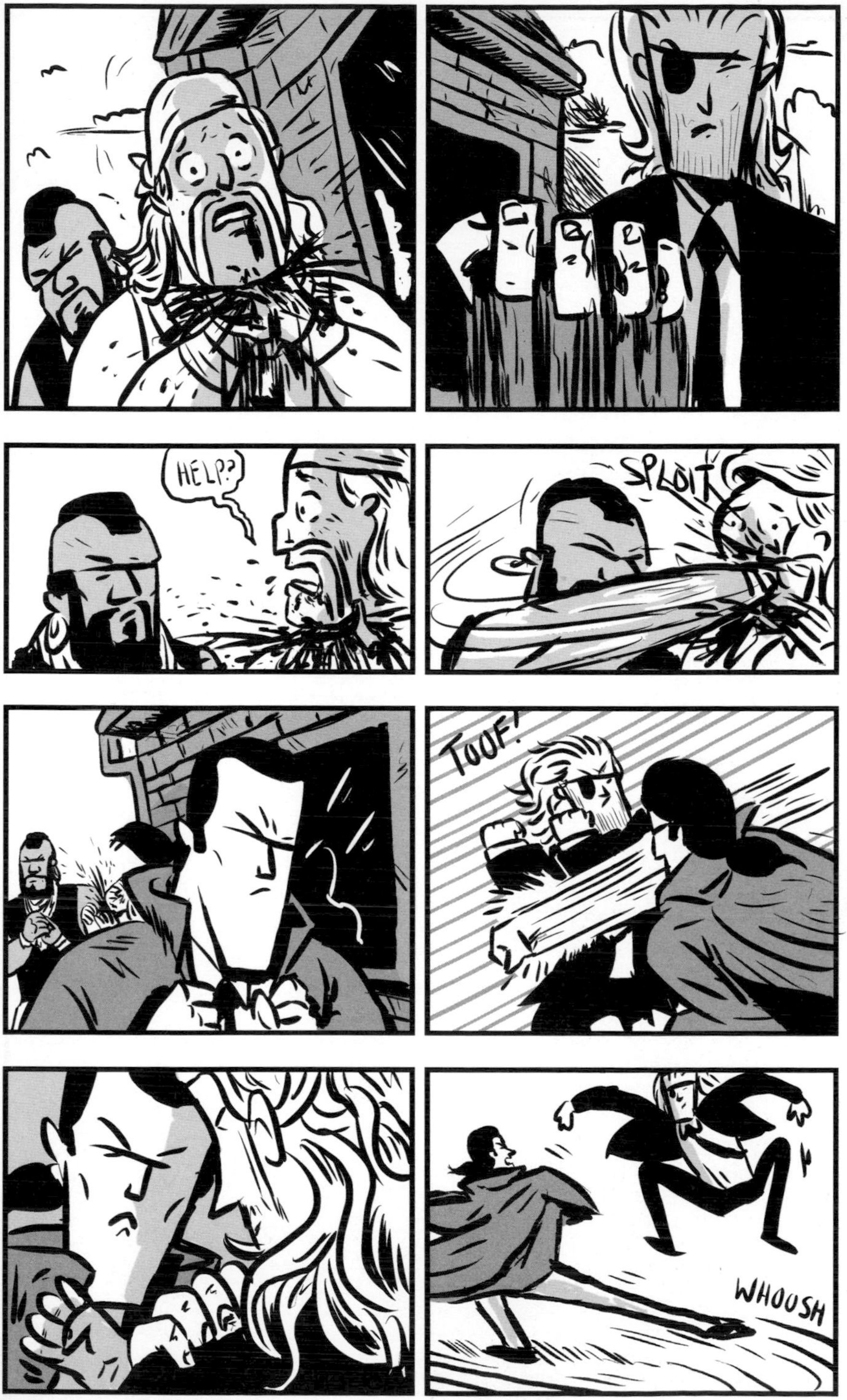
HELP??
SPLOIT
TOOF!
WHOOSH

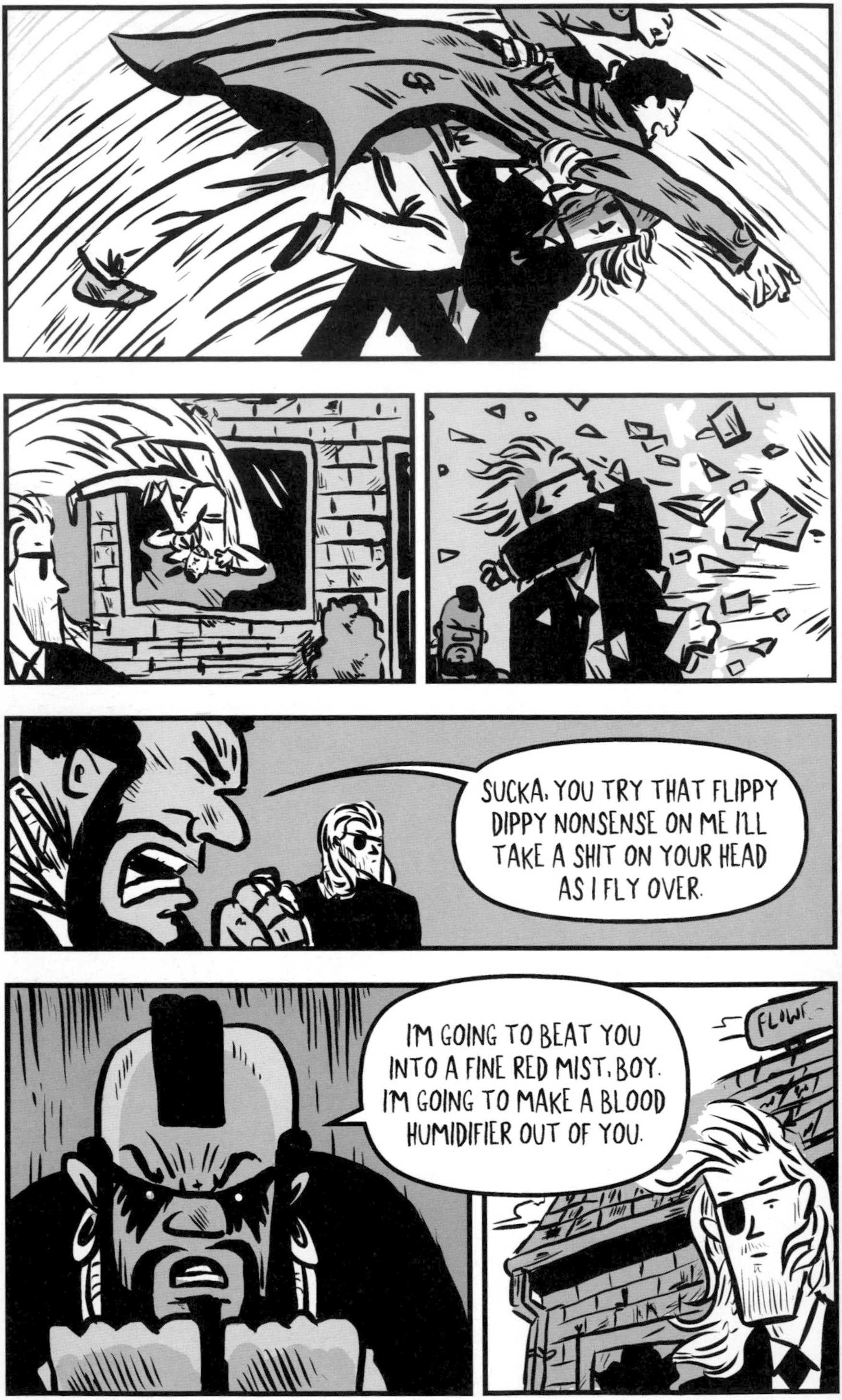
SUCKA, YOU TRY THAT FLIPPY DIPPY NONSENSE ON ME I'LL TAKE A SHIT ON YOUR HEAD AS I FLY OVER.
I'M GOING TO BEAT YOU INTO A FINE RED MIST, BOY. I'M GOING TO MAKE A BLOOD HUMIDIFIER OUT OF YOU.

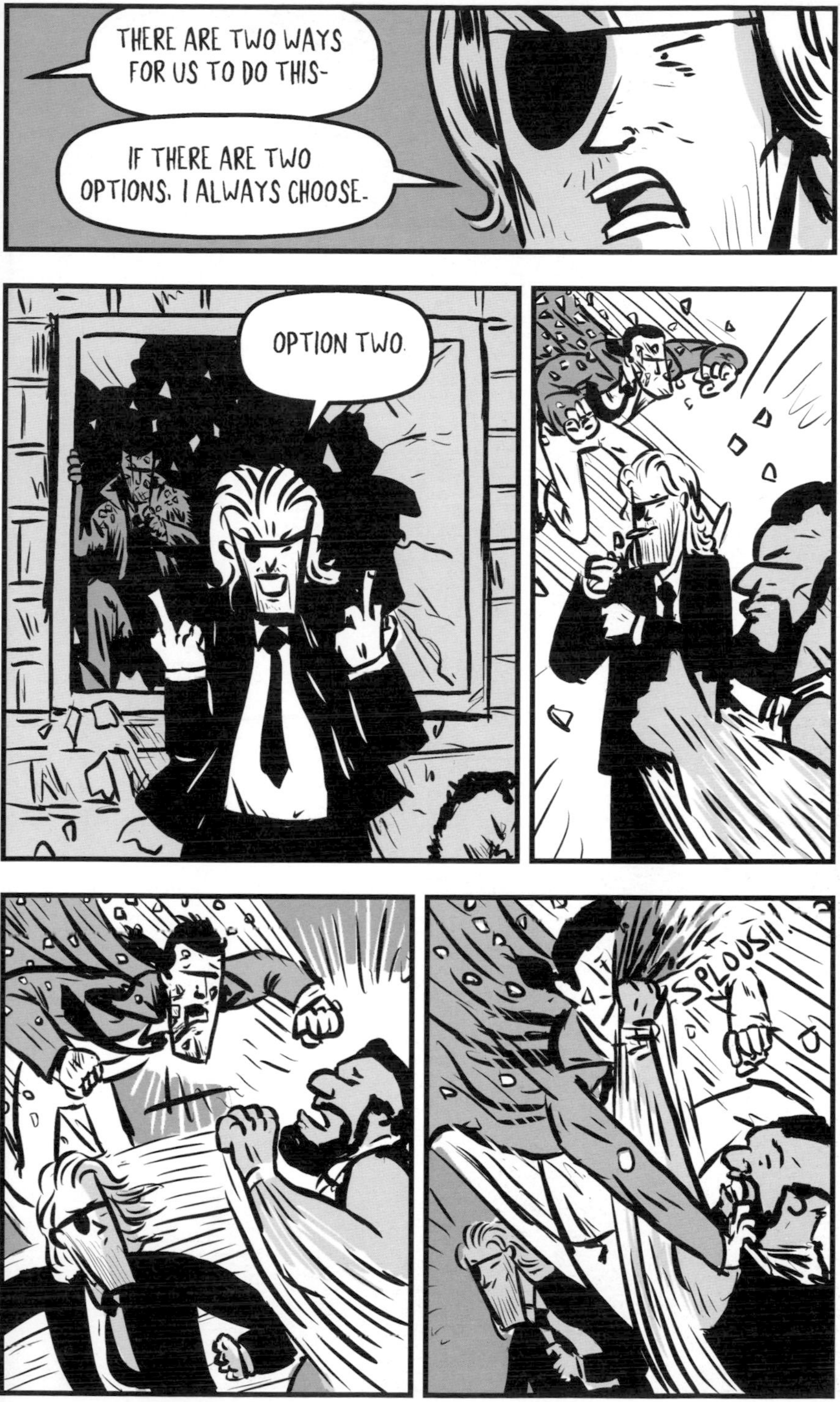
THERE ARE TWO WAYS FOR US TO DO THIS-
IF THERE ARE TWO OPTIONS, I ALWAYS CHOOSE-
OPTION TWO.
SPLOOSH!

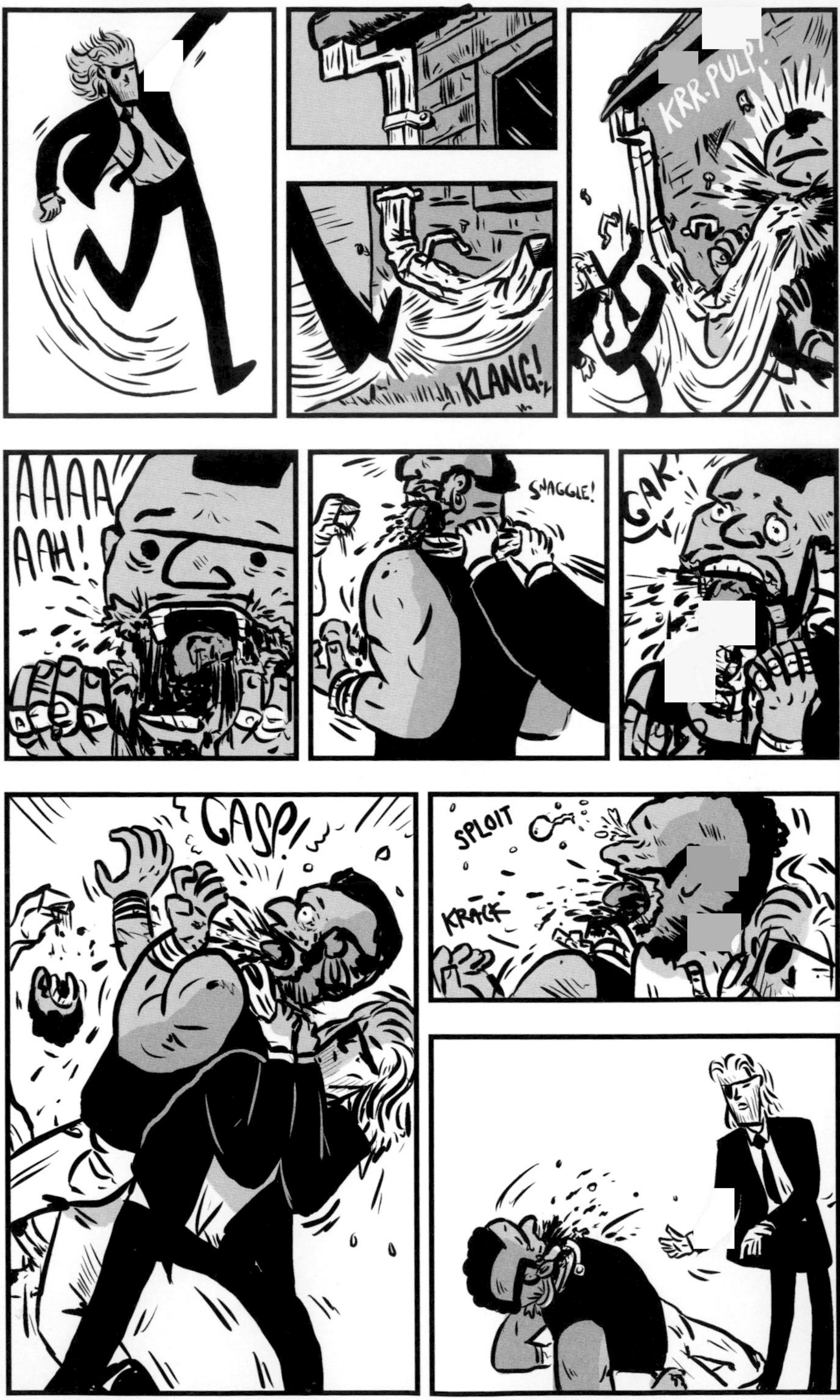

KLANG!
KRR-PULP!
AAAAAAH!
SNAGGLE!
GAK!
GASP!
SPLOIT
KRACK

SEXCASTLE!

GET YOUR PUSS-ASS OUT HERE SO I CAN CUT YOU UP.

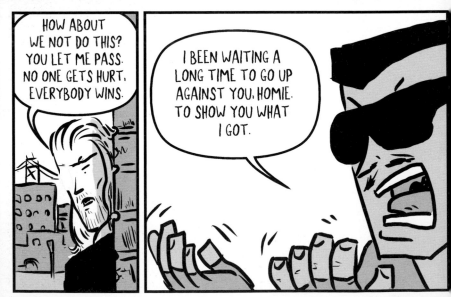

HOW ABOUT WE NOT DO THIS? YOU LET ME PASS. NO ONE GETS HURT, EVERYBODY WINS.

I BEEN WAITING A LONG TIME TO GO UP AGAINST YOU, HOMIE. TO SHOW YOU WHAT I GOT.

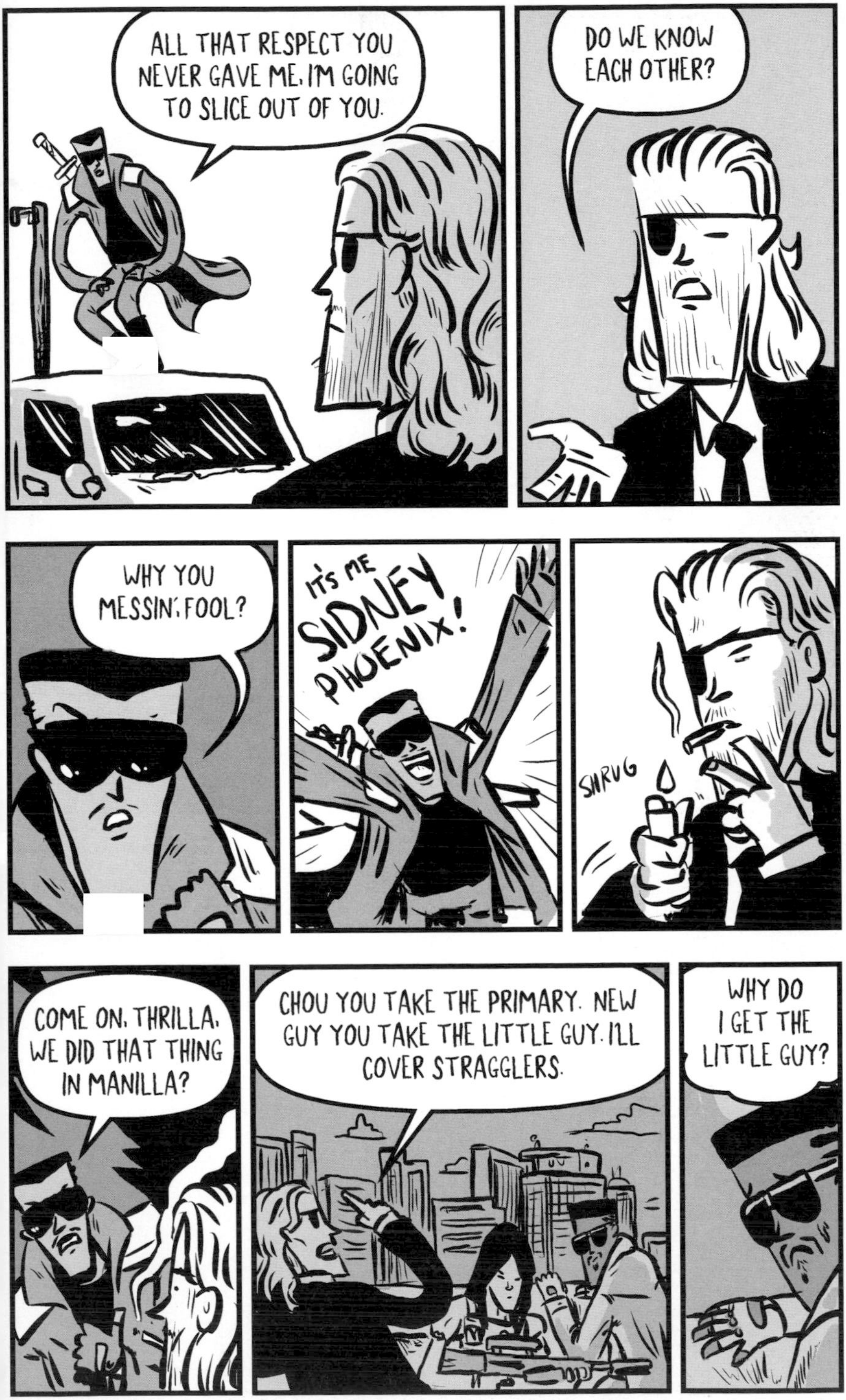
ALL THAT RESPECT YOU NEVER GAVE ME, I'M GOING TO SLICE OUT OF YOU.
DO WE KNOW EACH OTHER?
WHY YOU MESSIN', FOOL?
IT'S ME SIDNEY PHOENIX!
SHRUG
COME ON, THRILLA. WE DID THAT THING IN MANILLA?
CHOU YOU TAKE THE PRIMARY. NEW GUY YOU TAKE THE LITTLE GUY. I'LL COVER STRAGGLERS.
WHY DO I GET THE LITTLE GUY?

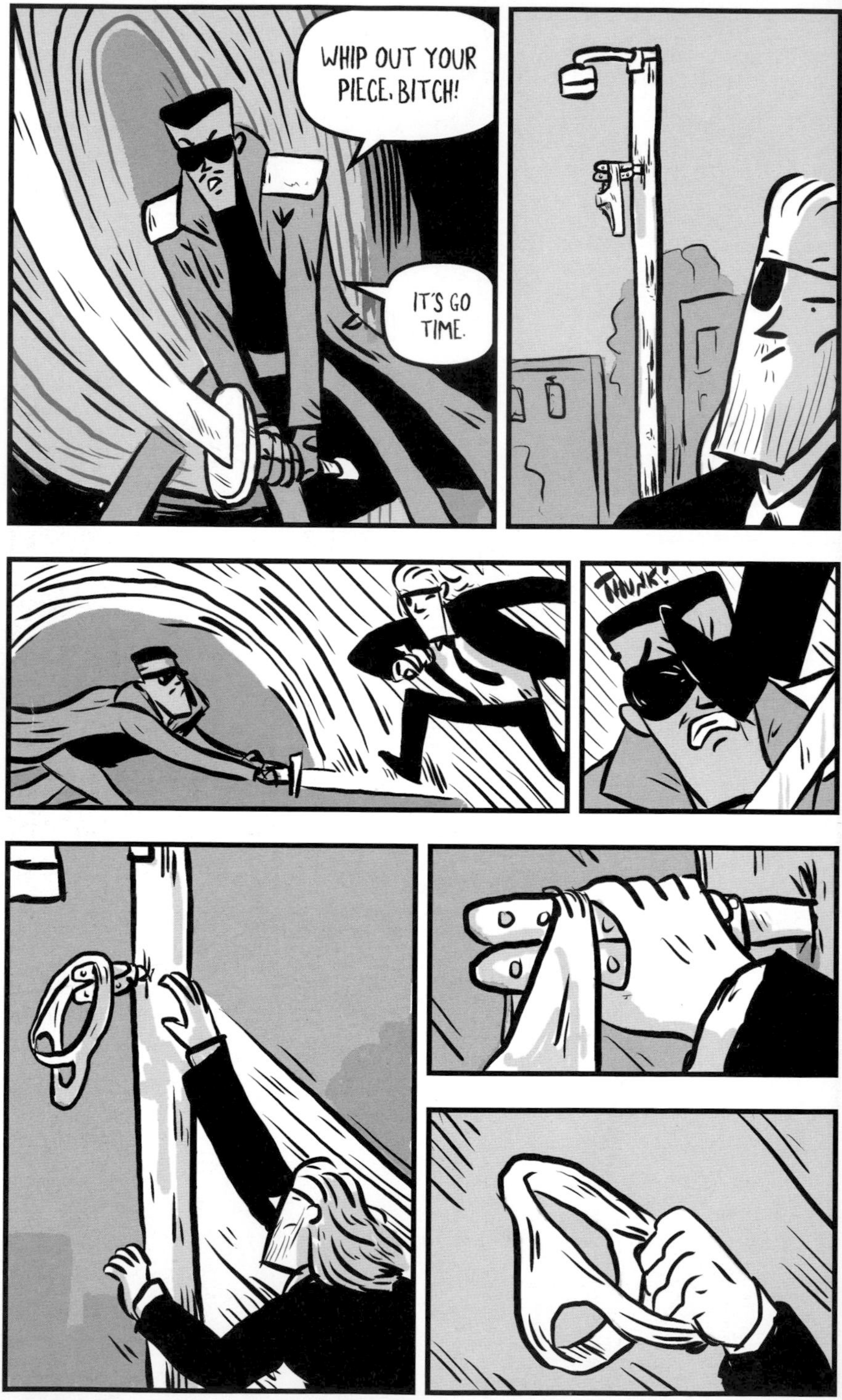
WHIP OUT YOUR PIECE, BITCH!
IT'S GO TIME.
THUNK!

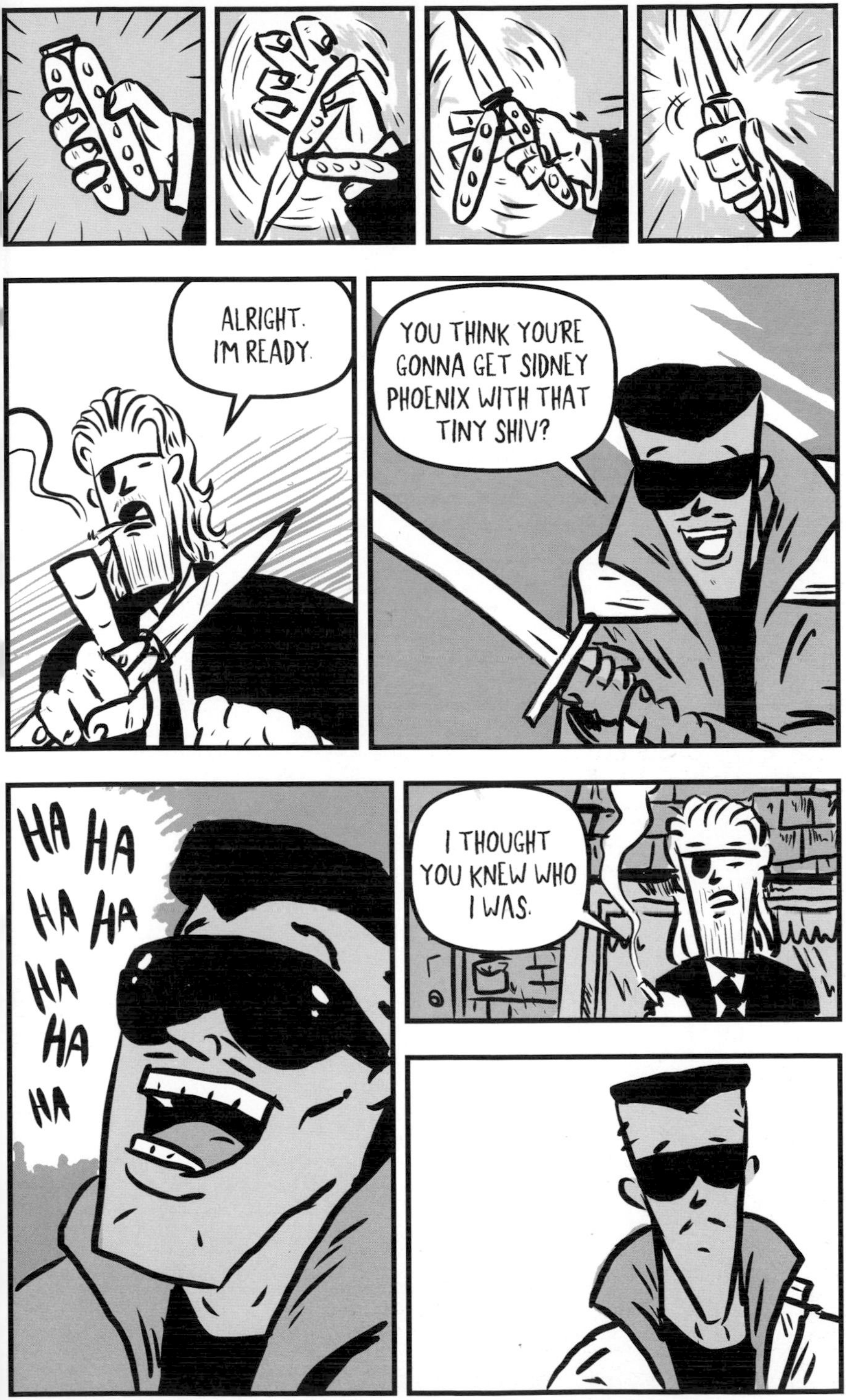
ALRIGHT. I'M READY.
YOU THINK YOU'RE GONNA GET SIDNEY PHOENIX WITH THAT TINY SHIV?
HA HA HA HA HA HA HA
I THOUGHT YOU KNEW WHO I WAS.

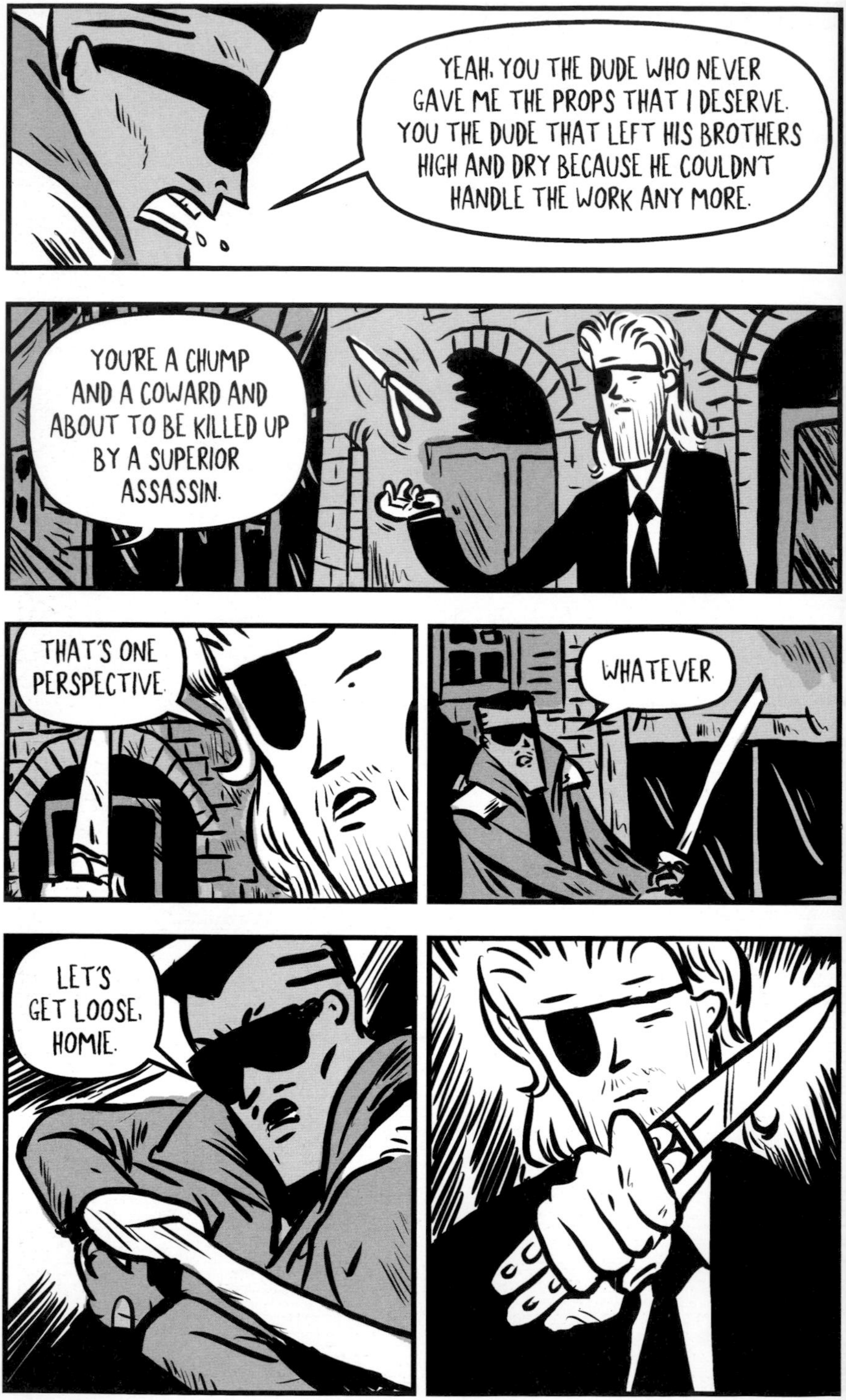
YEAH, YOU THE DUDE WHO NEVER GAVE ME THE PROPS THAT I DESERVE. YOU THE DUDE THAT LEFT HIS BROTHERS HIGH AND DRY BECAUSE HE COULDN'T HANDLE THE WORK ANY MORE.
YOU'RE A CHUMP AND A COWARD AND ABOUT TO BE KILLED UP BY A SUPERIOR ASSASSIN.
THAT'S ONE PERSPECTIVE.
WHATEVER.
LET'S GET LOOSE, HOMIE.

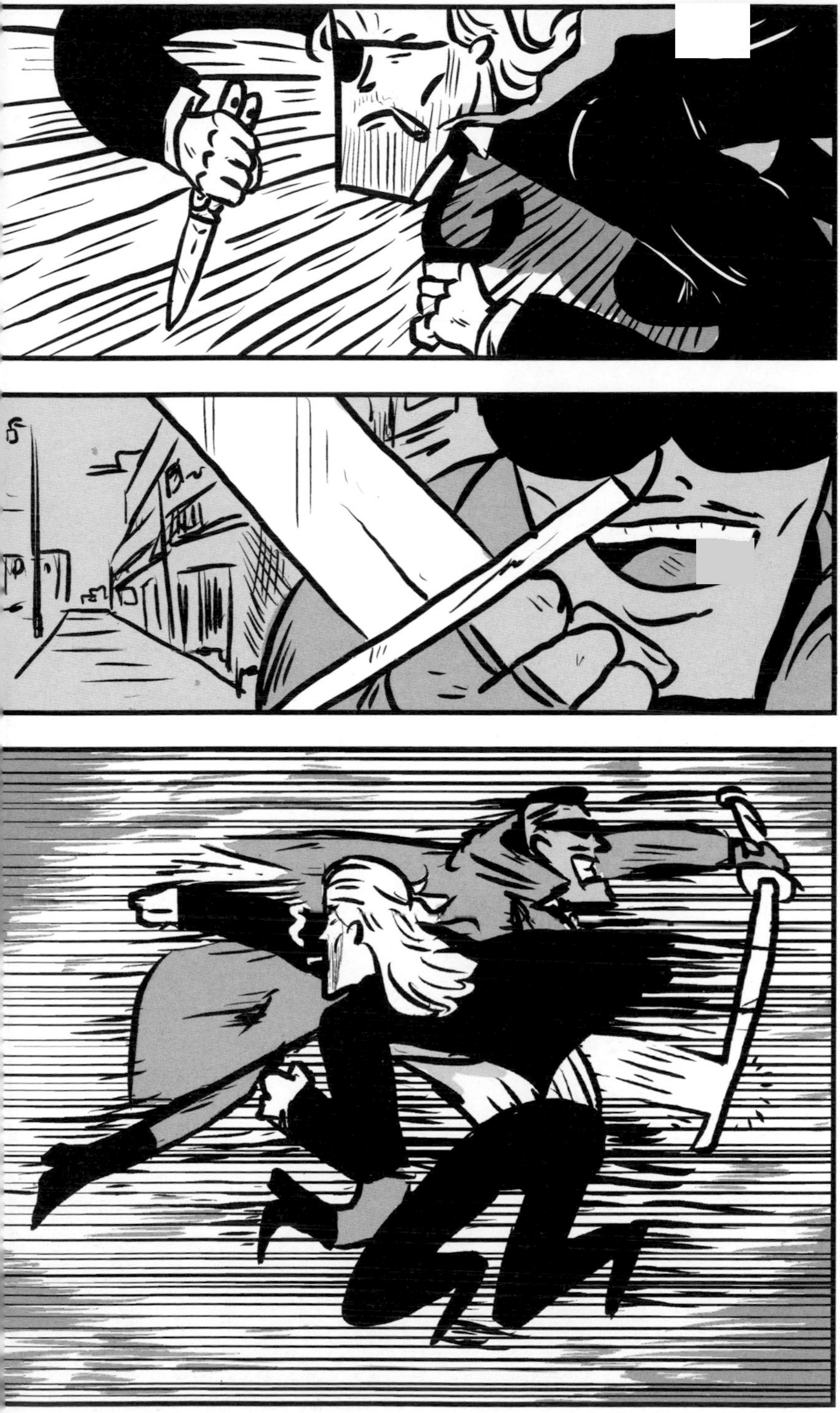

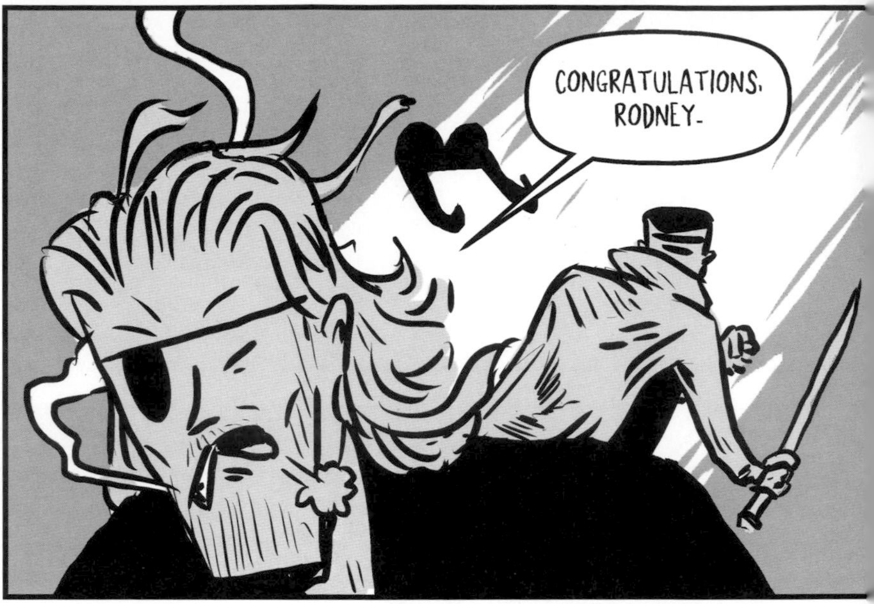
CONGRATULATIONS, RODNEY-

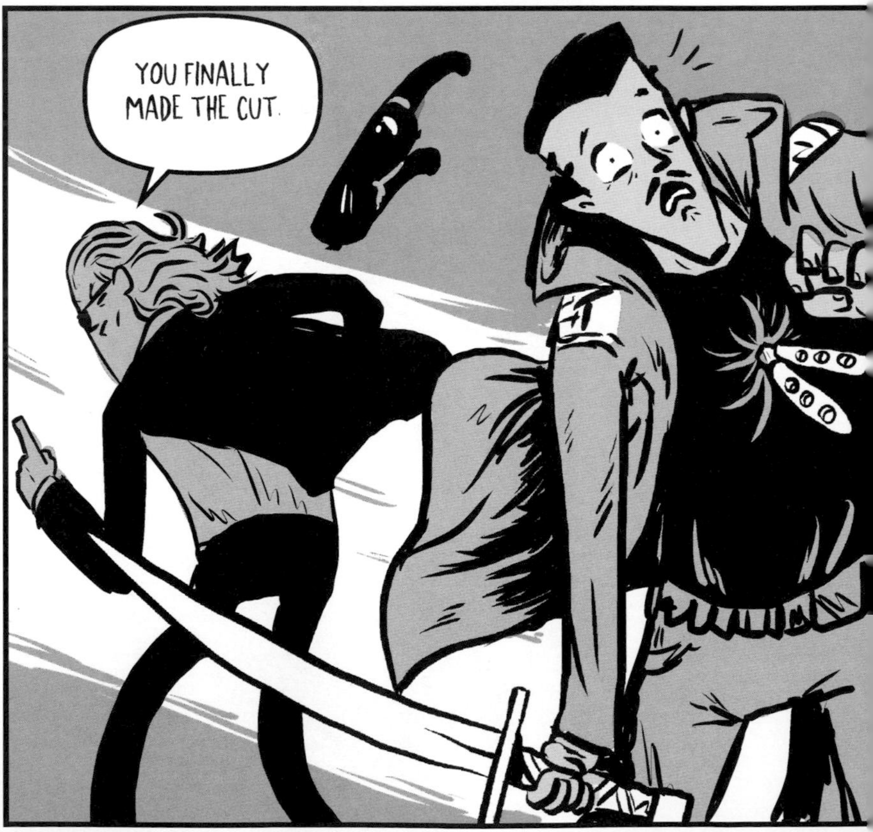
YOU FINALLY MADE THE CUT.

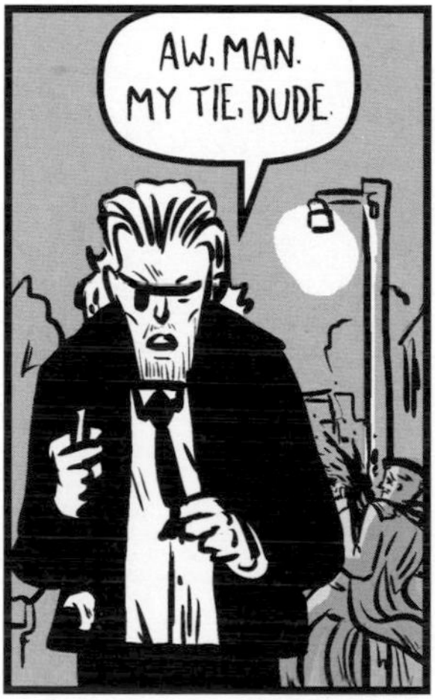
AW, MAN.
MY TIE, DUDE.

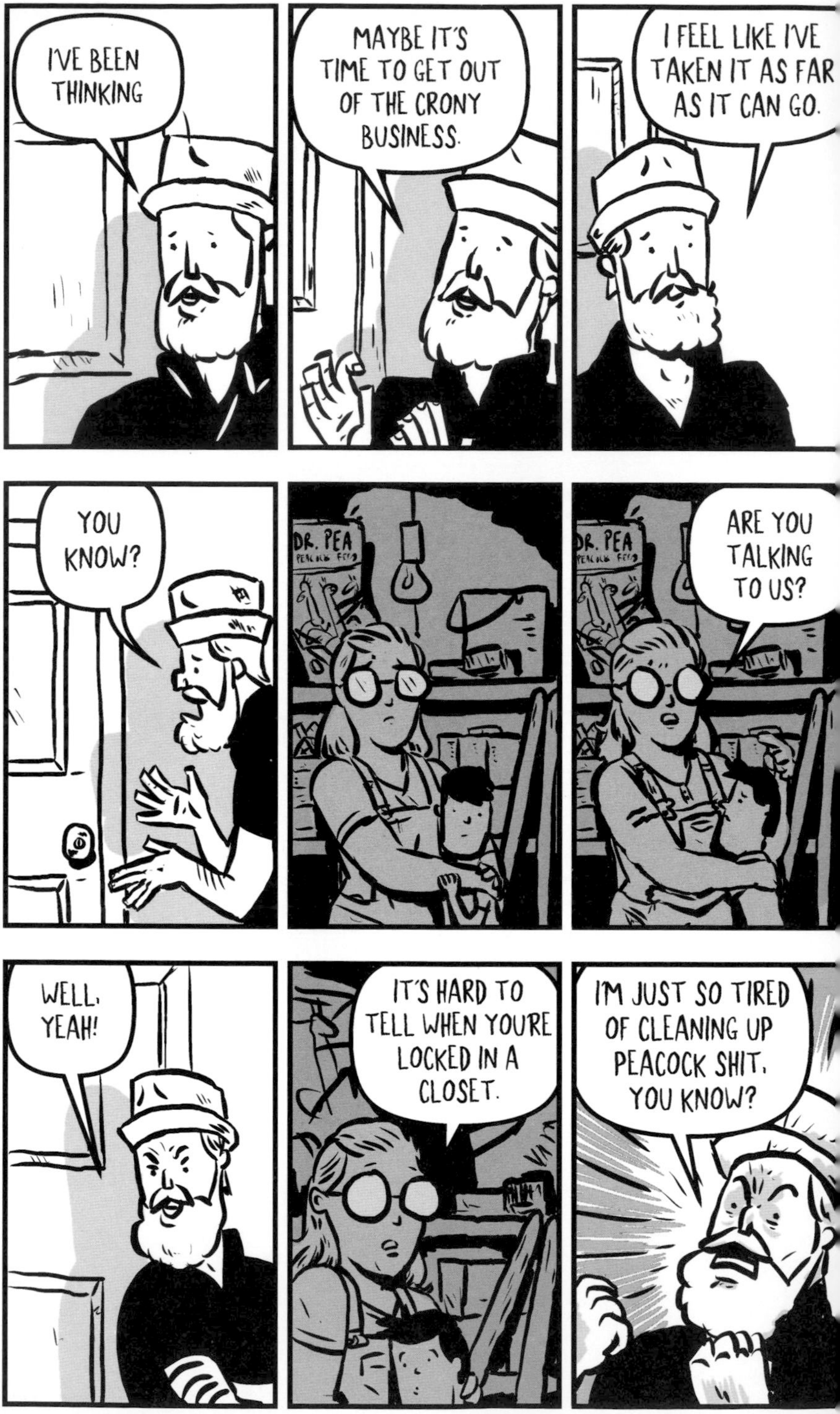
I'VE BEEN THINKING
MAYBE IT'S TIME TO GET OUT OF THE CRONY BUSINESS.
I FEEL LIKE I'VE TAKEN IT AS FAR AS IT CAN GO.
YOU KNOW?
DR. PEA
ARE YOU TALKING TO US?
WELL, YEAH!
IT'S HARD TO TELL WHEN YOU'RE LOCKED IN A CLOSET.
I'M JUST SO TIRED OF CLEANING UP PEACOCK SHIT, YOU KNOW?

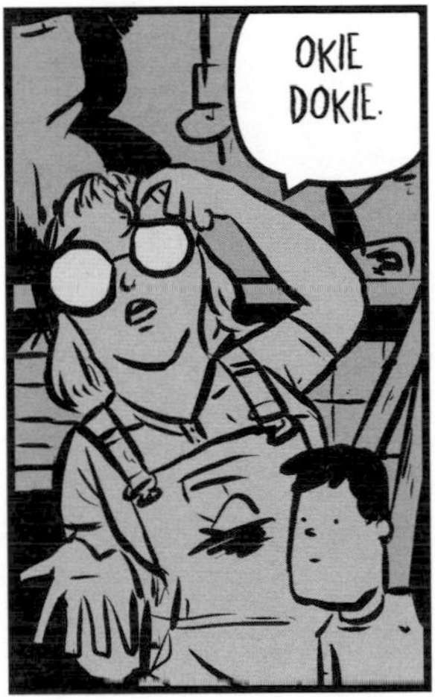
OKIE DOKIE.

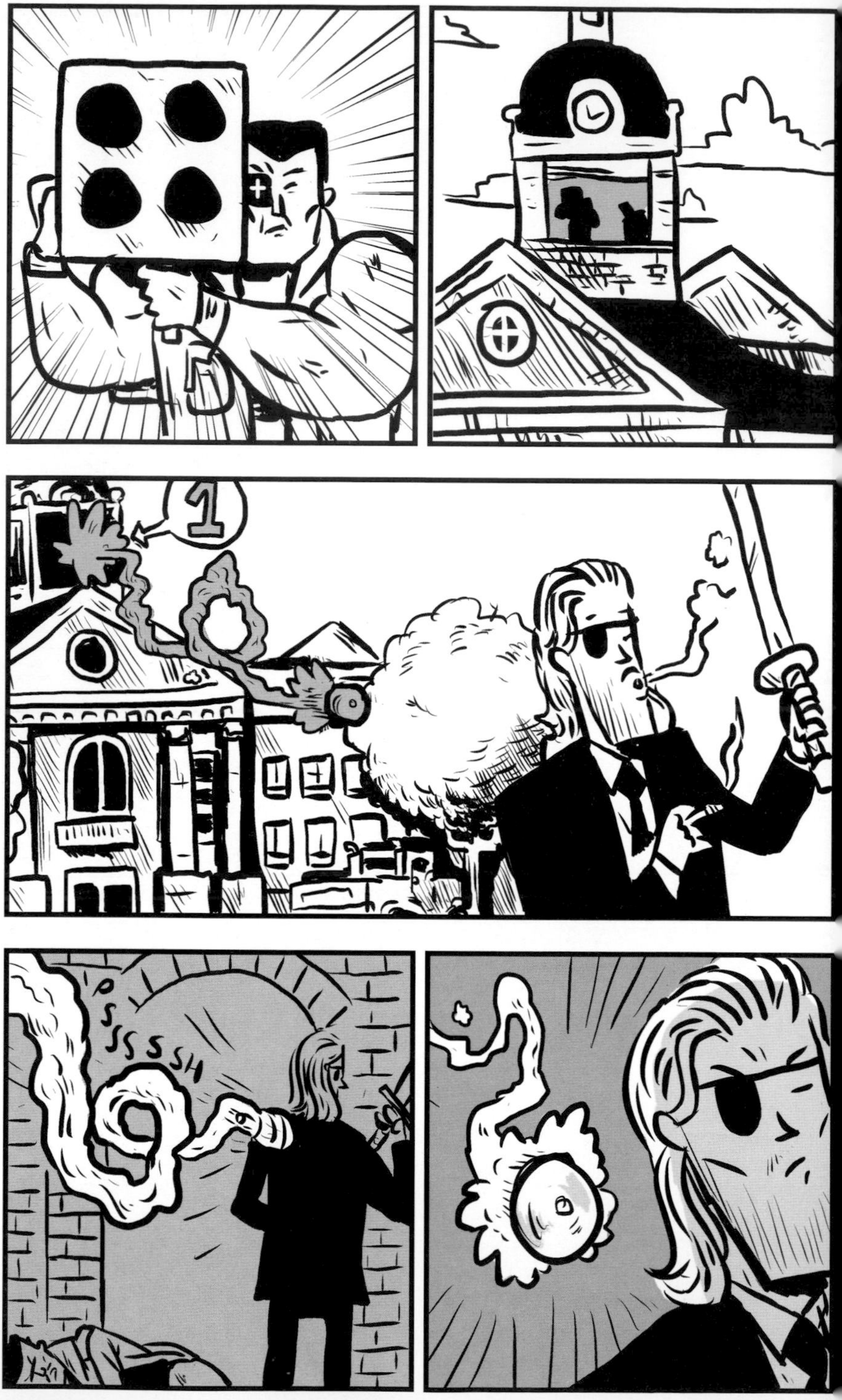
1
PSSSSSH

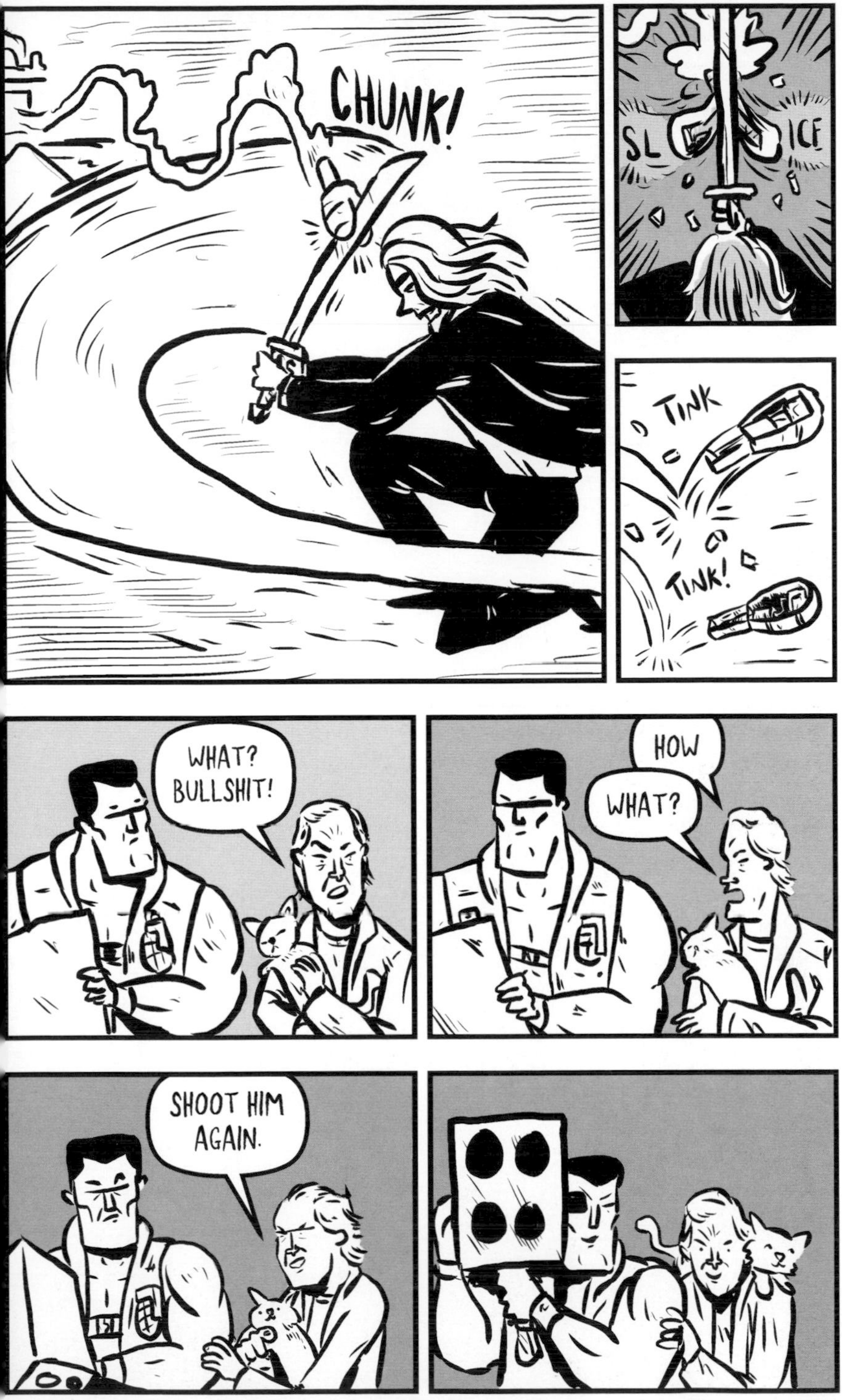
CHUNK!
SL
ICE
TINK
TINK!
WHAT? BULLSHIT!
HOW
WHAT?
SHOOT HIM AGAIN.

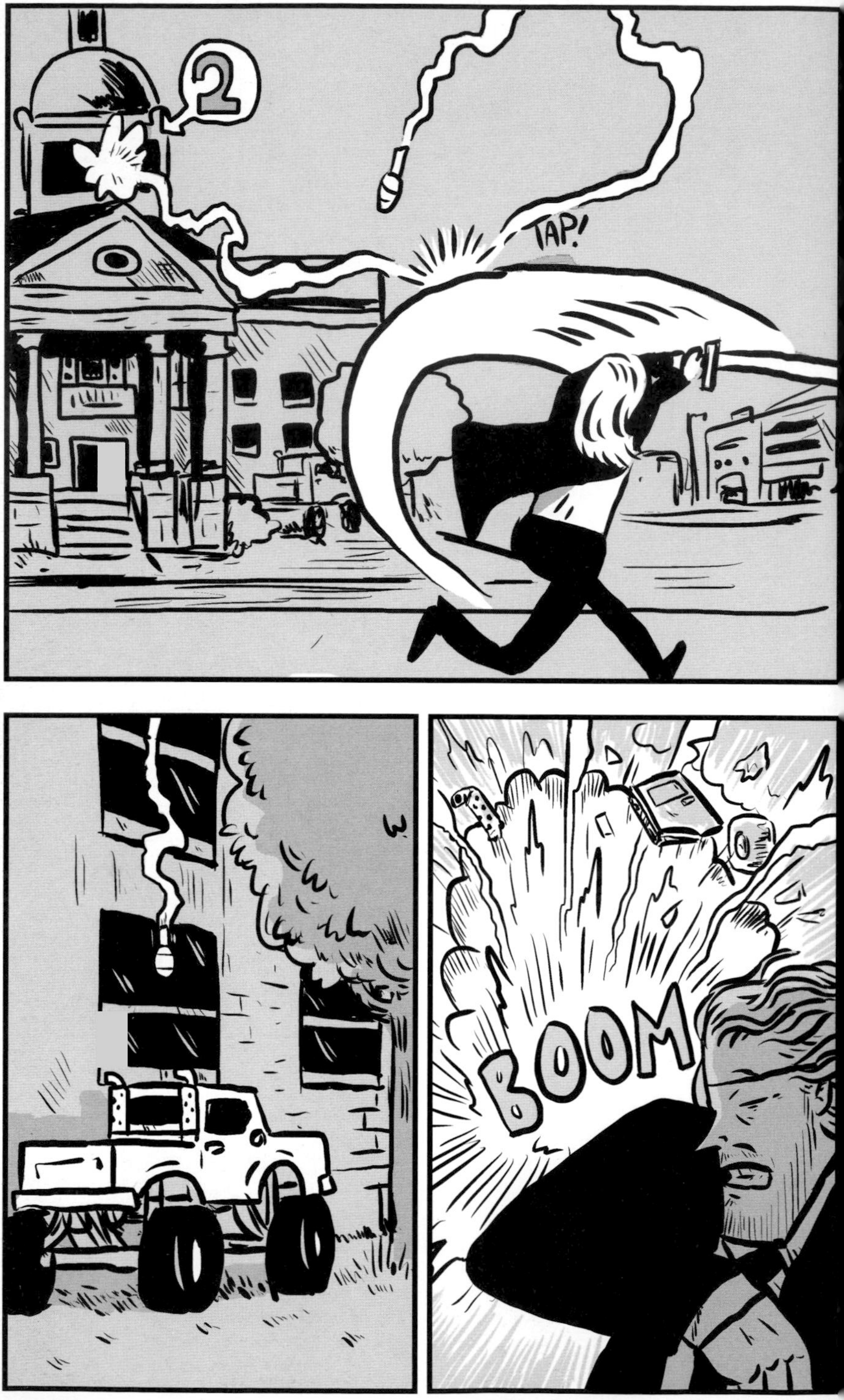
2
TAP!
BOOM

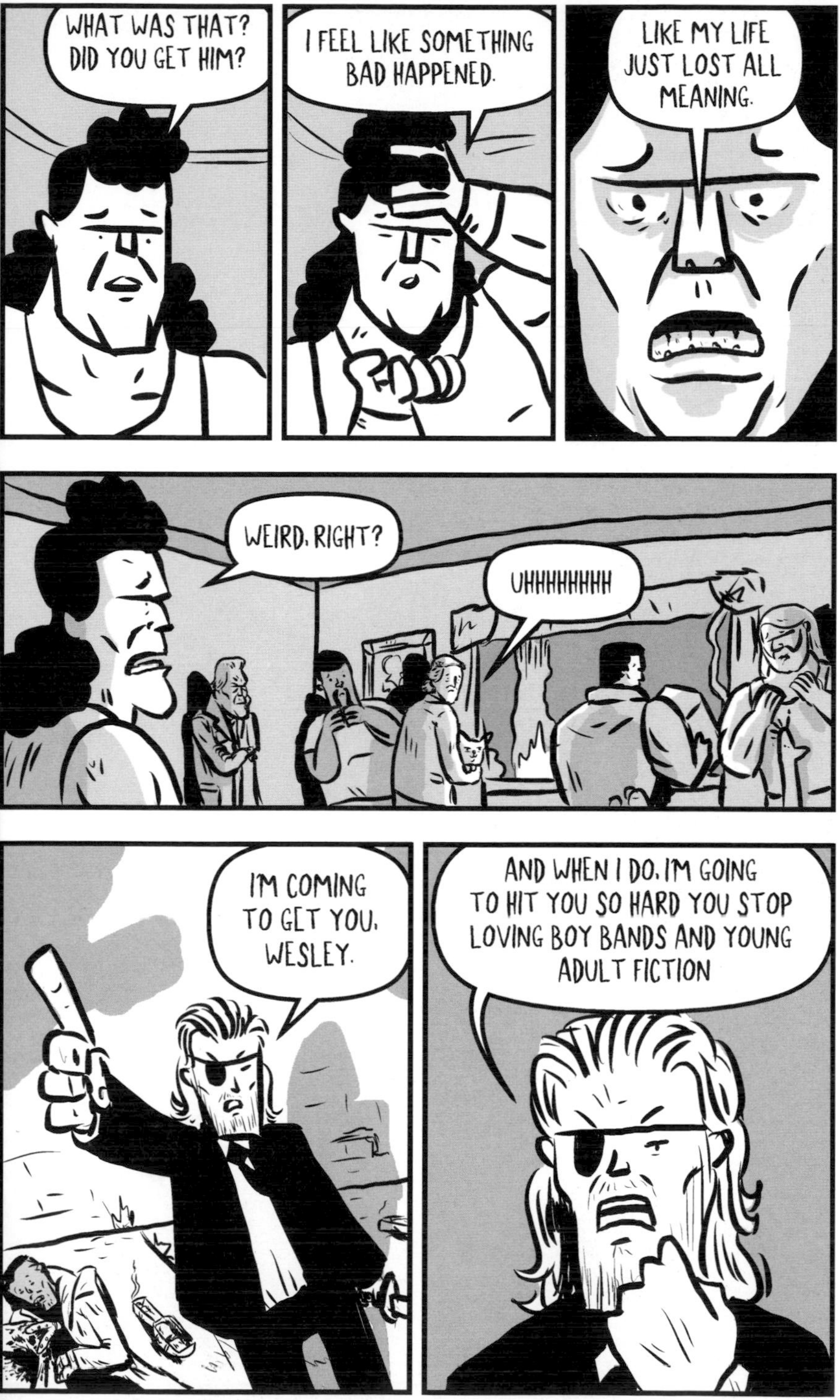
WHAT WAS THAT? DID YOU GET HIM?
I FEEL LIKE SOMETHING BAD HAPPENED.
LIKE MY LIFE JUST LOST ALL MEANING.
WEIRD, RIGHT?
UHHHHHHHH
I'M COMING TO GET YOU, WESLEY.
AND WHEN I DO, I'M GOING TO HIT YOU SO HARD YOU STOP LOVING BOY BANDS AND YOUNG ADULT FICTION

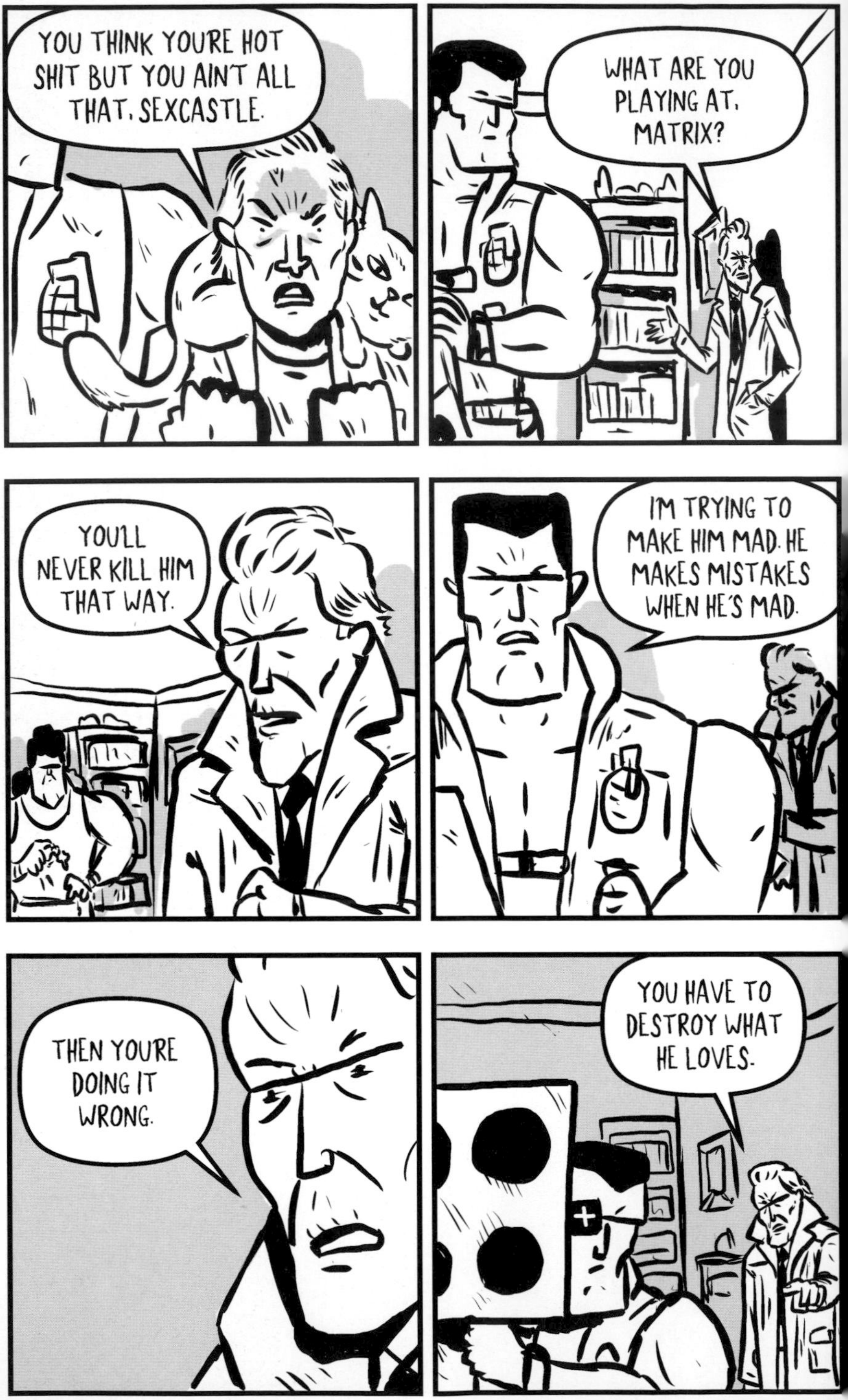
YOU THINK YOU'RE HOT SHIT BUT YOU AIN'T ALL THAT, SEXCASTLE.
WHAT ARE YOU PLAYING AT, MATRIX?
YOU'LL NEVER KILL HIM THAT WAY.
I'M TRYING TO MAKE HIM MAD. HE MAKES MISTAKES WHEN HE'S MAD.
THEN YOU'RE DOING IT WRONG.
YOU HAVE TO DESTROY WHAT HE LOVES.

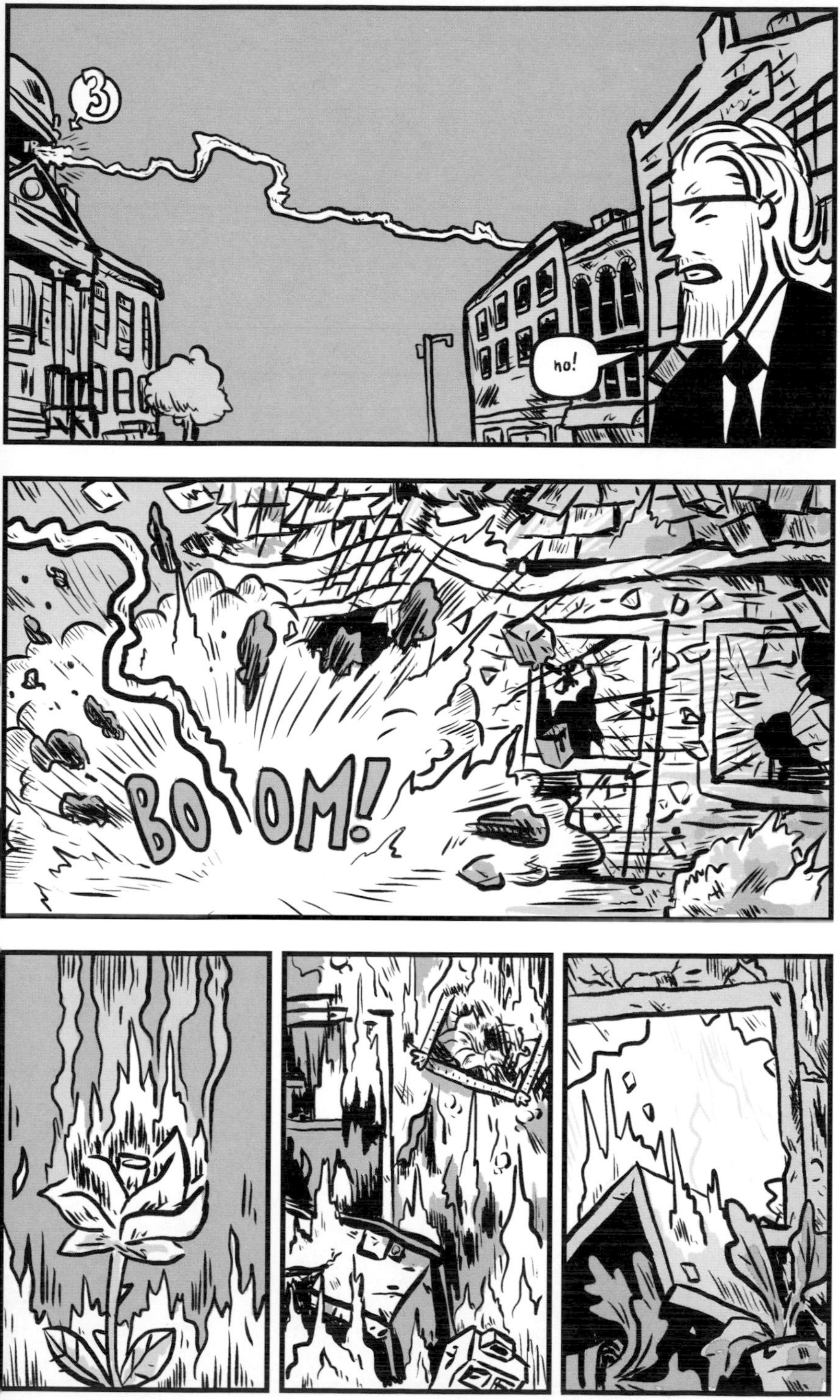
3
no!
BOOM!

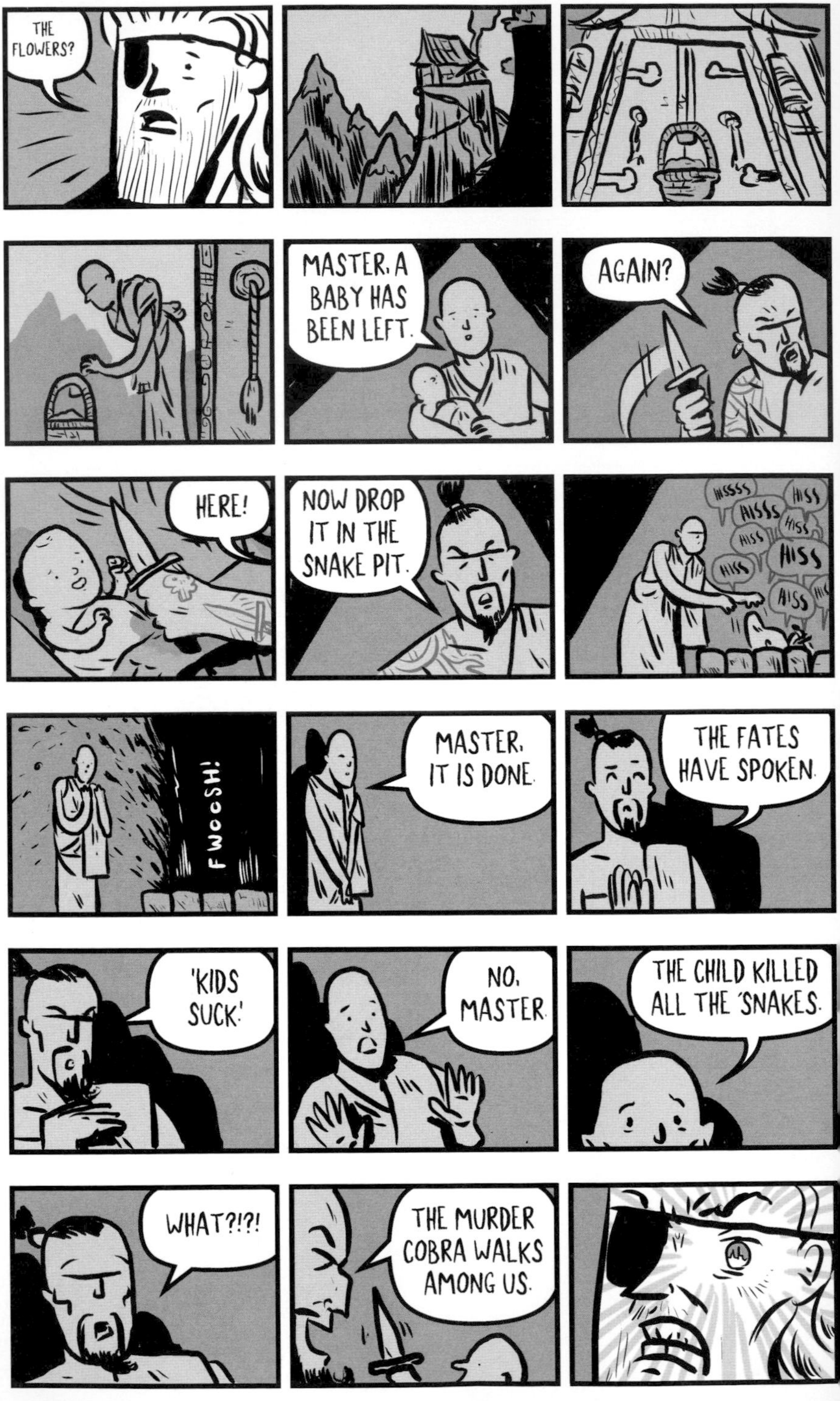
THE FLOWERS?
MASTER, A BABY HAS BEEN LEFT.
AGAIN?
HERE!
NOW DROP IT IN THE SNAKE PIT.
HISSSS HISS HISSS HISS HISS HISS HISS HISS
FWOOSH!
MASTER, IT IS DONE.
THE FATES HAVE SPOKEN.
'KIDS SUCK.'
NO, MASTER.
THE CHILD KILLED ALL THE 'SNAKES.
WHAT?!?!
THE MURDER COBRA WALKS AMONG US.

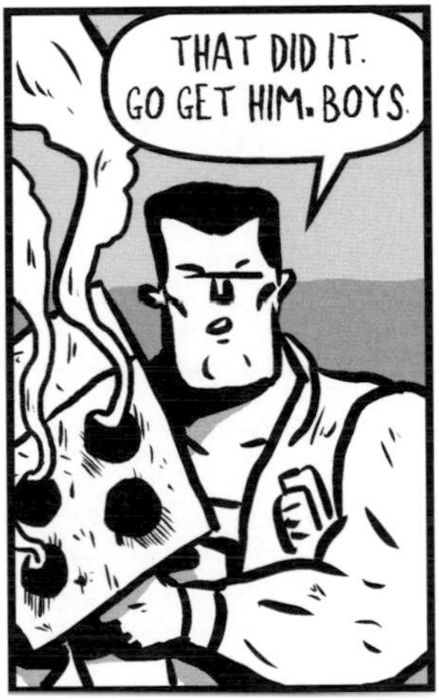
THAT DID IT. GO GET HIM, BOYS.

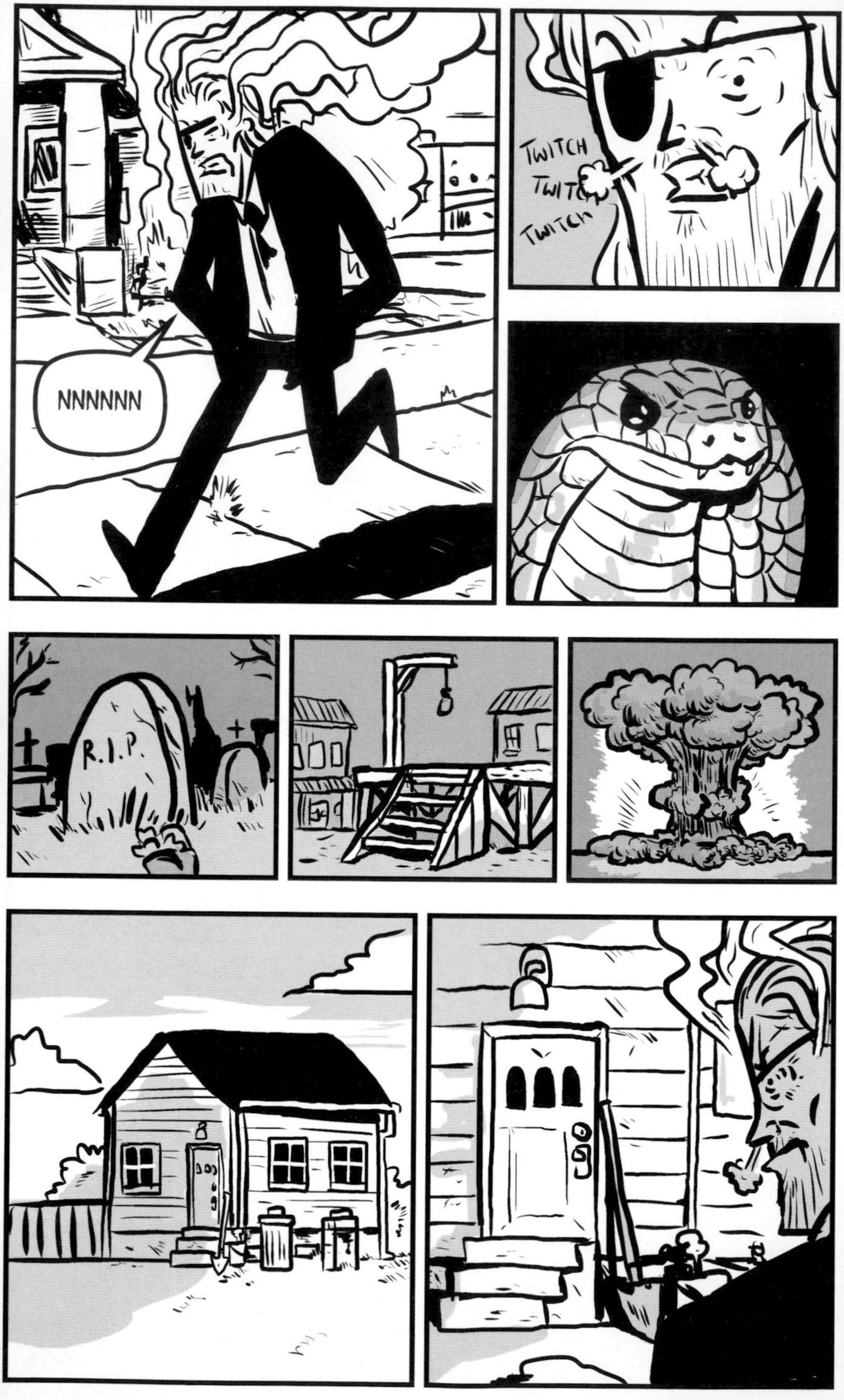
NNNNNN
TWITCH
TWITCH
TWITCH
R.I.P.

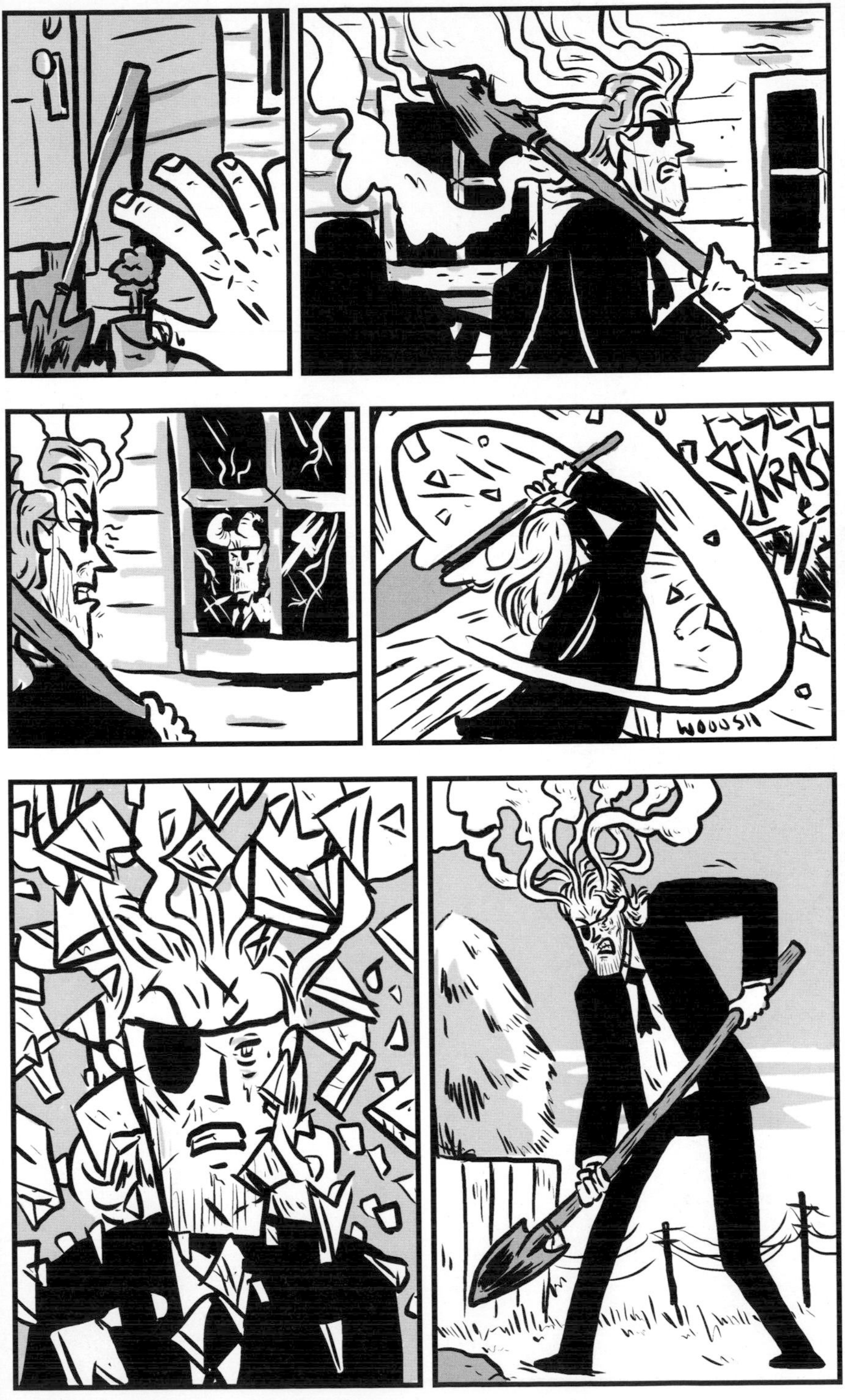
KRAS
WOOUSH

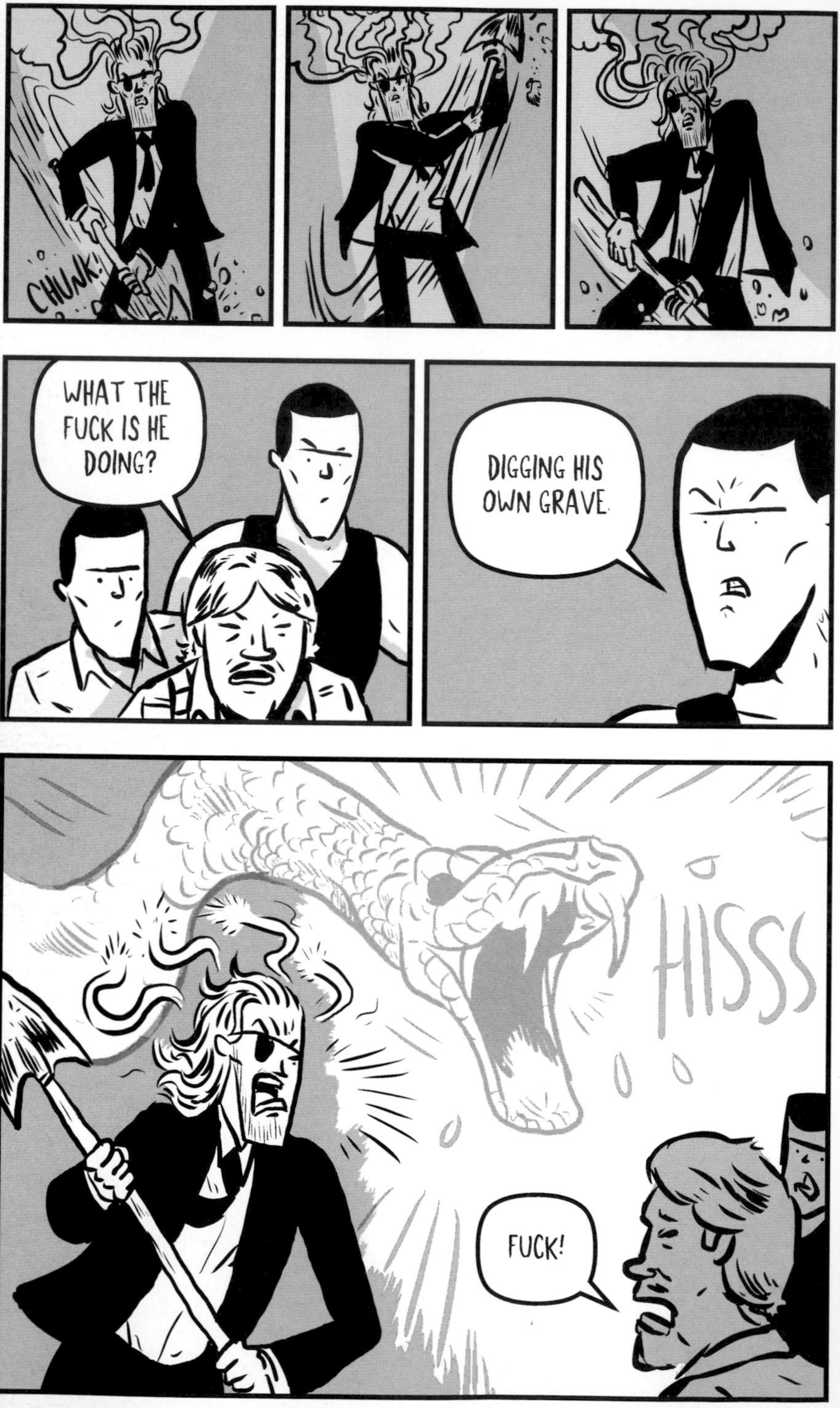
CHUNK!
WHAT THE FUCK IS HE DOING?
DIGGING HIS OWN GRAVE.
HISSS
FUCK!

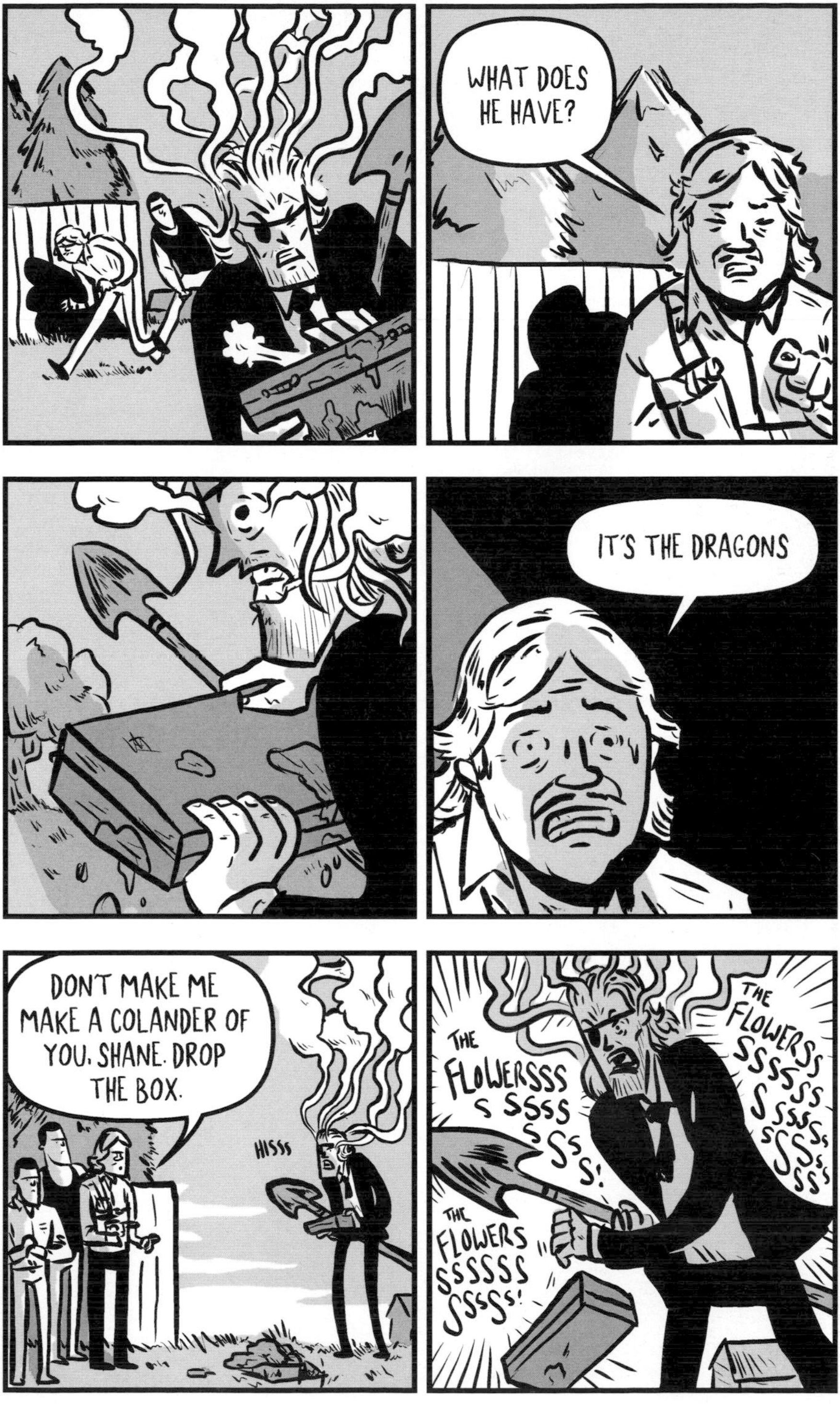
WHAT DOES HE HAVE?
IT'S THE DRAGONS
DON'T MAKE ME MAKE A COLANDER OF YOU, SHANE. DROP THE BOX.
HISSS
THE FLOWERSSS S SSSS S SSSS!
THE FLOWERS SSSSSS SSSSS!
THE FLOWERSS SSSSSS S SSSSS SSSSS SSSS

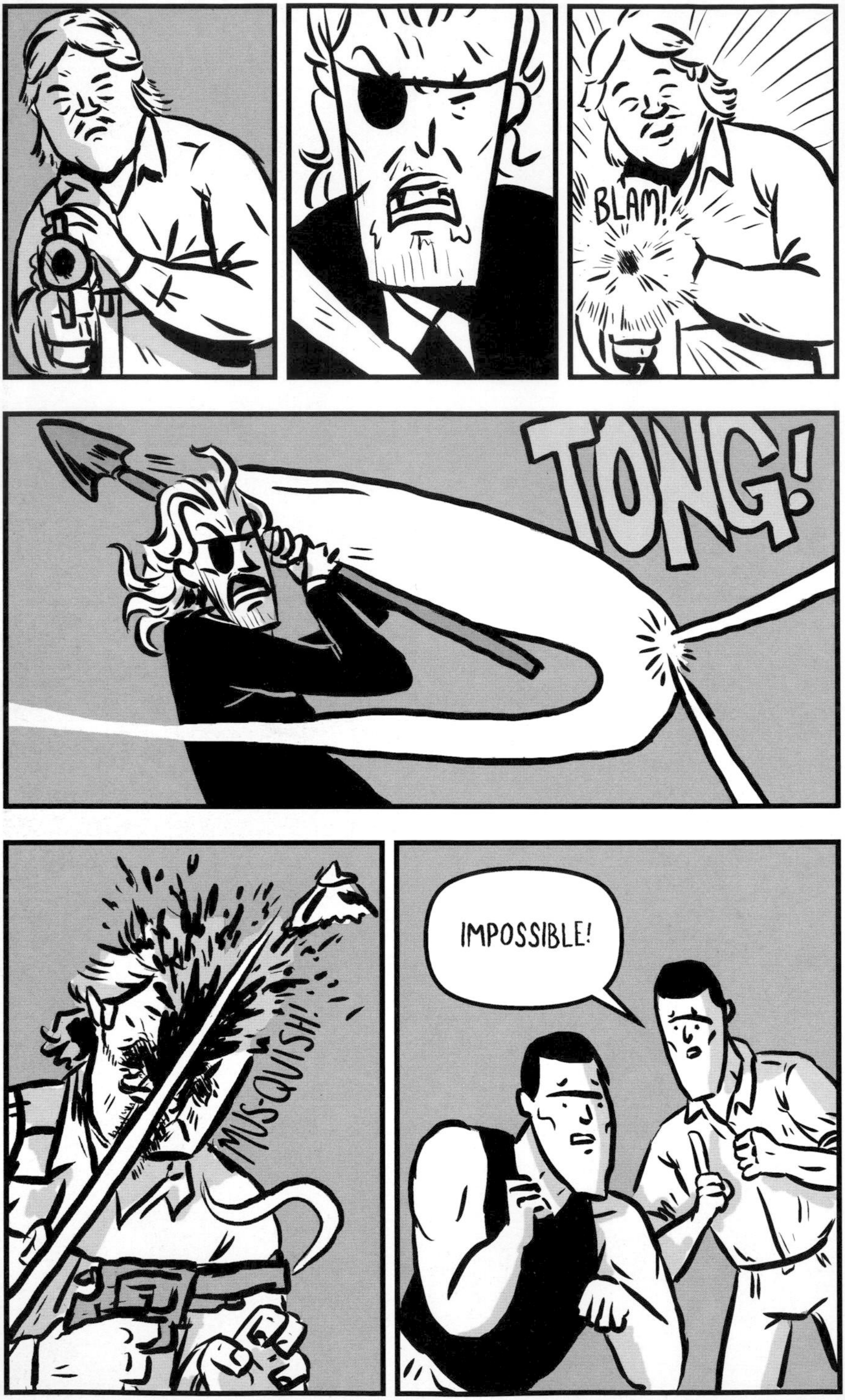
BLAM!
TONG!
MUS-QUISH!
IMPOSSIBLE!

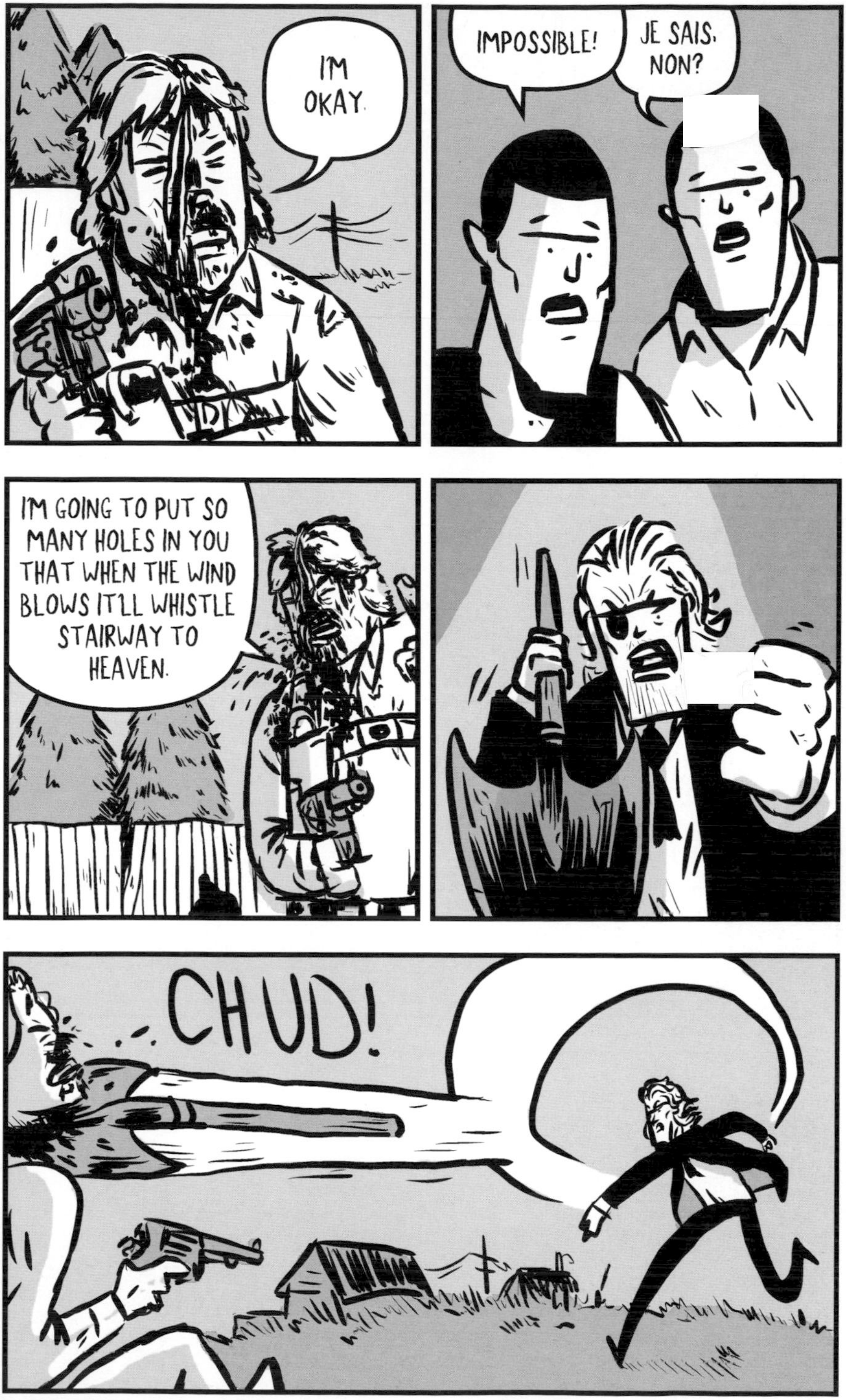
I'M OKAY.
IMPOSSIBLE!
JE SAIS, NON?
I'M GOING TO PUT SO MANY HOLES IN YOU THAT WHEN THE WIND BLOWS IT'LL WHISTLE STAIRWAY TO HEAVEN.
CHUD!

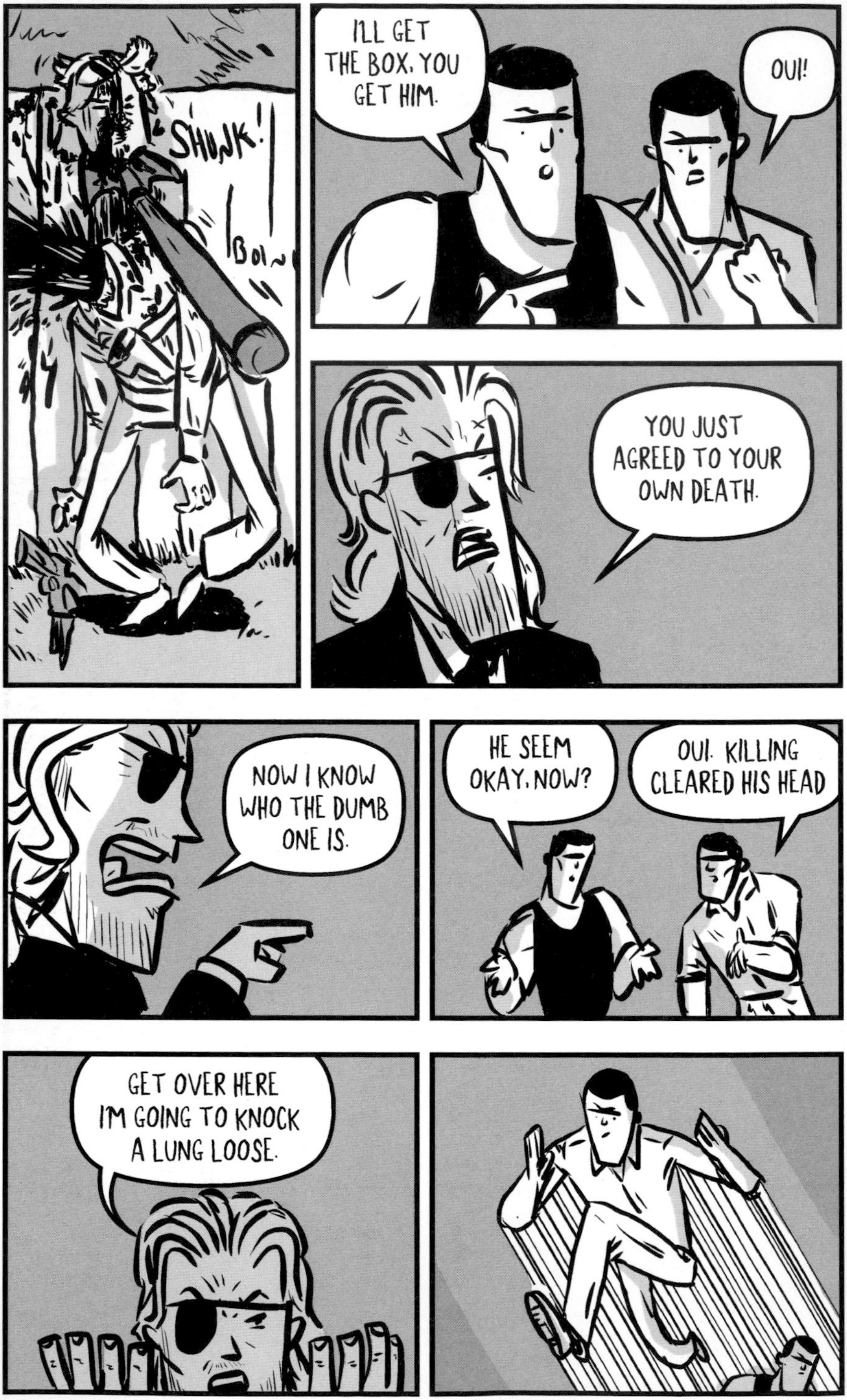
SHUNK!
BOI~
I'LL GET THE BOX. YOU GET HIM.
OUI!
YOU JUST AGREED TO YOUR OWN DEATH.
NOW I KNOW WHO THE DUMB ONE IS.
HE SEEM OKAY, NOW?
OUI. KILLING CLEARED HIS HEAD
GET OVER HERE I'M GOING TO KNOCK A LUNG LOOSE.

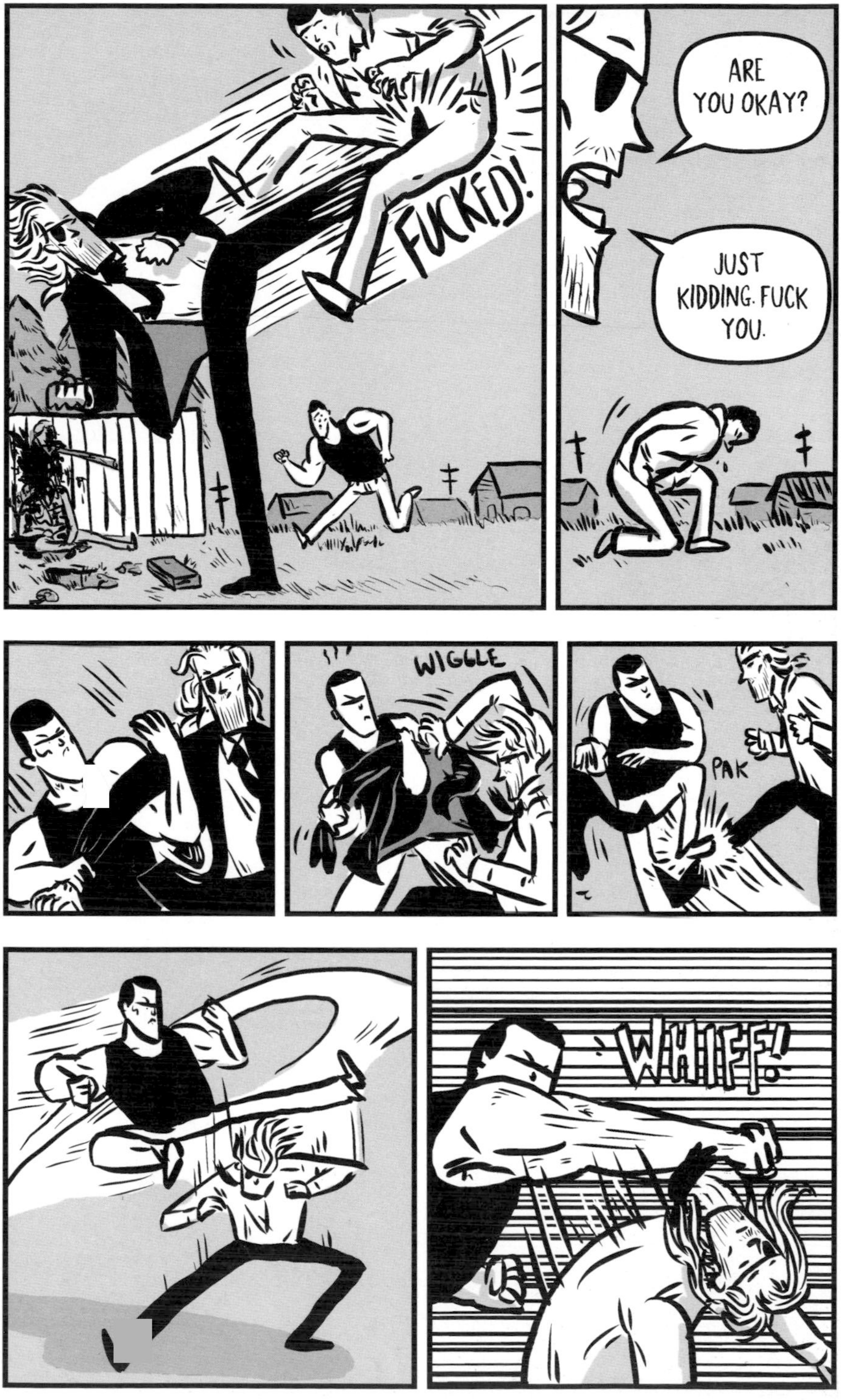
FUCKED!
ARE YOU OKAY?
JUST KIDDING. FUCK YOU.
WIGGLE
PAK
WHIFF!

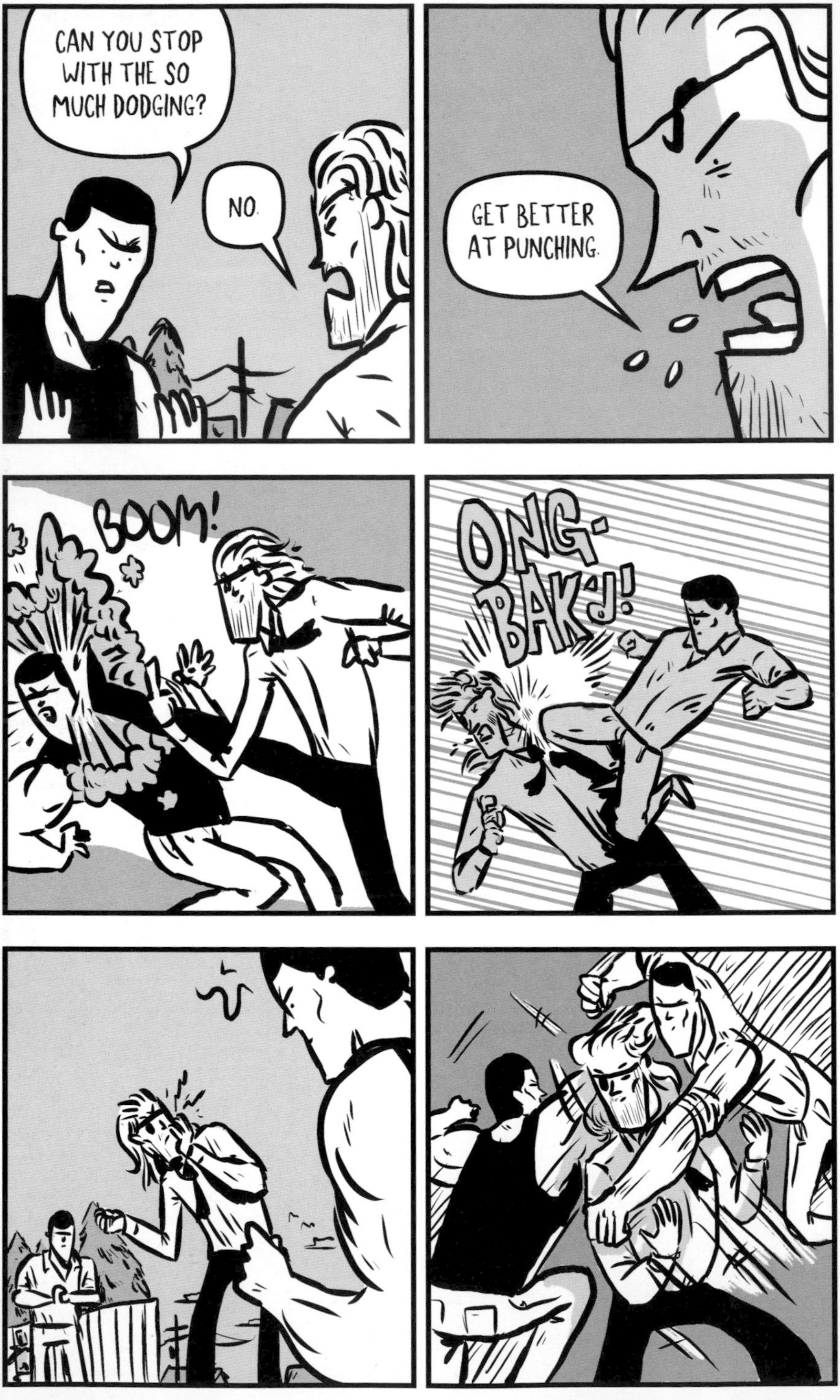
CAN YOU STOP WITH THE SO MUCH DODGING?
NO.
GET BETTER AT PUNCHING.
BOOM!
ONG-BAK'J!

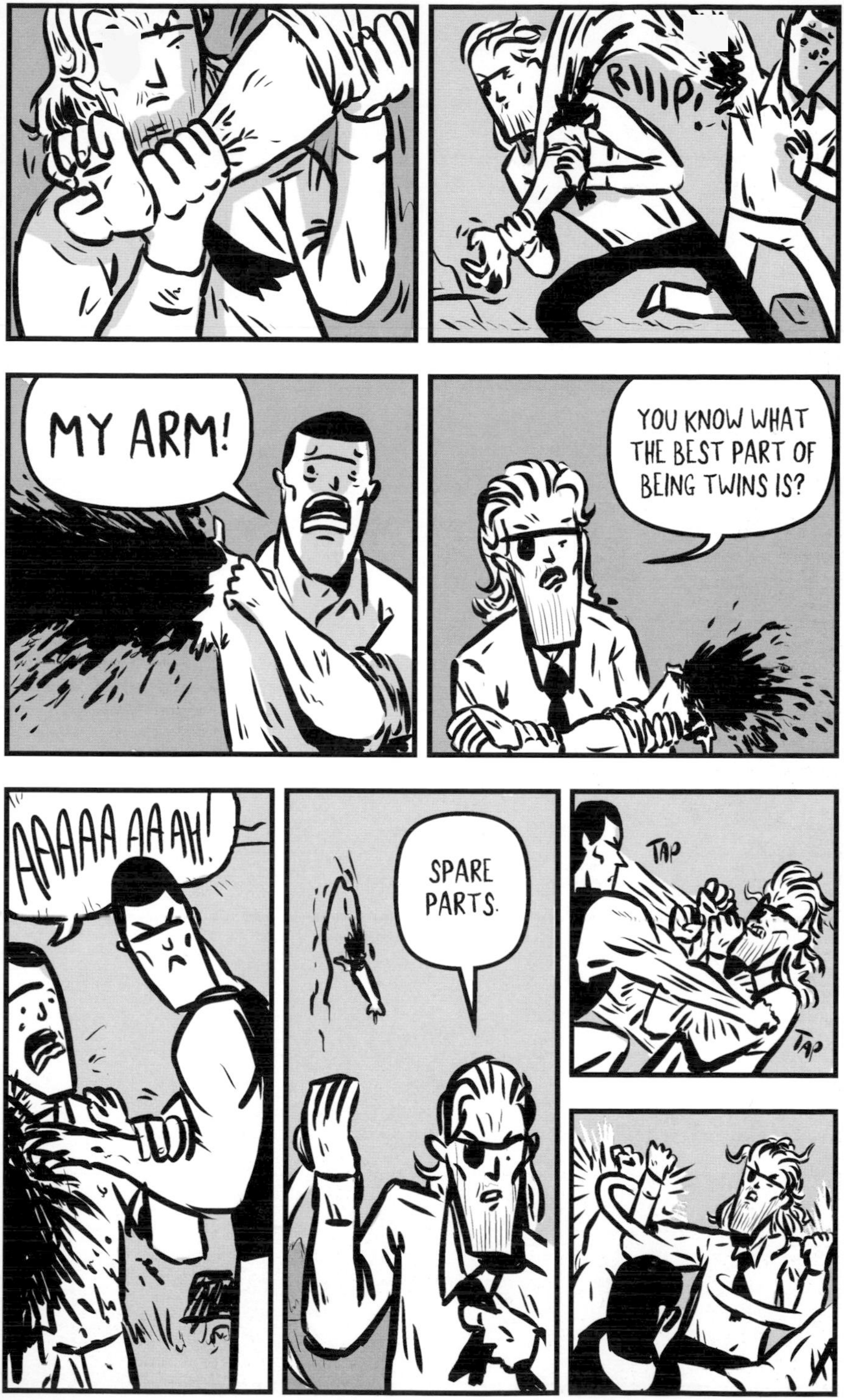
RIIIP!
MY ARM!
YOU KNOW WHAT THE BEST PART OF BEING TWINS IS?
AAAAA AAAH!
SPARE PARTS.
TAP
TAP

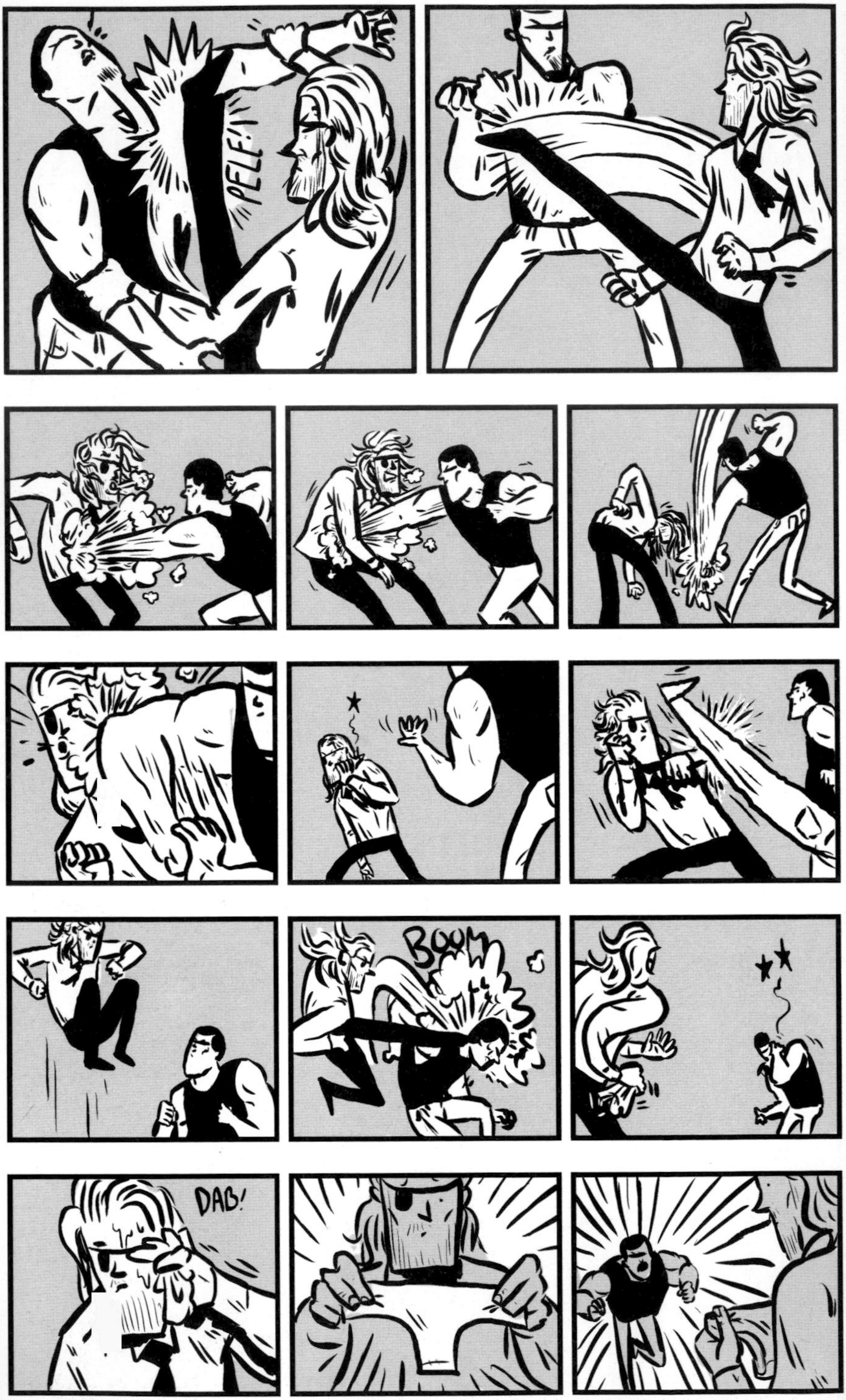
PELF!
BOOM
DAB!

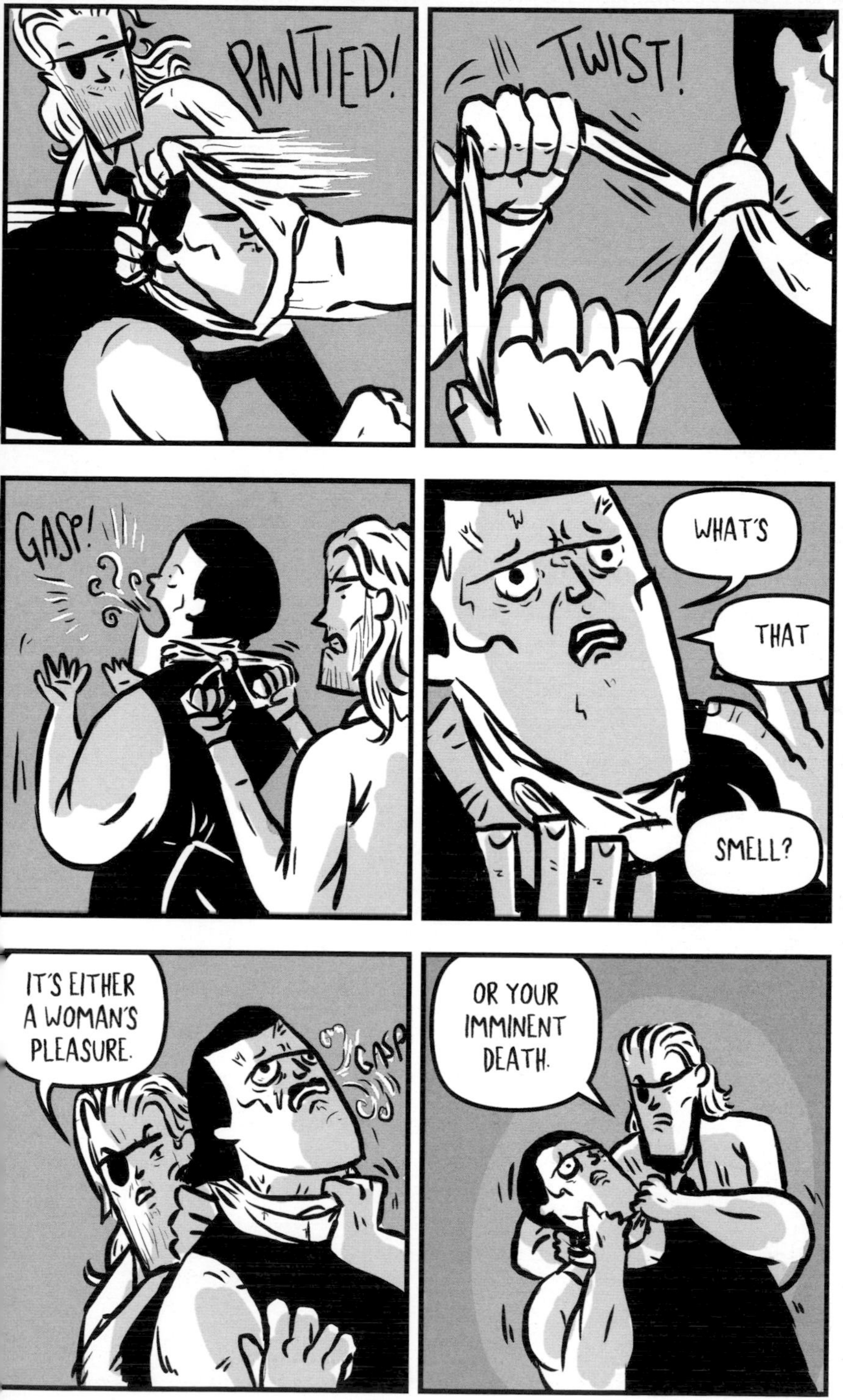
PANTIED!
TWIST!
GASP!
WHAT'S
THAT
SMELL?
IT'S EITHER A WOMAN'S PLEASURE.
GASP
OR YOUR IMMINENT DEATH.

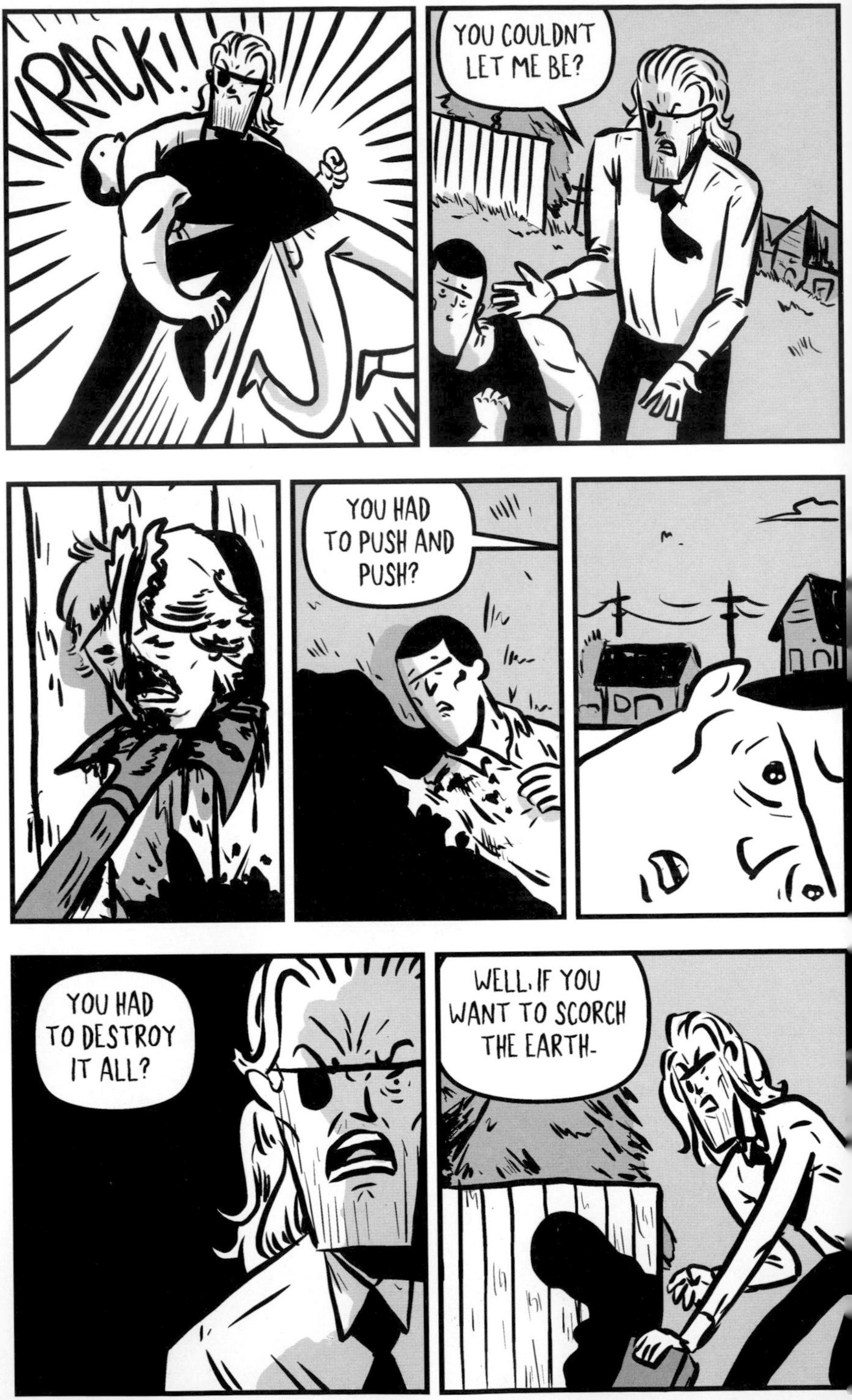
KRACK!!
YOU COULDN'T LET ME BE?
YOU HAD TO PUSH AND PUSH?
YOU HAD TO DESTROY IT ALL?
WELL, IF YOU WANT TO SCORCH THE EARTH-

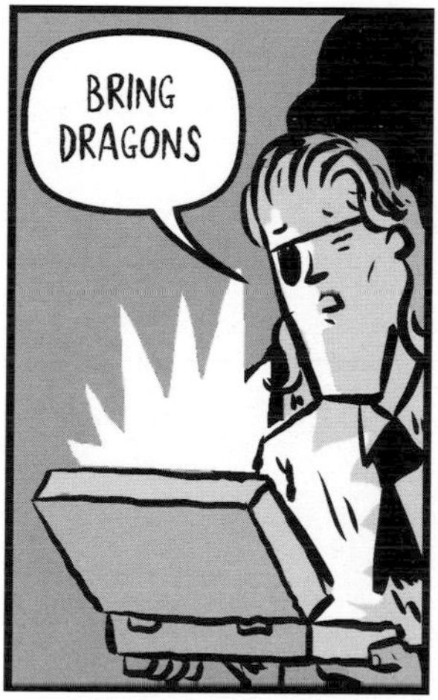
BRING DRAGONS

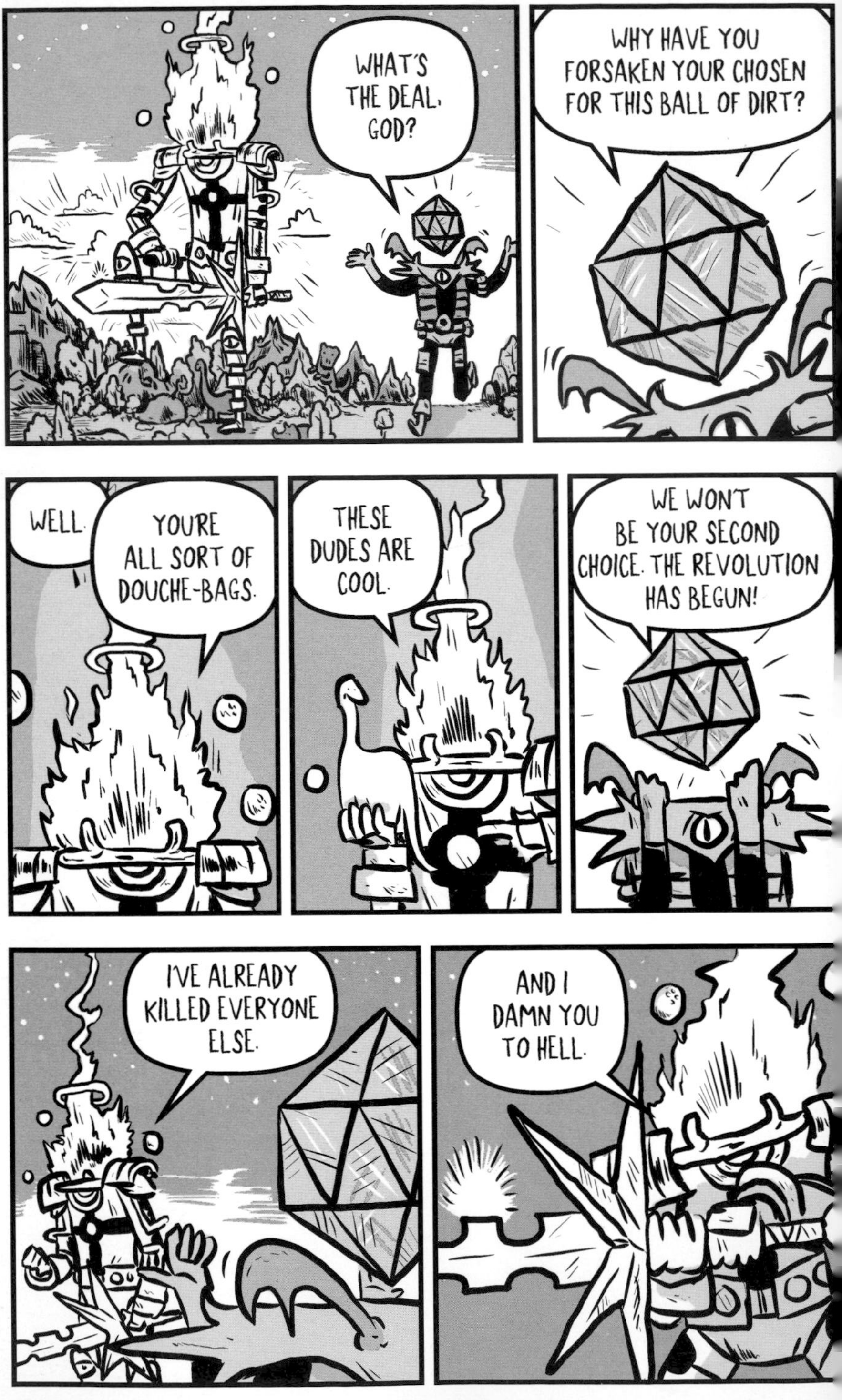

WHAT'S THE DEAL, GOD?
WHY HAVE YOU FORSAKEN YOUR CHOSEN FOR THIS BALL OF DIRT?
WELL.
YOU'RE ALL SORT OF DOUCHE-BAGS.
THESE DUDES ARE COOL.
WE WON'T BE YOUR SECOND CHOICE. THE REVOLUTION HAS BEGUN!
I'VE ALREADY KILLED EVERYONE ELSE.
AND I DAMN YOU TO HELL.

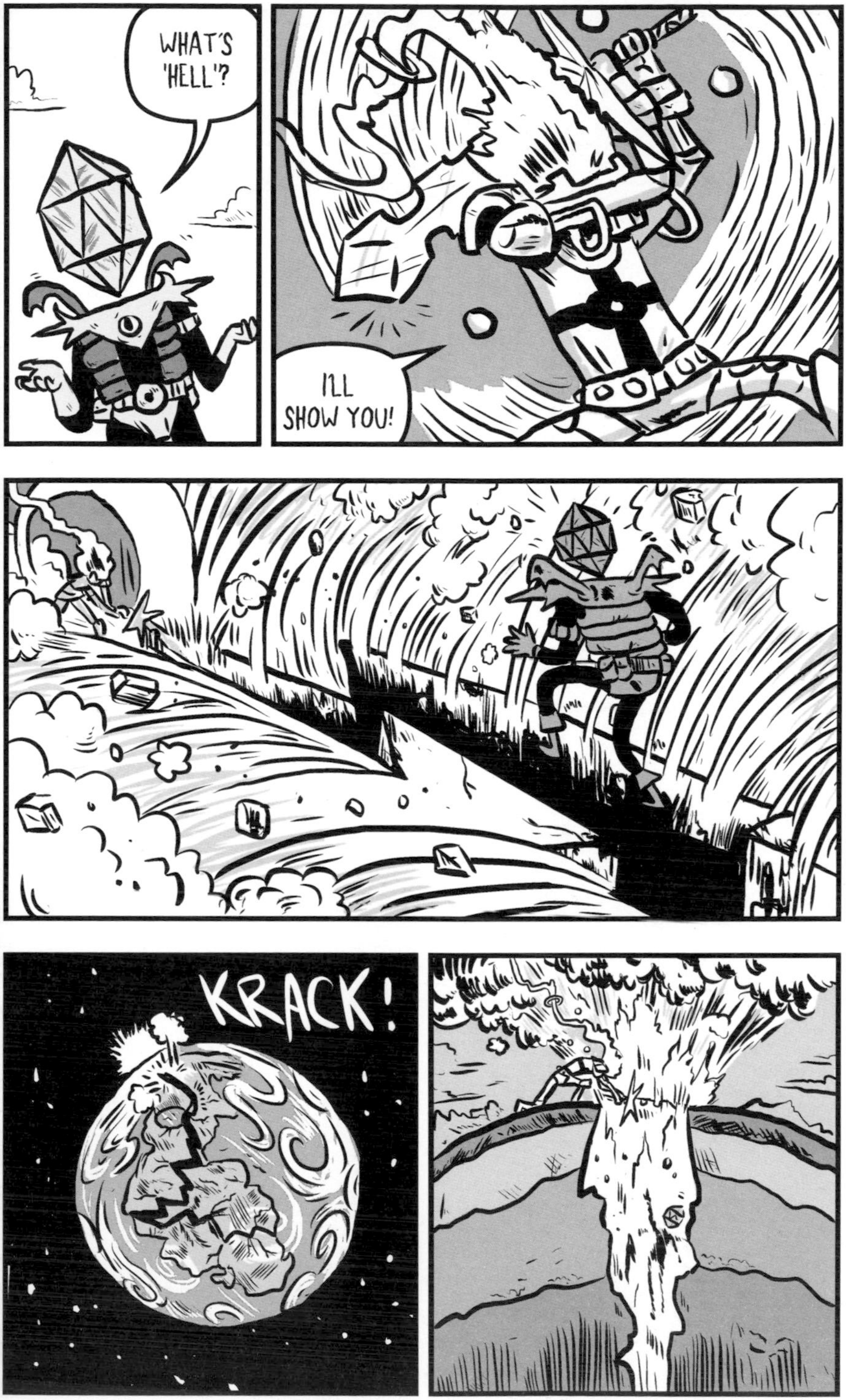
WHAT'S 'HELL'?
I'LL SHOW YOU!
KRACK!

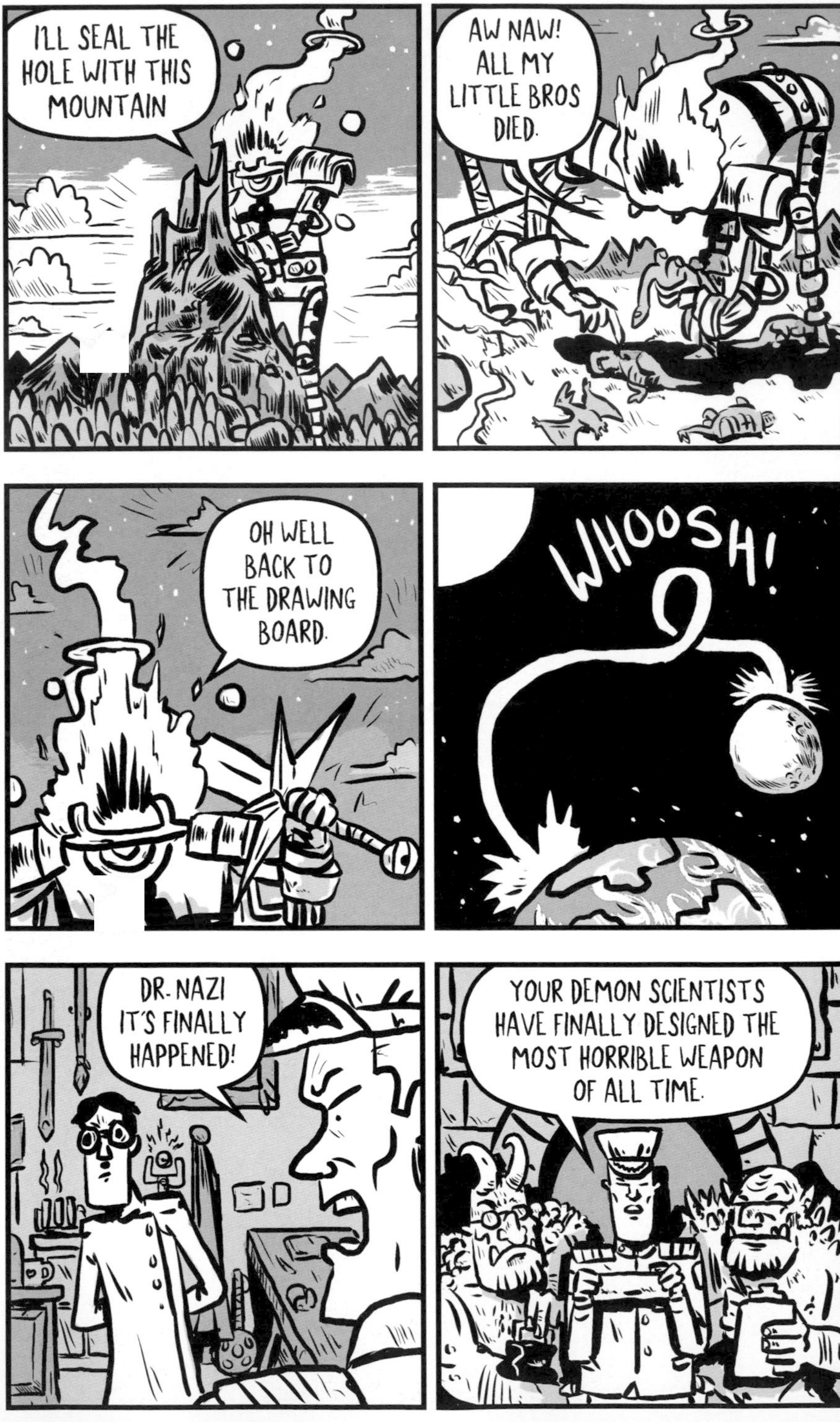
I'LL SEAL THE HOLE WITH THIS MOUNTAIN
AW NAW! ALL MY LITTLE BROS DIED.
OH WELL BACK TO THE DRAWING BOARD.
WHOOSH!
DR. NAZI IT'S FINALLY HAPPENED!
YOUR DEMON SCIENTISTS HAVE FINALLY DESIGNED THE MOST HORRIBLE WEAPON OF ALL TIME.

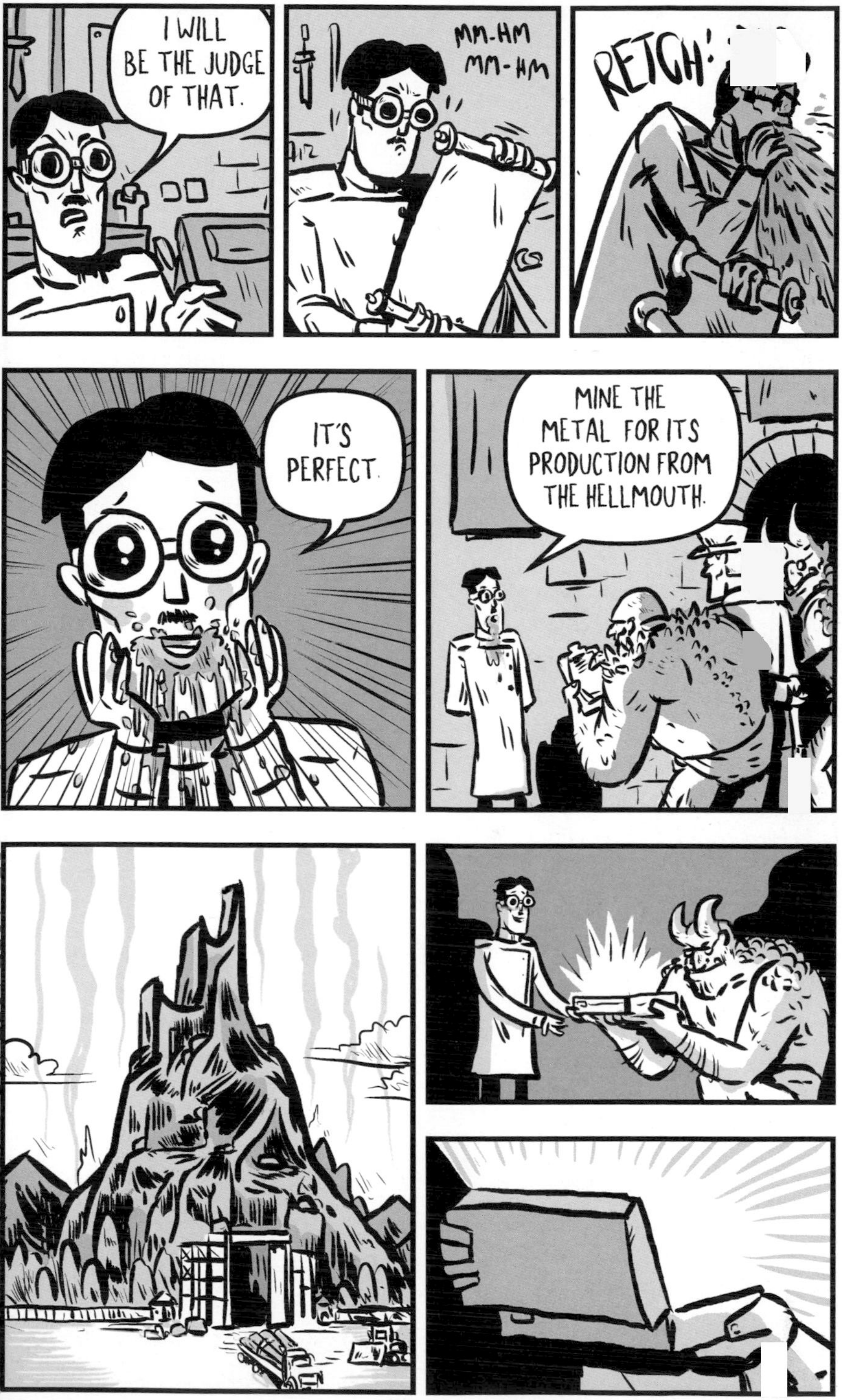
I WILL BE THE JUDGE OF THAT.
MM-HM MM-HM
RETCH!
IT'S PERFECT.
MINE THE METAL FOR ITS PRODUCTION FROM THE HELLMOUTH.

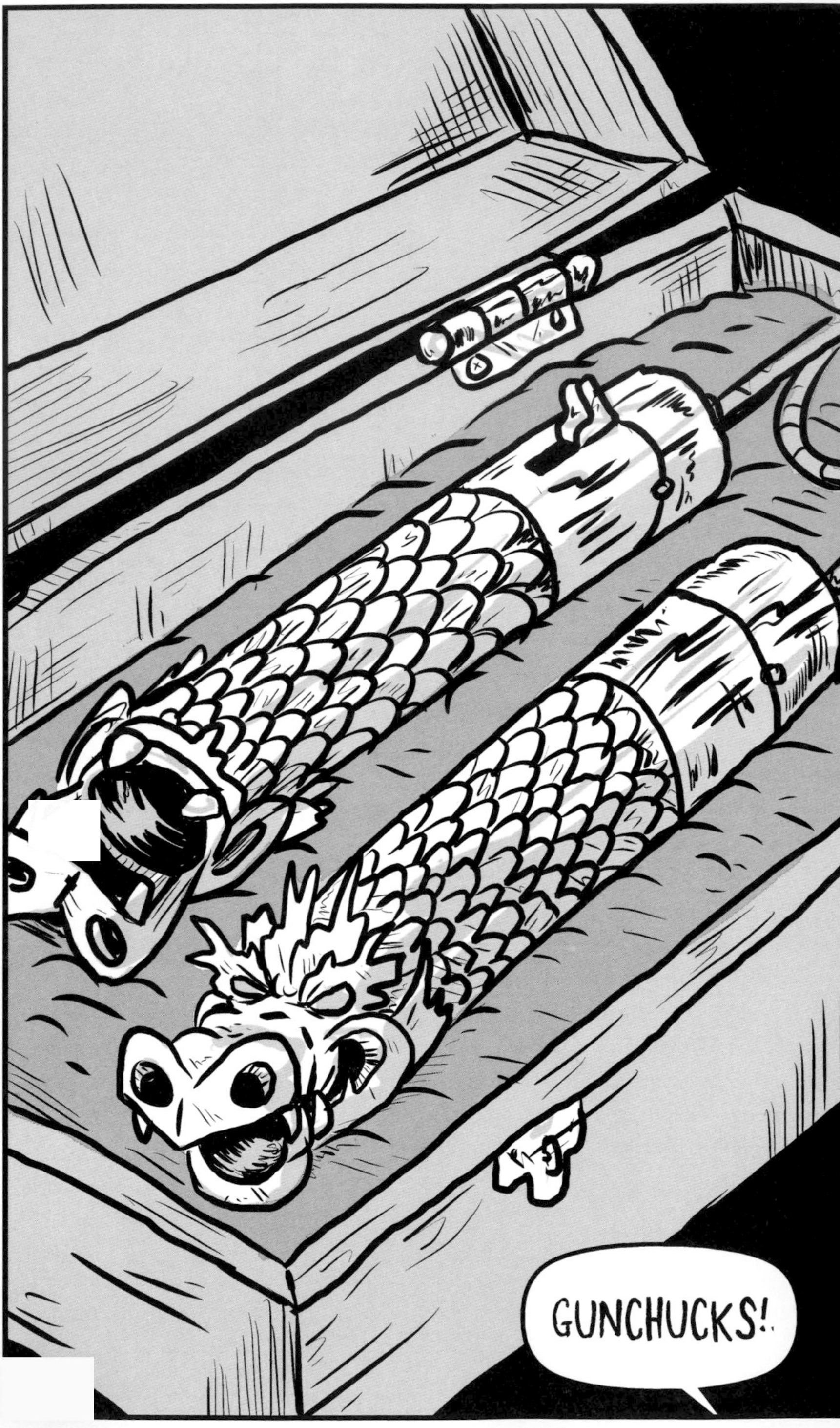
GUNCHUCKS!

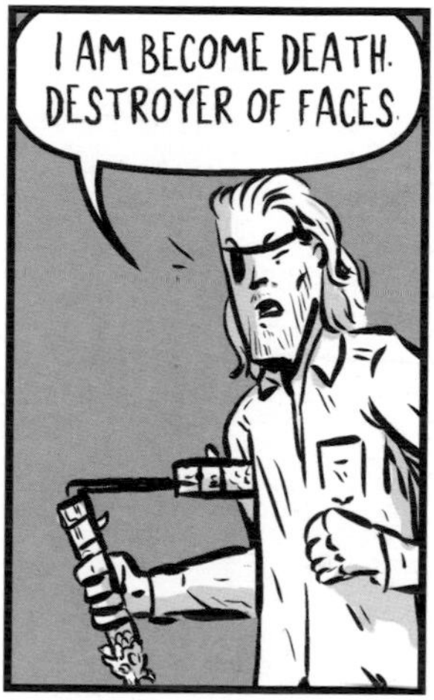
I AM BECOME DEATH.
DESTROYER OF FACES.

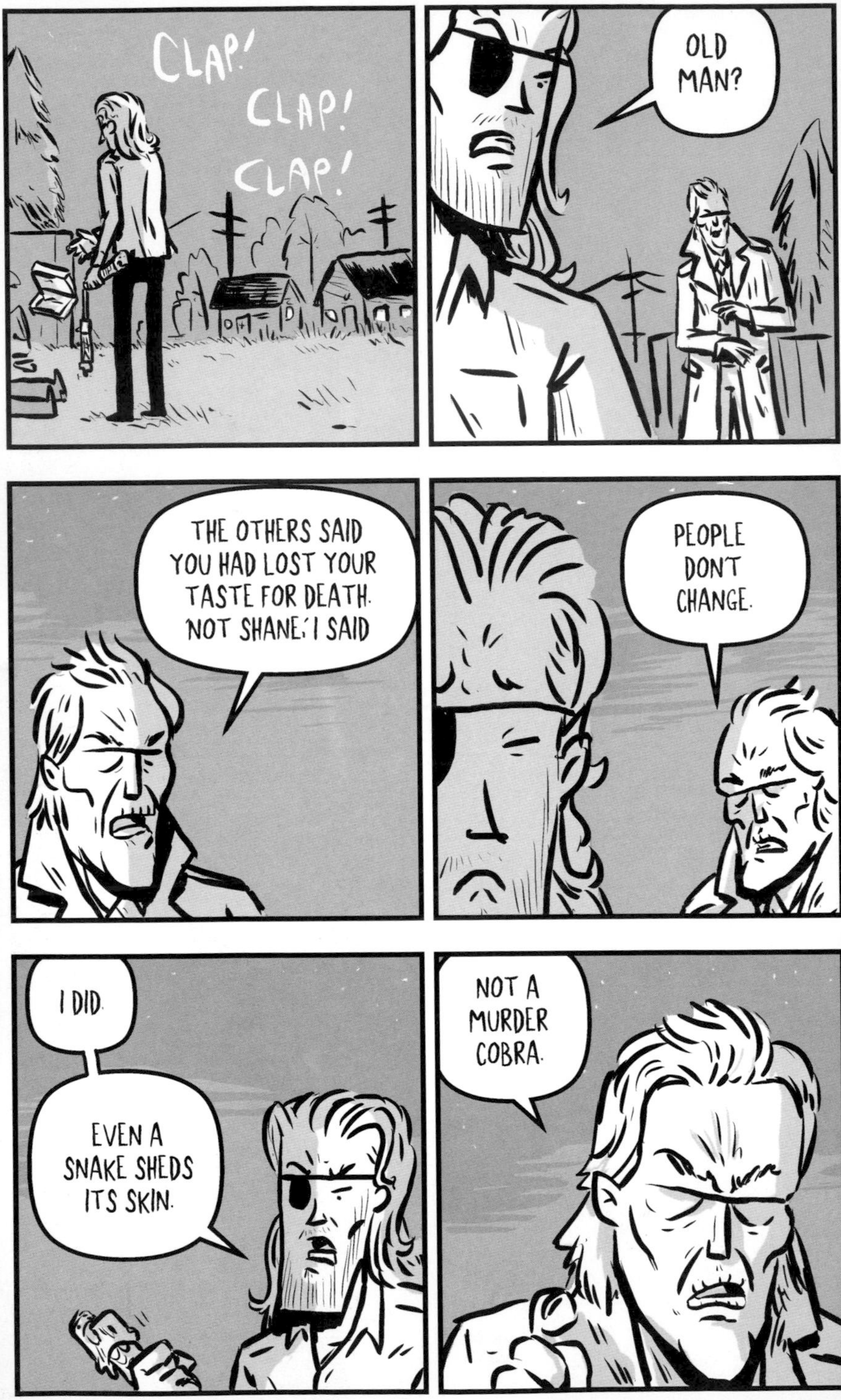
CLAP! CLAP! CLAP!
OLD MAN?
THE OTHERS SAID YOU HAD LOST YOUR TASTE FOR DEATH. 'NOT SHANE,' I SAID
PEOPLE DON'T CHANGE.
I DID.
EVEN A SNAKE SHEDS ITS SKIN.
NOT A MURDER COBRA.

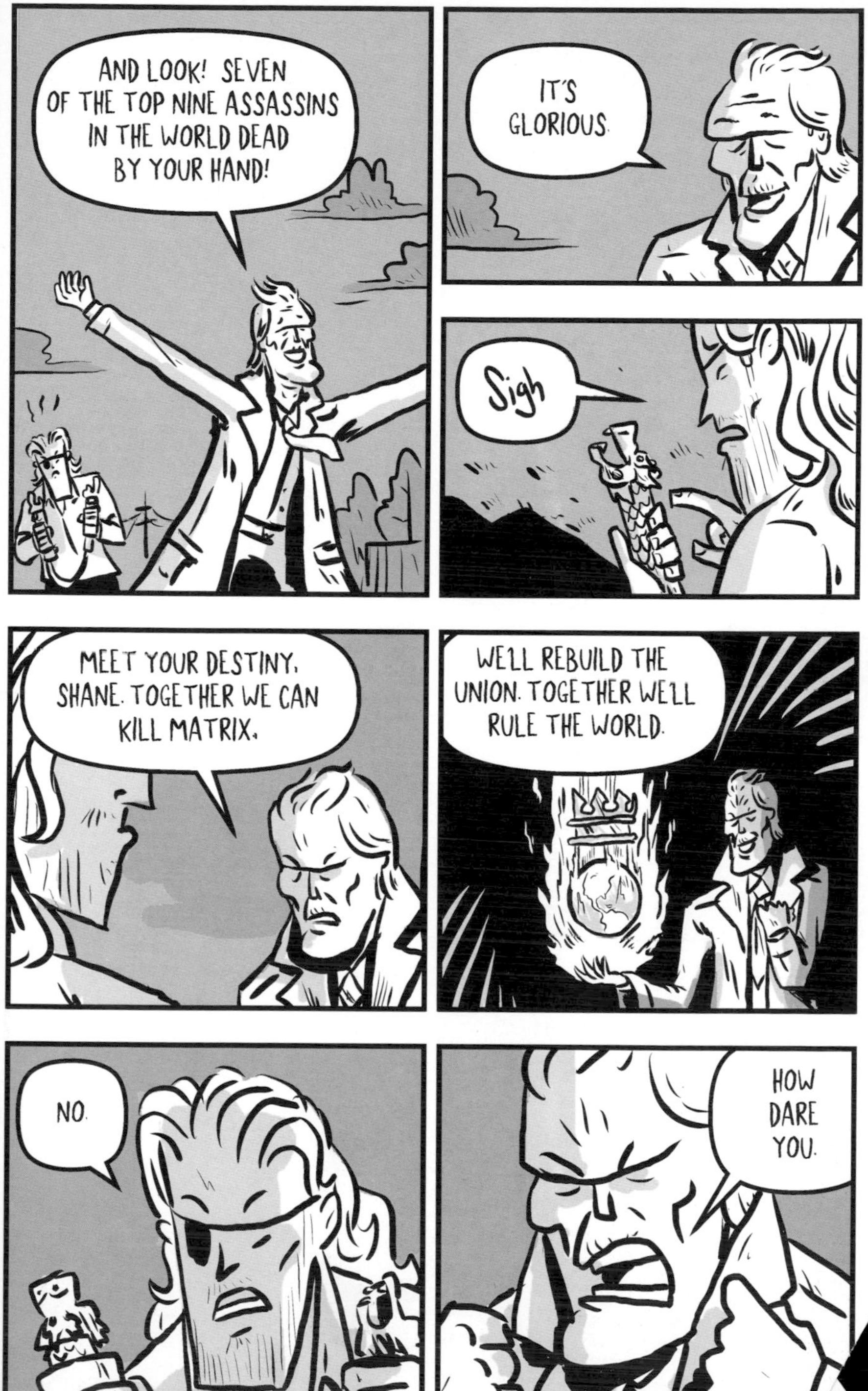
AND LOOK! SEVEN OF THE TOP NINE ASSASSINS IN THE WORLD DEAD BY YOUR HAND!
IT'S GLORIOUS.
Sigh
MEET YOUR DESTINY, SHANE. TOGETHER WE CAN KILL MATRIX,
WE'LL REBUILD THE UNION. TOGETHER WE'LL RULE THE WORLD.
NO.
HOW DARE YOU.

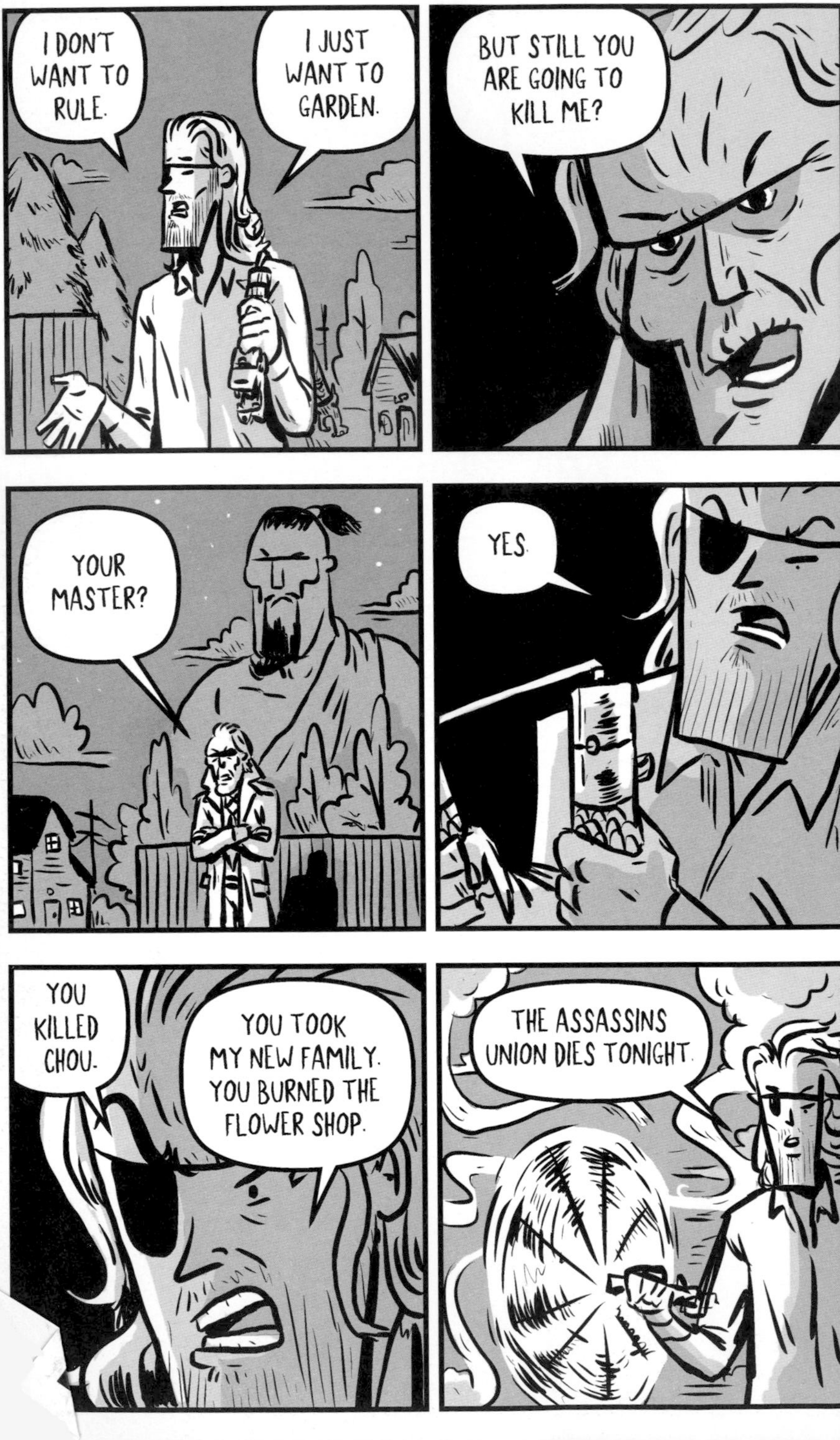
I DON'T WANT TO RULE.
I JUST WANT TO GARDEN.
BUT STILL YOU ARE GOING TO KILL ME?
YOUR MASTER?
YES.
YOU KILLED CHOU.
YOU TOOK MY NEW FAMILY. YOU BURNED THE FLOWER SHOP.
THE ASSASSINS UNION DIES TONIGHT.

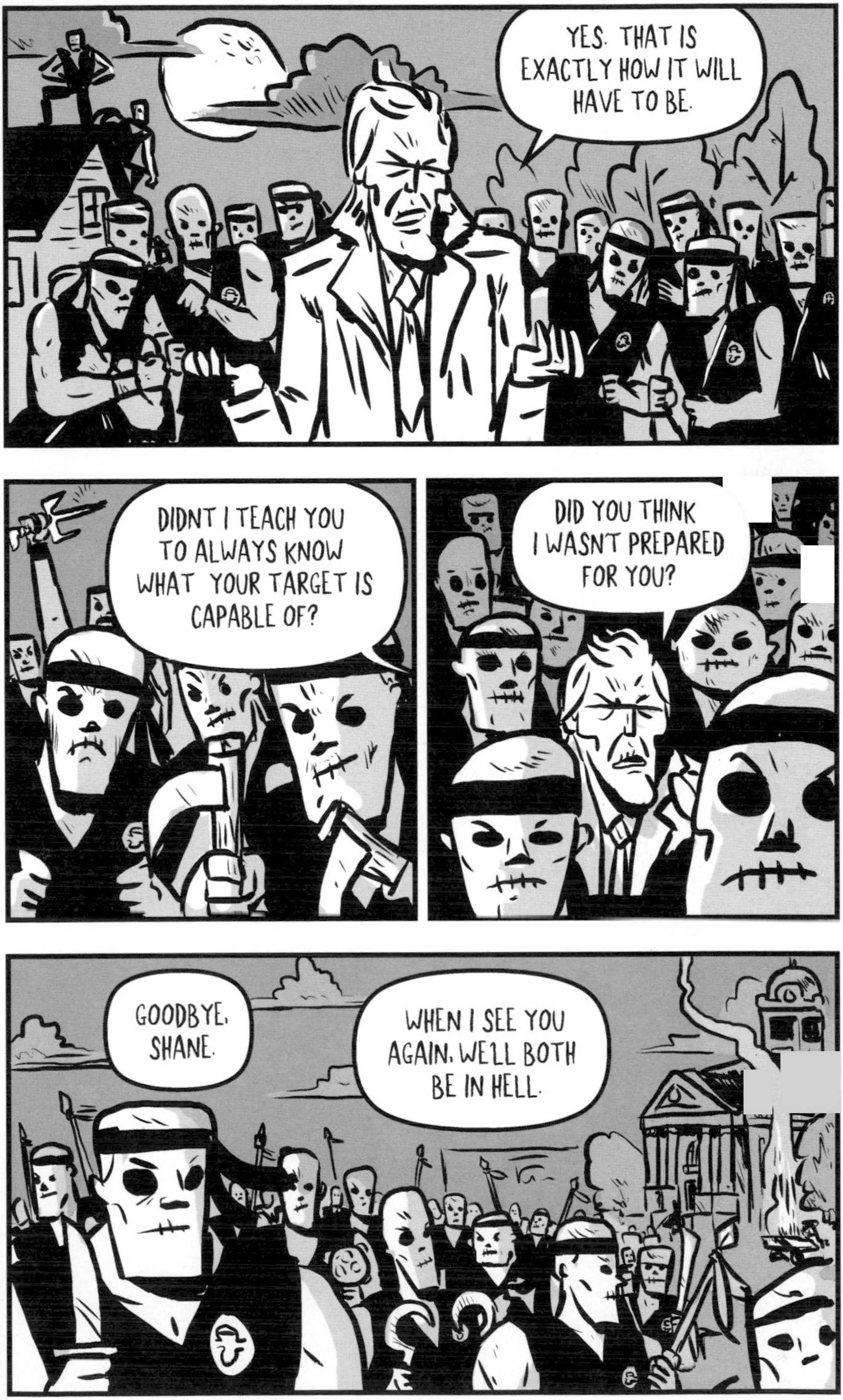
YES. THAT IS EXACTLY HOW IT WILL HAVE TO BE.
DIDNT I TEACH YOU TO ALWAYS KNOW WHAT YOUR TARGET IS CAPABLE OF?
DID YOU THINK I WASN'T PREPARED FOR YOU?
GOODBYE, SHANE.
WHEN I SEE YOU AGAIN, WE'LL BOTH BE IN HELL.

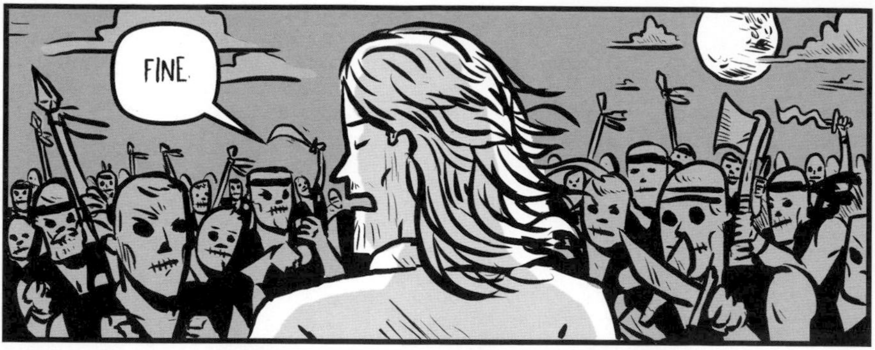
FINE.
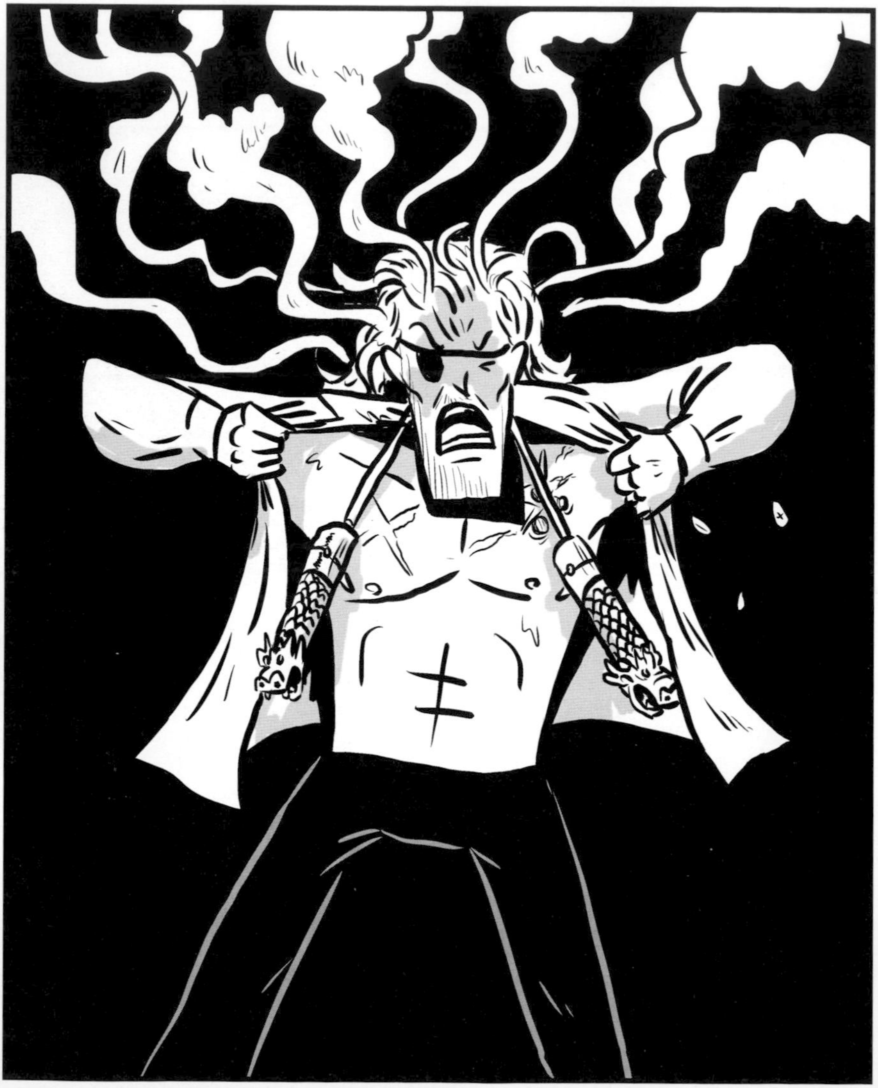

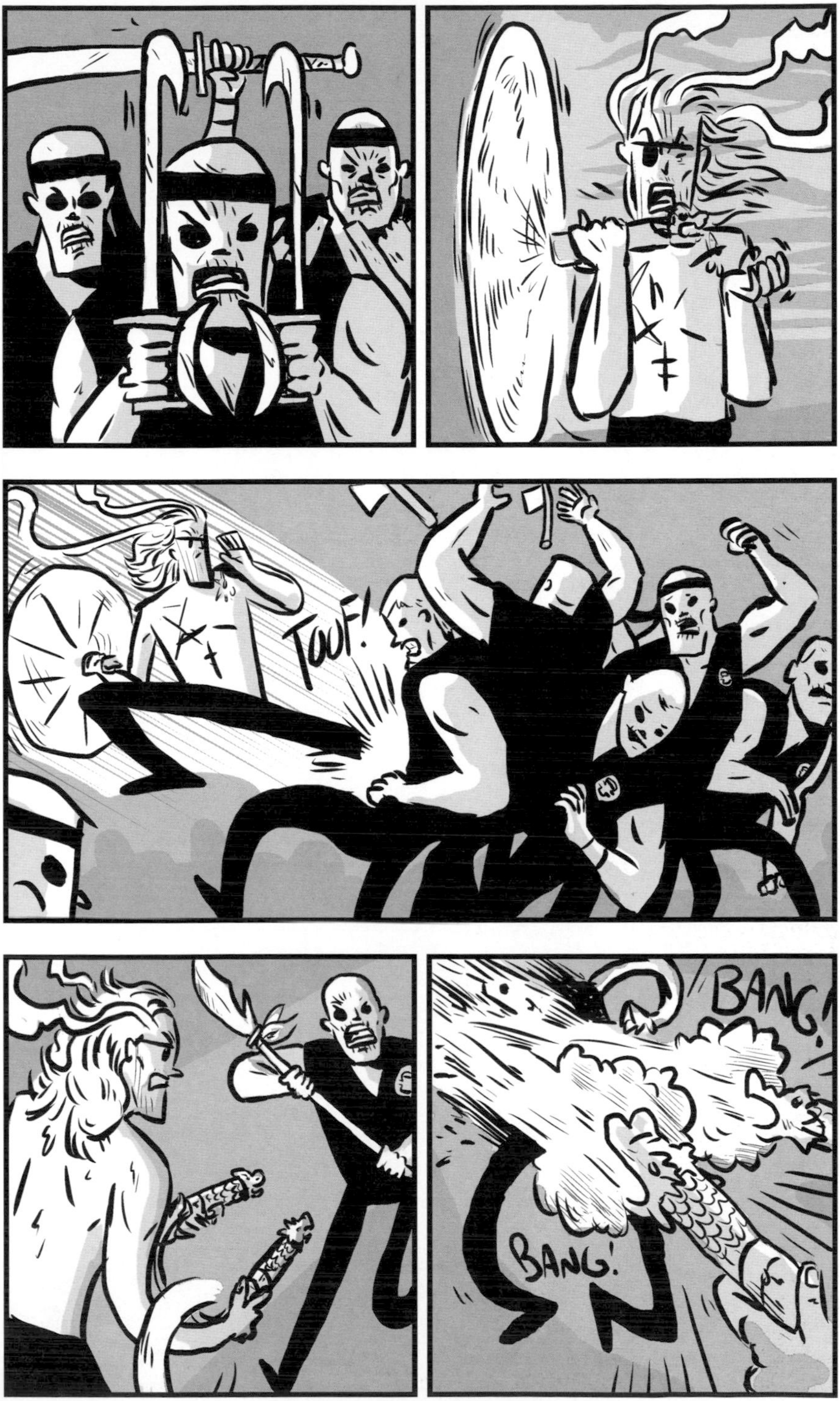
TOUF!
BANG!
BANG!

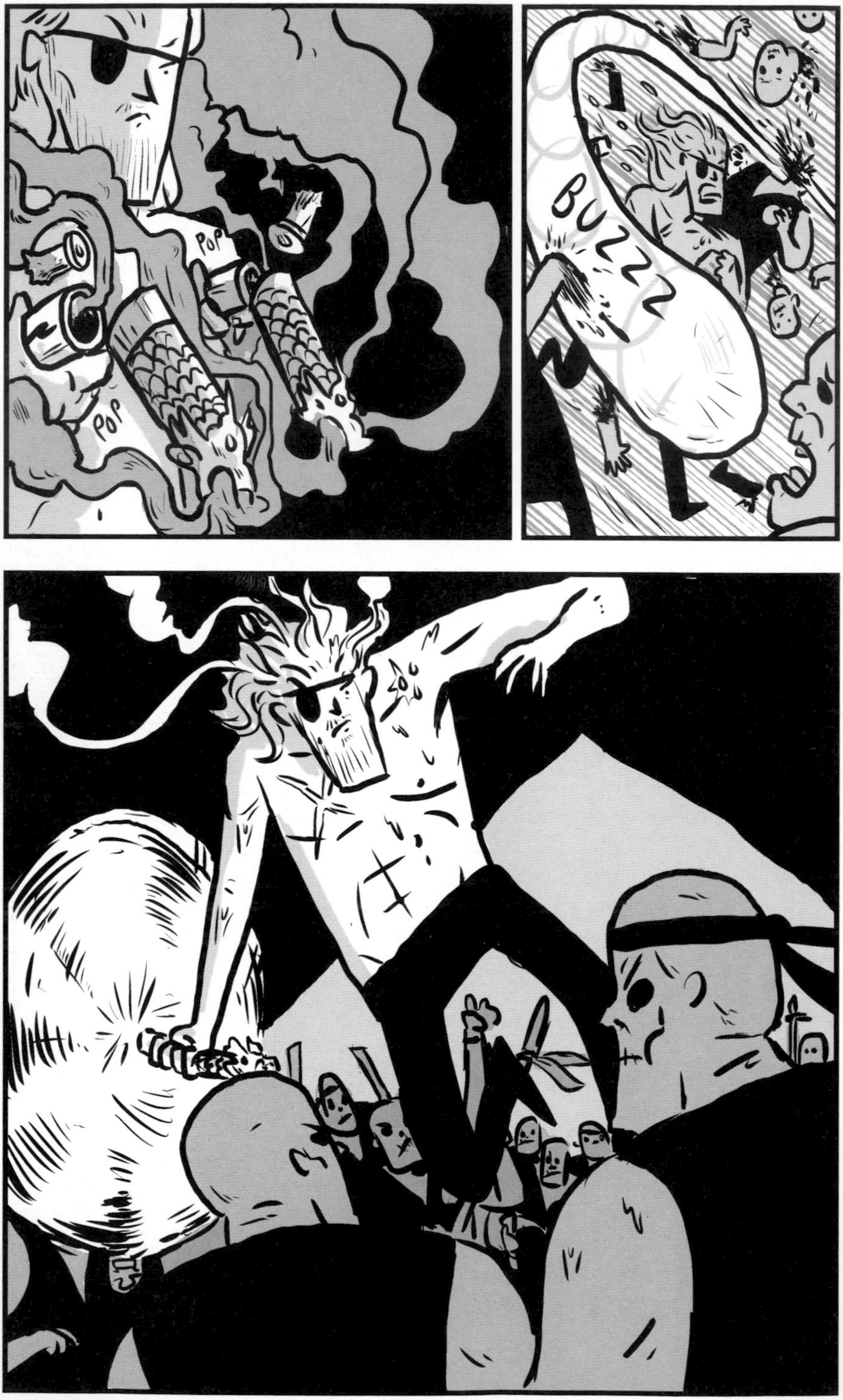
POP
POP
BUZZZ

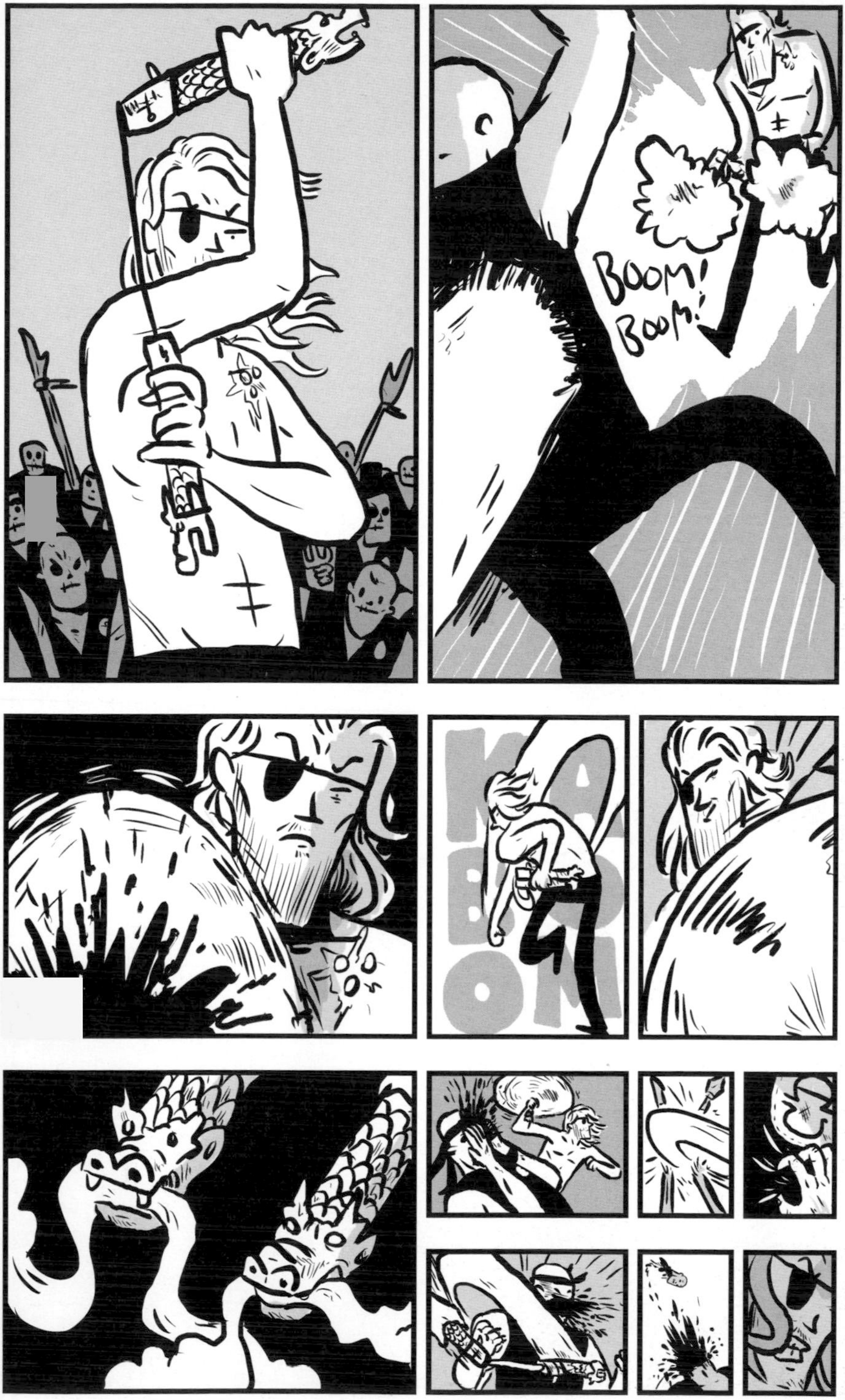
BOOM! BOOM!

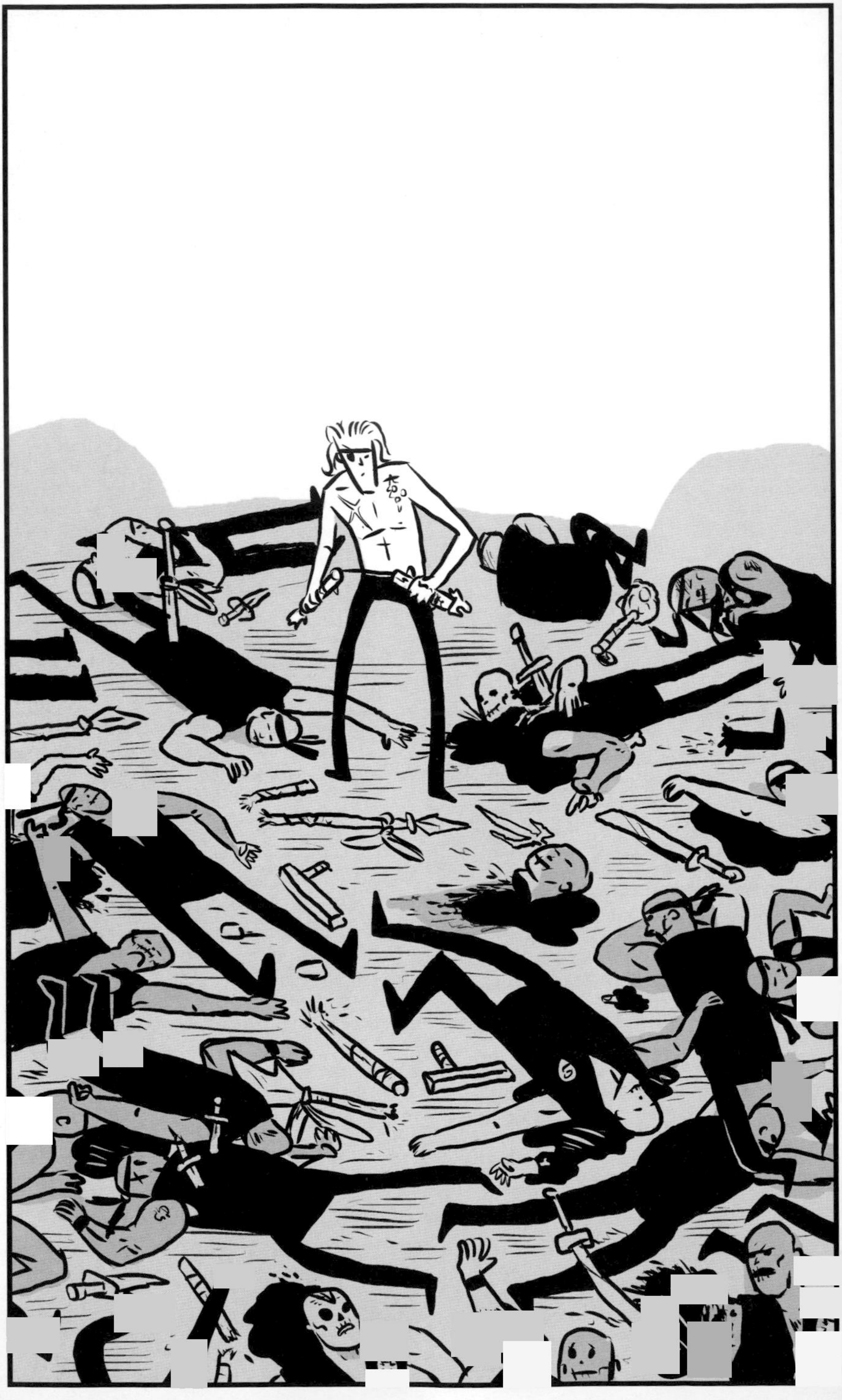

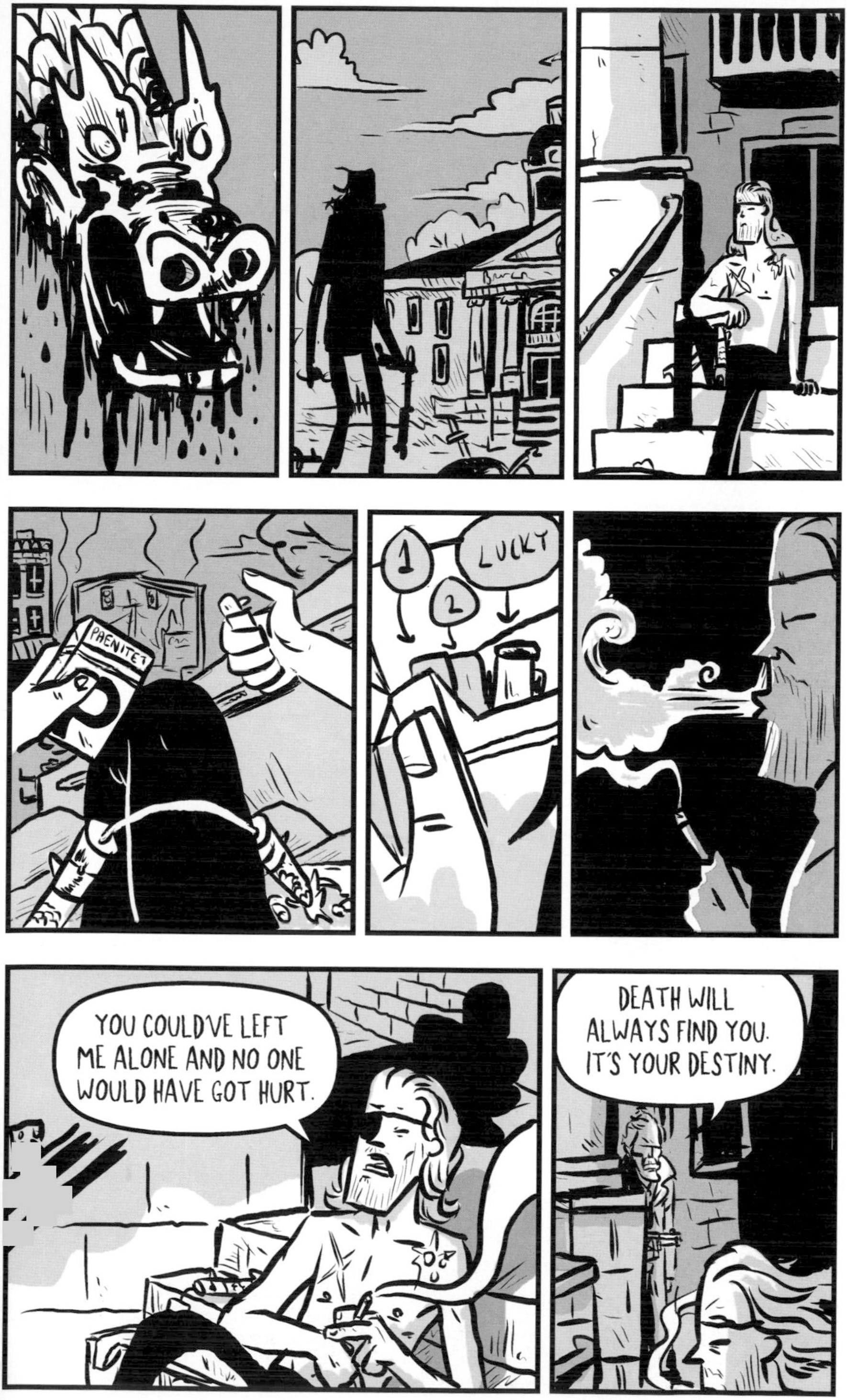
PAENITET
1
2
LUCKY
YOU COULD'VE LEFT ME ALONE AND NO ONE WOULD HAVE GOT HURT.
DEATH WILL ALWAYS FIND YOU. IT'S YOUR DESTINY.

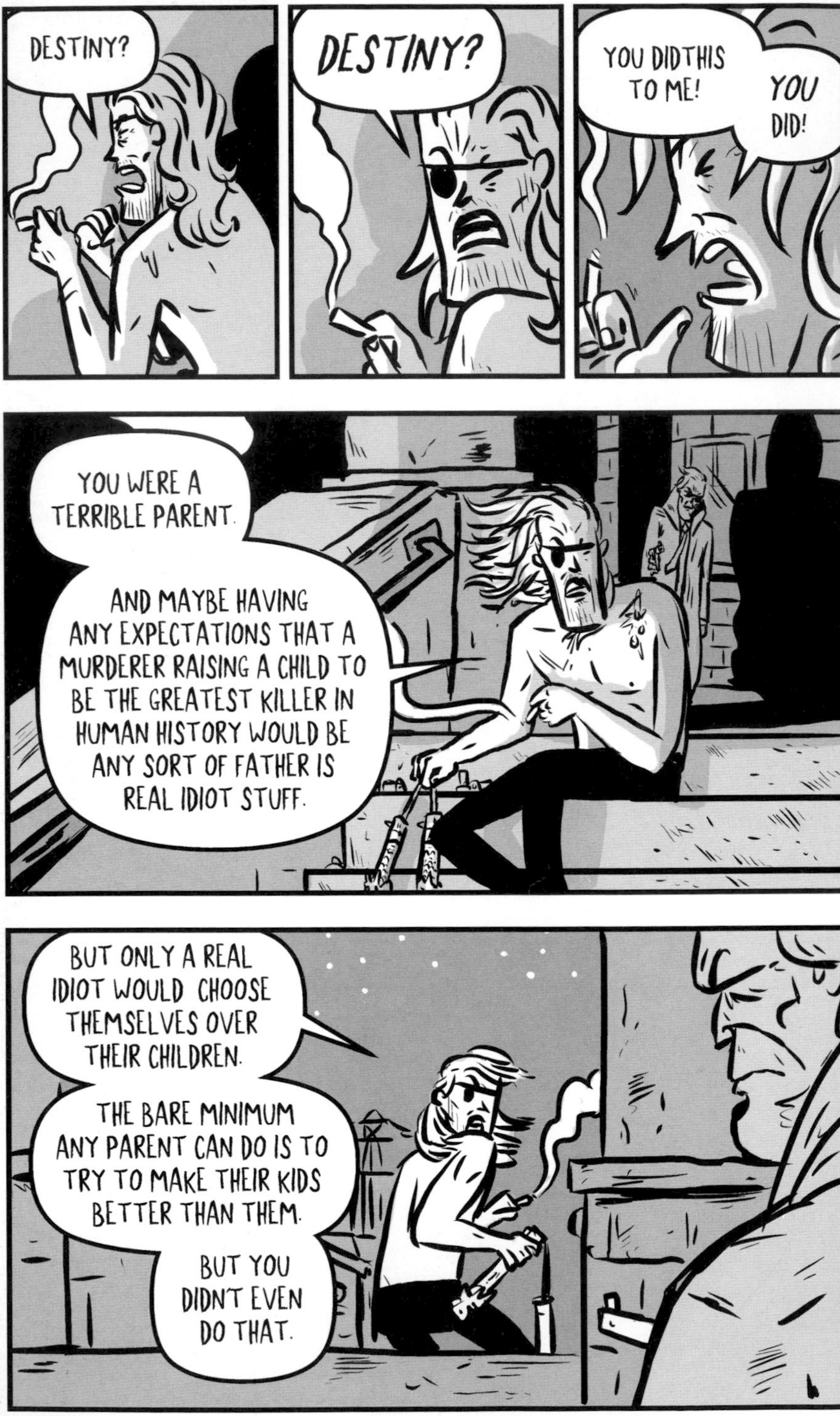
DESTINY?
DESTINY?
YOU DIDTHIS TO ME!
YOU DID!
YOU WERE A TERRIBLE PARENT.
AND MAYBE HAVING ANY EXPECTATIONS THAT A MURDERER RAISING A CHILD TO BE THE GREATEST KILLER IN HUMAN HISTORY WOULD BE ANY SORT OF FATHER IS REAL IDIOT STUFF.
BUT ONLY A REAL IDIOT WOULD CHOOSE THEMSELVES OVER THEIR CHILDREN.
THE BARE MINIMUM ANY PARENT CAN DO IS TO TRY TO MAKE THEIR KIDS BETTER THAN THEM.
BUT YOU DIDN'T EVEN DO THAT.

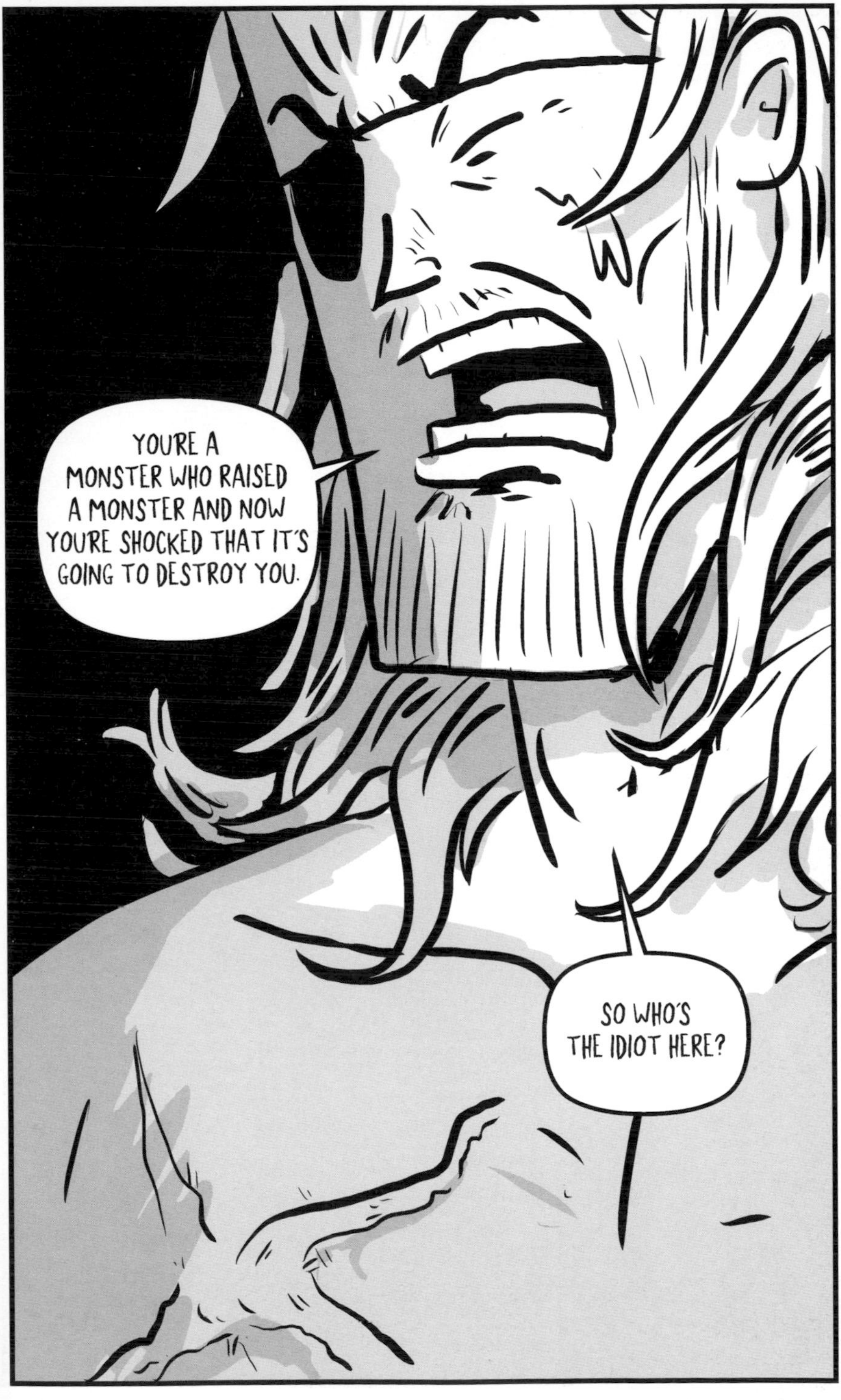
YOU'RE A MONSTER WHO RAISED A MONSTER AND NOW YOU'RE SHOCKED THAT IT'S GOING TO DESTROY YOU.
SO WHO'S THE IDIOT HERE?

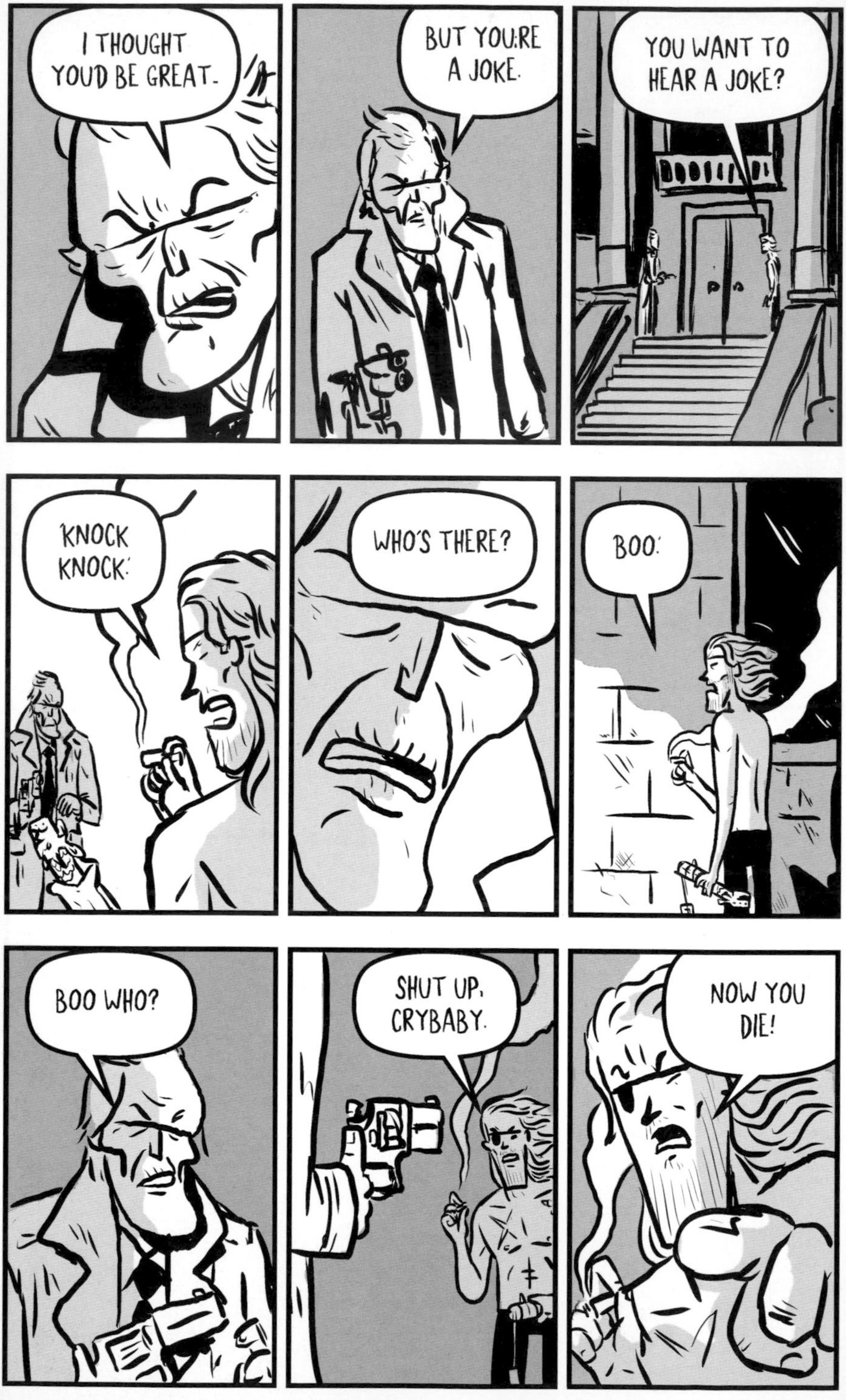
I THOUGHT YOU'D BE GREAT.
BUT YOU'RE A JOKE.
YOU WANT TO HEAR A JOKE?
KNOCK KNOCK!
WHO'S THERE?
BOO!
BOO WHO?
SHUT UP, CRYBABY.
NOW YOU DIE!

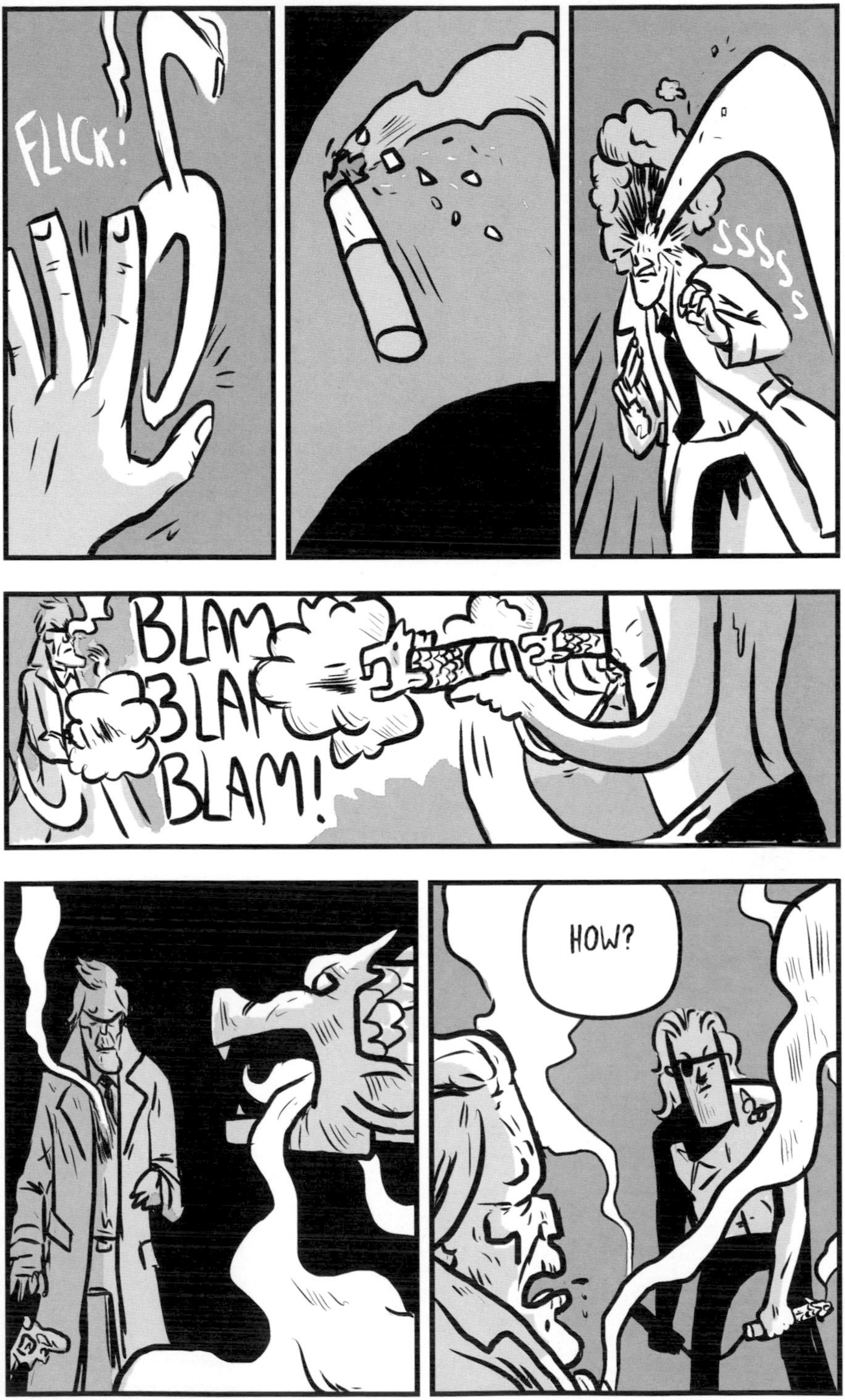
FLICK!
SSSSS
BLAM
BLAM
BLAM!
HOW?

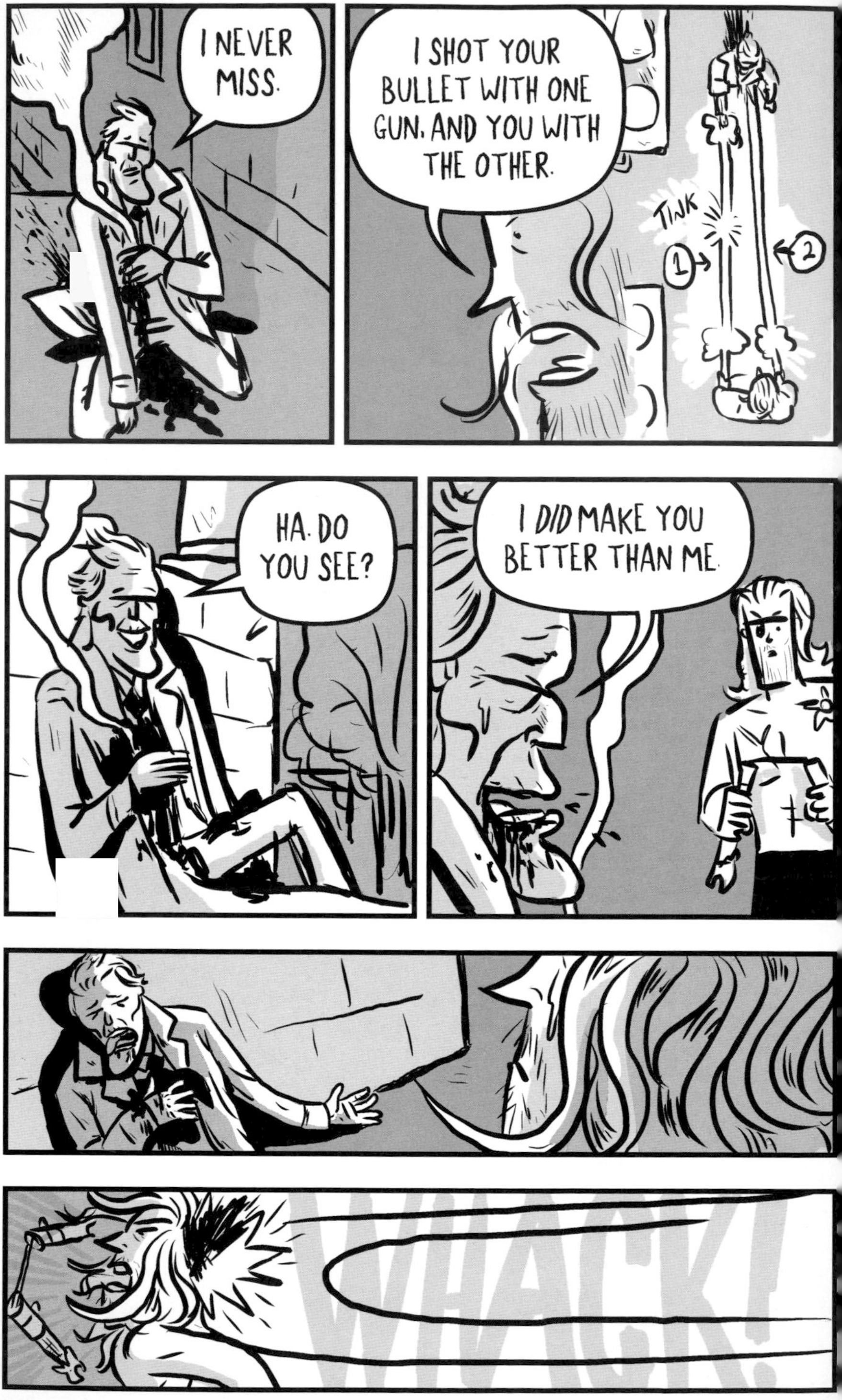
I NEVER MISS.
I SHOT YOUR BULLET WITH ONE GUN, AND YOU WITH THE OTHER.
TINK
1
2
HA. DO YOU SEE?
I *DID* MAKE YOU BETTER THAN ME.
WHACK!

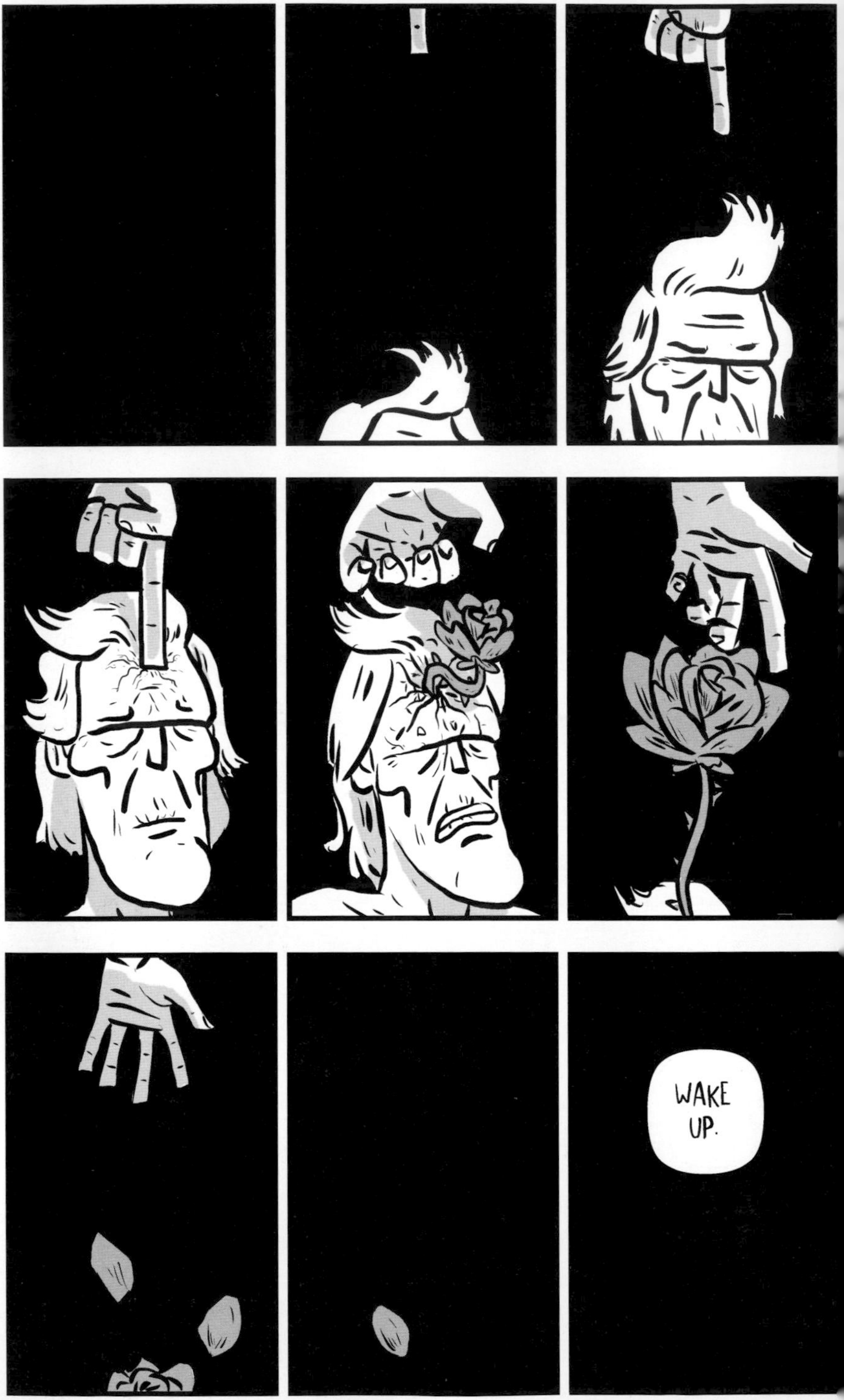
WAKE UP.

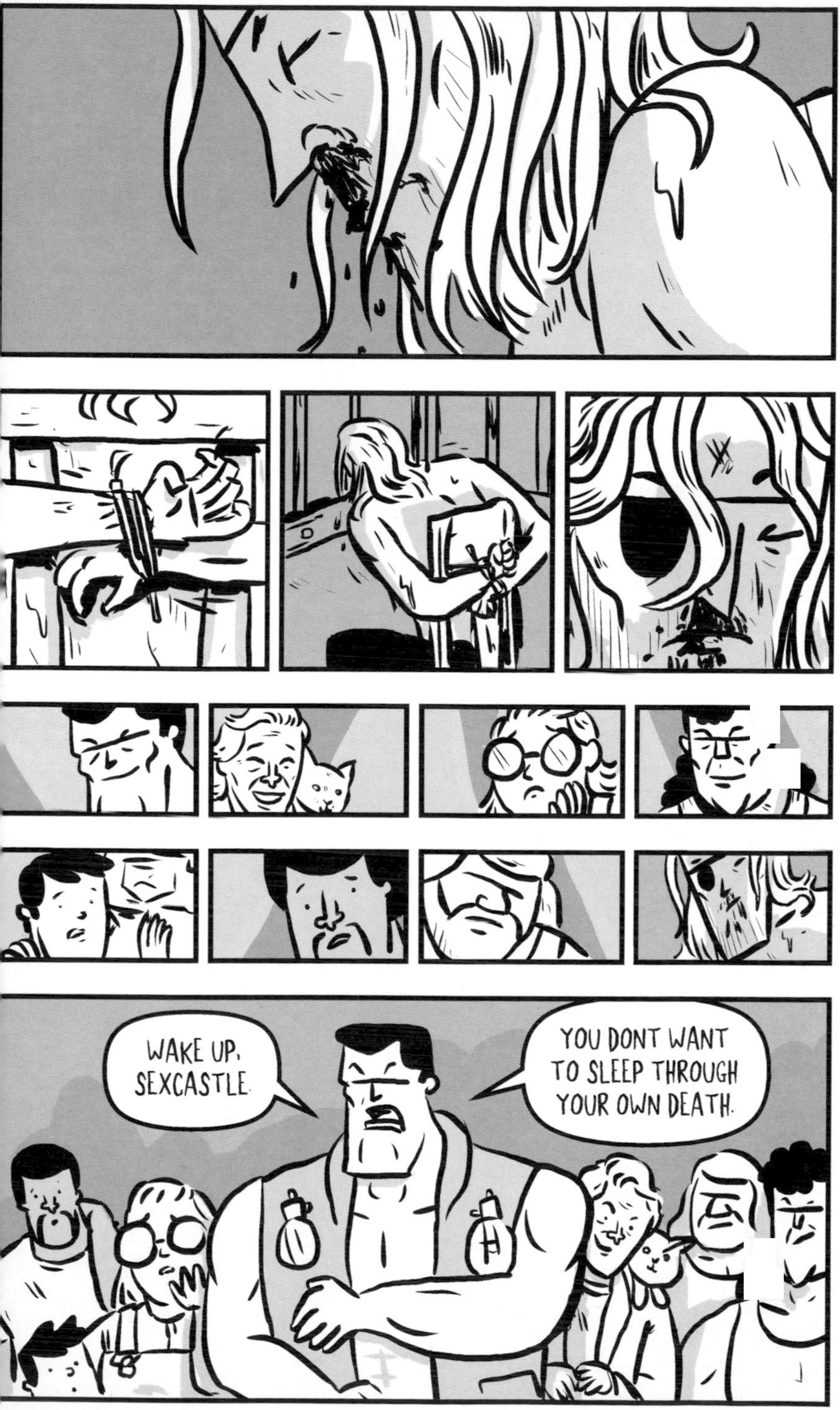
WAKE UP, SEXCASTLE.
YOU DONT WANT TO SLEEP THROUGH YOUR OWN DEATH.

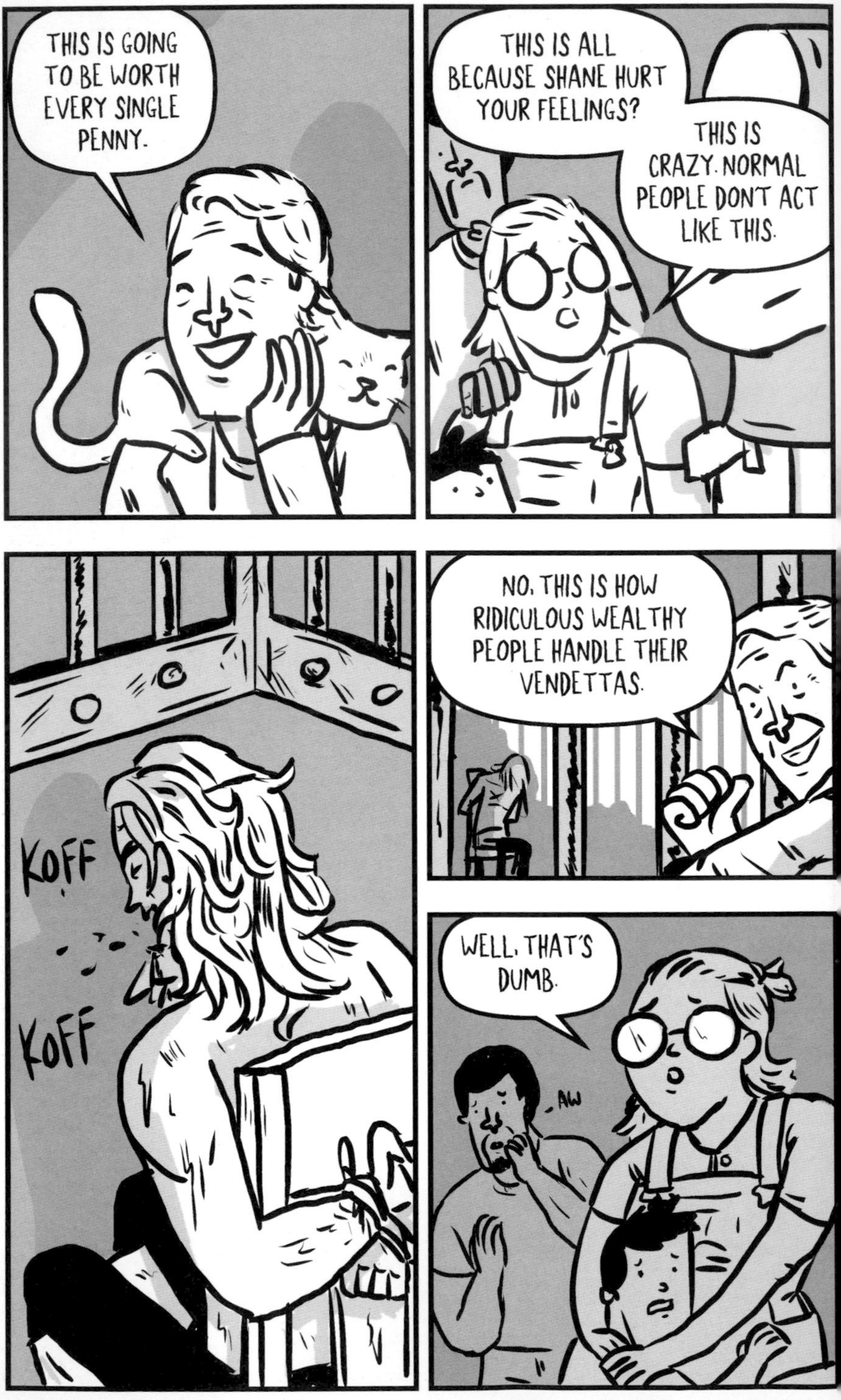

THIS IS GOING TO BE WORTH EVERY SINGLE PENNY.
THIS IS ALL BECAUSE SHANE HURT YOUR FEELINGS?
THIS IS CRAZY. NORMAL PEOPLE DON'T ACT LIKE THIS.
KOFF
KOFF
NO, THIS IS HOW RIDICULOUS WEALTHY PEOPLE HANDLE THEIR VENDETTAS.
WELL, THAT'S DUMB.
AW

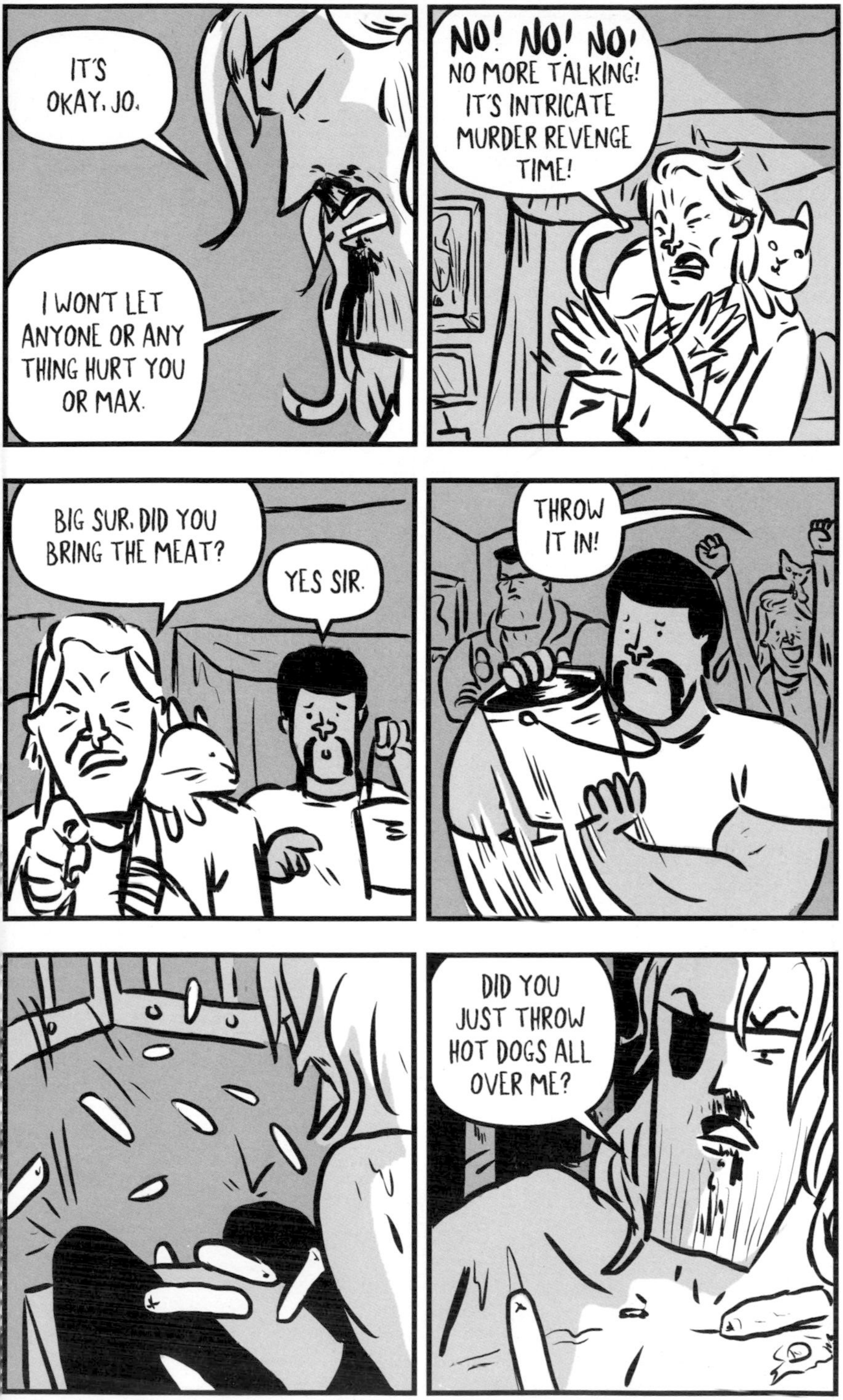
IT'S OKAY, JO.
I WON'T LET ANYONE OR ANY THING HURT YOU OR MAX.
NO! NO! NO! NO MORE TALKING! IT'S INTRICATE MURDER REVENGE TIME!
BIG SUR, DID YOU BRING THE MEAT?
YES SIR.
THROW IT IN!
DID YOU JUST THROW HOT DOGS ALL OVER ME?

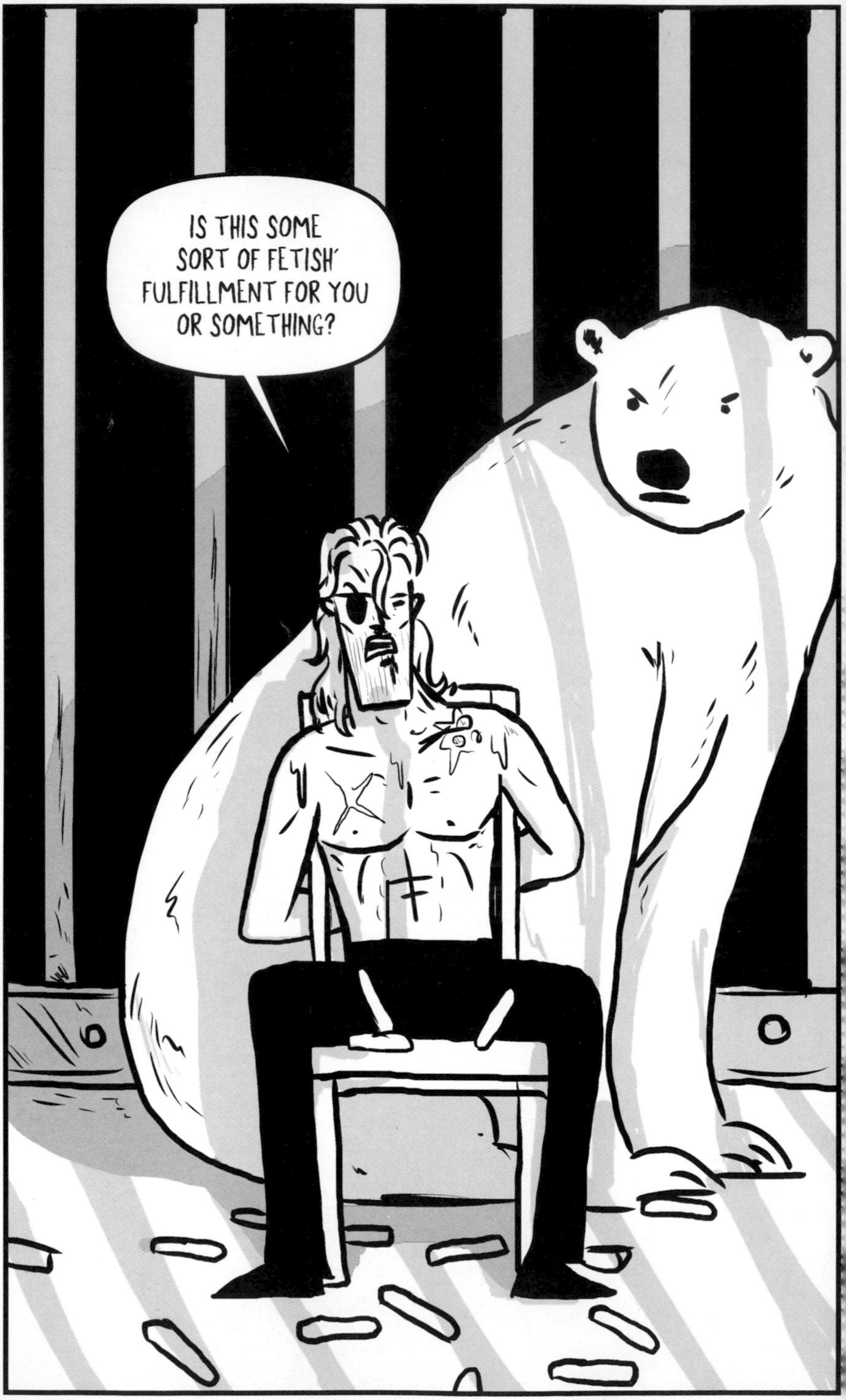
IS THIS SOME SORT OF FETISH FULFILLMENT FOR YOU OR SOMETHING?

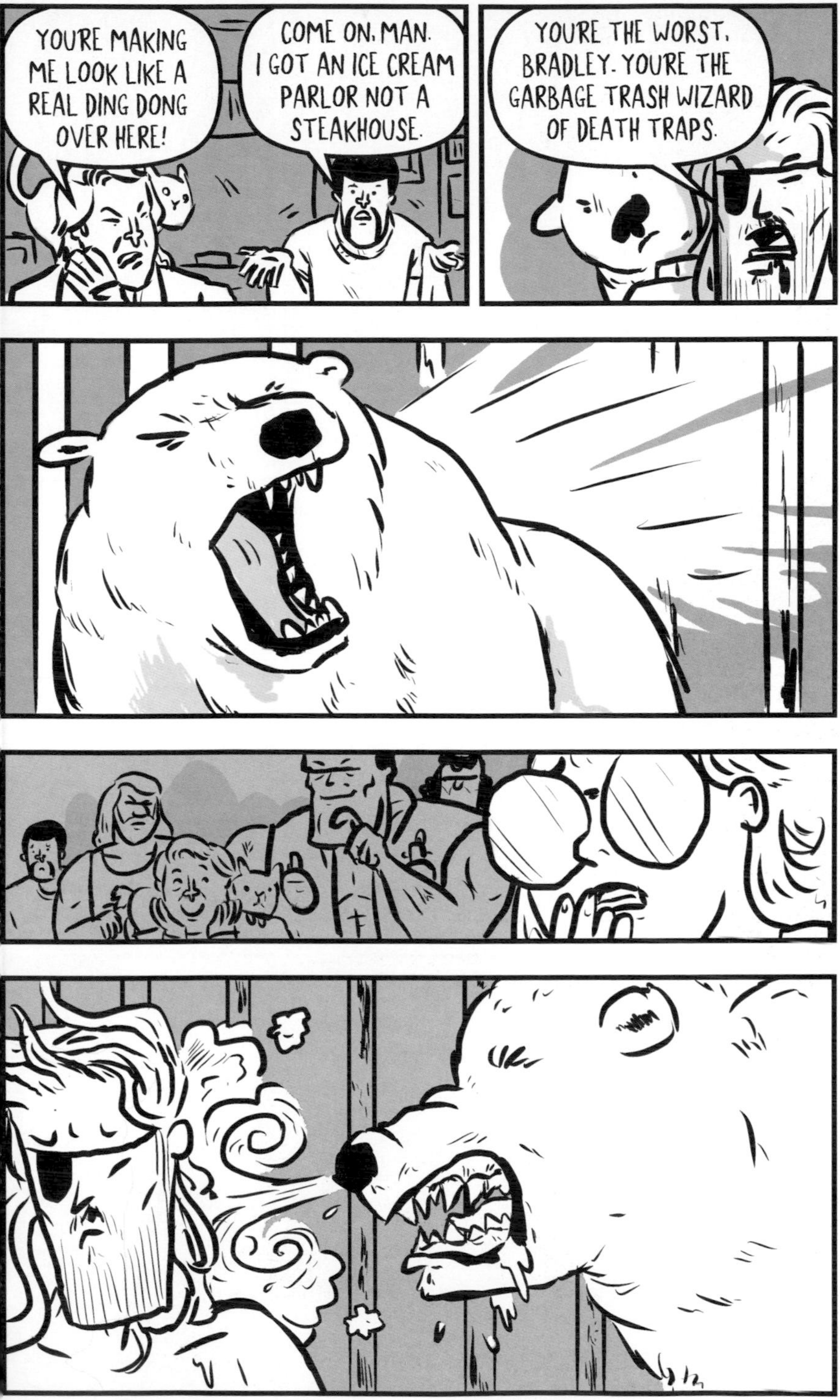
YOU'RE MAKING ME LOOK LIKE A REAL DING DONG OVER HERE!
COME ON, MAN. I GOT AN ICE CREAM PARLOR NOT A STEAKHOUSE.
YOU'RE THE WORST, BRADLEY. YOU'RE THE GARBAGE TRASH WIZARD OF DEATH TRAPS.

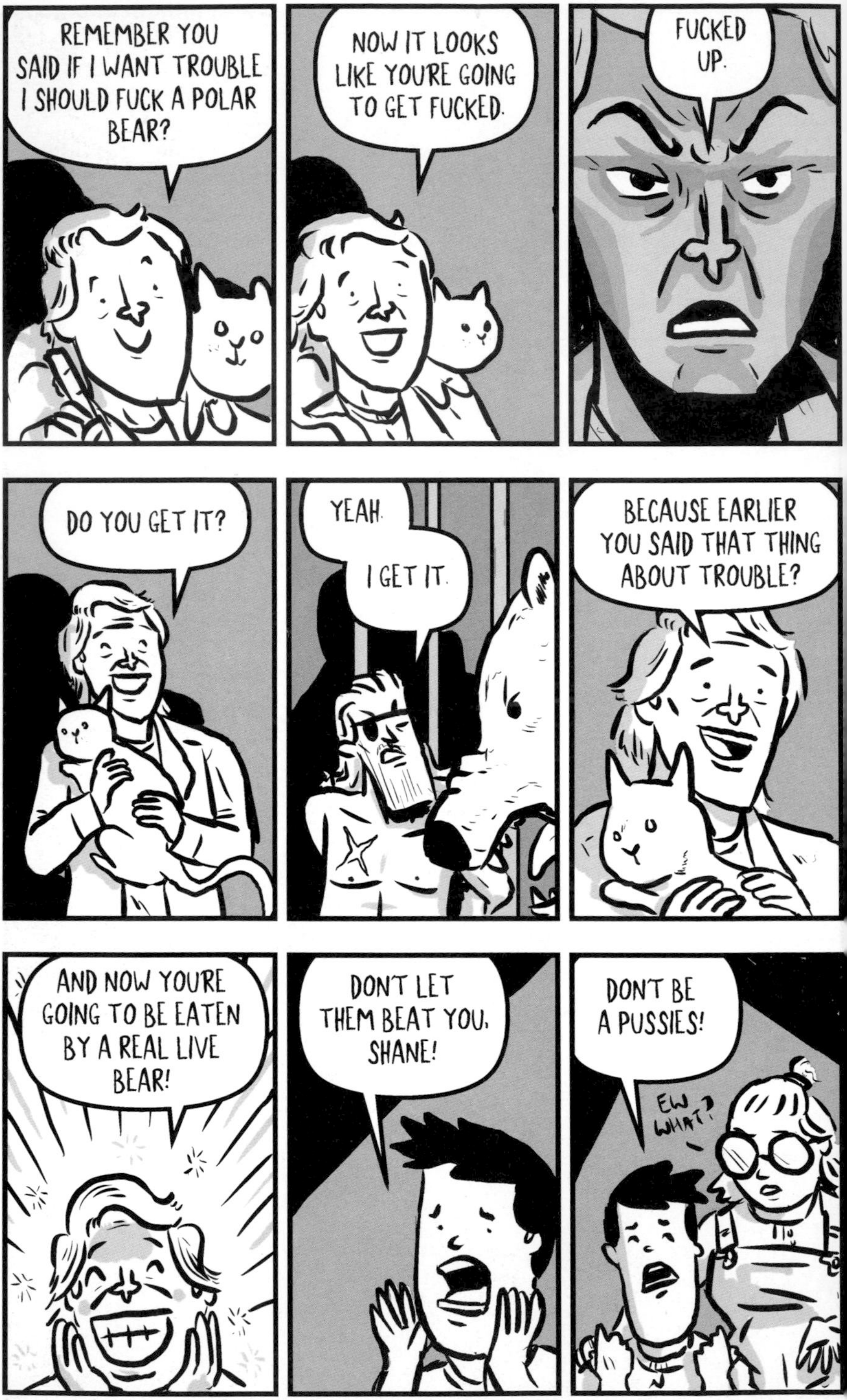
REMEMBER YOU SAID IF I WANT TROUBLE I SHOULD FUCK A POLAR BEAR?
NOW IT LOOKS LIKE YOU'RE GOING TO GET FUCKED.
FUCKED UP.
DO YOU GET IT?
YEAH.
I GET IT.
BECAUSE EARLIER YOU SAID THAT THING ABOUT TROUBLE?
AND NOW YOU'RE GOING TO BE EATEN BY A REAL LIVE BEAR!
DON'T LET THEM BEAT YOU, SHANE!
DON'T BE A PUSSIES!
EW WHAT?

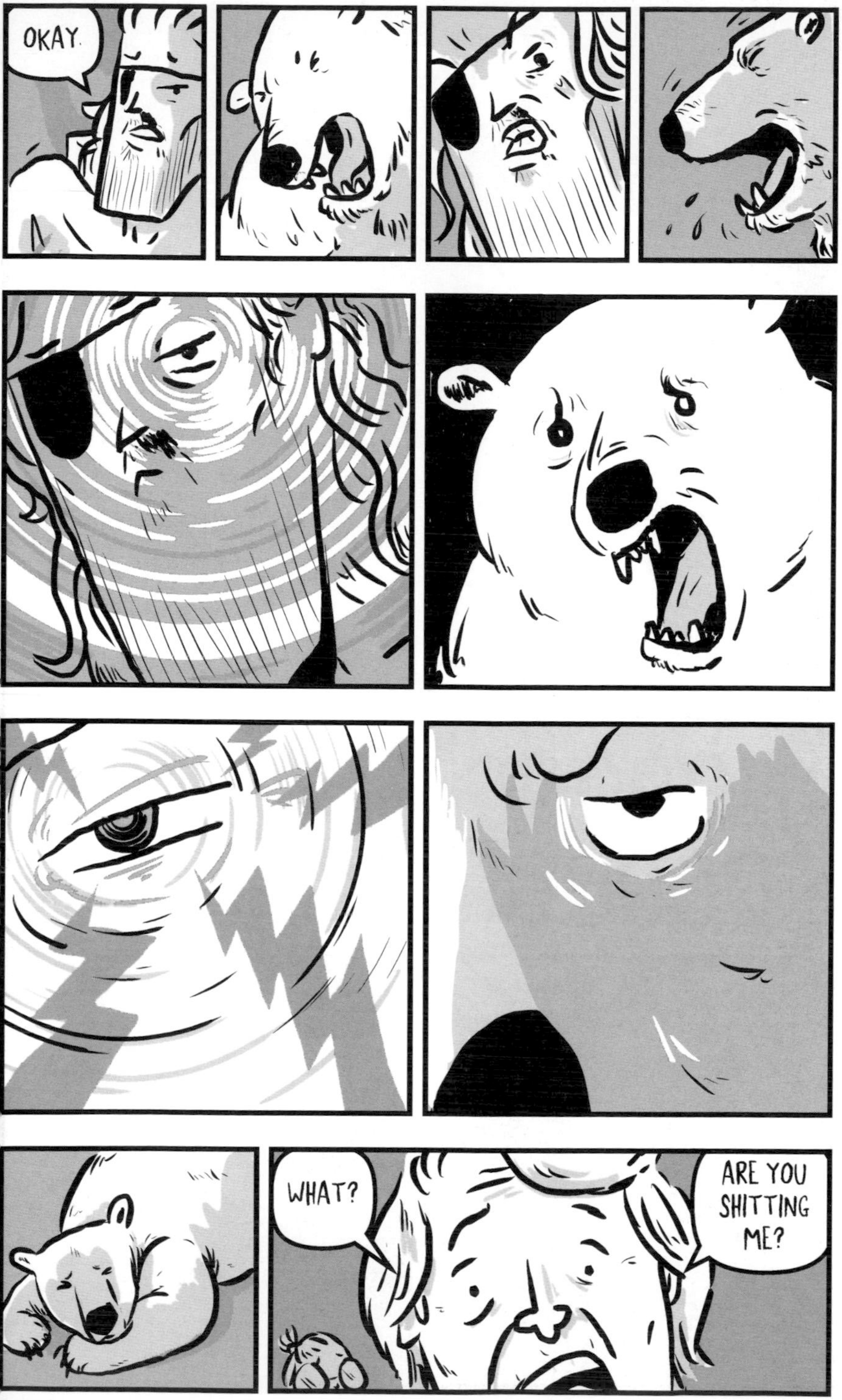
OKAY.
WHAT?
ARE YOU SHITTING ME?

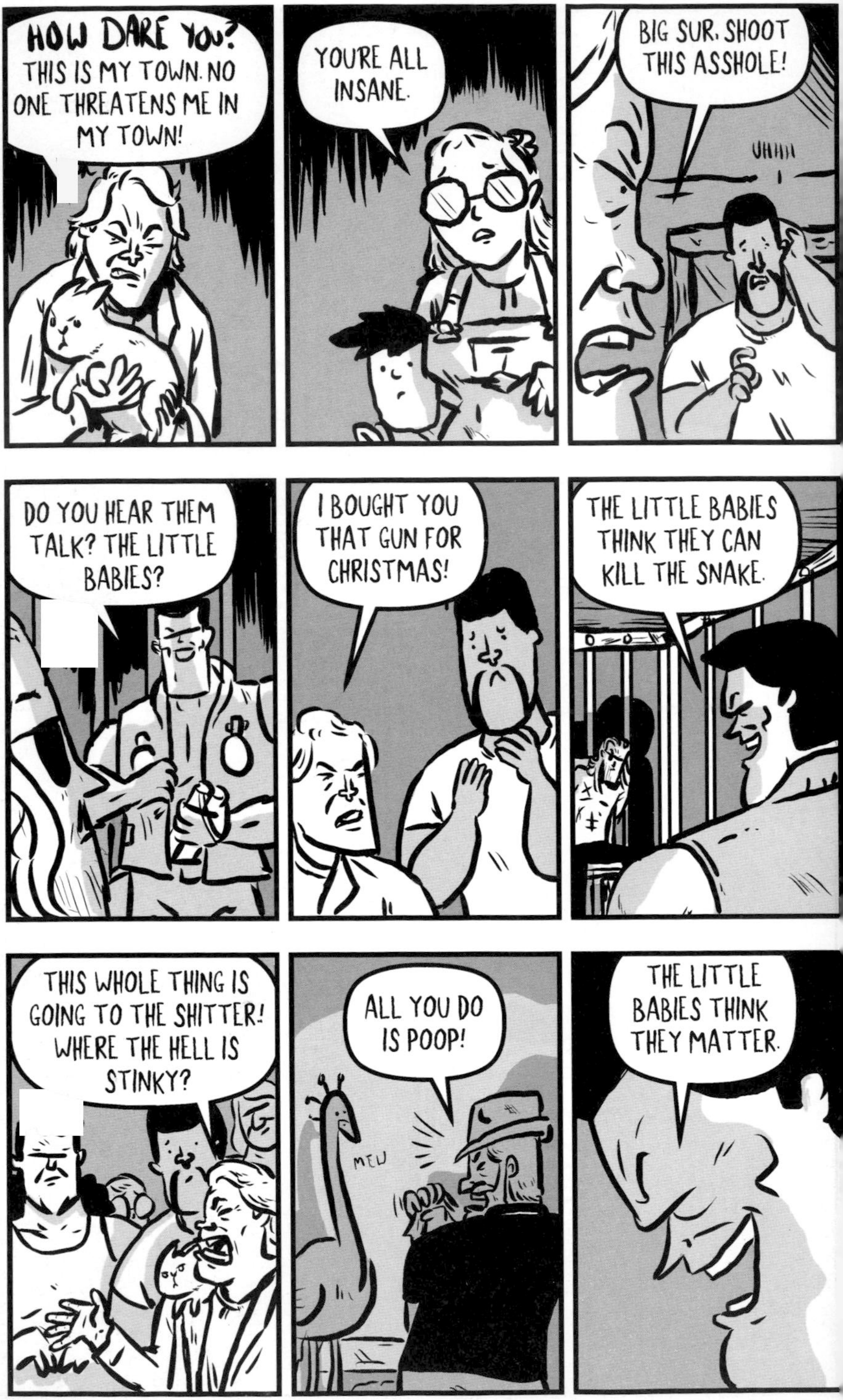
HOW DARE YOU? THIS IS MY TOWN. NO ONE THREATENS ME IN MY TOWN!
YOU'RE ALL INSANE.
BIG SUR, SHOOT THIS ASSHOLE!
UHHH
DO YOU HEAR THEM TALK? THE LITTLE BABIES?
I BOUGHT YOU THAT GUN FOR CHRISTMAS!
THE LITTLE BABIES THINK THEY CAN KILL THE SNAKE.
THIS WHOLE THING IS GOING TO THE SHITTER! WHERE THE HELL IS STINKY?
ALL YOU DO IS POOP!
MEW
THE LITTLE BABIES THINK THEY MATTER.

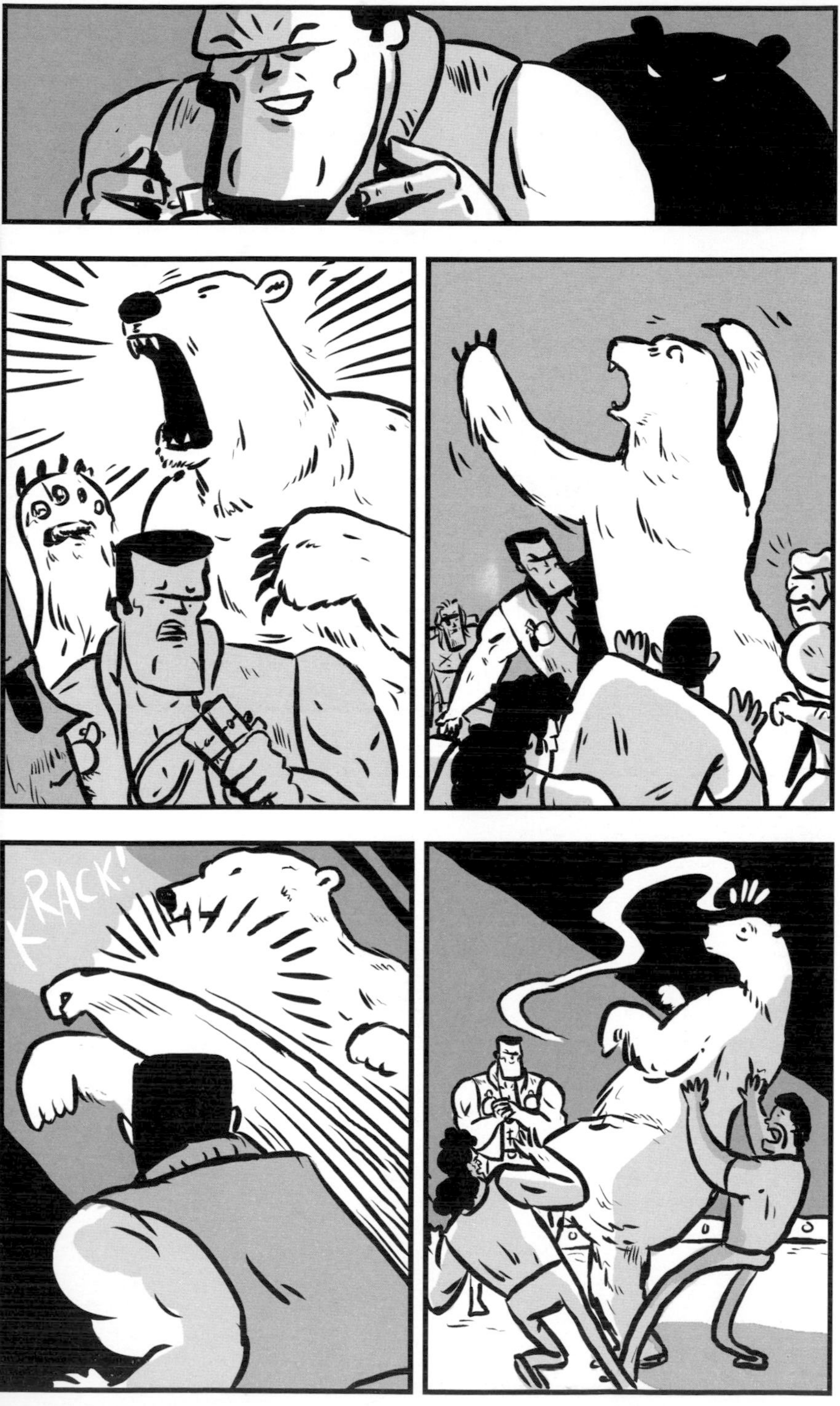
KRACK!

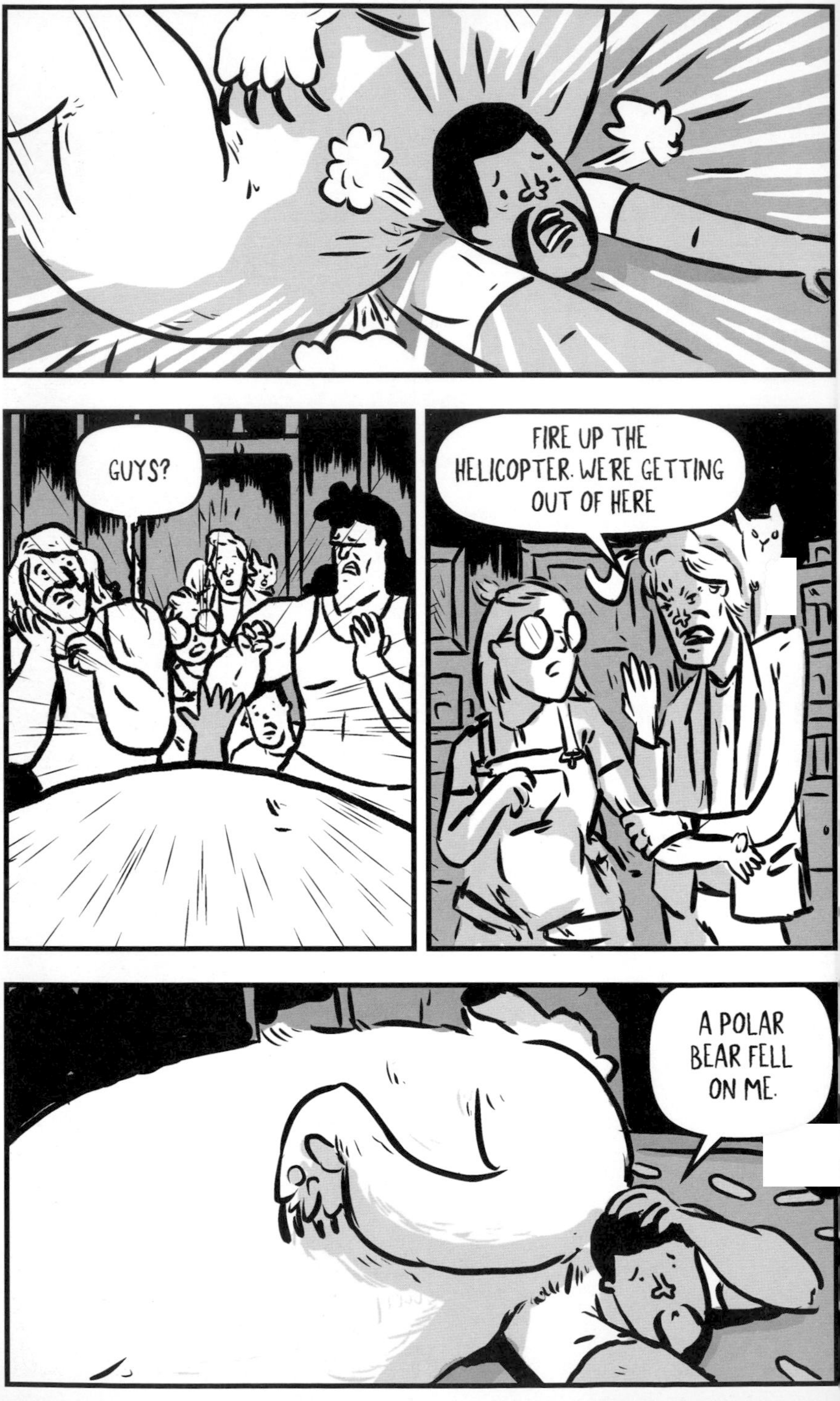
GUYS?
FIRE UP THE HELICOPTER. WE'RE GETTING OUT OF HERE
A POLAR BEAR FELL ON ME.

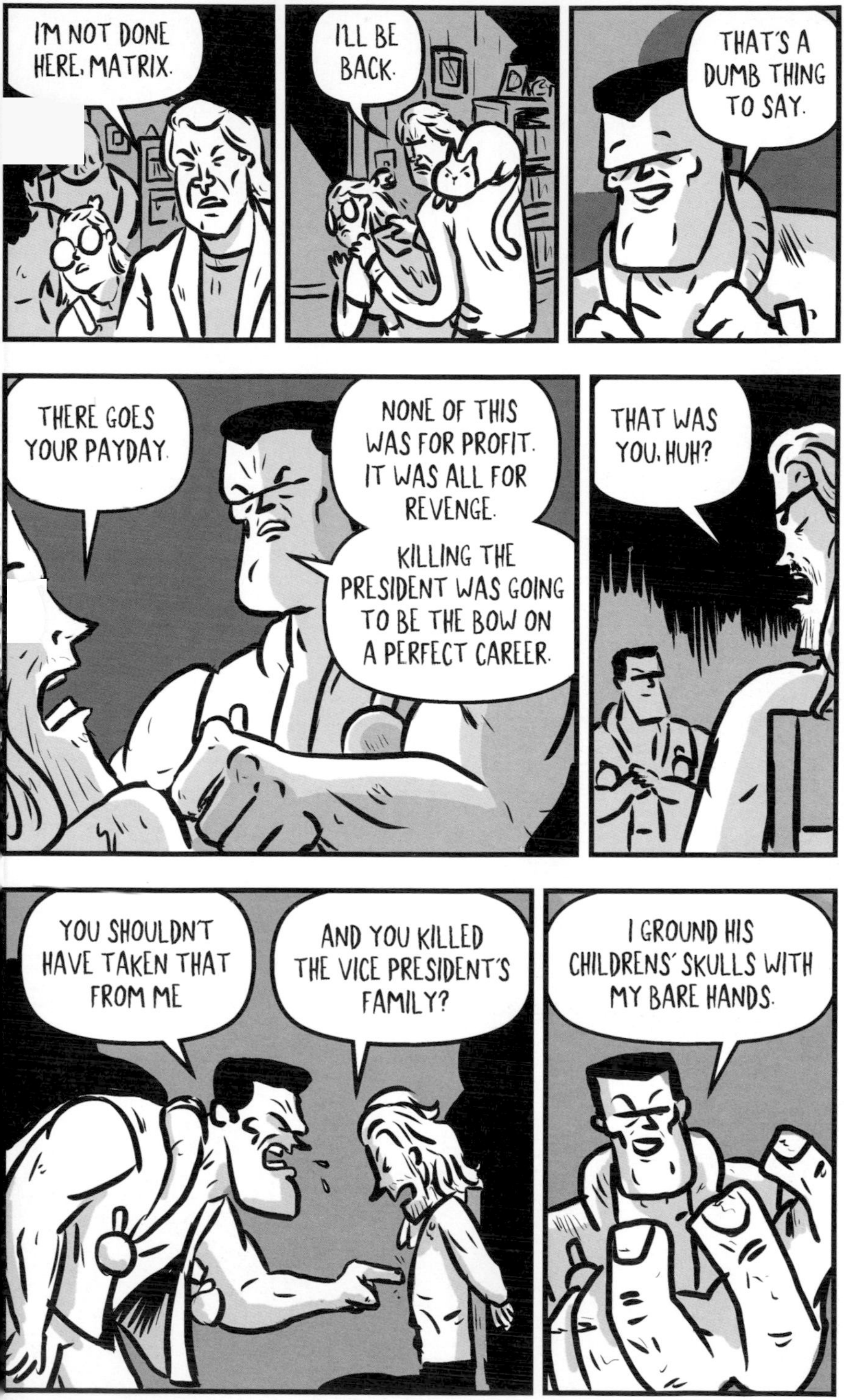
I'M NOT DONE HERE, MATRIX.
I'LL BE BACK.
THAT'S A DUMB THING TO SAY.
THERE GOES YOUR PAYDAY.
NONE OF THIS WAS FOR PROFIT. IT WAS ALL FOR REVENGE.
KILLING THE PRESIDENT WAS GOING TO BE THE BOW ON A PERFECT CAREER.
THAT WAS YOU, HUH?
YOU SHOULDN'T HAVE TAKEN THAT FROM ME
AND YOU KILLED THE VICE PRESIDENT'S FAMILY?
I GROUND HIS CHILDRENS' SKULLS WITH MY BARE HANDS.

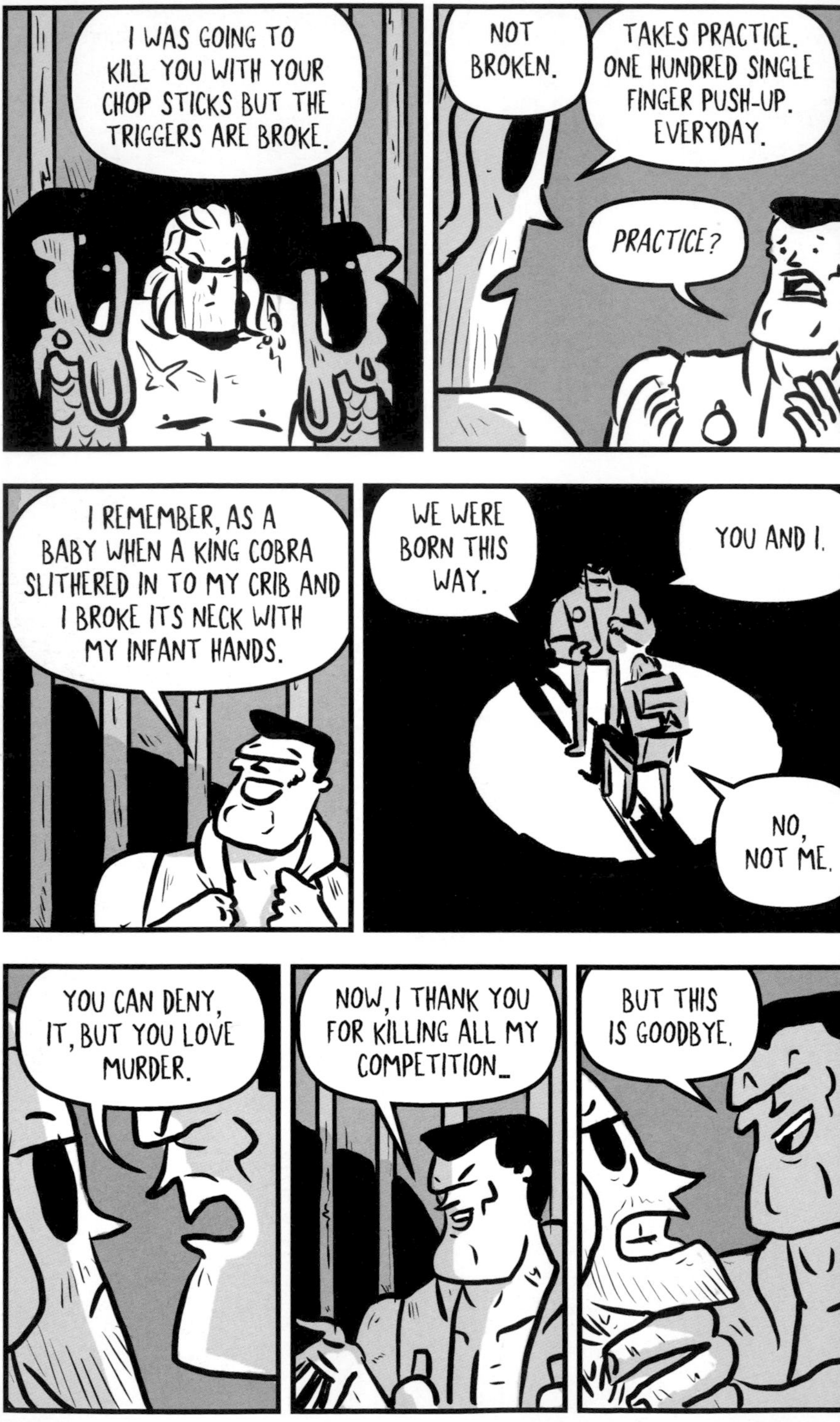
I WAS GOING TO KILL YOU WITH YOUR CHOP STICKS BUT THE TRIGGERS ARE BROKE.
NOT BROKEN.
TAKES PRACTICE. ONE HUNDRED SINGLE FINGER PUSH-UP. EVERYDAY.
PRACTICE?
I REMEMBER, AS A BABY WHEN A KING COBRA SLITHERED IN TO MY CRIB AND I BROKE ITS NECK WITH MY INFANT HANDS.
WE WERE BORN THIS WAY.
YOU AND I.
NO, NOT ME.
YOU CAN DENY, IT, BUT YOU LOVE MURDER.
NOW, I THANK YOU FOR KILLING ALL MY COMPETITION_
BUT THIS IS GOODBYE.

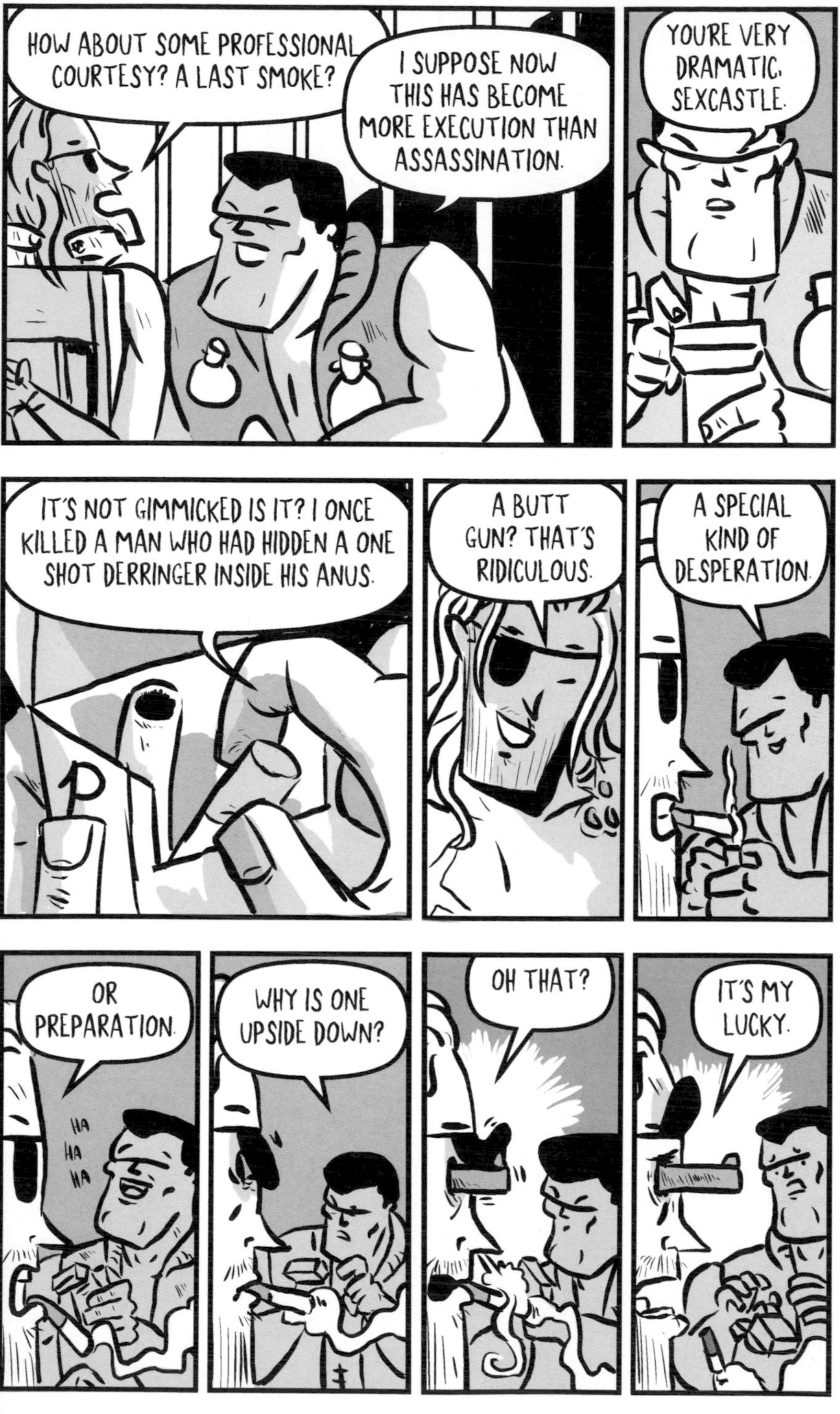
HOW ABOUT SOME PROFESSIONAL COURTESY? A LAST SMOKE?
I SUPPOSE NOW THIS HAS BECOME MORE EXECUTION THAN ASSASSINATION.
YOU'RE VERY DRAMATIC, SEXCASTLE.
IT'S NOT GIMMICKED IS IT? I ONCE KILLED A MAN WHO HAD HIDDEN A ONE SHOT DERRINGER INSIDE HIS ANUS.
A BUTT GUN? THAT'S RIDICULOUS.
A SPECIAL KIND OF DESPERATION.
OR PREPARATION.
HA HA HA
WHY IS ONE UPSIDE DOWN?
OH THAT?
IT'S MY LUCKY.

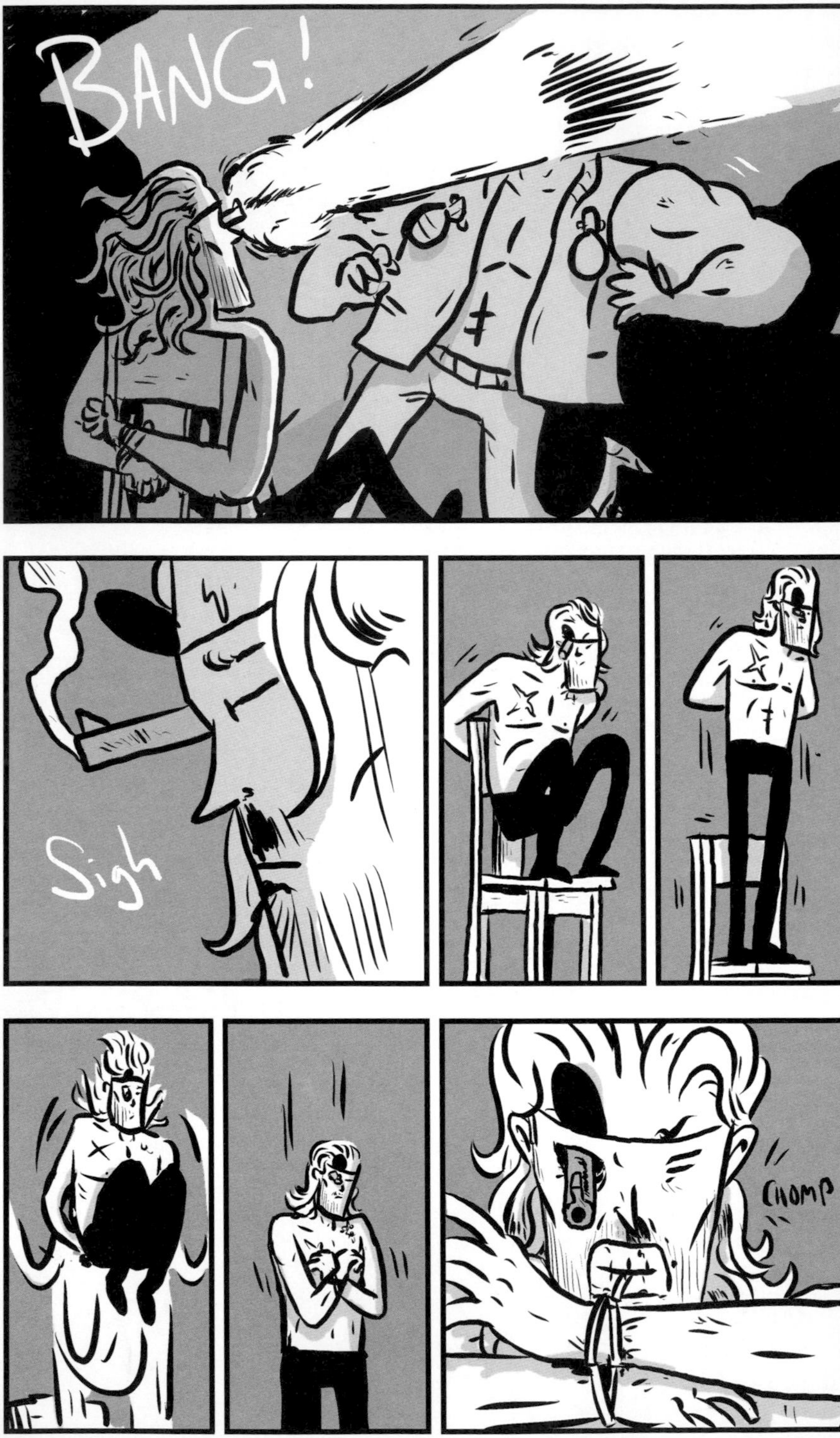
BANG!
Sigh
CHOMP

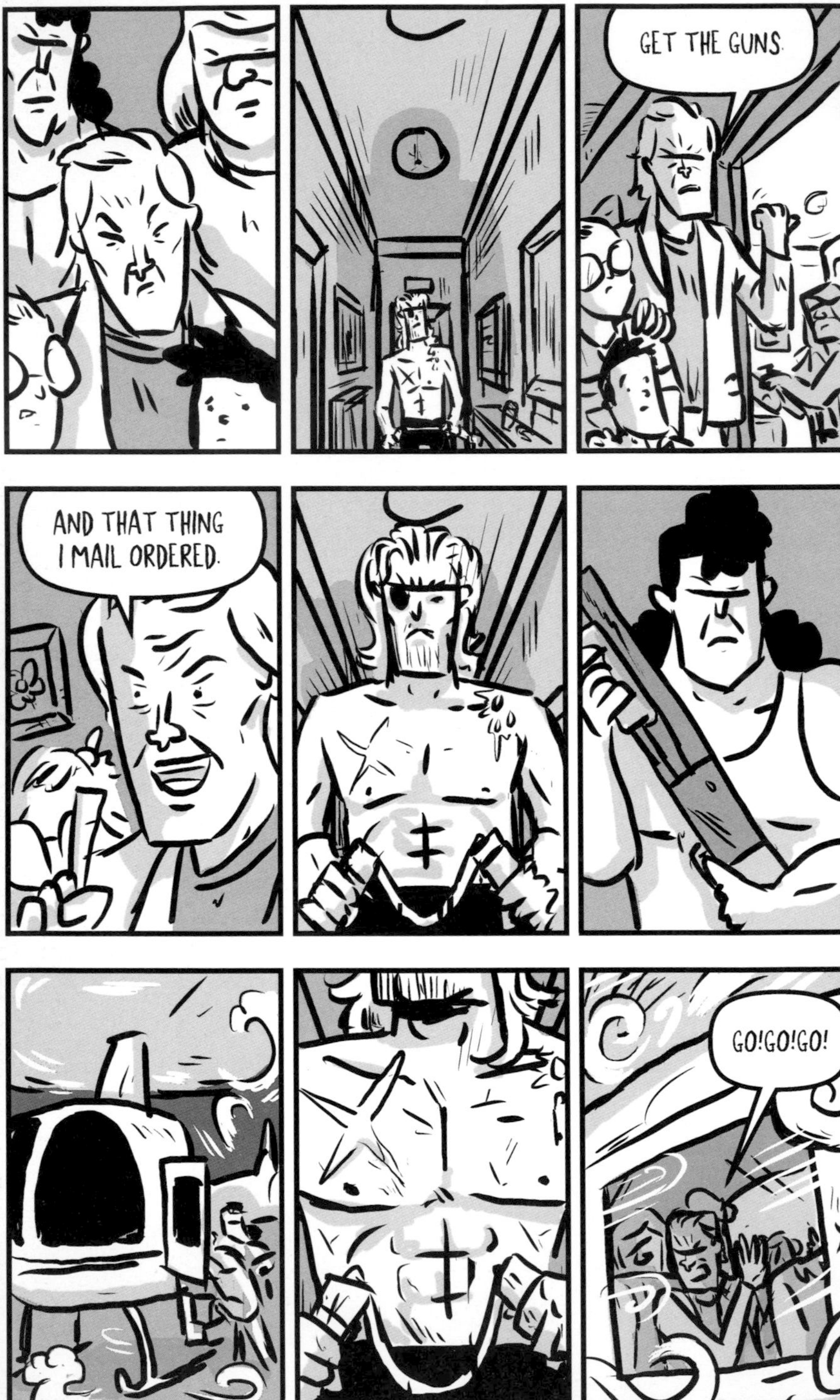
GET THE GUNS.
AND THAT THING I MAIL ORDERED.
GO!GO!GO!

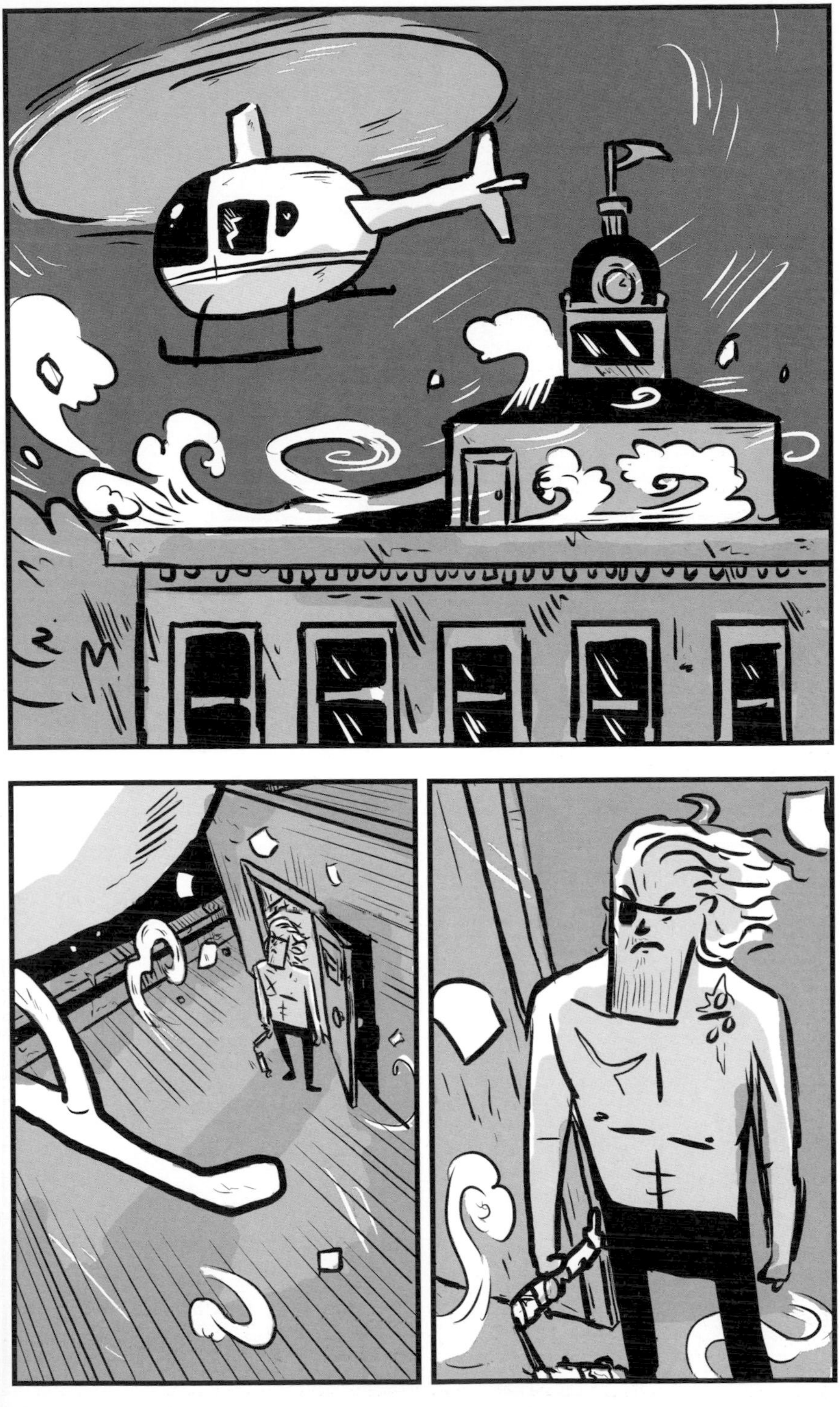

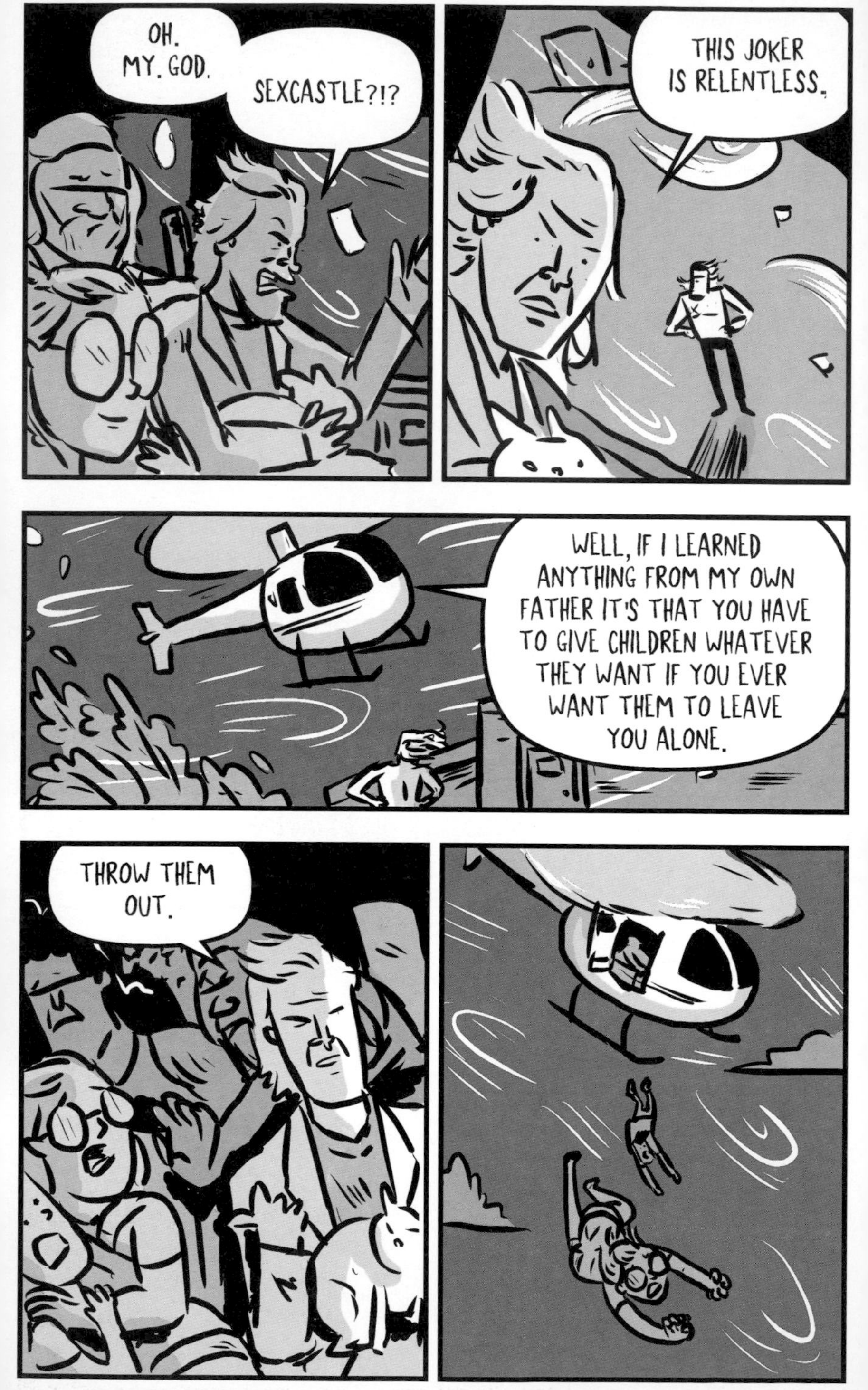
OH.
MY. GOD.
SEXCASTLE?!?
THIS JOKER
IS RELENTLESS.
WELL, IF I LEARNED ANYTHING FROM MY OWN FATHER IT'S THAT YOU HAVE TO GIVE CHILDREN WHATEVER THEY WANT IF YOU EVER WANT THEM TO LEAVE YOU ALONE.
THROW THEM OUT.

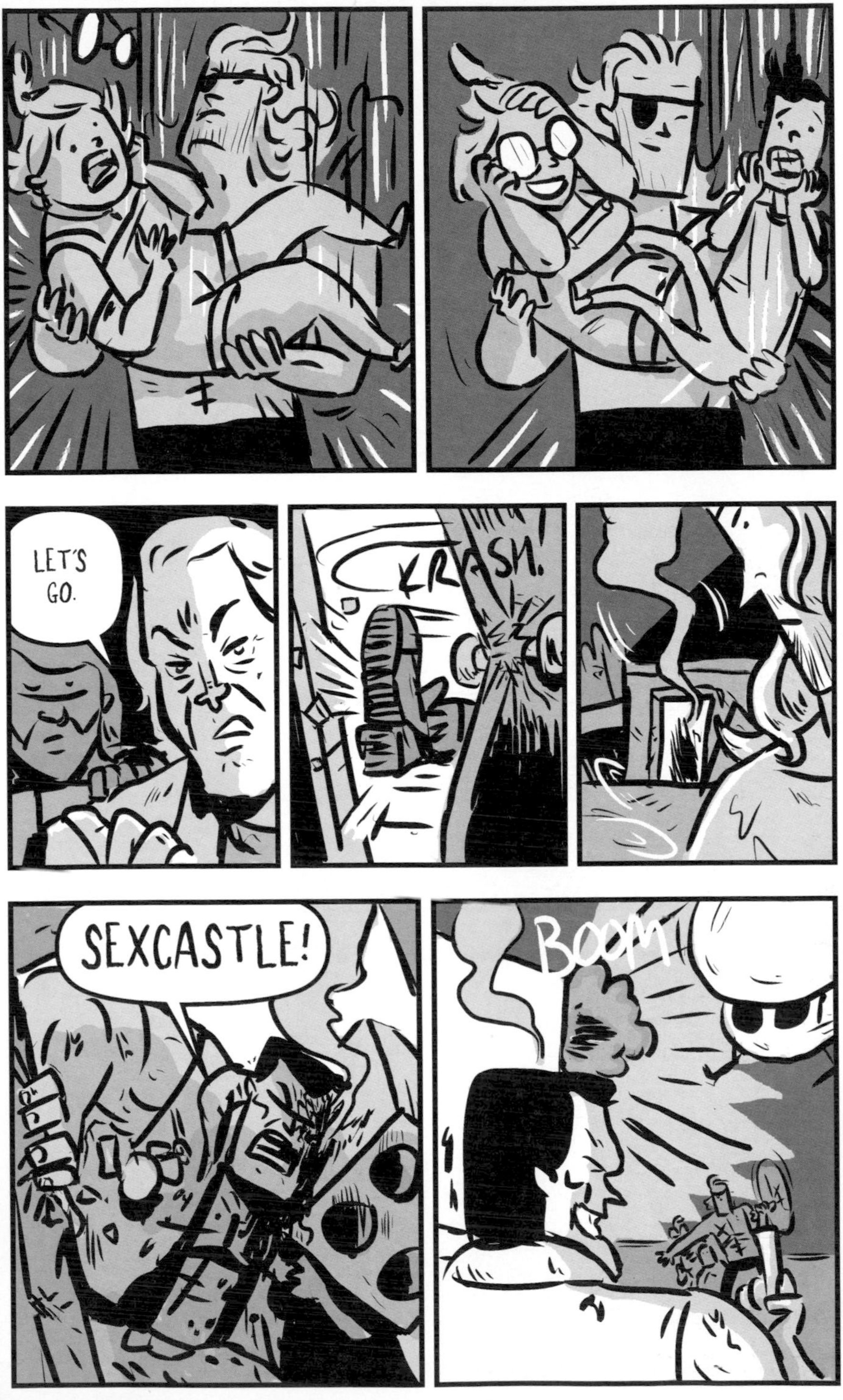
LET'S GO.
KRASH!
SEXCASTLE!
BOOM

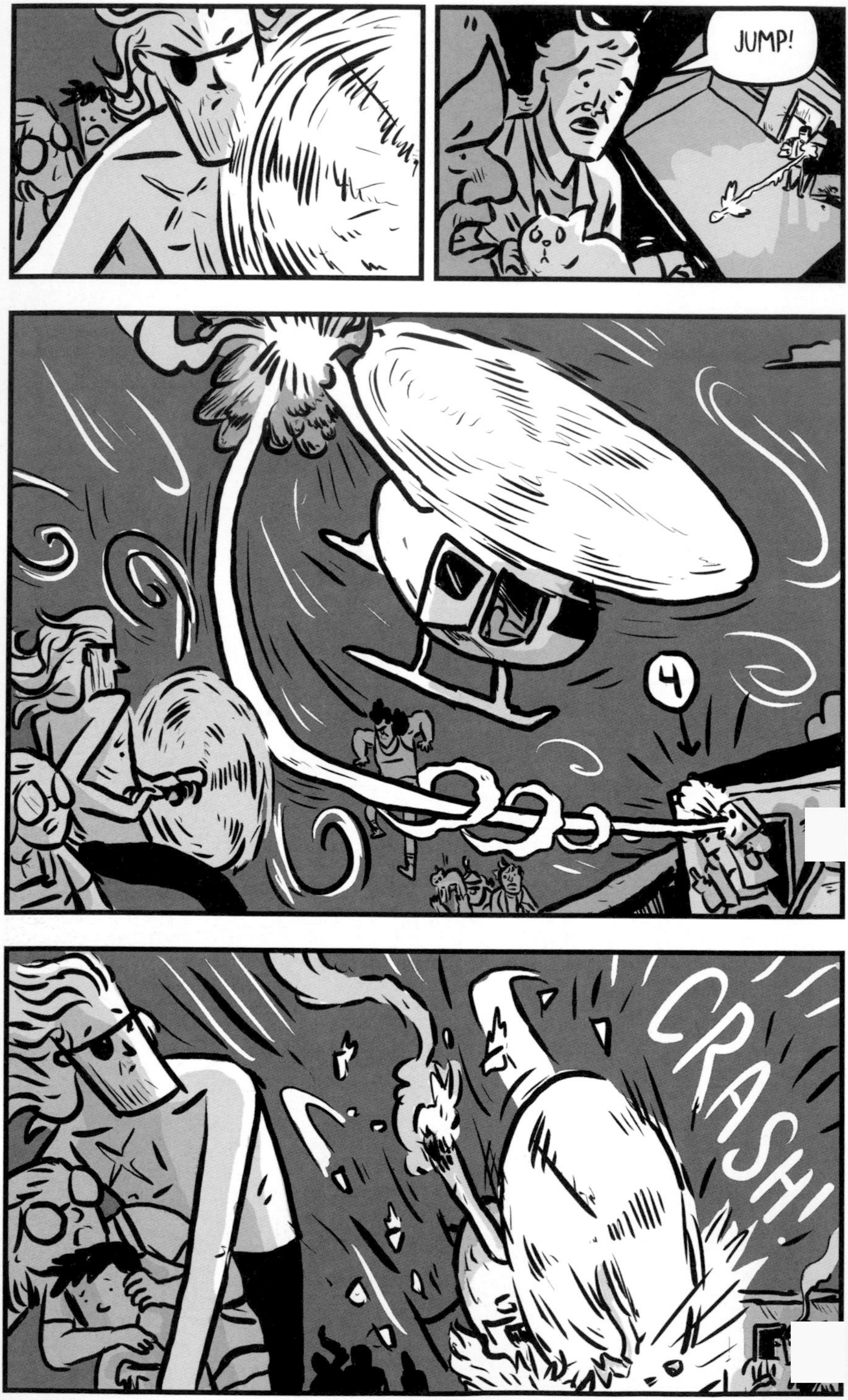
JUMP!
4
CRASH!

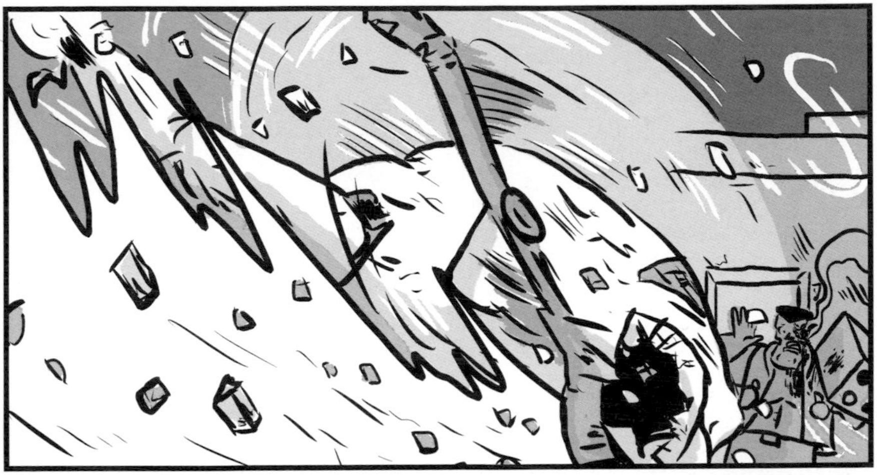

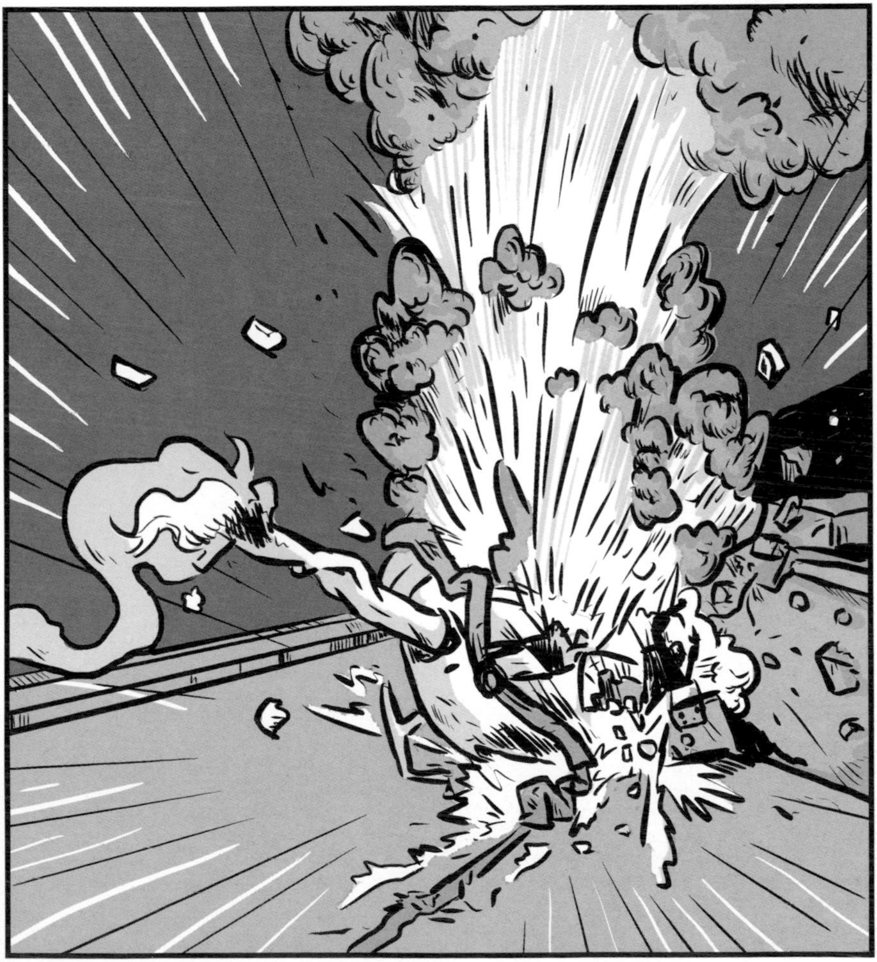

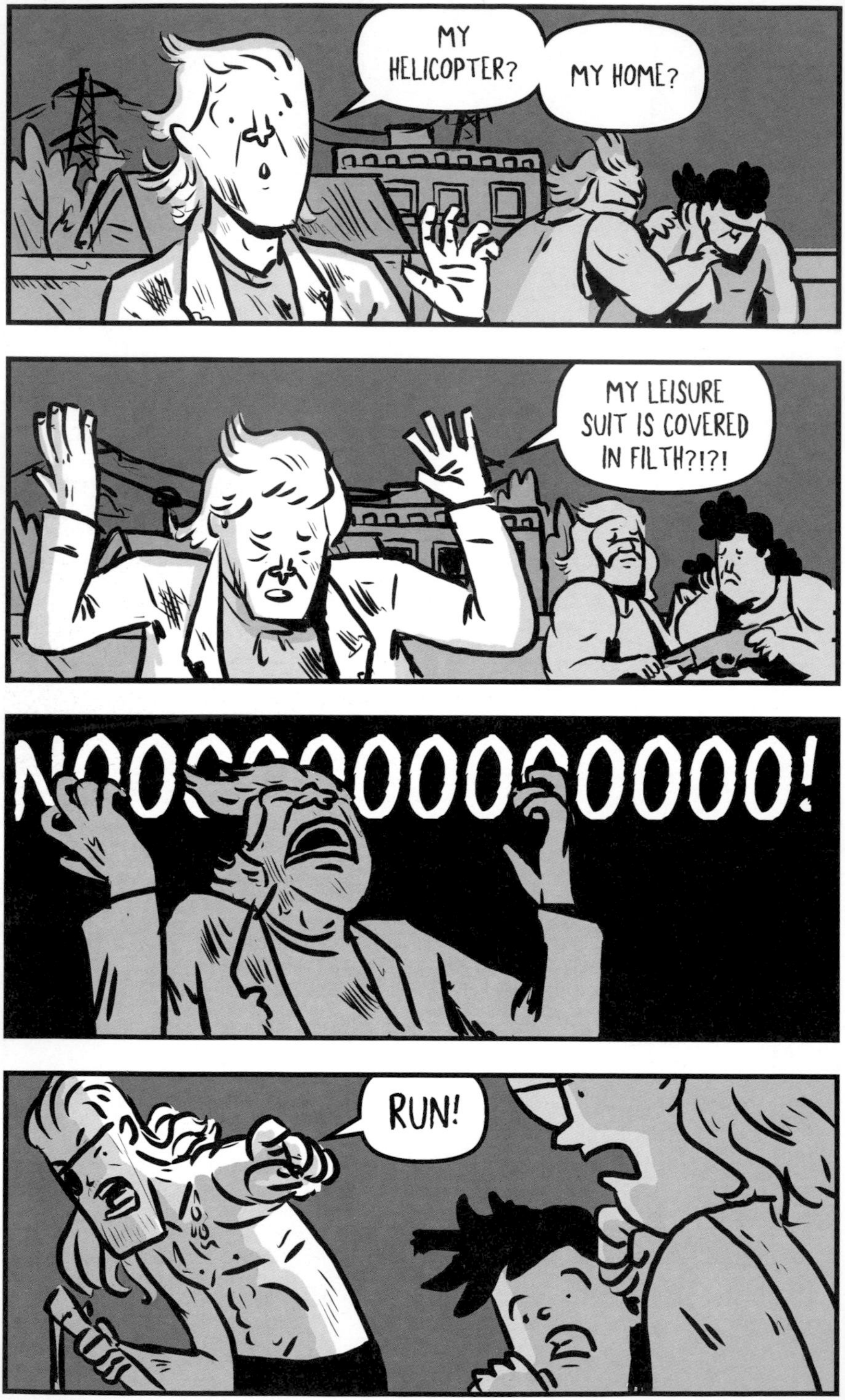
MY HELICOPTER?
MY HOME?
MY LEISURE SUIT IS COVERED IN FILTH?!?!
NOOOOOOOOOOOOOO!
RUN!

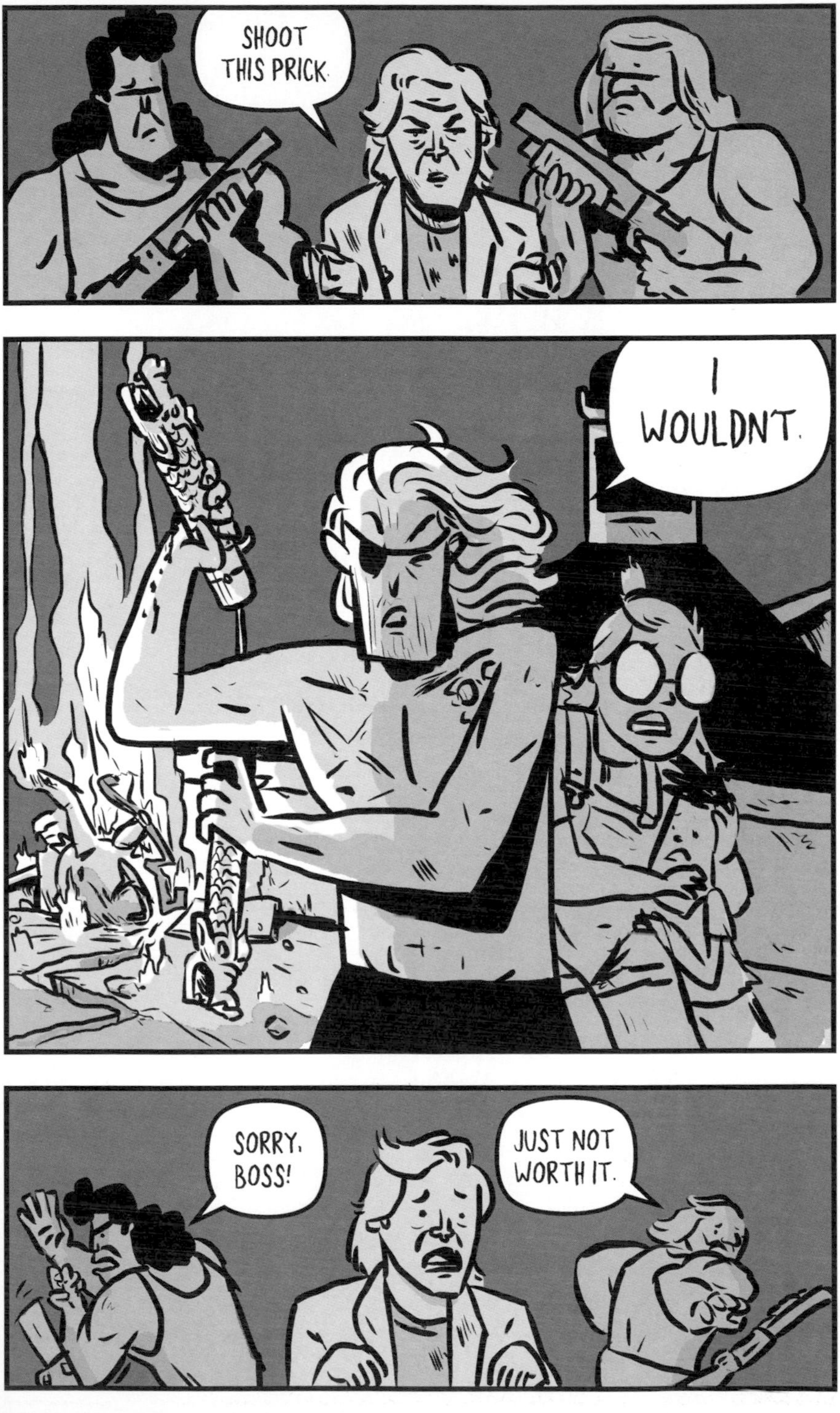
SHOOT THIS PRICK.
I WOULDN'T.
SORRY, BOSS!
JUST NOT WORTH IT.

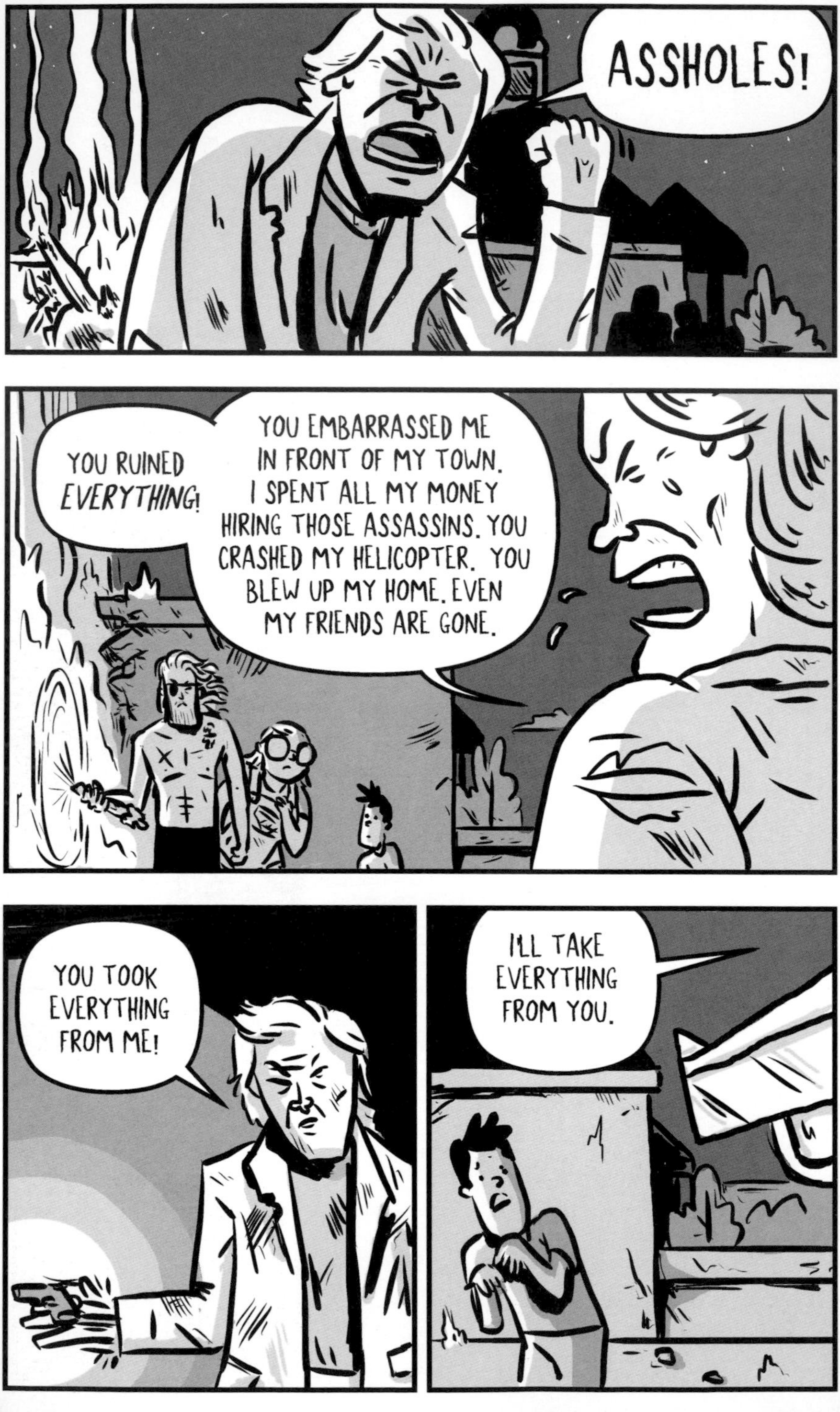
ASSHOLES!
YOU RUINED EVERYTHING!
YOU EMBARRASSED ME IN FRONT OF MY TOWN. I SPENT ALL MY MONEY HIRING THOSE ASSASSINS. YOU CRASHED MY HELICOPTER. YOU BLEW UP MY HOME. EVEN MY FRIENDS ARE GONE.
YOU TOOK EVERYTHING FROM ME!
I'LL TAKE EVERYTHING FROM YOU.

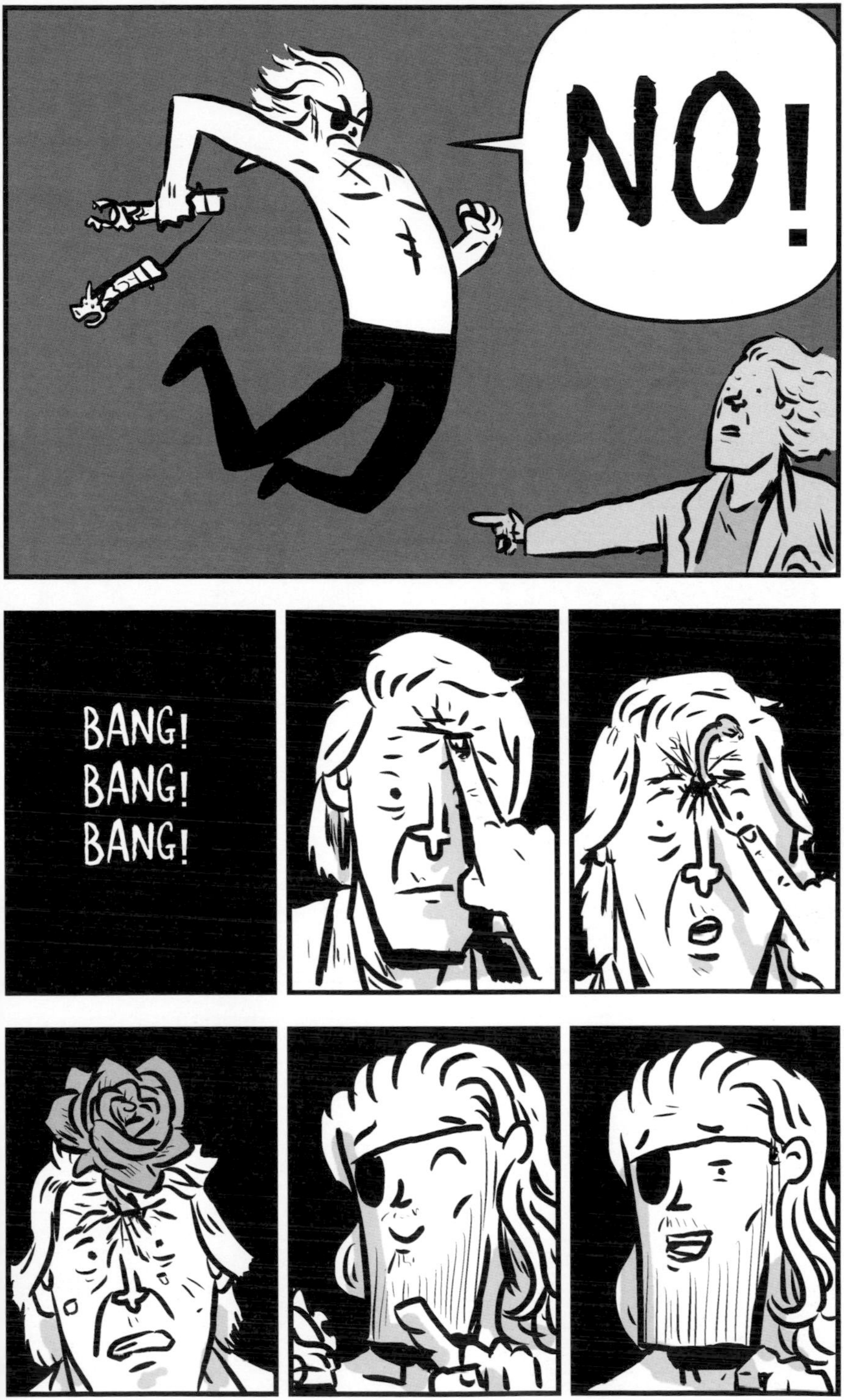
NO!
BANG! BANG! BANG!

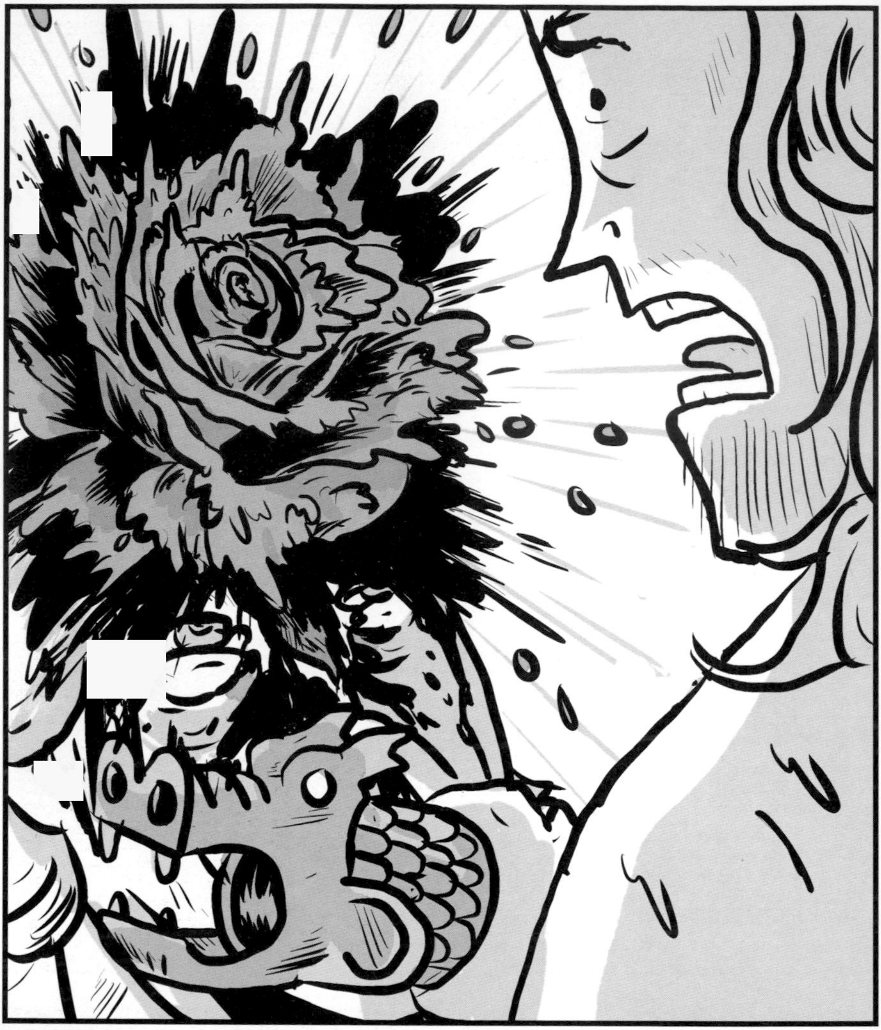

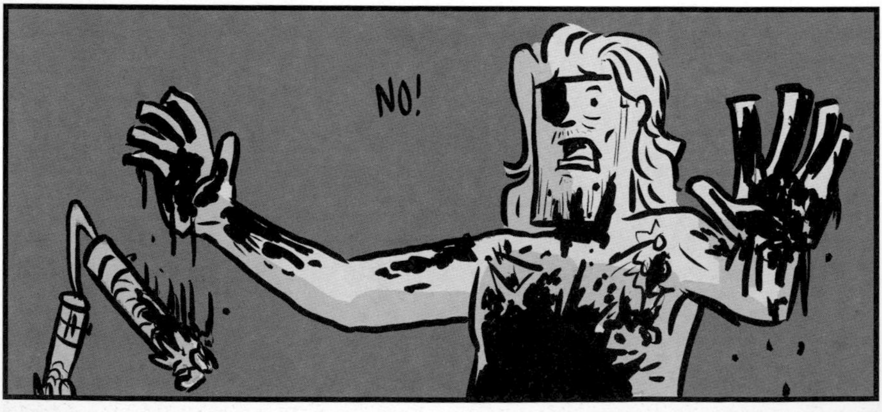
NO!

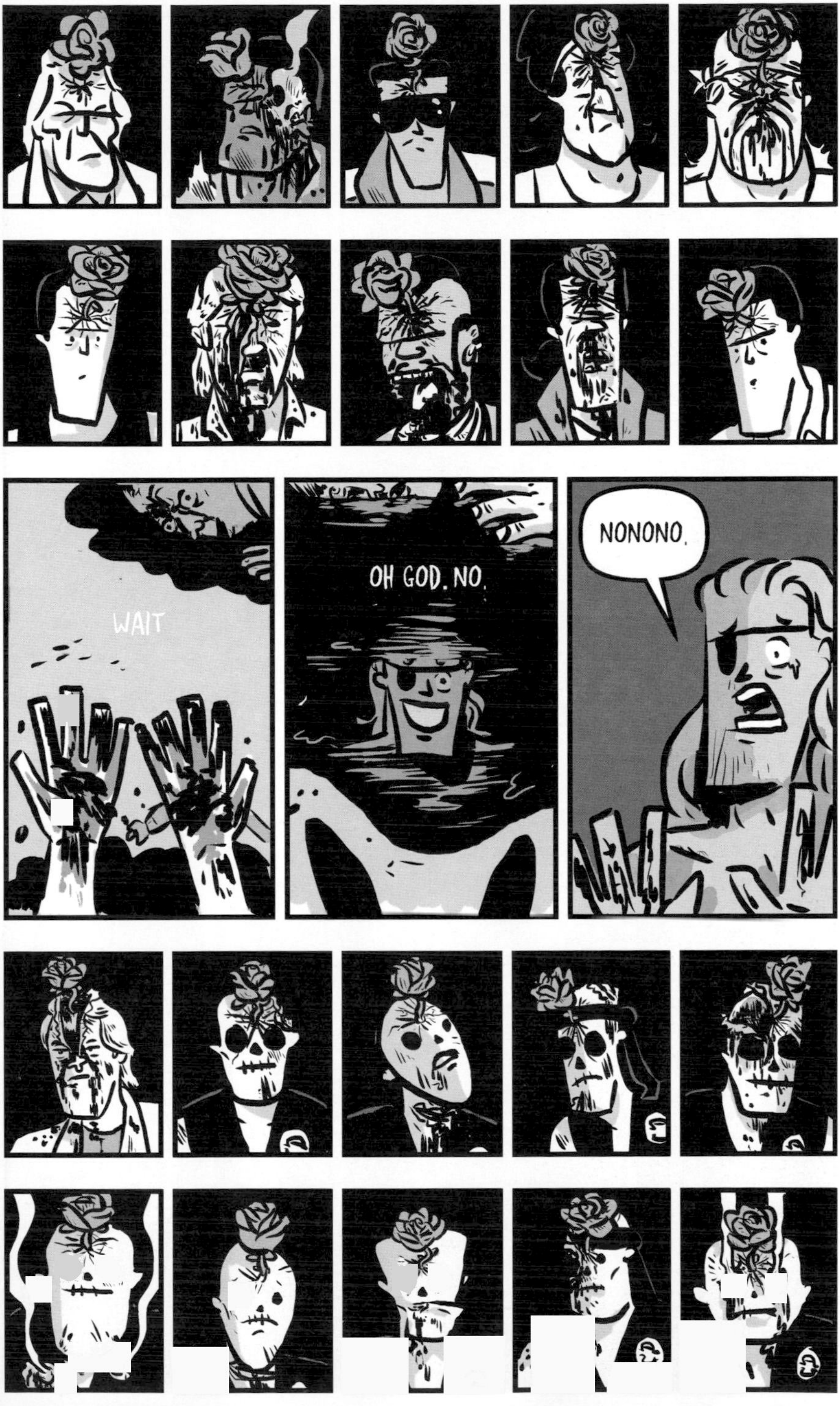
WAIT
OH GOD. NO.
NONONO.

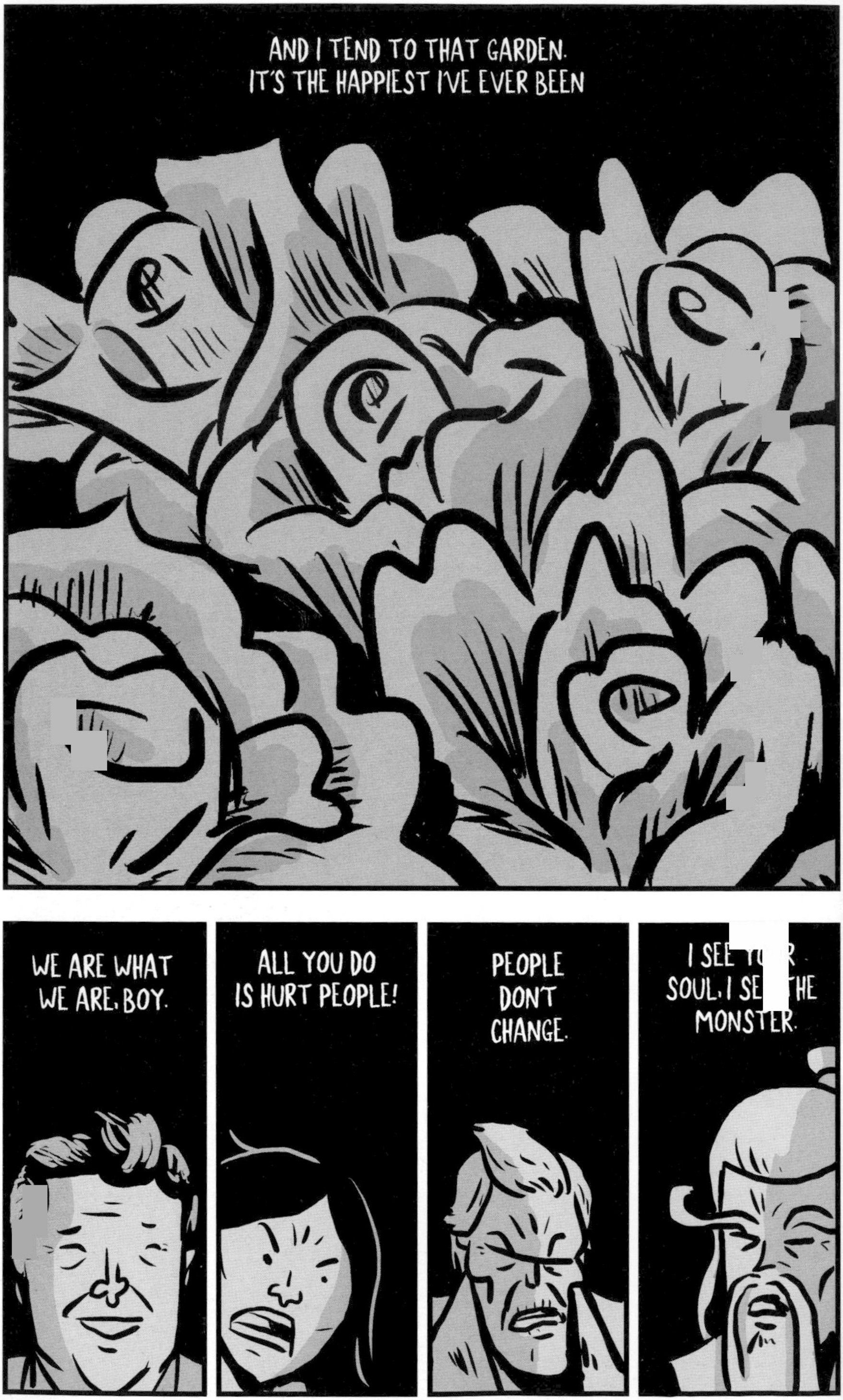
AND I TEND TO THAT GARDEN.
IT'S THE HAPPIEST I'VE EVER BEEN
WE ARE WHAT WE ARE, BOY.
ALL YOU DO IS HURT PEOPLE!
PEOPLE DON'T CHANGE.
I SEE YO R SOUL, I SE THE MONSTER.

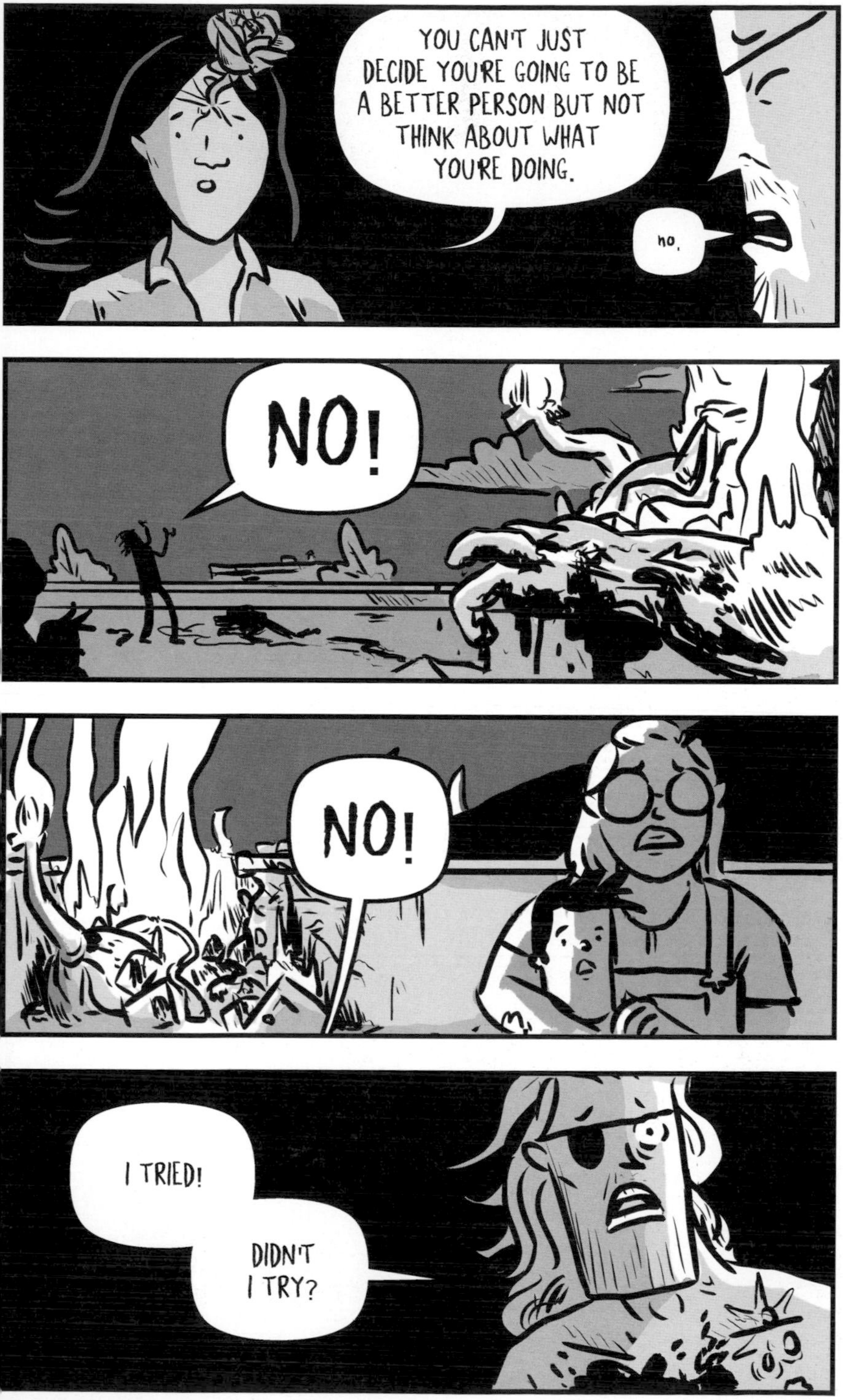
YOU CAN'T JUST DECIDE YOU'RE GOING TO BE A BETTER PERSON BUT NOT THINK ABOUT WHAT YOU'RE DOING.
no.
NO!
NO!
I TRIED!
DIDN'T I TRY?

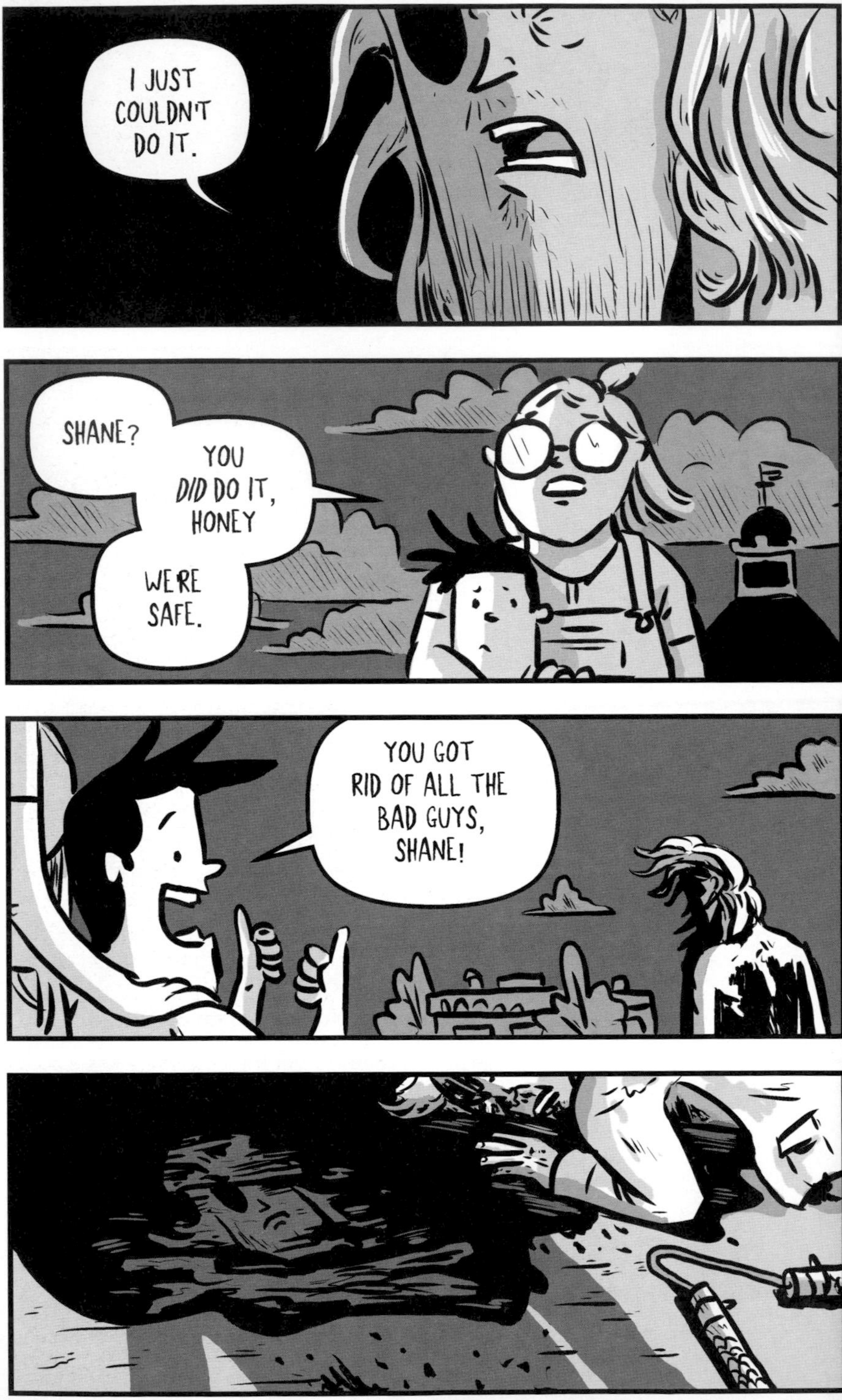
I JUST COULDN'T DO IT.
SHANE?
YOU *DID* DO IT, HONEY
WE'RE SAFE.
YOU GOT RID OF ALL THE BAD GUYS, SHANE!

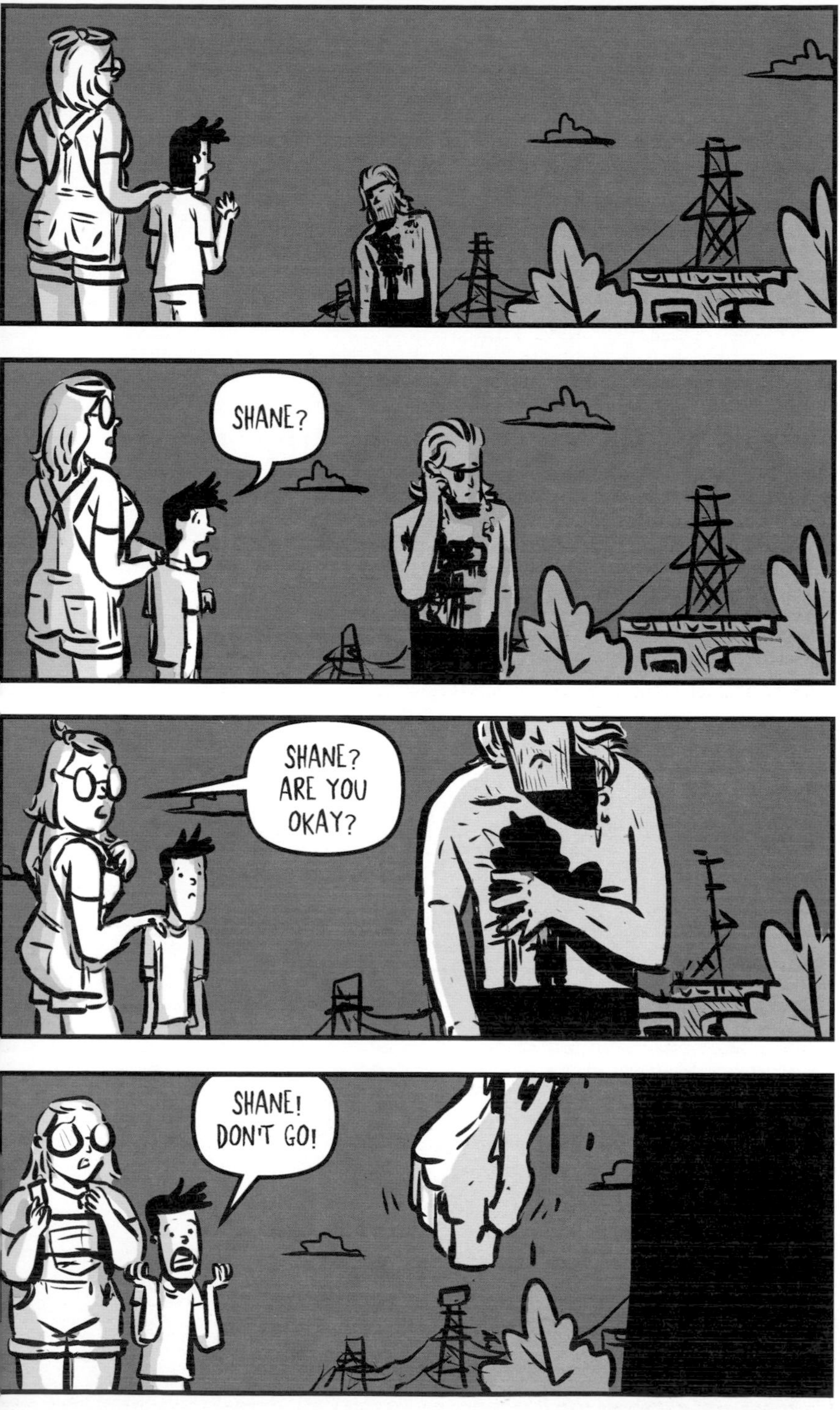
SHANE?
SHANE? ARE YOU OKAY?
SHANE! DON'T GO!

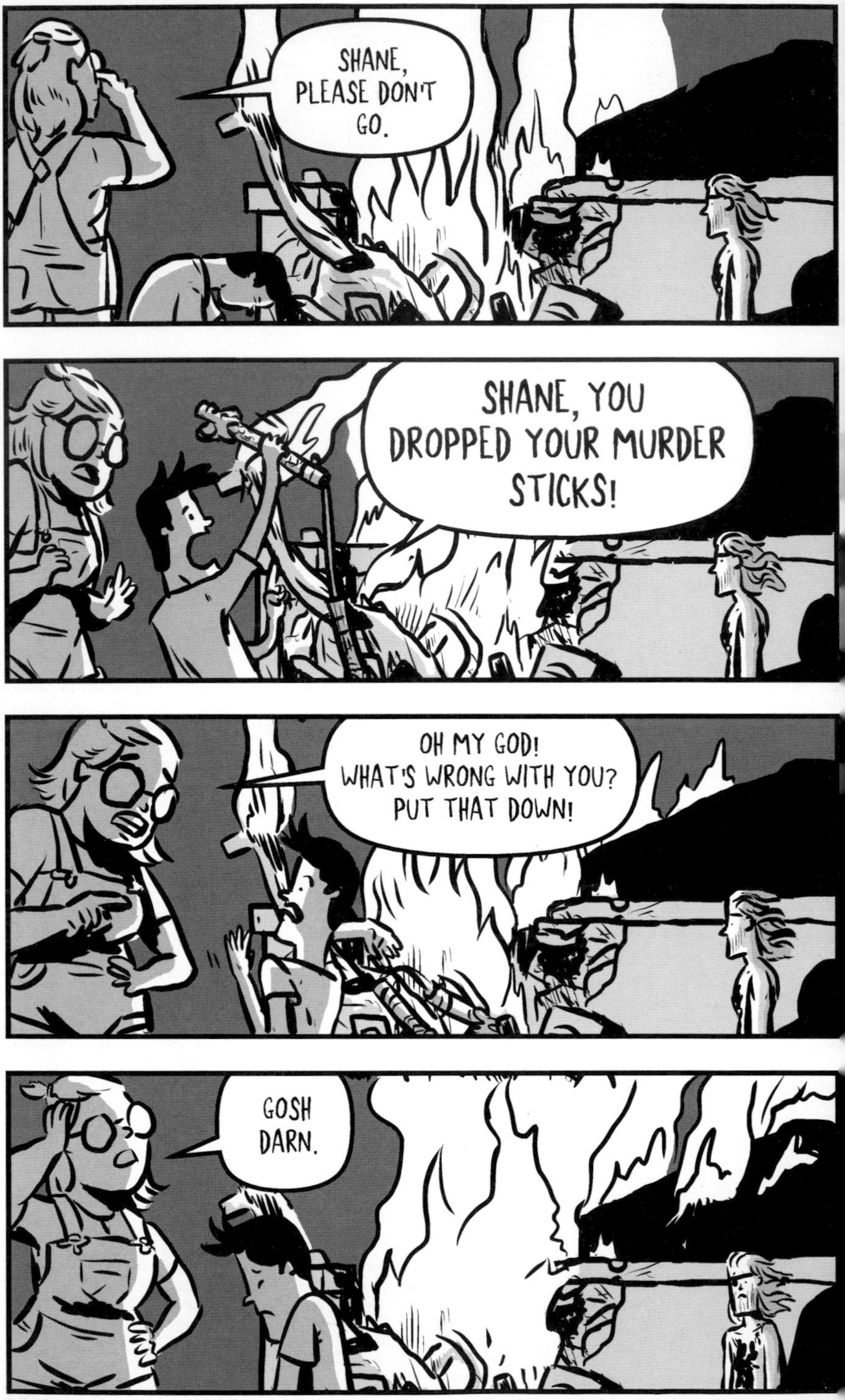
SHANE, PLEASE DON'T GO.
SHANE, YOU DROPPED YOUR MURDER STICKS!
OH MY GOD! WHAT'S WRONG WITH YOU? PUT THAT DOWN!
GOSH DARN.

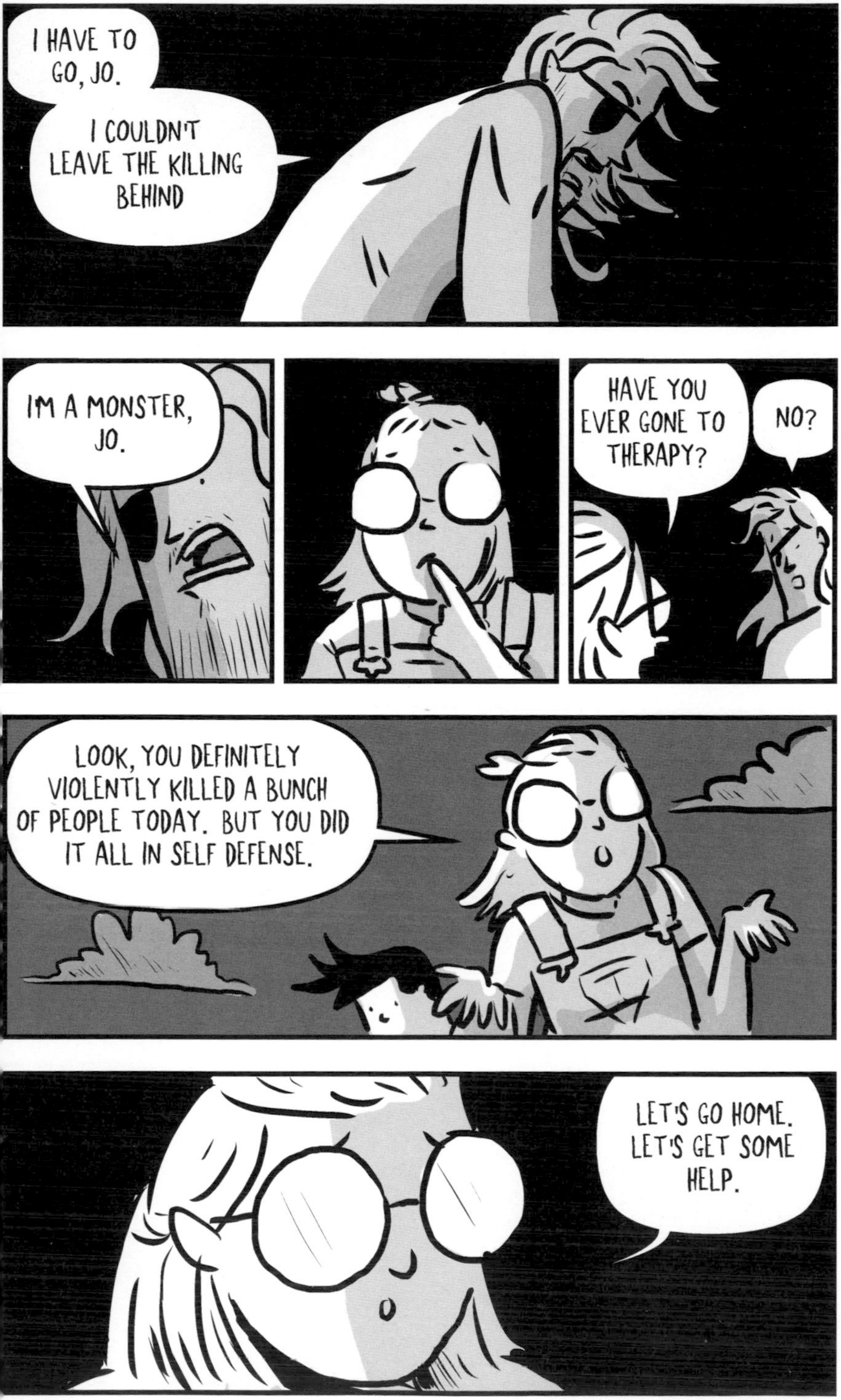
I HAVE TO GO, JO.
I COULDN'T LEAVE THE KILLING BEHIND
I'M A MONSTER, JO.
HAVE YOU EVER GONE TO THERAPY?
NO?
LOOK, YOU DEFINITELY VIOLENTLY KILLED A BUNCH OF PEOPLE TODAY. BUT YOU DID IT ALL IN SELF DEFENSE.
LET'S GO HOME. LET'S GET SOME HELP.

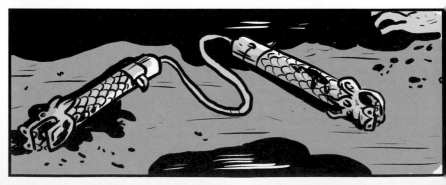

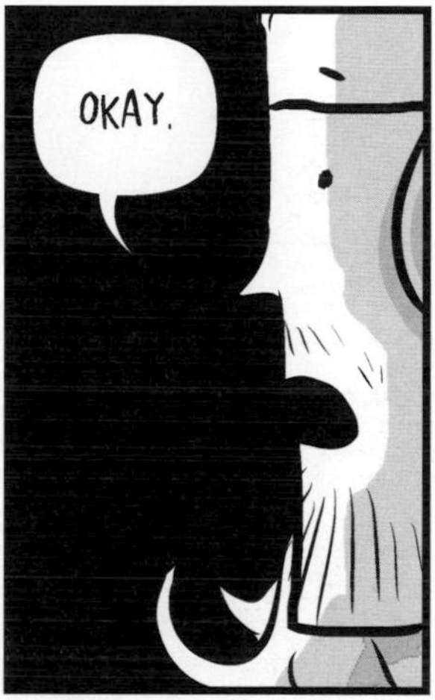
OKAY.

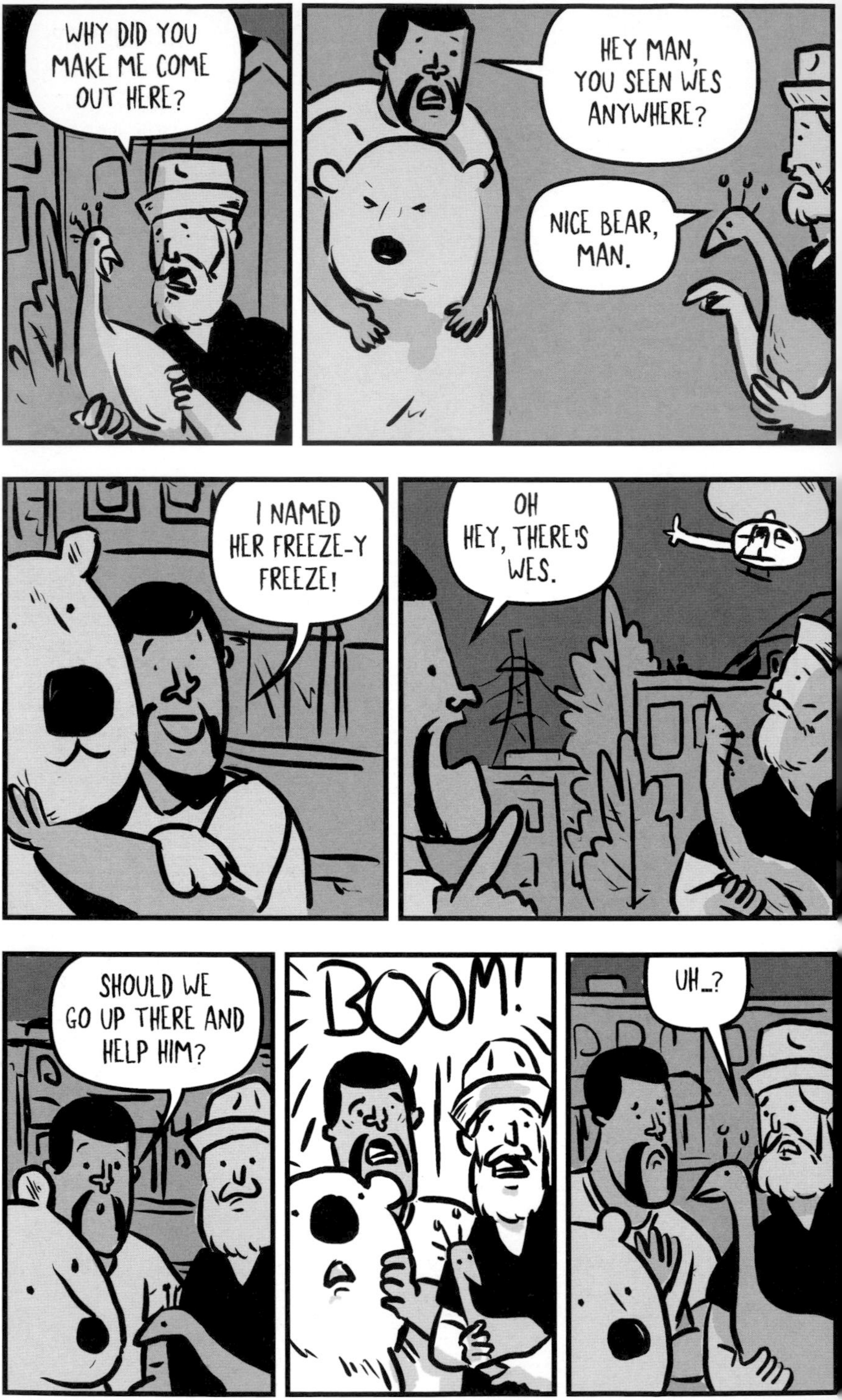
WHY DID YOU MAKE ME COME OUT HERE?
HEY MAN, YOU SEEN WES ANYWHERE?
NICE BEAR, MAN.
I NAMED HER FREEZE-Y FREEZE!
OH HEY, THERE'S WES.
SHOULD WE GO UP THERE AND HELP HIM?
BOOM!
UH...?

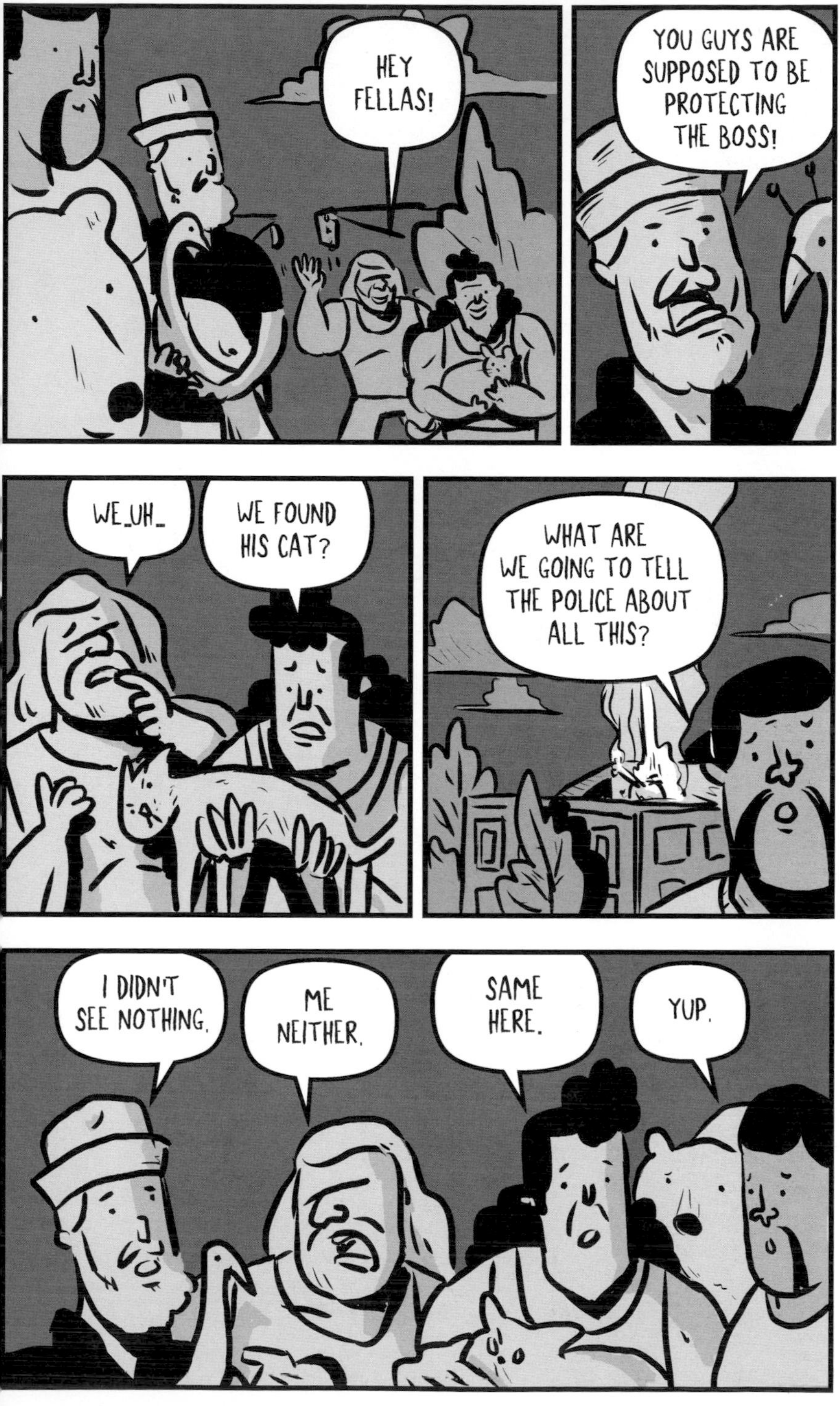
HEY FELLAS!
YOU GUYS ARE SUPPOSED TO BE PROTECTING THE BOSS!
WE_UH_
WE FOUND HIS CAT?
WHAT ARE WE GOING TO TELL THE POLICE ABOUT ALL THIS?
I DIDN'T SEE NOTHING.
ME NEITHER.
SAME HERE.
YUP.

AFTER ADDING FREEZEY FREEZE TO HIS
MARKETING FOR HIS ICE CREAM PARLOR, BIG SU
BECAME THE NEW RICHEST MAN IN TOWN.
HE ALSO STARTED A CHARITABLE GROUP TO
COLLECT AND DISPOSE OF HANDGUNS.

DUE TO HIS INTIMATE FAMILIARITY WITH THE
DAY TO DAY OPERATIONS OF RUNNING A CITY,
MARK "STINKY" MALONE WAS ELECTED MAYO
HE ALSO STARTED A PEACOCK FARM AND IS
WIDELY CONSIDERED NOW TO BE AN EXPERT IN
PEACOCKERY.

E AND THE BUS LEFT BRADLEY. THE LAST
ANYONE HAD HEARD OF THEM THEY HAD OPENED
A GYM SLASH CAR WASH.

SHANE, JO AND MAX
ARE HAPPY.

NO ONE KNOWS WHAT HAPPENED TO BRADLEY'S EVIL
CAT, BUT RUMORS PERSIST THAT IT'S BEEN BIDING IT'S TIM
PLANNING ITS BLOODY REVENGE.
IF YOU SHOULD SEE IT DO NOT APPROACH IT.
SERIOUSLY. THAT THING IS LEGIT EVIL.

THE END